Write To Woof
2014

Edited by Diana Kathryn Plopa
and Jennifer Koch

Grey Wolfe Publishing, LLC
PO Box 1088
Birmingham, Michigan 48009
www.GreyWolfePublishing.com

© 2014 Grey Wolfe Publishing, LLC
Published by Grey Wolfe Publishing, LLC
www.GreyWolfePublishing.com
All Rights Reserved

ISBN:978-1-62828-022-7
Library of Congress Control Number: 2014931327

Write To Woof 2014

Edited by Diana Kathryn Plopa
and Jennifer Koch

Dedication

We humbly dedicate this book to the dogs; big ones, little ones, and all those in between suffering in shelters, waiting for their "furever" homes.

Perhaps through the writing contained in these pages, more humans will come understand the unconditional love and selfless devotion you bring to our lives, and open their hearts and homes to you.

No more homeless dogs, this is our prayer for you today and always!

Acknowledgements

We would like to send out a special **Thank You** to all of the fine authors who submitted their work for this book. It is because of your dedication to dogs as well as the writing craft that we have been able to produce such a spectacular tribute to our furry friends!

We also want to thank the good people of **Almost Home Animal Rescue League** who fight tirelessly day after day to make sure that dogs find all the love, medical care, and comfort they deserve!

And finally, we want to thank **you**, the person who purchased this book and is about to read it. Because of your interest in dogs, or perhaps because of the relationship you have with one of the authors, dogs will be saved, cared for, and find a special place in loving homes!

Contents

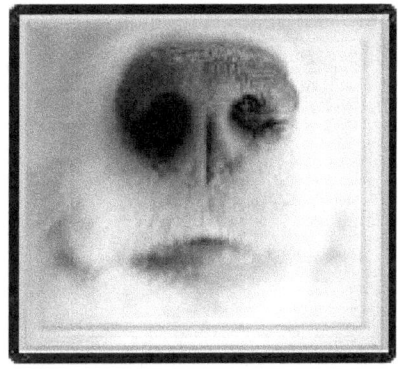

Thank You, Authors!

We believe in the power of the pen. We believe that literacy is an important part of a successful life. We are committed to saving dogs from death row, and we asked for your help. You responded with an enthusiasm we could have never predicted; and we are tremendously grateful!

The goal of this collection is to bring awareness to the plight of the thousands of dogs that are currently suffering in shelters and needlessly walked into the gas chamber. 100% of the proceeds from the sale of the *2014 Write To Woof* anthology will support the work of *Almost Home Animal Rescue League*, a no-kill animal haven in Michigan, as they save dogs from a fate that is death. Their important work is supported entirely through the generous hearts and hands of people like you.

This book is a collection of poetry, short fiction stories and personal essays about dogs. The guidelines were simple: write something that includes a dog as a character, or a no-kill shelter as a locale. We were thrilled to receive such a diverse collection of words that will most certainly make a difference in the life of dogs!

The wet noses and wagging tails of the dogs you have helped, we hope, will be incentive for you to foster, adopt, donate or perhaps volunteer at a no-kill shelter in your area.

Thank you, again. Your words have made a tremendous difference in the lives of these precious souls!

A Boy and His Dog
Robert Bickmeyer

It was a few days before my tenth birthday so it had to be 1939 during the Great Depression. I was sitting on our front porch with Mom, Dad, my sister Claire and our little mixed breed dog, Blackie. A cat ambled along on the other side of our street. Seeing him, Blackie gave chase, darting across the street. Dad emitted the whistle he had always used to call Blackie and he stopped his chase, immediately returning. As he entered the roadway from behind a parked car, the driver of another car did not see him. We all saw the accident. Blackie must have sailed ten feet into the air and died on impact. His obedience caused his demise.

Heavy of heart, this little boy wanted only one thing for his birthday - another Blackie. We found a few puppies in a cage in the basement of a small department store. One was black. He was my dog for the next fifteen years. He grew to look like he was part wolf, but with a long, curly tail.

It was not the norm to leash dogs in those days. Blackie had two pals on our block, Pinto and another Blackie, but my Blackie was territorial. When a strange dog wandered onto our block Blackie chased him away. If he didn't leave, a dog fight broke out and I had to reach into the fight to grab Blackie's curly tail and lift him out of the battle to carry him home.

The only other problem we had with him was his fixation to chase boys on their bicycles and nip at their ankles. If three bites were reported on a dog the law required that he be "put down." After two bites my mother shrewdly bought him another license with the name Duffer. Blackie was, legally, no more.

Over the years, I often shared a bag of peanuts with Blackie. I'd throw a nut above my head and catch it in my mouth, but not always. When a nut fell to the floor it was Blackie's. He made out quite well.

My father often parked the family car at the curb in front of our house. Blackie would hop onto the running board, scramble onto the fender, and then the hood before jumping up onto the roof where he would lay as if to say, "This is my car" because he never did this on any other car. Our neighbors chuckled when they saw this. He was known and friendly to them all.

I taught him to jump into my arms when I thumped my chest with both hands and said, "Blackie, jump." I never dropped him. My mother tried it once, but she did not catch him. He never jumped for her again.

My days with Blackie were a joy, but so were my nights as he slept on the foot of my bed. His end came fifteen years later, one week before I married.

A Brand New Chance
Heather Moser

Today is my day! My dream has come true!
Today is the day I go home with you!
My time in this shelter has been rough.
Don't get me wrong, they provided enough.
I was given food, a roof, and time to run.
I even had a few moments of fun,
but I needed and deserved more
than to sleep every night on a cold concrete floor.
Before I closed my eyes each night, I would dream
of a family willing and wanting to redeem
me away from here, away from this cage
even though I am more advanced in age.
Puppies get adopted quickly, and for them, I am glad,
but I cannot deny it made me sad
to be reminded I was once that youthful, too.
I was cute with an energy I never outgrew.
I had a warm home for quite a while,
but I guess, as I aged, I just fell out of style.
When the shine and novelty of my fur began to fade and dissipate,
my former humans decided a shelter would be my new fate.
I always thought we were a pack, a family,
until that horrible day they abandoned me.
I spent days with no appetite and utterly depressed,
until I realized I deserved the best.
Not all humans, surely, would change their mind,
and I deserved to have a better friend this time.
Yes, I knew it would happen! I could be loved!
When suddenly, just like an angel from above,
you walked through the doors and looked at me!
I was so excited! Could it be? Could it be?!
Yes, you wanted me! You chose to take me away,
and forever a part of your family I will stay!
So, thank you, my lovely human, my new best friend.

You have saved me from a very lonely end!
You will never know how much you have lifted my heart.
Please know my excitement now is only the start
of many days filled with love, joy, and laughter
because I know, as yours, we will live happily ever after.
So, with love I say thank you for that first warm glance.
You have given this old dog a brand new chance!

A Day In The Life
M.K. Sukach

Dedicated to Syrah, 1997-2013. You will always be quirky and beautiful to us.

no, i'm not making you another saucer of coffee...
dogs don't have regrets, i don't think...
stop looking at me like that...
i heard you the first time...
why don't you ever pee on her side of the bed...
quit fussing, lay down...
you can't drive, get off the wheel...
i don't know what that look means...
you smell like bologna...
i'm not sure why you don't like other dogs...
i haven't seen your ball...
well, if the shower is on, you're getting in...
yes, dog is god backwards but...
i'm not sure why you have more than one name...
it's late, go to sleep already...

i know your ears hurt...
i'm trying

A Hound Maybe
Wendy Taylor Carlisle

Light falls away from the desk that holds piled up pictures
of all the dogs they owned in those collapsed years when
the Rottweiler's baying advertised the FedEx truck
idling in the drive, a nightmare crack and tear in
the house where regret stalked the red, blue and white mailer
containing their visions and aversions. The dogs were
hostages then, forfeit to righteous notions: Trilby,
Skid Row, insistent wedge heads, noses at their owners'
thighs. She pastes what's left of them in soft, black albums:
halo of wet light around a muzzle, gleaming pelts
beside a palm, sun through a venous ear. Here they are,
a snap of dogs next to a Kodacolor couple,
in which a man shows up as the usual mongrel:
paw for adventure, slick tracker, a buccaneer for voles.

Abby
Michele Theisen

It was Father's Day, 2010. My son had just left for work and called me to tell me he almost hit a puppy. I got off the phone and jumped in the car, hoping I wouldn't find this little dog. Across from our subdivision is a county gun range and out of the corner of my eye down this dirt road, I saw something moving. I turned down the road and there was this dirty little mini lab hanging around. I got out of my car and tried to talk her into coming to me but she wouldn't. So I jumped in my car went home, got dog food and water and came back. She was still there and still wouldn't come to me. I was getting discouraged. Finally, I lay on the ground and started patting the ground with my hand and she came belly-crawling over to me and I scooped her up.

I brought her home and put her in the garage trying to figure out what I was going to do with her. I called my daughter from her bedroom and told her to come downstairs and not to bring her dog with her. When she opened up the door to the garage, she saw the blackest eyes staring back at her. When our other daughter came home, she met her also and the three of us sat on the deck with this dirty little emaciated dog trying to figure out what we were going to do with her.

We knew she wasn't going anywhere, and when my husband got up, we told him we had a surprise for him. This was his Father's Day present; and it was the best present he could have ever gotten. He adores her. My son that found her named her Abby. We took her to the vet right away, got her cleaned up; all her shots and a little ways down the road, had her spayed. She is a bit skittish but she is like the little sister to three male dogs that just love to play with her. They are her best friends. At night she snuggles up in our bed; and I know without a doubt, she loves her home and we love her.

Am I Okay?
Gay Pawlak

When I started volunteering at Almost Home I guess Hershey was just going in for hip and knee surgery on her left leg, that's a lot of surgery at one time, yikes! I didn't really know about her until Almost Home started asking on their Facebook page for a special needs foster for their sweet girl. Many comments went back and forth and it seemed to me that she would be better off with a foster other than me, since I am gone from home ten to twelve hours a day, and I felt she needed to be with someone who had more time than I did. Well, after about the third day it seemed she wasn't getting anyone to raise their hand to take on the task she needed; so since I went into this to give back, I raised my hand to take her. I basically chose the little dog that needed help. I had an extra bedroom she could have, where the other volunteers didn't have the space she required. They all are wonderful and do so much for all the animals there; actually most do much more than I, so hats off to them all.

I also have two little noisy Shih Tzu's and two sweet cats that Hershey really didn't need to be bothered by each day. Since I had an extra room that was all for her, since she couldn't be crated and needed room to move around in on her leg; this was a good fit. I figured, *so what if she is in there while I am gone, she is safe, warm, fed and when I get home, she gets belly rubs, my attention and walks, that's pretty good!*

Her Journey to being okay. ..

Okay, is such a simple little word, but in the life of an animal, it's huge! When I picked Hershey up, that was the first time she laid eyes on me, her eyes asked, "am I okay with this person?" She was fearful as any being would be. I took her home and got her into her very own room, she laid on her big comfy bed and again it looked like she was thinking, "who is she, am I okay?" For a few weeks, she didn't make a sound, she was happy to be left alone, she felt safe alone. Each day when I got home, I changed her water, fed her and cleaned up her wee wee pads (she couldn't get outside with our stairs), and that was fine, I was happy to do it for her. She got petted and comforted and made to feel loved and cared for. We bonded day by day when I walked her up and down the hallway, keeping her up on that leg.

Then as family and friends would stop over to visit, I would see her expression change again asking, "am I okay?" And of course, she was. She is getting used to people now but I introduce her slowly and with ease, so she is comfortable and not scared.

About six weeks in though, she got to where she wasn't doing so well on that leg. I called Gail, the owner of Almost Home, and she got her quickly into therapy. Almost Home does so much for the animals they take in and it shows in their happy, little faces. I took Hershey in to be evaluated by the doctor and again, she looked at me with her big brown eyes asking, "will I be okay here?" She didn't know what was going on, but when she was being taken away she whimpered for me, asking again "will I be okay?" But, I had to let her go to be helped and I knew she was in the best possible hands and facility to get better.

The facility she was at was an hour and a half away, so I couldn't get over to see her while she was there, but they kept me updated on her progress and after about five weeks they had gotten her in good shape and I went to pick her up. When she saw me, her little body just swayed back and forth and her "excited whimpers" were of joy to see me, plus she was happy with all the staff there so I know she had a great time, bless her little heart after all she had been through. She practically ran to my vehicle to get in, it was so precious. She and I talked and barked most of the way home, person and dog talking, it was the funniest thing and I knew she was thinking, "I am really okay?"

So she is still with me and will be forever. Now when she hears me come into the house, she is barking for me just like the little dogs are. She knows she is okay in our home; whoever comes into our home is good to her and loves her.

Her favorite place is laying on the comfy rug in front of my chair.

Thank you Almost Home staff and volunteers who give your daily lives to helping those in need. If only 1% of people could measure up to your standards, the world would be a better place for all beings.

And a big thanks to my perfect husband, Ron, who is my rock and has been a huge help with Hershey, as well as my brother, Tim, who helps out as I need him, too. Hershey knows we both love her and we are happy she is part of our family. Unfortunately though, none of us really know her journey up until she came to Almost Home as a stray, she is a really good dog, she listens, waits for commands so I pray she was loved and cared for in her past. She will certainly be cared for in her future, Hershey will be okay.

Arvin the Talking Dog
Clyde Liffey

"You need a dog, Eva, not necessarily a talking dog."

"But he's so cute!"

"No he's not." I observed him in his big cage littered with barking dogs and their offal. Though he was well past middle age he assumed his best sad puppy face, the look that hooked my wife. "He's ludicrous."

"Stop, you'll hurt his feelings."

I was about to apologize when the keeper came in. "It's five after four: viewing hours are over. If you haven't made up your minds, you'll have to come back on Monday."

"But I work on Monday."

"So do I, buddy."

Eva widened her eyes, sad kitty style. One of the side effects of her illness or her medication, I'm not sure which, is that she exudes a sensuality far out of proportion to her moderate good looks. A tall man, the keeper crossed his thick short-sleeved arms authoritatively, narrowed his eyes as though to belittle me. I knew Eva was turning him on. She hung her head, batted her eyelashes. I could never tell if that was a tic or conscious flirting. I was always too anxious to ask her. She didn't say anything. I was fed up with visiting pounds, worried and most likely misinformed about my wife's worsening condition.

"Does the talking dog cost more?" I asked.

"They all cost the same. This one might be cheaper since he's already neutered."

"Okay, we'll take him. What's his name?"

"Arvin," said the dog.

If only his vocabulary was limited to his name! He didn't say anything on the way back. After signing the papers and writing the check, we placed him in the cage we brought, secured the cage in the back seat of our old compact car, and quietly drove to the pet store. Eva stayed in the car while I bought a twenty-five pound bag of the dog food the keeper recommended.

I could see Eva talking as I put the dog food in the trunk. She paused occasionally as if listening to what Arvin said. "What are you two talking about?" I asked as I slid into the driver's seat.

"Nothing."

"It must have been about something."

"I was just trying to make Arvin comfortable in his new home. It's a big adjustment for him." Arvin kept his silence. Eva told me to keep the radio turned off so that he wouldn't get overstimulated. I protested, she pouted, and we drove home listening to the sounds our car's engine made.

"What was that rattling in the car?" Eva asked me when we got home.

"I don't know. I'll take it to the mechanic next Saturday. It's due for an oil change anyway."

"Why don't you look at it yourself?"

"You know I'm not good with cars."

"My father is. My brothers are."

"Yes, but I'm your husband and the rest of your family lives three states away."

We heard some voices in the living room. When we walked in we saw Arvin on the couch watching TV. The remote was on the armrest.

"Arvin, get off the couch."

"Let him stay, honey. He has to get used to his new surroundings."

"But I wanted to watch the game."

"There are games on every week. Let Arvin watch his show for once."

I came home deflated the following Saturday.

"Is the car still making that rattling noise?" Eva asked me.

"No, it was a minor repair."

"Then why so glum?"

"The timing belt was due for another replacement and while he was there the mechanic recommended a new water pump and all the other things he could reach down there. I ended up spending much more than I thought I would. I can never tell if I'm being snowed."

"Didn't you know you were due for a timing belt?"

"If I had a sense of timing"

"Yes, I know, we'd be rich."

Arvin whispered something to my wife. She took the keys from me. "Thanks honey. Arvin and I have to drop some things off at the soup kitchen."

While they were gone, I turned the game on and perused the mail. We were invited to a family reunion in three weeks. I had a sandwich and a can of beer for lunch, fell asleep on the couch before the end of the game which I later found out was very exciting. I awoke when my wife entered the living room weighed down by shopping bags. She put them on the floor by the couch, sat on the nearby armchair. Arvin grabbed the remote, sat on the other side of the couch from me, and changed the channel on the TV. "Was the soup kitchen closed?"

"No, Arvin and I stopped at the supermarket on the way back. They had a huge sale on canned goods."

I rummaged in one of the bags. "But we don't eat this stuff."

"It's for the soup kitchen."

"Why this sudden interest in soup kitchens?"

"It's important to help those less fortunate than us."

I rose from the almost threadbare couch, paced back and forth. "We're one missed paycheck away from eating our meals there."

Arvin knocked my beer can over, spilling the little left in it. "We'll be all right," Eva said. "Why don't you clean up that puddle then give Arvin a walk while I start cooking dinner?"

"Why can't he use the toilet?"

"He's not a cat."

While Arvin and I strolled around the neighborhood, I reflected that talking dogs behave more like cats than like other dogs. I'd read on the Internet that they'll often attach themselves to one owner and ignore or be actively hostile to the other. Many of them can be toilet trained. Only the spiteful dogs insist on needing walks. It was a mild afternoon. Arvin and I had wandered into a tony part of town, a neighborhood watch area. "Excuse me a minute," Arvin said. He sat under an azalea and did his business. It was messy. The plastic bags I'd brought could hardly hold his output. I worried about the cameras trained on me while I tamped down the soil round our wealthy neighbor's prize shrubbery.

Eva wasn't happy when we returned. "You stained your pants at the knee."

"It must have been while I was cleaning Arvin's business."

"That never happens to me. I must walk him three or four times a day during the week."

"That's because he likes you."

She blew air over the hair hanging in front of her face. I was aroused. I could tell she wasn't in the mood. She rarely is. "Never mind. Come and eat. Arvin, please change the channel so we can see the movie that we agreed on at eight. If we're not done with dinner by then, you can catch me up during the commercials."

"Yes, mistress," he replied in a voice deeper and more resonant than mine.

"Mistress?"

"It's a joke we have."

Arvin sat in the living room watching TV. "We've got to curb our spending. We can't afford to donate so much to charities."

"But I'm only buying specials. I'm watching the budget."

I looked at my meat, a low quality cut. "Where did you get this beef?"

"You said we need to watch our expenses. I'm going to buy less meat from now on anyway. We should be eating lower on the food chain. Are we going to your family's reunion?"

"Are you trying to change the subject?"

"I'm just asking. You left the invitation on the kitchen table."

"I left it there for you to see. It's a landmark birthday. We have to go even though it means driving three states away then coming home and driving three states more the other way to see your family."

"It will be good for Arvin to travel."

"Why can't we put him in a kennel?"

"I thought you wanted to cut expenses."

"I do." I looked at my uneaten inedible meat, the sodden canned vegetables surrounding it. As Eva's sexiness waxed, her culinary skills waned. "I know the doctor said you should have a pet but our insurance doesn't pay for it. Now on top of dog expenses we have to give to charity? Did Arvin put you up to this?"

Eva looked down at her clean plate, carefully patted her hair into place. I was flummoxed and desirous. "Arvin knows about poverty and what it does to people," she quietly said. "He lived on the streets for months before Animal Control picked him up."

"That's probably because his previous owners got fed up," I thought but didn't say. I wanted my arousal to find an outlet. I silently picked at the remainder of my meal. We heard the overture from Eva and Arvin's musical blaring from the TV. "I'll wash the dishes," I said. "I can make popcorn if you'd like."

We wash the dishes at the sink because I'm too worried about expenses to get the dishwasher repaired. Eva could have let the dishes drip dry but she probably felt guilty about our tiff. I scalded my hand while scrubbing the pot that cooked the soggy vegetables. "Ow, that damn dog! At least he won't live much longer."

"That's a terrible thing to say. What if he heard you?"

"You know of course that dogs have exceptional hearing," Arvin said.

"He didn't mean it, Arvin."

I didn't say anything.

My relation with Arvin never recuperated from that *faux pas*. We left for my family's reunion three weeks later. My wife packed the laptop and some other materials she needed for her home business in the trunk, hopped in to the passenger seat. "No, I didn't forget anything," she said.

"That isn't what I was thinking."

"Oh."

"I was wondering if you're going to miss ogling your sexy musician friend," I said. We have a new neighbor who suns himself on fair afternoons on the small patio behind his townhouse.

"You mean Gabe?"

"You know his name?"

"Of course I know his name. He's a local celebrity."

"I think he's just a womanizer."

"Not every tall young sinewy handsome trumpeter is a wolf."

"I thought getting a dog would keep you from straying."

"Who says I'm straying?"

"Arvin," I asked, "male to male, can you tell me if Eva is behaving herself?"

"I don't see how Eva looking out the window is so different from you looking at naked starlets," Arvin said.

"They're not naked. How do you know, I mean, what are you talking about?"

"Your browser history," Arvin replied.

"Did you teach Arvin how to search browser histories?"

"He taught me," Eva said.

"There's nothing wrong with looking at pictures of pretty girls in bathing suits."

"Did I say there was anything wrong with it? Did I even bring up the topic?" She looked out the window. It was still a partly cloudy day. We had one hundred-eighty miles to go before our rest stop.

Veterans of this route, we stopped at a place with cheap gas and outdoor benches. Eva retrieved the cooler from the trunk and chose a table for us while I filled up the car. Arvin was already sitting next to Eva when I joined them. She was feeding him the meat from her sandwich.

"I thought the doctor said you weren't getting enough protein," I said as I tucked into my sandwich which appeared to be thinner than usual.

"Posh."

We said very little after that. Arvin didn't finish his kibble.

I took Arvin for a walk through the small pine wood next to the picnic area while Eva cleaned up. He didn't leave my side, showed no interest in the other dogs being walked there.

A half hour later, he announced that he had to go.

"But you could have gone in the woods at the rest stop," I said.

"I didn't have to go then."

"You're doing this to punish me."

"Don't believe everything you read on those dog advice web sites," Arvin replied.

"There's another exit in five miles," Eva said. "Can you hold out that long, Arvin?"

"For you I will."

A few raindrops hit the windshield. I saw some thunderheads ahead of us. "It will be raining pretty hard when we pull off the exit. Did you pack an umbrella?" I asked.

"I didn't think we'd need one."

Arvin as was his wont with me did his business messily. "I don't think we're required to clean up after dogs in this State," I said as I let him back into the car.

"You'd better clean up anyway. There's a police car parked a few car lengths behind us. Take these plastic bags."

"I don't think they're big enough."

"It's all we have."

I knew better than to ask what they were laughing about when I returned. The police didn't follow us onto the highway.

Both sides of our family keep animals though for different reasons. Arvin didn't associate with any of the other pets at the picnics and barbecues we attended. Since the adults were mostly interested in each other, Arvin spent most of his time with the young children for whom he was a novelty. He occasionally acted like a normal dog. I once saw him on his hind legs begging for a doggy treat. Since his face was inexpressive, I couldn't tell if he was playacting or if he was at one with his canine identity. It seemed that whenever I forgot about him and started to enjoy myself that he would tug on my shoes or a pants leg and ask to be taken for a walk.

Eva's family kept dogs for hunting and cats for killing vermin. They understood why Eva would want a talking dog: she was the artsy member of the family. That's why she moved nearly two hundred miles away to live with me in a suburb of a regional arts hub far away from both the tastemakers of the country and the real people. They thought I was a namby-pamby because I worked in an office and allowed her to keep such a useless animal.

I was drinking beer with George, Eva's tolerant uncle, when Jem (as a toddler Eva couldn't pronounce James; the name stuck) her youngest brother, approached us.

"Your dog tells me you had some car trouble recently," he chuckled.

"It was a minor repair and some routine maintenance."

"How much did it cost you?"

I told him the sum.

Jem whistled. "Hell, I could have found those parts for next to nothing and fixed it for you for a bottle of whisky or two."

"I would have liked to come but we'd just gotten Arvin and he needed to get acclimated."

Jem guffawed, clapped me drunkenly on the shoulder. "You are funny! Come on, let's go inside. I want to show you the latest additions to my taxidermy collection. I'm getting really good at it."

I saw Arvin out of the corner of my eye sitting near Eva's lap, waiting for me to feel comfortable so that he could ask for a walk.

"I'm glad our summer visiting is over," I said when we finally got home.

"It was nice seeing everybody again."

"I enjoyed it," Arvin said from the TV room.

I plopped down on the armchair. "Well I'm exhausted. Driving through six States takes its toll on you."

"But they're narrow States."

"They're still States."

Eva came in with a tray of cookies, placed them on the coffee table in front of the couch Arvin sat on. "I was checking my email and," she hesitated.

"Is something wrong?"

"No, no, it's just"

"Tell me now so I can deal with it." I'm not normally so stern.

"My charity group is being recognized for its work. We're invited to a reception at Le Gril. I feel awful. It costs twenty-five dollars per person and with all the money we just spent on the trip." She sank deeper into the couch. I wanted her. Arvin patted her gently on the thigh.

Le Gril is a fancy new restaurant, part of a small chain, that opened in our town about six months ago. We'd both always wanted to eat there but never felt we could afford it. "That's not so much money."

"It's probably a limited menu. There's a cash bar."

"You deserve the recognition for all the work you did. We'll go."

"Thanks, honey." Eva pecked me on the forehead and ran off to unpack.

A hard rain, the outer fringe of a hurricane that had veered off into the sea, fell the day of the dinner. Le Gril's parking lot was full. I circled it a few times then parked in the lot of the huge shopping mall across the street. We had to make several detours around deep puddles. We almost got splashed by a car speeding along the street between the mall and the restaurant. The left sleeve of my blazer was wet when we got to the entrance but we were otherwise dry. The maître d', a tall thin balding man, sniffed his disapproval at our approach. "No dogs allowed, monsieur."

Eva was crestfallen. Neither of us realized that dogs, especially talking dogs, were considered gauche in philanthropic circles. "You go in," I said. "You earned it. I'll watch Arvin and drive up to the restaurant at ten to pick you up."

The guests and honorees were mingling in a small reception area behind the haughty major-domo's stand. Gabe, mixed drink in his left hand, gallantly held Eva's right hand in his and kissed it. Charmed, she curtsied.

"What is he doing here?" I muttered as I descended the steps.

"I believe he's the entertainment," Arvin said.

We stopped at the edge of the street, waited for the light to change. A car sped through a puddle thoroughly drenching us. "Tell me, Arvin, what's really going on between Eva and Gabe."

"I don't know. I'm neutered."

"You must know something."

"I'm just a dog."

His voice was so toneless that I couldn't tell if he was being evasive or honest. The light changed. We crossed the street. I held the umbrella up and my head down, smelling wet dog.

At The Foot Of Her Bed
Beth Ford Roth

When my dying mother left California to move in with my husband Alex and me in Atlanta, our dog Bodhi was a very young and energetic five-year-old. We adopted him when he was barely a year old. We were told he would calm down by the time he was two. That was the first of the many ways we were misled about Bodhi.

I first saw Bodhi's handsome mug online, scrolling through the hundreds of dogs up for adoption, about a week after Alex and I got married. Bodhi, with his human-like eyes that went in slightly different directions, big pink-tongued smile, and yellow fur, looked like the perfect family dog.

I had two cats from before I married Alex, and it was important to me that our new dog treat the feline duo with respect. Alex and I also planned to have children at some point, so we wanted our new dog to be gentle with little humans as well. The woman who rescued Bodhi from a high-kill shelter near the Mexico-California border described him in her Petfinder.com ad as a lab-mix who was "great with kids, great with cats."

I filled out an online application and was almost immediately sent back an email with the subject line: Approved! I spoke briefly with Bodhi's caretaker on the phone, and she agreed to drop him off later that evening for a quick meet-and-greet.

Just a few hours later, the woman was unlatching Bodhi's cage from the back of her pickup. He burst out of his carrier like a jack-in-the-box, leaping off the back of the truck and running immediately over to the woman. He jumped up on her and licked her face. He then did the same to Alex, then to me (nearly knocking me over), and then without an invitation ran into our condo. Maybe he wouldn't be so great with kids.

My cats were watching all this unfold on the landing of the stairs. Bodhi immediately raced towards them, chasing them under the bed in one of our spare bedrooms. It didn't look like he was great with cats.

I was about to pull Alex aside and tell him this dog was just too hyper for us. Before I got the chance, the woman was back behind the driver's seat of her pickup truck. She handed us a paper bag.

"Here's his food and a leash. He sleeps on the floor. I'll give you a call tomorrow to see how your first night together was." She burned rubber and was gone before we could protest.

Alex and I took Bodhi on a walk around our neighborhood. He pulled on the leash the entire time, yanking it especially hard whenever he saw a cat, squirrel, or critter of any kind.

When we returned home, Bodhi ran upstairs to our bedroom, jumped on the bed, rolled on his back, and began to snore, his googly, human-like eyes partially open.

****

We never did send Bodhi back to the woman who rescued him from the shelter. The cats learned to steer clear of him, and Bodhi them – as they weren't afraid to swipe at him with their claws if he got too close. Bodhi, to his credit, began to view the cats as members of his pack instead of critters to be chased.

Every weekend was a challenge, trying to figure out the best way to tire out Bodhi so we could get a good night's sleep. We were living in California then, and would take him to the beach, throwing tennis balls in the ocean for him to fetch until our shoulders were numb. We took him to dog parks, where he usually ended up trying to hump the other neutered males. Alex went on long runs with

Bodhi. It didn't seem to matter what we did. After his afternoon nap, Bodhi was recharged and looking to play again.

About three years after we adopted Bodhi, we all moved out to Atlanta for Alex's job. It turns out Atlanta is a squirrel haven, and Bodhi would chase them in Piedmont Park, trying to climb the trees into which they scurried, crying loudly and tearing the bark off the trees in frustration when he couldn't catch them.

We'd been in Atlanta about a year when I found out my mother had terminal throat cancer. She'd had it twice before and beaten it back both times. This time, though, her doctors were giving her just a year to live. I flew back out to California, and brought Mom home to Atlanta with me, where Alex and I could take care of her.

When Alex, Mom, and I arrived home from the Atlanta airport, it was late afternoon, prime squirrel-watching time for Bodhi. He greeted my mother with all the unbridled joy with which he greeted every human being.

We got Mom settled in our guest bedroom, and Bodhi followed. Instead of heading out to the backyard to bark at his furry-tailed nemeses, he hopped on the bed next to Mom, circled a few times, and then lay at the foot of the bed.

My mother was tiny to begin with – just five feet tall, but the cancer had taken away her ability to eat, and she relied on me to give her liquid nutrition and pain medication through her feeding tube. The liquid had a sour vanilla smell to it that permeated her room and kept the cats away. But Bodhi remained.

Our perpetually-in-motion dog had taken on a new role - that of calm, nurturing companion. Mom wasn't much bigger than Bodhi at that point, and she loved to put her arms around him and hold him tight. Bodhi would always hold still just as long as she needed him to.

My mother's condition deteriorated much more quickly than the doctors predicted, and at a rate I wasn't ready for. We enrolled her in hospice care, although she remained at home with Alex and me. When Mom began to stumble out of her bed in the middle of the night, we had to order a hospital bed with bars to keep her safe. Soon, she slipped into a coma.

The hospital bed was in our living room. I slept on one side of our sectional couch, Bodhi on the other. He and I kept a vigil on Mom. I was afraid to leave her side, afraid that she would die when I was not in the room. When she did finally pass, just six weeks after she arrived in Atlanta, it was in my arms, with me telling her gently to let go.

The morning after she died, I was in a panic. I went from room to room, looking for her, yelling that I still needed her. My heart knew she was dead, but my mind still couldn't grasp the concept.

But somehow, Bodhi knew. He could also sense that it was now me who needed to be taken care of. During the next several months, when I would collapse on our guest bed, sobbing, searching any remnants of Mom's scent, Bodhi would hop on the bed. Instead of circling to the foot of the bed, Bodhi would lie next to me, licking the salty tears from my face.

****

When we adopted Bodhi, his name had been Peyton. Alex picked the name Bodhi from one of his favorite bad movies, *Point Break*. Bodhi was Patrick Swayze's surfer character. With Bodhi's blond hair, it seemed to fit.

It wasn't until years after my mother died that we learned what Bodhi means in the Buddhist religion. The word Bodhi means "be enlightened, and awake to our purpose on earth, and knowledgeable on how to liberate oneself from earthly suffering."

I don't believe it to be a coincidence that our dog, with such a name, displayed a transcendent understanding of what was happening when my mother was dying. I'm just grateful he was by our side.

At The Poetry Reading Where I Imagine Dogs
M.K. Sukach

Our neighborhood scholars
who live in the third person
patrol in panoptic circles
about their garrisoned yards at night
who nuzzle the soiled paragraphs of earth
decipher signs of the dark
discern one car from the next
know what's wrong in the house down the street
lick wounds, theirs or another's because it's a wound.

I'll never be as good as that I think
listening from the back of the room
where I should be
patrolling around chairs
nuzzling bared ankles
deciphering pauses
discerning breaths
knowing the ineffable
licking tendered hands.
At least the dogs know your life is not a literary event.

Blessed By The Dog
Stefanie Freele

She greets the others at the dog park with wiggles, *I'm here – let the party begin!* She leans over from the passenger seat, *Thank you for taking me.* She sniffs cool air through the cracked open window, *The world is magnificent.* She does her business in the wrong yard, *The grass was soft. You should try too.* She runs along the beach, *Hurry. We can sniff everything.* She takes bites from the dish and brings them close, *They taste better over here.* She sneaks onto the end of the bed at night *I'll keep your feet warm.* She perks up her ears when the keys jangle, *Lets go. Me and you.*

Canine Yoga
A.J. Huffman

My Chihuahua does his best to stay
fit when he can. Lying in his bed,
he practices his stretches . . .

Position 1: Frankenpuppy

Roll onto back. Front and rear paws
rigidly extended. Straight out. Close
eyes. Hold till owner checks for vitals. Move
to

Position 2: Pretzel Puppy

Stay on back. Bend front paws to semi-
relaxed extensions. Arc to side till nose
touches toenails. Hold till owner comments
on cuteness and concedes to rub belly. Move
to

Position 3: Broken Neck Puppy

Relax paws. Roll onto side. Extended
stretch of torso. Bend neck back to extremely
awkward angle. May use coffee table
or chair leg to assist with appearance of
discomfort. Hold till owner starts to worry, takes
pity, picks up onto lap, and proceeds to provide
post-workout rubdown.

Repeat as desired.

Celia P. Ransom
Corkie

Oh, how little feet did scurry
When thunder released all its fury.
And where did doggie quickly tuck her head?
You know, I bet, 'twas under the bed.

Deity
Michael L. Kamrath

I met a dog the other day
a nice russet colored short-haired blend
curved tail arcing over his broad back
square head, held high and regal
    and his eyes
almond shaped   golden brown
rimmed with black mascara, lines extending back
from each corner
a full inch
like an Egyptian tomb guardian
standing beside Anubis
protecting the dead

Dog and Cat
Gillian Lee

Dog and Cat lying out in the sun,
Dog said to Cat, "I think you should run."
"Why should I run, what can you hear?"
"They're coming to bathe you.
I hear them, they're near."
Cat ran.

Dog and Cat lying out in the sun,
Cat said to Dog, "I think you should run.
The dog groomer's coming, I heard them say.
They're going to clip your toenails today."
Dog ran.

Dog and Cat lying out in the sun,
Both now tired by all of the fun.
Cat was now clean, and Dog's claws were trimmer.
With tummies empty, the call comes,
"Dinner." Both ran.

The Dog-Fur Coat
Molly Tamulevich

Mrs. Angela Mertz carefully placed three boxes of chocolate chip cookies into her cart and felt the hair on the back of her neck stand up. Someone was watching her. She turned swiftly and found herself face to face with her neighbor, Ms. Elizabeth Carter, a woman she only knew from front porch hellos and the occasional late night peek into a perpetually uncovered bedroom window.

"Angela!" Ms. Carter clasped her slim hands around Mrs. Mertz's shoulders and kissed her cheek. "How *are* you?"

"I'm well. How..."

"Dan's just *fine*. Thank you for asking. He's taken Mackenzie and her friends up north for the weekend to go fishing." She rolled her eyes dramatically, "Which leaves me free for a girl's night. I can't remember the last time that I had the house to myself. If it isn't soccer, it's benefits or meetings or projects. I even told Martina to take a vacation! I'm going to be scrubbing the floor all by myself!" She paused for a moment, her eyes locking in on something just below Mrs. Mertz's face. "My goodness. Your coat. I didn't know we had so much in common!" She stepped back and twirled. "I just bought it last month. Ermine! I never thought I would be able to wear it in public after all the nastiness of the past few decades, but things have changed! Fashion isn't a crime anymore. Aren't people fickle?" The heavy bottom of her coat thumped into a row of peanut butter and softly batted them out of rank. The fur glistened under fluorescent light. Ms. Carter grasped the collar and rubbed her cheek against the material, follicles so dense that Mrs. Mertz could almost hear the razor thin sound of them slapping her skin. A sales woman walked by and glanced over at them, shaking her head as she passed. She stopped at the end of the aisle and looked back as she spoke to a coworker. Mrs. Mertz couldn't hear their conversation, but the energy was clearly full of disapproval.

Ms. Carter seemed oblivious to the controversy. She was inspecting Mrs. Mertz's coat with her eyes, then her fingers, running them up and down the sleeves and lingering at the cuffs. "I love it. Vintage." Mrs. Mertz was at a loss for words, and the truth would surely disappoint, so she nodded and garbled her response into a dainty cough. Ms. Carter beamed her blue eyes into Mrs. Mertz's. "Come over tomorrow night. I'm hosting a presentation for some of my friends-a business venture. I suppose you could say it's going to be a fashion night. Please come! We'll have food. Vegan options of course. Gluten free. Raw. Whatever it is you eat, I can make it happen." She patted Mrs. Mertz's arms excitedly and then walked away, still chattering. "I feel like I've discovered something about you just now and I would love for you to join us." Her black hair tumbled over the shimmering coat and Mrs. Mertz didn't have the heart to say no. She nodded and agreed to be there at eight and to bring a bottle of sulfite-free wine and to just be herself because everyone would love her.

As she passed by the cheese island, Mrs. Mertz noticed that many other customers were inspecting her coat with frowns and whispers. She became embarrassed, the unknown conversations following her like shuffling feet in the leaves. *It was my grandmother's!* She wanted to shout. *I only wore it because I miss her!* She reached for a block of tofu and the sleeve rubbed against the arm of a young woman standing next to her. The woman recoiled. "That's ironic, "she said, glancing between the coat and the cold block of soybeans in Mrs. Mertz's hand. "I thought that people like you don't give a shit about animals. Oh wait, I forgot. It's all about the image, right? The bag, the diet, the coat? They're cute until they can do something for you and then they're just pieces to rip up and use. Do you know how your coat died, Ma'am? Someone shoved a cattle prod up its ass, electrocuted it, skinned it, and left the body in a pile. Judging by the size, you've probably got thirty bodies on there at least. Thirty wasted lives. Good thing you care about your cardiovascular health, though. We definitely need people like you eating healthy and living for a long time, teaching your children how to be just like you."

Mrs. Mertz jogged to the checkout with tears in her eyes and drove home as quickly as she could. She threw herself on the couch and hugged the fraying, faded garment in her arms, thinking of her grandmother wheeling herself down the halls of the hospital, grey hair akimbo, still wearing her pinkest lipstick.

At seven fifty the following night, Mrs. Mertz slipped her feet into her best boots, shrugged the coat over her shoulders and clasped the wine bottle in her hand. She made her way carefully down the sidewalk, nervous about slipping, although the maintenance man always salted thoroughly. There were other women approaching Ms. Carter's doorstep, and she fell in behind them as they chatted, swallowed up by white folds as plush as marshmallows. The door opened and Ms. Carter appeared, effortlessly graceful. She wrapped an arm around each of the women and squeezed them together. "I'm so happy to see you" she squealed, head sandwiched between their collars. She noticed Mrs. Mertz standing on the last step and glided outside, shooing the other two in. Her arms were heavy with silver bracelets, and as she embraced Mrs. Mertz, they chimed gently together. "I'm so happy you could make it, Angela. Come inside and let's eat. Jasmine should be here in half an hour and we can get started."

Ms. Carter's house was the same model as Mrs. Mertz's, but the choice of décor was several shades pricier. Instead of eggshell, there was mahogany; instead of cotton, pashmina. Ms. Carter took her coat with a sigh of appreciation and sent her towards the kitchen with a wave of her hand and a command to eat. Seven other women mingled around a circular table, their angular wrists pendulums that supported delicate flutes filled with pomegranate arils and bubbling champagne. Mrs. Mertz smoothed the front of her dress and stepped into the mix. The first to introduce herself was Meryl, a longtime friend of Ms. Carter and manager of a local boutique that Mrs. Mertz had never believed herself wealthy enough to set foot in. Meryl had brought Naomi, who had brought Courtney, who was on the board of the community theatre. Rachel and Brooklyn were sisters from Savannah who complained about the lack of anything stronger to drink and began raiding Ms. Carter's cabinets with familiarity. Within minutes, Mrs. Mertz felt relaxed enough to share her experience at the grocery store, and the women all laughed and reassured her that it happened to them every time they wore anything luxurious in public. A giant sexagenarian named Loretta shouted from a corner chair that they were lucky they hadn't lived during the seventies when activists had a free pass to harass anyone they liked. "Those were the days" she shouted "when red paint was made with lead and mercury. Imagine! Splashing me with a carcinogen in order to spare a few rodents. You don't even want to know what they did to my Louis Vuitton! You have to understand, girls, that these people want nothing more than to have what we have. They're sandwiched between a glass ceiling and a glass floor. They'll never be able to be where we are, but they can always look down and see where they'd fall if something goes wrong."

"You have the best stories, auntie" chirped Lily, a short, slender black woman with finger waves. "If someone tried that now, they could be charged with domestic terrorism!"

"The flannel they all wore was already domestic terrorism!"

Mrs. Mertz laughed along with the group and bit into a slice of bruschetta. The champagne warmed her chest and the dim light glowed on the assorted metal and stone on the bodies around her. Brooklyn reached deep into a cupboard and triumphantly lofted a bottle of whisky above her head as her sister grabbed an armful of tumblers and ice. Everyone was so busy talking and drinking that they didn't hear the fight until it reached domestic disturbance levels.

"...If you *never* cared about me, this would still be a big deal. No one will support you in this." The voice was a woman's, raspy as a match scraping the box. The kitchen fell silent and they heard Ms. Carter's voice, but the words were lost.

"A waste. You think what I do is a waste? I've spent my entire life working to make the situation better. Did you ever help me? Where were you when I was covered in vomit? When I cried because I had to make that call, when no one would help. You were in *goddamn Finland* buying some purebred bitch so you could fit in at the club!"

Ms. Carter's voice was an angry hum in the foyer. Loretta turned to the other guests and whispered, "That'll be Eleni"

"Who's Eleni?" Mrs. Mertz inquired, drunk on the new bond formed by their collective voyeurism.

"An ex-friend of Elizabeth" Lily responded.

"A very very close ex-friend" Courtney elaborated

"She's the executive director of the Allen County Humane Society. Wonderful lady. She does so much." Naomi chimed in

"She helped me adopt my Sasha!" Meryl whispered, "I didn't think that she'd be invited."

"I don't think she was."

"Does she still feel...friendly...toward..." Mrs. Mertz began

"Oh no no no!" Loretta interjected, "it's Elizabeth who still wants to be friends with Eleni. "

"It's 2013" Brooklyn interrupted, "Can't we skip the bullshit and call a lesbian a lesbian? Even if she still acts like it's a secret?"

Loretta huffed and ignored her, "The problem is that love pales in comparison to other drives. You get what I'm saying? Eleni is one of those people I just described, except she handicaps herself. She has the brains and connections to have anything she wants, but she keeps looking down, not up. She doesn't put herself first. She works all day for nearly nothing, gets herself tangled with the worst kinds of people, puts herself in physical danger... it's like she sabotages everything she could be. Elizabeth tried to remove her from the squalor she works in, but..."

"But what?" Mrs. Mertz asked, captivated.

"But can you imagine the shame if Ms. Elizabeth Carter was to leave all this behind for an animal rights activist? No more yacht club, no foie gras, no shark fin soup, and certainly no fur. She'd be looking down into the abyss, and we all know how ugly that can be. Elizabeth isn't suited to craning her neck to see what might make her uncomfortable"

"But if she's in love, isn't it worth changing..." Mrs. Mertz began, but Naomi talked over her.

"No future. No luxury. No mystique. Just dog shit and sad appearances at $50 a plate charity dinners. I mean, what would they even serve? Some green beans and a baked potato?"

The women laughed quietly as the fight raged on outside. The last discernable comment was Eleni screaming , "Cruella Deville!" before the door slammed shut. Mrs. Mertz set her glass down and felt herself drift out of the shared merriment, dirty dishes in her sink dancing through her mind- frozen mixed vegetables, stir fry, water. She stepped backwards, her mind made up to leave before the presentation began, but Ms. Carter appeared in the doorway, her hair pinned back from her ears with a glimmering dragonfly.

"Jasmine should be here any minute, ladies. Are you ready?"

"Ready!" They all replied, smiles dancing.

Ms. Carter poured herself a glass of champagne and smiled at Mrs. Mertz as everyone filed into the den. "Are you enjoying yourself?"

Mrs. Mertz just nodded and shuffled along behind them, mouth dry and feeling very out of place.

As they piled onto couches and chairs, the doorbell rang and Ms. Carter leapt up to answer it with an excited, "She's here!"

There was a moment of unseen greeting and then Jasmine rounded the corner, blonde hair thick over her shoulders, steps confident despite a confining, charcoal pencil skirt. Ms. Carter walked behind her, rolling a large black tote and smiling.

"Good evening," Jasmine greeted them warmly. "How are you all tonight?" Mrs. Mertz, who had once worked as a Tupperware party hostess, recognized the voice of a person who was ready to sell. "On behalf of Greenwear Luxury Apparel, I'd like to introduce myself. My name is Jasmine Gorden, and I am here to revolutionize the way that you dress." The women quieted down and sipped their drinks. "How many of you have censored yourself and your closet due to public pressure? I did. I worked my way up the ladder for years only to find that when I made it to the top, no one wanted me to wear that success on my sleeve." She extended her hand emphatically. "I started to feel like I had succeeded for nothing. I woke up every morning and put on the same outfit. It didn't matter if I was wearing Dior, Gucci or Sears; it was a black pantsuit and it was awful. I wanted to feel sexy. I wanted to feel proud of my work, but when I bought that first fur vest, I felt shunned. I felt judged. By people who had no idea what I had achieved, friends who hadn't come nearly as far as me. Do you know what I'm talking about?" The women all raised their hands. "How many of you feel torn between luxury and political correctness?" A few members of the audience nodded, "None of us want to hurt animals, none of us want little children to slave away over our clothes, none of us want to kill off a species! Unfortunately, it's sometimes necessary to ask for sacrifices in order to stay current. Look at Beyonce. Look at Vogue. Is it fair that you should have to deny yourself what everyone in your circles is wearing simply because it may involve the quick, painless euthanasia of a few animals that no one wants? I don't think it's fair! I don't think it's right! I can't wear my mink to run errands because of some serious stigma, but here's where I think things could change. "

Jasmine opened the tub and pulled out a scarf. It was a series of spheres all sewn together. Some were red and some were mottled. She passed it around and the women oohed and aaahed, rubbing it against their faces and necks. Mrs. Mertz passed it along quickly, feeling suspicious. Once it had returned to the tote, Jasmine continued, "I heard that someone here works in theatre."

"I do" Courtney volunteered.

"And I heard that your company will be attempting a very ambitious production."

"Yes. Next winter, we will be staging a musical adaptation of Braveheart."

"It sounds like you'll need a lot of costumes. Period pieces."

"Oh yes."

Jasmine reached in the tote and pulled out a roughly made fur cape. It was brown and black, short and patchy. She swirled it around Courtney's shoulders and fastened it with a small, metal clasp. "Do you feel like William Wallace?" Courtney giggled. "What if I told you that I could supply you with two hundred of these capes at five dollars apiece?"

Courtney gasped. "How?"

Jasmine silenced her with a raised hand. "I was also told that we have a few shop owners in the audience tonight. Meryl, Rachel and Brooklyn raised their hands. Jasmine reached in the tote and pulled out two pairs of fuzzy boots and a fur vest as black as sable. Except it wasn't sable. Mrs. Mertz was sure of that. The vest was quoted at twenty dollars and the boots at thirty. Jasmine then provided a soft, blonde blanket for Loretta and Lily's massage studio and an insulated glove prototype for Naomi's spiritual retreat center. For a long moment, the women were preoccupied with the items in front of them. Jasmine looked at Ms. Carter and then glanced at Mrs. Mertz. "She's just here as a public test." Ms. Carter assured her, and Mrs. Mertz noticed how Jasmine furrowed her eyebrows slightly.

Jasmine opened her briefcase and withdrew some paper. Soon, she had everyone's rapt attention. "Now for the statistics." She began. "I'm sure that all of you are aware of the controversy surrounding our industry, so I'd like to show you the big picture. Every year, between six and eight million unwanted cats and dogs are surrendered to animal shelters in this country. Of those, about two point seven million are euthanized. Of the almost eighty four million dogs owned in the US, only twenty percent are adopted from a shelter. This means that people do not want these animals. Why would they? Does everyone want a pit bull? Does everyone want an old mutt? No! Even when a purebred ends up in a shelter, there's no telling what they'll be like."

Mrs. Mertz felt her hair begin to stand up as she remembered Eleni's shouted condemnation.

"The fact of the matter is that we are wasting an enormous retail opportunity. Fur has been a luxury since human beings first wrapped themselves in buffalo skins and wolf pelts. If you own it, you know. If you've ever felt the difference between the real thing and a synthetic, you know why fashion designers the world over prefer it. Now imagine- with the competitive prices that Greenwear Luxury offers, you could not only pass on the luxury to your clients, but you could appeal to markets that are now out of your reach. Envision this: Old Randy the German Shepherd down the street has finally been captured. He's been terrorizing the neighborhood for years. There's no way anyone would want him. Who would spend the resources to adopt a dog like that? Now instead of just throwing his body away after he's euthanized, what if it went to a Greenwear processing plant? We could turn a public health risk into gloves for mountain climbers, winter boots, a scarf, even a costume. All those pit bulls from the fighting ring downtown? Statistically, no one wants them. Who wants the risk? Wouldn't it be better to turn them into a purse? No petroleum byproducts, no fur farming, just reusing and recycling."

"Stop." Meryl interjected. "Just stop. I adopted a dog from the shelter who used to be aggressive and now she comes with me to work. Are you telling me that she's not worth it? That it would be better to make her into a coat than a companion?"

Jasmine shrugged, "Minks, foxes, stoats, beavers, wolves and rabbits are all considered intelligent, and many are domesticated. You think they're cute, but you also wear them. What's the difference? Pigs, cows and chickens are all important characters in children's books, but then you eat them. What's the difference?" There was a pause. Jasmine continued. "The difference is that you know your dog and you wanted to make it work for her. That's great. That's one dog. What about the other two point seven million? We aren't a nation of Good Samaritans; we're a nation of consumers. As a business owner, you should know that. The quickest way to turn controversy into something bland is to offer it at a reasonable price to the middle class. They already wear faux fur in spades. You don't think they'd jump at the chance to try the real thing?"

"She has a point." Brooklyn interjected. "Do you know how many people would want this stuff? It's high quality. Once someone famous does it, everyone will follow right along. Why do we order based on celebrity style? It's what people want."

"I can't believe you're defending this!" Meryl responded, "You have dogs!"

"Purebred dogs."

"What if they ended up at a shelter and became someone's coat?"

"That's unlikely. Most of the animals she's talking about aren't worth the time it would take to rehabilitate them."

"Are you telling me that Sasha wasn't worth the time?"

"She's sweet, Meryl, but we don't all want a sob story. My animals reflect my success." She flipped her hair, "I think it's a great idea, Jasmine. I can think of several celebrity sponsors we could approach about this." Brooklyn stroked the boots in her lap, agitated.

"We already have some in mind," Jasmine reassured her.

The room was still, tension high. Ms. Carter broke the silence. "Angela, what do you think? You're the public's voice on this issue. The fur-wearing public, that is." All eyes turned to her. The white sheets of statistics, the golden blanket, the merle patterned cape.

"I think," Mrs. Mertz began, "I think that I need to go home now. I'm not who you think I am." She rose and walked to the door as the women around her began to bicker amongst themselves.

"Angela!" Ms. Carter followed her out onto the stoop. "I didn't mean to offend you. I just wanted your opinion."

"My opinion," Mrs. Mertz began, "is too vast for you to understand."

"Please tell me." Ms. Carter asked, "This could be my future, you see. This could be my claim to fame, my million dollar idea."

"All I see is a lot of people scheming about how to step on the backs of the less powerful to make themselves more powerful."

Ms. Carter scoffed, "They're animals, Angela. They're as good as dead. They keep us company, we get bored with them, and then we drop them off for someone else to deal with. For most people, they're as disposable as the coats we would make them into."

"Only because people like you believe that."

"The statistics prove it."

"No." Mrs. Mertz asserted. "The statistics prove that we aren't valuing life for life's sake. I lived in a shelter for a time as a child. I had to be rehabilitated. Does that make me any less worthy than you? Does it make me disposable because no one wanted me?"

"Angela... you can't make that argument"

"I can. I did. You are the worst kind of predator; you see the possibility for change and instead choose to exploit the status quo. How many disposable children overseas will sew coats in the name of your bottom line? How many disposable people will labor over your disposable animals? It's all the same; it's your foot on all of our backs. It isn't the shelter's fault that those animals die. It's people like you who treat them like they're less-than."

Ms. Carter was silent and then she shivered. "You forgot your coat. I'll get it for you."

Mrs. Mertz's heart broke at the thought of leaving her grandmother's coat behind, but then it swelled with the realization that her sense of right and wrong was as much of an inheritance as any material thing. "Keep it."

Mrs. Mertz hugged herself on the short walk home. While her chilly hands fumbled with the key, she heard the excited tap tap of her dog's nails on the floor. She pushed inside and sat down, stroking the long, smooth fur, feeling the warm body wiggle against her in delight. "I love you," she crooned, "You matter." She stayed there for a long while, feeling her dog breathe as she replayed the last two days. Car doors began to slam next door and the women filed out, some walking quickly and some lingering and exchanging cards with Jasmine and Ms. Carter. As she was getting ready for bed, she peeked through the window and saw Ms. Carter propped up, reading. She had never noticed before that her meticulous beauty was as cold and stony as starlight, and equally unattainable, a frown dragging her face into a study of disappointment. The next day, Mrs. Mertz visited the shelter and filled out an application to be a foster parent. When asked to state her occupation, she simply wrote : Good Samaritan. She walked through the rows of cages and saw the faces there, imagined the faces of all the foxes and rabbits and children the world over and said a silent prayer that they would one day be offered the chance to be seen as more than garbage. *To all of us who are overlooked,* she prayed, *all us orphans, may we recognize each other, and when we do, may we help each other the best that we can.* A week later, she opened her home to a mottled six-year-old who would have made a lovely hat. Instead, he made a fine companion.

Dog Women
A.J. Huffman

Most of us prefer solitary
confinement, relish its tangible
ability to contain our natural aggression,
allowing only canine trespass into
our fortresses. The dogs speak
guttural growls that make perfect sense
to our ears. Bursts of rapid-fire barking
re-enforce mutual disdain for external
activities. Ours is the only world that matters.
Quickly assimilating into each other's lives,
each adapts to familial roles. We offer food,
warmth from blankets, studded collars, rewards
for good behavior. They call us
mother, lick our face when they are happy,
retreat to the bedroom without a word
when they are not. We call them baby
and pumpkin when they are curled in laps or
splayed across chilly feet, smile proudly
when they chase off less-respectful children
who wander inside our boundaries, bite
mailmen who attempt to deliver
hate-mail from exes and bill collectors. At night
we become mirrors, restlessly dreaming
of the chase. Feet and fur fly in the wind,
no restraints, just adrenaline-driven freedom,
room to run.

Dogs Don't Send Flowers
Gary Beck

When my dog was a year and a half old I discovered that he needed sex. Like a good master, I tried to obtain female services for him, but my efforts resulted in failure. My frustration level was probably growing higher than his, but it was hard to tell. After all, Pard didn't look up suddenly from gnawing a bone and say: *Master, master, this deprivation is killing me.* In general, though, our relationship was satisfactory. Pard followed the basic hygiene rules indoors. He even allowed me to slip newspaper under him outdoors, when he squatted for doggie business. I expressed my appreciation for not having to carry a cumbersome pooper scooper, or messy plastic baggies, by liberally distributing dog yummies whenever he cooperated. It was an excellent arrangement that benefited both of us.

Pard was a medium size, brown and white, haphazard mix of terrier and shepherd, with trace elements of other breeds. He was a clever dog, a valid testimony to the melting pot theory. I often took him to my drama classes at Gotham University's School of the Arts. Sometimes I would challenge my well-fed student actors to display more facial expressions than my dog. Once the initial humiliation of their acting skills being compared to a dog was over, some students showed a keen zest to prove themselves. If one came close to rivaling Pard's expressiveness, he blew them away with the 'sad look' of woeful eyes, sagging mouth and drooping ears. To date, no vanquished young thespian, resentful in defeat, had complained to the university about my unorthodox teaching assistant. When I brought Pard to school I always wore sunglasses. If security tried to prevent our entry, I told them I was blind. The underpaid guards of the sons and daughters of prosperity weren't about to be politically incorrect and deny admission to a blind man and his faithful Seeing Eye dog.

I first met Pard in the sixth floor hallway of my east village walk up, one of the few remaining ungentrified buildings on East 9th Street. The tenants were under constant pressure from the landlord to vacate the premises. His goal was to replace them with yuppies. He knew yuppies would eagerly pay seven or eight times more for the privilege of living in a chic ex-slum. The Olmedos, my neighbors across the hall, were the current target for eviction. We shared a bathroom in the hall. Their courteous apologies for its frequent use by their four children had led to friendship. The Olmedos still believed in the American dream, despite being persecuted by the landlord. Raul and Elena left the Dominican Republic to build a better life for their children. Raul worked long hours as an orderly in the psych ward at Malvue Hospital. Elena sewed in a sweatshop. I became fond of the oldest son, Armando, a bright youth who I tutored in English. Armando got a puppy from a friend and kept it in a cardboard box in the hallway. His parents wouldn't allow Perro in their tiny, three-room, vastly overcrowded, but spotlessly clean apartment.

The Olmedos finally tired of the landlord's harassment and purchased a house in the South Bronx. It wouldn't be ready for a few months, so they temporarily moved in with relatives. Naturally, Perro was unwelcome. Armando begged me to take care of him for a few days, until he could make other arrangements. It seemed simple enough to give him food and water, and to change his newspaper toilet once a day. I agreed and the Olmedos departed, leaving Perro behind. That night, the landlord pounded on my door and demanded to know who owned the dog in the hall. I told him it was the Olmedos'. He got furious and said he would have it removed. I requested a few days' grace, but was refused. After two lawsuits and one personal confrontation that almost became violent, we were in the midst of a temporary truce, but it was fragile. I saw no other alternative, so I gave Perro sanctuary.

My efforts to reunite Perro and Armando were futile. Raul politely but firmly rejected my request to bring them the dog. "I am sorry, my good friend, but it is impossible for us to take him. My sister-in-law will not allow it. I will call the pound and they will take him." An image flashed into mind of the tiny cells that held the prisoner dogs and cats, until they went to the gas chamber at the A.S.P.C.A. I was trapped. "There's no need, Raul. I'll see if I can find another home for him."

"Thank you, my friend. You have been a good neighbor. As soon as we move into our splendid new house, you must come to dinner." I promised to come to the housewarming, although the thought of going to the Bronx was intimidating. All I knew about the Bronx was from horror stories in the media: fires, drive-by shootings, crack houses. Well, that was in the future. Right now I had to find a good home for abandoned Perro.

I put a notice on the school bulletin board: 'loving puppy seeks adoption.' No response. I asked all my friends. They said no. I phoned my ex-girlfriend, Anitra, a flighty painter who knew every artist in Soho and requested her help. Her suggestion that I keep the puppy, since it would teach me to be more caring, wasn't appreciated. I tried animal adoption centers, but they were overpopulated. Meanwhile, Perro was transferring his affection to me. He followed me around the apartment, tripping over his large paws, wagging his tail vigorously when I set him on his feet. He would flop down when I was working at my desk and send ESP messages until he attracted my attention. I would look down into those large, soulful brown eyes and they beamed rays of unmitigated adoration. The ruthless manipulator worked his way into my heart.

I never had a dog before. Throughout my childhood, my parents had opposed anything animal, vegetable, or mineral that I brought home. I vaguely knew that dogs had to be trained, so I visited the Tompkins Square Library and browsed the dog book section. One unexpected side benefit was that I picked up a great looking girl. She was impressed that I was sheltering a needy puppy and we arranged to get together later that week. I took two books home, read them carefully and concluded that it didn't seem difficult to train a dog. Then we began the next phase of our relationship. First, a new name. Perro no longer seemed suitable for my best friend to-be. In the back of one of the books there was a list of the twenty most popular doggie names. They were even more vapid than the twenty most popular human names. I considered several literary candidates: Patraclos, Horatio, Uncas, but rejected them. I thought of the old western heroes and their loyal sidekicks, and came up with Pard. I told Pard his new name and he wagged enthusiastically, confirming the wisdom of my choice.

Pard's debut at the Tompkin Square Park dog run was less than distinguished. He was attacked by the male dogs and ignored by the females. He tried everything in his meager repertoire to make friends; groveling, whining, following, sniffing, wagging and crying. None of his displays made the other dogs relent. My human debut wasn't much better. I was scorned by the males and ignored by the females. We obviously hadn't obtained the right passports for the land of dogwalkers. It was a strange world indeed: pretentious maidens with overbred companions; macho men with vicious killers; weirdos with surrogate children; fascists with obedience school compulsives. All of them, human and canine, primped, preened, posed and role-played. This wasn't anything like the dogdom I imagined. The main dog walking sessions were at three fixed times: before work, at seven o'clock; after work, at six o'clock; late night, at ten o'clock. Due to the vagaries of my schedule, the only regular session I could attend was at night. This was a coincidental consolation, since the dogs and humans were more relaxed, whether from combat fatigue after a taxing day, or gentler moods fostered by lunar tides.

It was painfully clear that I had no practical alternative to the Tompkins Square Park dog run. The only other nearby park, the East River Park, necessitated walking through public housing to get there. It was a hazardous passage past urban pueblos, mostly inhabited by Hispanics, whose endurance of poverty had been shattered by yuppie wealth flaunting. If I survived the obstacle course, I would have to cross a walkway over the East River Drive. My silhouette at night would provide the murderers, perverts, muggers, junkies and mentally ill homeless with early warning identification of a high priority target. I had always been a loner, which partially explained my lack of advancement in my chosen profession, theater, a networker's orchard. Now, I was compelled to become a socializer for my pal Pard.

When Pard was approximately three months old, we started training sessions in the park. They were periodically interrupted by bullying dog attacks, which I had to fend off by myself. The instigating owner of Thor or Fang would accuse puppy Pard of provocation. What was more obnoxious was that everyone urged their dog training methods on me, from Nazism to Zen. There were two main types of advice givers: those who sent their dogs to obedience school, and therefore had no idea how to do it themselves; those who championed the natural system, and whose dogs were always out of control. This group was the most amusing, since they invariably had to chase their dogs to take them home. This was always an entertaining spectacle of impatient vocal exercise and inept pursuit. But Pard and I gained a modicum of acceptance from the less-socially scrupulous night crowd. I did notice, however, that the dogs of the daytime princesses never had to do doggie business at night.

I used the K-9 obedience training system and Pard quickly learned 'sit,' 'come,' and 'heel.' It took longer for 'stay,' since he got nervous when he saw me walk away. We got over his insecurity, added several more commands and by his sixth month he was a reasonably well trained animal. It was during this training period that he began to reveal his true nature, that of a hedonist pig who wanted his pleasures. Whenever I left the apartment he scorned the comfortable doggie mat that I had purchased for him, climbed onto the bed, pulled the covers into a nest and snoozed underneath. I never caught him because he always met me at the door, wagging a loving greeting for my safe return. He countered all my attempts to break this habit, including liberal admonitions of 'no', 'bad dog' and 'disgusting swine', with looks of innocence, confusion, or hurt. I resolved to catch him in the act. After I left one day, I waited, then quietly snuck up the stairs and threw open the door. Pard was sitting there, wagging cheerfully. I went to the bed and it was still warm where he had been nesting. In this struggle between man and beast he was as stubborn as the Viet Cong.

Many dog owners warned me about psychos who went around the city poisoning dogs. I could believe almost anything in this shared habitat. I trained Pard not to take food from others and not to eat anything on the ground. Pard complied willingly, but compensated by helping himself to food in the refrigerator and the cabinets at home. He would gorge on delectables like roast beef, breakfast cereals, cooked vegetables, baked goods, fresh fruit and any leftovers. He developed a fondness for Chinese food, especially tofu and shitake mushrooms, in garlic sauce. Fortunately for both of us, Pard had a cast iron stomach and digested these non-traditional dog foods without the inevitable belching, burping, gaseous emissions, nausea, vomiting, diarrhea or unscheduled bowel movements. I figured out how he opened the refrigerator and cabinets. He hadn't figured out how to clean up the spill from the ravaged containers. This was becoming a growing issue between us, until his heroism earned him full dining room privileges.

We were leaving the park a little later than usual one night. I had indulgently left Pard off the leash until we crossed Avenue B. Two junkies darted out from behind a tree and demanded my wallet. One of them waved a knife in my face. I was terrified. My entire body started shaking, but a portion of my mind still functioned. I said soothingly: "Sure. Sure. Be cool, man. I'll give it to you." Before I could even reach for my pocket, Pard came out of the darkness, growling ominously, looking twice his size. He lunged at the surprised muggers and one of them turned and ran. The knife wielder threatened Pard, but then saw large fangs snapping menacingly and fled. The barely-out-of-puppyhood Pard had saved me. I petted and praised him lavishly. When I stopped shaking we went home. I couldn't find a suitable commendation plaque, so I gave him all the leftover roast pork lo mein. I decided to rethink my bodyguard's household rights.

Pard made his first friend, Boris Yeltsin, when he was nine months old. Boris was a devilish mix of labrador and coyote. He and his master had been exiled from the day sessions because Boris nipped the little lapdogs. Boris appointed himself Pard's mentor and began to teach him adult dog values. Pard was a quick study and a bond rapidly formed between them. When they met, they would exchange formal stretch bows, then run and frolic. Pard couldn't keep up with the nimble Boris at first, and he would trip over his big paws trying to wheel and turn. As Pard grew stronger and more agile, they would play-fight. Soon it was all out combat training. They would duel as they ran, slashing and parrying, stop abruptly, reverse direction and continue the running battle, attacking and defending. They would take turns lying down, while the other practiced the coup de grace. They growled, snarled, snapped and foamed ferociously. People would scream for us to stop them. When the demand for intervention reached its peak, the two dogs would get up, shake off and trot off happily together, leaving the agitated spectators completely confused. But dog friendship is even more ephemeral than human friendship. Boris moved, Pard was on his own again and he couldn't e-mail.

The tutorial months with Boris had built skills and confidence. Though just a yearling, he tolerated no more bullying from other dogs. The masters reluctantly accepted this emancipation and sought easier victims. One vicious obsessive stalked us for a while, egging his dog to attack, but we learned to avoid him. Then Pard started training me. When he wanted dog biscuits, he would suddenly raise his hackles, growl, run to the door and bark. If his reward for defending the castle wasn't forthcoming, he would come to me, poke me with his paw to get my attention, look me in the eye, then turn and stare at the cabinet with the biscuits. I generally gave in first. He used different expressions to fulfill his needs. My favorite became the forlorn look of dejection when I left him at home. I finally realized the range of his talent and I trained him to show happy, sad, angry, perplexed, loving and other expressions. One day in class, exasperated with a student as emotive as a middle-class zombie, I said: "My dog is more expressive than you." My challenge was accepted; Pard appeared on the field of honor and vanquished his opponent with the poignant ears of 'sad.'

Pard's excursions to school entertained both of us and dog/human relations were at an all-time high. Then something changed. He reacted strangely to my selections of female companionship. One night, I was making love with the current girlfriend in my apartment. He lay down nearby and watched. When he heard the animal sounds of our sexual encounter, he jumped on the bed, mock growling and demanded to play. He scratched the girl with his pawnails and she departed in a huff. A little later, I was standing near the window and Pard stood on his hind legs, wrapped his front paws around my leg and began to push against me. I didn't feel like playing so I started to push him down. He growled, held on tighter and rhythmically pumped my leg. I noticed that his red, shiny thing had emerged from its sheath and I realized that I was being sexually abused. I don't know whether it was because of my example, or normal hormonal stirrings, but doggie sex had reared its head.

I went back to the Tompkins Square Library, but none of the dog books discussed sex. I went online, assuming I would find the ubiquitous know-it-all, whose moment had finally come on the World Wide Web. The only response was from a disgusting degenerate, who wanted to do vile things to my innocent dog. I browsed newspapers, magazines, periodicals, but there was no helpful information. I tried radio call-in shows. One host called me a pervert and disconnected me. Another thought I was cleverly disguising my need by pretending it was for a dog. She requested explicit sexual details and I disconnected her. I phoned my ex-girlfriend, Anitra, the flighty painter who knew everything about anything, without ever studying. Her suggestion that we both practice abstinence, since it would teach us self-control, wasn't appreciated. I thought wistfully that if Boris had only stayed long enough to lead Pard through this vital coming-of-age ceremony, things might be less stressful.

I spent hours thinking of schemes to relieve Pard's tension. I considered adopting a comely female dog at Bide-a-Way, letting her service Pard for a few days, and then returning her to her cell. But the cruel deception of her feeling rescued, then being subjected to sexual exploitation, deterred me. But it was a tempting idea. I knew there was a time honored philosophy of love them and leave them. There were ample historical precedents for abduction and rape. Sexual predation has become a recognized, contemporary urban activity, especially near bus terminals. The thought entered my mind that Pard and I could lurk at Port Authority, swoop down on some country bitch right off the bus, abduct her, let Pard have his way, then abandon her on the street. I didn't feel comfortable with that plan, but it started a new trend. For a few days I got caught up in a fantasy about a doggie cathouse. The girl dogs lounged around in provocative garments, while the doggie madam, a blowsy old Irish Setter, negotiated with the customers. I began to think I was losing it.

I learned one critical fact about canine sex from a wolf documentary: the only time bitches respond to sexual overtures is when they're in heat. The rest of the time it's tough nuts for the guys. I spent hours comparing bitches to human females, who did not come into heat. Did this explain why human females were always, never, often, seldom, sometimes responsive to sexual overtures? I was getting confused. When wolf bitches put out it was only to mate. They didn't engage in casual sex. They didn't require a wedding ceremony. It was man who went rim-ram, thank you ma'am and departed. Did that mean that the only way to provide Pard with sex would be for him to get married? Would that make me a beastial procurer? Would I be up to my ass in puppies, since I didn't think Pard could use a condom? I kept coming back to the fantasy of the doggie cathouse. I staffed it with working girl dogs from the Tompkins Square Park dog run. There was this beautiful, standard size, black French poodle. I visualized her in red lingerie... I definitely had to get things under control.

It was easier said than done. Pard's urges were occurring more frequently. I approached the late shift female dog owners with various proposals. I tried simple requests for sexual accommodation, pleas for compassion for a sex-starved pooch, offered to share his talented dog genes and reminded all and sundry that females had obligations to fulfill male needs. My entreaties were rebuffed with scorn. However, I didn't let my personal discomfort deter my efforts for my best friend. I offered cash for services rendered, but was refused with complete contempt. I wasn't even allowed to raise the offer. The owners were not simpatico. Out of discretion, I avoided the dog run for the next two weeks. Pard's attempts to satisfy himself on my leg were becoming more demanding. He had already torn one pair of my pants and scratched my leg twice in his progressively more urgent sexual assaults. I don't know why he made my leg a love object. Perhaps he was confused about his needs, but it was becoming more difficult to fight off his advances. I was getting desperate.

During my self-imposed exile from Tompkins Square Park, I took Pard to other neighborhood dog runs. We went south to the Mercer Street run in Noho, where I surveyed the new prospects like Kublai Khan, seeking a suitable concubine for the crown prince. But the dog walkers at Mercer Street were more pretentious than the Tompkins Square crowd. They had even better radar for possible threats to their dogs. I didn't conclude that it was class snobbery, pedigrees looking down on mutts, though I harbored my suspicions. There was just something about the quest for doggie sex that immediately alerted all owners to danger, as if by ESP. We went north to Madison Square Park, where we lurked in the shadows of trees, waiting to spring on the unwary bitch who might wander too far from the protective eye of the master. We never got lucky. I filibustered to approachable dog owners, hoping to distract the custodian, while Pard would snatch the booty. We both failed dismally.

Months passed in fruitless endeavors. My life was unraveling. My students were feeling neglected. My department head, who I nicknamed 'Ernest the emoter,' reminded me nastily that 'Adjunct instructors can't slack off.' My latest girlfriend left me because she felt I was more concerned with Pard's sex needs than hers. Pard was growing increasingly impatient and had nocturnal emissions that I had to clean. He howled during the day when I was out. This annoyed the landlord, who was already yearning for my departure and the subsequent gentrification of my apartment. I had temporarily exhausted all resources while I reassessed the problem. I succumbed to fantasy again. There were hundreds of dog owners out there with horny dogs. Maybe thousands. We were victims of a pernicious system that denied sex to male dogs. This was an issue that should concern others. I imagined filing a class action suit against the A.S.P.C.A., on behalf of the horny dog class. It would compel the A.S.P.C.A. to provide requesting dogs with sex partners, selected from their female prisoners who were confined on death row. Perhaps the females who serviced a certain number of males could win a pardon. The legal procedures were becoming too tedious, so I pictured Pard as the Scarlet Pimpernel, rescuing condemned bitches who would gratefully reward him with their favors... I was in trouble.

We went back to the after-work session at Tompkins Square Park and managed to conceal our crass motives for a few days. Our subterfuge went up in smoke when Pard mounted a pampered fluff ball a fraction of his size, the spoiled pet of an indulgent princess. His extended member rubbed her head and he ejaculated all over her well groomed coat. The shrieks of moral indignation and disgust were deafening. The howls of accusation were daunting. It looked as if a lynch mob was forming. I had a dreadful vision of Pard and me dangling side-by-side, at the end of a rope, on a shabby sycamore tree. I pleaded innocence, endured the threats and abuse, collected the lugubrious culprit and dejectedly headed out of the park. I petted Pard reassuringly. "Don't worry. I won't give up trying." One righteous defender of the violated fluff, currying favor with the pretentious princess, called after me.

"You should keep that mutt away from purebreds. We don't want his kind here." If I kept my big mouth shut, we probably could have returned to the after work session in a week or two. Instead, I had to be a smartass.

"You wuss. What do you want him to do, say it with flowers?" As we crossed Avenue B, I looked back at the scene of our debacle and rededicated myself to finding a solution to Pard's sex problem. My only consolation was that at least this time I didn't have to clean up after him.

Dyson
By Kevin Theisen

My wife and I started volunteering at Almost Home Animal Haven in April of 2013. We started just walking some of the dogs, getting used to them and them to us and learning from the staff. While making new friends, walking the dogs and just spending a lot of time at the shelter, I started to take notice of one dog in particular. His name is Dyson and he is a Staffy mix (what most call a Pit Bull). Every time I showed up at the shelter I noticed two things: 1. He looked and acted like he wanted me for lunch, and I don't mean as a guest. 2. His eyes never left me no matter what I was doing or who I was with. At the time he was a Staff Only dog, meaning he was to be handled by experienced staff only.

After about a month or so of letting all the dogs get used to seeing me around and feeding them and giving them treats I asked if I could walk Dyson. I had noticed that whoever came to his kennel with a leash he would immediately sit and calm down because he knew he was going for a walk. So I grabbed my leash and walked toward his kennel (secretly saying to myself "please don't eat me, please don't eat me") and when I reached for the handle he sat down and looked at me like I was his best buddy. I opened the gate and he practically put the leash on himself and away we went.

Dyson is a very striking Staffy, both in looks (he is extremely handsome) and in strength (he is extremely muscular) so the first few walks were just that... walks. Dyson commands attention when he walks because he marches. No petting, no eye contact, just walking with me saying to myself "please don't eat me, please don't eat me."

After several walks we started becoming pals; he was learning new commands and we started playing but most of all we started to trust each other. I learned from the staff that he had been given up by his owner and that hit me hard. After several weeks I asked my wife to think about fostering or adopting Dyson. We did a meet and greet with our other two dogs and adopted him in July. He has become part of our family, loved by all of us and our other dogs. We had no idea how much love and affection this boy had to give. He now has six humans to share it with as well as three fur siblings (we have since fostered Nigel, another senior dog from Almost Home). Dyson is a wonderful dog and a wonderful story.

Thank you Almost Home!

Excising Guilt From Morning Rituals
By Shelley Kahn

The warm dog sleeps curled by my side,
Dreaming of bacon before the sun comes up.
I sweat slightly beside her, thinking of the day to come.
The smell of coffee stirs my sluggish heart, so
I rise to the radio's tune.
Members of the House of Representatives are talking
To me about the glorious works
They have recently completed in the Philippines
For the devastated Filipino people, so far removed
Yet suffering in ways I cannot fathom.
As I peel back the covers, I see
An image of defoliated palm trees and ragged clothing,
Then blink it away. I catch
A whiff of excrement and impending disease, then
In my half sleep, I creep along downstairs
To rejoin the family dog now on the couch, television blaring,
Still she snores softly beside me.
Nothing but promos for discounted shopping,
Singing of sales and expositions, of hot tubs,
Of Santa Claus and of insurance and stealthy
Luxury cars to hold all of our excess. Trying to fill up
That void, I listen to the forecast for our times.
Here in our warm home, only a high of 50 or so,
With scattered clouds, no hint of past disasters.
The suffering across the globe, surely forgotten now,
By the members of the House of Representatives and almost
By me, as I dress for my job and pour myself another cuppa
To erase what I heard and what I thought I saw and smelled
When I awoke from dreaming with the lucky dog.

Finding Nacho
Judith Gille

One of the many things I appreciate about San Miguel de Allende's expatriate community is the unspoken agreement among them that says, *if you take up residency here, you will give something back to the community.* Practically every foreigner living in the charming Mexican hill town volunteers for one charitable cause or another. They raise money for scholarships, literacy programs, clean water projects; they build houses for the poor, volunteer to teach ESL, run medical programs; they work with orphans and in battered womens' shelters. They organize free spay and neuter clinics for dogs and cats and take in the town's mangy, starving street dogs.

I've visited and lived abroad in many wonderful and interesting places and have never found a community of people so committed to doing good.

During a six-week sojourn one winter in San Miguel, I decided it was time my family and I volunteered for something. When I read one day in *Atención*, the town's bilingual newspaper, that the Sociedad Protectora de Animales (S.P.A.), was looking for help, I figured it was perfect. We are all animal lovers in our family and I thought our lack of pedigree among San Miguel's wealthier expats wouldn't matter to folks running an animal shelter. I also imagined a shelter was likely to have real use for volunteers and that few skills would be required. An abundance of enthusiasm, and strong backs and arms, should be enough. We could provide those.

My husband Paul opted out, but the kids were up for it, so the following day, my son Will, daughter Hannah, and I took a taxi across town to #7 Los Pinos, where we found a single-story, grass-green building with windows secured by iron bars, and a torn screen door hanging loosely from its hinges. Inside the shelter's tiny office, behind a makeshift desk, sat a grim-faced, chain-smoking woman who was talking on the phone. She ignored us, while her cigarette burned down amid the pile of butts spilling over the ashtray.

We moved outside, where the smell of urine mixed with disinfectant filled the air and rows of four-by-eight-foot cells with chain-link gates lined the interior of a dusty lot. The din of attention-hungry dogs was deafening. There was little grass or other vegetation, and the handful of trees was sickly and leafless. Yet, as void of greenery as it was, the floors of the kennels had been freshly hosed, and the dogs appeared well-fed. Their coats were shiny and free of mange, which is rampant in Mexican street dogs. It was clear that the poor, abandoned creatures were well cared for.

A few minutes later, a tall, enthusiastic woman with a Canadian accent hustled up and asked if we needed help.

"We're here to volunteer," I said.

"Great!" She quickly sized up my strapping, eighteen-year-old son. "We could use a strong fellow like you to exercise the big dogs."

Hence, Will was roped into a job he adored. It didn't take him long to bond with a number of the shelter's lop-eared mutts and choose favorites: a Bluetick hound mix named Hank and a sweet-tempered bitch named Lola. Lola and Hank took turns dragging Will uphill every day to a junk-littered lot above the shelter.

Over the course of the next two weeks, Will exercised the dogs while Hannah and I volunteered for a few of the shelter's easier jobs: playing with kittens or walking the smaller dogs up to the *jardín* on Thursdays, where we chatted up people who showed interest in adopting them. When Lola was adopted by a gay couple from Connecticut, Will lobbied hard for me to let him to adopt Hank. I reminded him that Katy, our golden retriever, was enough big dog for our small backyard in Seattle. But the thought crossed my mind that a smaller companion for our aging retriever might be something to consider.

One sunny afternoon, Hannah and I were "socializing" the puppies—our favorite job at the S.P.A. But after a while, we grew tired of the mass of wriggling furballs shredding our shoelaces and nipping at our fingers with their needlelike teeth. So we wandered around to a group of kennels housing the smaller adult dogs.

As we approached, a goofy-looking miniature gray poodle, sequestered behind a chain-link fence with a long-haired, brown and white mutt straight out of the annals of Dr. Seuss, ran up to the gate. Hannah and I amused ourselves watching the little fellow perform tricks behind the chain-link enclosure. All twelve pounds of the wriggling mass of gray fur seemed to be showing off for us. Like a dog auditioning for a circus, he walked on his hindquarters, turned elaborate circles, paddled his paws in the air as if swimming. The only thing he lacked was a little sign that read, *Will Dance for Food.*

For some reason, the dog was tagged with the unfortunate name Major Mosby. Major Mosby, an officer in the Confederate Army, was nicknamed the Gray Ghost for his rapacious, surreptitious activities. How a Mexican street dog came to be named for a Confederate scalawag was a mystery. There were many mysterious things about the little gray dog. Like how he ever survived San Miguel's traffic-choked streets in the first place.

I found out from Karen, the Canadian volunteer, that Major Mosby had been living off garbage and dodging cars in San Miguel's cobblestone streets when he was brought to the shelter. Even harder to believe was what she told us next: this dog, with his Tickle Me Elmo personality, had viciously attacked a shelter worker when he was first brought in.

As is my habit, I ignored the alarming bit of information and relied instead on my intuition and the evidence curled up in my lap. Compared to the other small dogs, including a frantic male poodle that refused to pack up his privates, and another that yapped relentlessly, Major Mosby looked like a winner to me. Hannah agreed.

As soon as Will returned from walking Hank, we eagerly introduced him to Major Mosby.

"Let's do it!" he said when I told him Hannah and I wanted to adopt the little gray dog. Having spent the first eight years of his life—before we got Katy—lusting for a dog, Will would have been up for bringing home the shelter's entire canine population.

We tracked Karen down again, and in the smoke-filled office she gave us the paperwork we needed to fill out to adopt Major Mosby. She told us adoptive families were required to make a donation to the S.P.A., which I was happy to do. Then Will, Hannah, and I left the Gray Ghost to sacrifice his manhood for the comfort of a new home and family. We were told to come back two days later, and then we would then bring him home to Casa Chepitos.

****

"No way! We're not getting another dog!" my husband declared, when the three of us arrived home with the news that we'd just adopted the cutest miniature poodle. For a guy who'd been a pretty good sport about me liquidating my retirement account to purchase a house in Mexico that he'd never seen, I thought he was being a little recalcitrant. I decided to back off and let the kids battle it out with their dad. Normally, he caved in to their requests with enough persistent begging.

"Come on, Dad, you'll like him when you see him. He's really cute," Hannah said. "His name is Major Mosby, but we're going to call him Nacho."

My son was more contentious. Like a pair of alpha males, he and his dad went head-to-head a lot during his teenage years.

"How can you make up your mind just like that!" he shouted at Paul. "You haven't even seen him!" They went back and forth, arguing for a long time.

"Katy is the only dog we need," Paul said with finality. I was beginning to think we'd lost the battle. Then Will piped up again.

"Okay, let's put it to a vote," he said. I immediately saw through my son's ruse. He was relying on our family's tradition of running things democratically. Majority rules in our house.

"All those in favor, raise your hand," he said. Three hands flew into the air, none belonging to my husband.

"I guess you're outvoted, Hon," I said, giving him a little hug. He stomped off to the living room to sulk and read the *International Herald* I'd brought him. And Nacho, the little circus dog, had a new home.

For An Old Dog At The Shelter
John Aylesworth

They will care for you, the college students
and volunteers, until you die.
Your white maw, cataracts, brown skin scarred
but still as soft as your ears,
say you were loved.
Your tail keeps thumping while you wait,
legs ready to run, eager for dog dreams.

Forgotten
By Jane Panich

Lying on the cold cement,
Within this metal cage.
At least I am not hungry.
And not running for a change.
I don't know how I got here,
and I don't know where I'll go.
But at least it's cooler than the sun
and warmer than the snow.
The hours pass with faces.
I cower low with fear.
They look left, and they look right.
They never look down here.
I was once a wiggly puppy.
"How adorable," they'd say.
I slept in cozy blankets.
They would snuggle me all day.
But as I started growing,
the attention grew to fade.
Sometimes my bowl sat empty,
sometimes I sat in the rain.
And then one day, the gate ajar,
I wandered from my home.
I used to do this all the time,
on my leash they'd let me roam.
At first it was so glorious.
I ran free a little ways.
But my recall is not what it was,
back in my younger days.
So now I'm here and so alone.
They haven't come for me.
I long so much for contact
Even though I might look mean.
If I were a wiggly puppy,

maybe I'd go home today.
They always take those puppies.
They're so cute and love to play.
I just need someone to love me
And put food into my dish.
I don't play but need a place to rest.
Do you think I'll get my wish?

Fred
Renee Moxlow

Discarded at the shelter

Foggy eyes
Deaf ears
Legs that won't support me

Scared, cold, confused

I was loyal
I loved my family
The only thing I did wrong was get old

Rescued

Warm bed
Lots of love and scratches
Fur brothers and sisters

Thankful

Tail wags
Kisses
Peace

Heaven on earth before I leave

Frenchie Love
By Shelley Kahn

My Frenchie is the baby dog
Who sniffs everything with an eye
Toward
      taking its measure
                  as a toy.
Then chews the lucky object
She selects
      With an unrelenting vigor
Born of puppyhood games and
        Dining room chair legs.
My sweet French Bulldog
      Licks my face
In a manner never studied or coy.

There is much we can learn
From her loving and open ways:
How to best appreciate each
And every person and day.
To treasure each other in every kiss
And nurture the inner puppy in us
We otherwise might have missed.

Getting Lost With Spike
Mark Burgh

A small, old dog, almost black
with white streaks on his jaw,
trotted among bushes cut carefully
as insults to a friend,
seeking a trace of other
dogs where the foliage meets
brown spines and fertilizer hopes,
where the sign of the dog
written secretly from humans who
know only shapes not scents
that make the dog growl
or stand still and wag.
I follow him,
abased by my ignorance,
sure that he
will lead me
home better than a map,
GPS, or directions from
any human.

Gifts
Terri Simon

My dog lies across the doorway
like a furry border guard.
She tells me very clearly
that I know the rules.
Tolls are paid
with one tummy pat
or two ear scratches
or one long, luxurious
head to tail rub.
Once properly paid,
she rises and stretches,
head down, tail up,
then reverses.
She moves to the side
so I can get by.
She wants to see what adventure
I may lead her to -
a couch snuggle
or a treat
or, best of all,
to get her sister
and head outside.
She rescued me,
like all her four-footed siblings.
They teach me what's important –
food, shelter, someone
to share play time,
the value of simple touch.
They teach me that love
and absolute acceptance
are possible and real.
I am firmly convinced,
in the great ladder of reincarnation,
humans are one or two rungs
below dogs.

Girl Going to College, Saying Goodbye to the Dog
Kathy Ewing

Her face is an inch away
as you doze,
the girl who was here when you arrived as a puppy.
She was little then, and would run.

Big now, she peers at your face,
trying to figure you out one last time.

You lie still, snoozing. She strokes your soft ear,
your muzzle, places her lips against the side of your head.

She is solemn,
contemplating, for a moment, the break she's soon to make,
leaving you behind with your two old caretakers.

She rests her forehead on yours, while you sleep on,
as you do most days, all day,
dreaming of a little girl.

Good Company
Edward Ahern

Frank retreated from the house into the back yard, his eyes wet. *I should've told her, "Ashley , I'm not lazy or weak, quit picking at me. It only hurts me, and doesn't help you." But instead, I backed off. She's carving pieces off me every time we argue.*

He bagged up hedge cuttings and grass clippings and stuffed the bags into the back of their vintage SUV. The drive to the town dump took fifteen minutes, most of which Frank spent staring towards a visualized Ashley. She'd been slender when they married, but with the hint of coming fullness. But over time she'd puckered and soured into a caricature.

He dumped off the clippings, being careful to remove every trace of plant and dirt. Ashley would inspect the car later that day.

The access road to the dump went past the town dog pound, which in over thirty visits Frank had barely noticed. But this day he pulled into the small parking lot and went in. The man behind the desk was comfortably frumpy. "Looking for a pet?"

Ashley hated the idea of an animal making a mess of her house, and had refused to consider getting one. "Yeah, maybe. Could I look at the dogs?"

The attendant opened a counter-weighted metal door, pointing Frank onto a gangway with ten cages on each side. The yapping and howling made talking impossible, and the man just waved for him to go down the line of cages.

The dog in cage eleven didn't bark, just padded slowly toward Frank and stared at him. The dark brown eyes were calm, the body posture loose. They studied each other as if it were a first date. He walked back out through intensified barking and baying.

"What can you tell me about cage eleven?"

"Which one is that?"

"Wolfy-looking black and gray shepherd."

He went to a card file. The desk top computer apparently was there for show. "Yeah, we'd been trying to trap that one for months. Wily devil, kept eluding the guys. Unaltered male, maybe eighty-five pounds, maybe three years old. Nobody has gone for him, and he's scheduled to be put down at the end of the week. You want him, you have to sign that you'll get him his shots and remove his testicles, plus pay us twenty three dollars."

"Let me think about it."

Frank knew he couldn't get a dog; he already had too many problems. *Big dog, big food bill, die by the time he's ten or eleven. Looks like a shedder. No collar or tags when they trapped him, could be wild. Ashley will rip me up. Bad idea, Frank.*

He broached the possibility that evening. "Honey, I'm thinking about our getting a dog."

Ashley flipped open her verbal knives. "You're an idiot. We don't have the money to repair my car and you want to get a dog. And who would take care of it- me, probably, because you don't take care of anything on a regular basis, not the yard, not fixing things around the house, for sure not me. Once you get a job and make enough money to feed us you can talk to me about getting a dog."

Her cuts stung and Frank shut up. But the next day he drove back to the dog pound. "Can I go in his cage and see how the dog and I get along?"

"No, but I'll put a choke leash on him and you can walk him around the exercise cage."

The animal was densely furred, with a thick mane. It moved with feral grace and not a dog's self-consciousness. It neither recoiled from Frank nor fawned on him, but took his pats and stroking calmly, as if its due, as if it knew that Frank gained as much as it did.

The dog held eye contact with Frank like few people had done in his life, his father perhaps a few times, a boyhood friend now gone away. Frank slipped the leash off its neck and the dog held its position at his side. "When is it being put down?"

"Day after tomorrow."

Bad idea, walk away. "I'll take it."

Ashley was at work when Frank brought the dog home. He expected it to sniff through every open room, but it held its position next to him, pacing with him from living room to kitchen to Frank's cubbyhole office, where it lay at his feet.

Both man and dog were watching television when Ashley returned home. Frank noticed clumps of gray fur on the egg shell carpeting, and hoped Ashley wouldn't.

"Frank! How could you? Get that goddamn dog out of my house!"

Frank had jumped, but the shepherd merely raised its head. "He's a good dog, Ashley, he'll protect us."

"Bullshit. I told you not to get it. Take it back. If you don't, I'll call the police and have them take it back."

Frank felt like he'd waded into an ebbing surf, with the sand running out from under his feet. He glanced over at the shepherd and felt the bottom firm. "I don't think so, Ashley. The neighbors would see the cops come and I'd make sure to tell them all about it." He started speaking faster, forcing his ideas to be heard before Ashley shredded them.

"Let's give it a couple weeks before we decide, it'll be companionship for me while you're at work, look at it, it'll make a good watch dog…"

"No pets! We agreed. Keep to your word for a change. You'll just get to love it and it'll die. You take it back first thing tomorrow morning. Meanwhile, stick it in the basement." She stood breathing heavily, arms still waving, as if she'd semaphored her orders.

Frank realized that his shoulders slumped and straightened up. "I'm not going to argue with you, Ashley, but I want to keep it. I'll sleep in the living room tonight, along with the dog."

The skin was stretched tautly over Ashley's facial bones. "You soft-dicked little parasite, you can't even afford the dog food. If it wasn't so much trouble I'd of dumped you years ago. But it's not too late."

The dog had remained crouched next to Frank, its hackles unraised. Apparently arguments between humans were of no concern. Ashley prepared her own supper, as did Frank after she'd left the kitchen. Without speaking again, it was understood that the upstairs was hers, and Frank could only briefly visit to retrieve clean clothing and brush his teeth.

Frank sat back down and pointed his eyes at the television. The words were drowned by the roar in his ears, and the images flickered without comprehension.

Shortly before midnight he realized that the dog needed to go out. The dog sensed Frank's purpose almost before he reached for the leash, and put its head next to his leg. The night was overcast and dark, the dog a well camouflaged blur at the end of the line.

It held close to Frank, putting no strain at all on the leash, following his lead like a dance partner. *Maybe Ashley is right. I can't even buy this dog a bed. It was wild before, maybe I could just let it go, and say the collar was too loose. It'll probably run away, but if it stays it's meant to be.*

He stepped over to the dog, reached down and unsnapped the collar. "Your call, buddy. You stay with me, I keep you. You run off, we're both back where we were."

The dog looked intently at Frank, but didn't move. Then it loped off to sniff a neighbor's yard. *That's that, it's gone.* But as Frank turned to walk away it bounded back over to him, and paced with him down the sidewalk.

The animal strode with a grace that stumpy-legged humans lack, and ran like God or nature meant running to be, the paws invisible, the muscles beautifully flexed. Frank realized that he'd brought the dog back into its element, into the night when it hunted. He realized that while the dog was with him he need fear nothing, for it would frighten away any coyote or robber.

They moved together for two hours, the animal disappearing into darkness and reappearing like a second shadow. *That's it, I'll call you Shadow.* "Time to go back, Shadow" He repeated the name all the way back to the house, but the dog had seemed to recognize its title from the first utterance.

Frank set an alarm early enough to make peace-offering coffee for Ashley, but she came downstairs already dressed for the office, and blew through the living room and out the front door while slinging barbs. "That animal stinks. You take it back or get out of my house, both of you. You've actually gone beyond useless to harmful..."

He walked the dog in the post-dawn sunshine on a leash so it wouldn't frighten the neighbors. He drank three cups of coffee, his increasingly caffeinated nerves clamoring that he prepare for what seemed inevitable, that Ashley would throw him out. Frank made a telephone call.

"Collin? Frank. Yeah, listen, things aren't going so good here, and I need to get some work. Are you still looking for people for your landscaping crews?... I know it's minimum wage, but I've got to earn some cash... Thanks Collin. Oh, and I'm going to need a cheap place to stay, one that takes pets... That much, huh? What do you know about the shelter at Operation Hope?... No pets?... Thanks Collin, it would only be until I got on my feet, and I'd be glad to pay you something."

Frank was scared but focused, like a parachutist must feel right after he'd jumped from a plane. He carried his clean clothes downstairs and stacked them in unusually neat piles, then stuffed his dirty clothes into a plastic trash bag. He made a few more phone calls, and then took Shadow into wooded acreage near their house.

Frank slipped the leash, and Shadow immediately caught the scent of something and loped off. It glided without a snag through the brambled underbrush and disappeared. Frank stood still in awe. *How wasted its grace is on flat lawns and sidewalks.*

He waited ten minutes before beginning to worry, and was about to call the dog when the underbrush rustled to his left, the opposite direction from which Shadow had disappeared. A spike horn deer burst out of the thicket, almost running into Frank in its panicked flight. Shadow streamed behind it, blurred and almost soundless, and was gone again. The two animals had transited past him in under three seconds.

Frank waited five more minutes and started calling Shadow. He'd yelled the name a dozen times before Shadow loped back into sight, panting almost uncontrollably. There was no blood on his muzzle, so presumably the deer had escaped. But Shadow seemed content. He'd committed every muscle fiber, every nerve twitch possible to the chase, and had lost his prey. But there seemed to be no disappointment, no chagrin, only an exhausted satisfaction with the effort. Frank snapped the leash back on and they walked slowly home.

Ashley burst into the house at five thirty, glaring at them both. Shadow made no move toward her, seeming to sense that anything it did would be misinterpreted. *Just like me,* Frank thought.

Her voice was ominously calm. "I talked to a lawyer today. You've finally broken my patience. You've moving out, right now. This is my house, my car, I make the payments on both of them. You get nothing, and good riddance.

Frank surprised himself. He was resigned to the probable doom of his marriage; emotionally distancing himself far enough that Ashley's knives could barely touch him. "Ashley, I've checked with some guys who've gotten divorced. This is a community property State. Fifty-fifty. Plus you'll have to provide support while I find a job. I won't even have to argue much about it."

Shadow sidled nearer to him as he spoke. Ashley stared at the two males, then the piles of clothes. She began to silently cry, and then angrily wiped off the tears. Frank couldn't recall ever having seen her cry.

"Get out of my house or I'll call the police!"

Frank squeezed his lips together in a hard smile. "Good luck with that. I haven't abused you and am not a drunk. The cops will be men with a few marital issues of their own. I'll have their sympathy."

Ashley arms flailed while she searched for the words that would rebind Frank to her. None came. "Don't come near me, you or that insect-riddled beast. If you can't behave like my husband I want you out of my house, my life."

For just a second Frank saw Ashley as he'd hoped for when they got married. But the vision withered back into caricature. Frank glanced at the laying dog and with a jolt realized that Ashley was staring at caricatures as well, of an ineffectual and parasitic mate and a dangerous looking animal that violated the purity of her house. His voice softened.

"Ashley, there's no point anymore in hurting each other. Let's just kill the marriage and divide up the carcass. I won't be gluttonous. I'll move out as soon as I can."

They stood three feet apart, sparring distance. It'd been three months since Frank had touched Ashley with suggestive affection. He'd been rebuffed then, and was sure she would reject him again.

They cohabitated for another two weeks as the marital glue slowly leaked out of the house. Frank moved out when Ashley was at work, leaving a note- *I'll Call If I've Forgotten Anything. F.*

Collin was already divorced and sympathetic, although he'd been ditched because of serial philandering. "Frank, I know a couple of divorced women I can put you in touch with."

Frank realized that he was being offered Collin's culls. "No thanks, Coll, I'm not ready for dating, besides, I'm still married."

"Who's talking about dating? You really are out of touch. Take an example from that dog of yours- he'd hump any bitch in heat."

Collin had that part wrong. Despite the vet's encouragement and his signed commitment, Frank had left Shadow unaltered. But even though genitally intact, Shadow hadn't expressed sexual interest in other dogs, male or female. *Two celibates abstaining without understanding why. Or maybe I understand too well.*

The landscaping work suited Frank, who had an eye for garden layouts. He began taking side jobs, and then started up his own business, buying a used truck and equipment in installment payments.

Shadow usually came with him on a job. He would lay unleashed next to Frank and move back and forth with him. The dog made human and animal friends easily, and Frank was convinced that he was given at least some of his work because customers trusted a man that a dog trusted.

Ashley called one evening. It was the last married conversation they had without lawyers present. "Frank, you're being crazy. All this expense and work. Just get rid of the dog and we can try to put thing back the way they were."

The way things were. When did the absence of pain become a pleasure? "Ashley, I wish, I wish we'd done things differently. But we contorted ourselves into something unsustainable. Let's just let the process grind."

After the divorce, Frank moved from Collin's house to a rooming house that accepted pets, then to a larger apartment that he furnished mostly with customer cast offs. Five years slid past without seeing Ashley; until the post-funeral luncheon for a former neighbor. They came face to face in the swirling body surge of the reception.

"Hello, Frank. I see you still fit into the same suit. How's the landscaping business?"

"Ashley. You look good, a little more filled out than when we were together."

"It's because I don't worry as much."

"I heard you got remarried. Did he come?"

Ashley waved her arm. "He's over there, trying to sell insurance."

Frank could see former neighbors watching them, waiting for the fireworks. "I, I think you did the right thing to divorce me."

"Cost me enough."

"I wonder sometimes if we'd had survived by having a honeymoon yelling and screaming argument and then wrestling down onto the couch. Or if you'd have just had me arrested."

Ashley was silent for a few seconds. "I still get mad at you sometimes. I assumed you sat around without a job just to piss me off. I hear you live together with that dog better than you did with me. How is the hair ball?"

"You were right, he died young. Lung cancer. I had him put down a month ago." His lips pursed in a sad smile. "I wouldn't let them handle Shadow after he was injected. Picked him up and carried him out to the truck myself. Then drove it into the woods and buried him in a hidden grave. He would have liked that."

"So what now, another dog? A trophy wife? Guess you can afford her now."

"Don't think so. One wife, one dog. Figure that's enough bittersweet leavening. Nice seeing you, Ashley."

Grandma Dog And Squeakers
Charlotte Mielziner

Researchers have recently declared dogs the most perceptive observers of human body language than any other species, including ourselves. Nearly every dog owner swears their dog can tell when they are getting ready to leave for work as opposed to a walk in the park, or if they are sad, frustrated or tired at a single glance. Dogs quietly take the information they've gleaned from us and use it to solve problems. Well, I'm here to tell you at least a few dogs are also great observers where cats are concerned.

Cats can be the bane of many a dog's day. A six pound cat can settle like a broody hen in the middle of a hallway and keep a ninety pound German Shepherd at bay with nothing but "The Look." This is the serene gaze positively jet puffed with self confidence that says, "One more step and I'll make your face hurt." The poor Shepherd that would gallantly throw himself at a two hundred pound armed burglar stands whimpering in the hall, begging the cat for mercy. But, for those dogs who truly know the feline mind, getting what they want is no problem.

Our dachshund, Grandma Dog was a keen observer of cats. She had researched, taken copious notes, analyzed, tested her findings and published the definitive paper on how to manipulate cats. I think she was secretly famous in the canine world for her well-practiced methods. Dogs from far and wide would gather at her conferences and sit rapt with attention on how to move cats when they don't want to leave the area.

Cat on a lap? There is always the Wide Yawn in the Face Technique useful for cats who are hogging human attention. A blast of bad breath in the face is an excellent way to convince the cat to evacuate said lap. However, should that fail, no problem, settle down next to them butt to nose and simply pass gas. The cat will be happy to donate your lap already pre-warmed by their fluffy little tummies.

Our house in Pittsburgh had a sunshine patch that called for an animal to bask in it every morning. It would start as a gleam through the curtains and slowly crawl across the floor widening and warming the area as it went. It was the preferred spot for all three of our animals, Grandma Dog, Scruffy our terrier mix and Squeakers our large black and white cat; sure he was king of all he surveyed.

One early morning, Scruffy had claimed the still small patch of sunshine for herself. Just as she completed her grooming ritual, carefully licking her curly hair coat into some level of hygiene, Squeakers decided a nap in the sun's warm rays was in order. He entered the living room and circled the worried little terrier noting that there was only room for one animal.

Then, he gave her The Look. Stalking slowly towards her, ears laid back and golden eyes flashing, Scruffy quickly gave up the spot and retreated to safer quarters.

Happy for now, Squeakers settled into the sunshine patch, briefly making bread on the carpeting and circling into a perfect donut shape. Life was good as far as he was concerned. Scruffy watched from afar, the same injured look on her face that third graders have who just survived a wedgie by the school bully.

But, Squeakers time in the sun was limited; Grandma dog was waking from her post breakfast nap. First, there was the flappity - flap of her leathery ears coming from the bedroom. Then, there was the trit -trot sound of her crossing the kitchen floor. Squeakers' eyes were closed, but his ears radared around to the oncoming dachshund.

Grandma Dog circled the sunshine patch, noting there was only room for one animal. She nudged Squeakers in the shoulder which got the combination Look with Growl. From the corner, Scruffy whined a plea for me to intervene before her elderly mentor could be shredded and served up like cheese on a salad. But, this was Grandma Dog who was not daunted by a mere cat that outweighed her by two to one and sported quite an impressive array of weapons.

Our clever little dachshund, circled once more trotting around Squeakers as he followed the action. Then, she did the unthinkable, she defiled the cat with that most disgusting of all techniques. The one that instantly produces such revulsion that that it is guaranteed to open the coveted sunshine patch. She licked his face.

Squeakers flew across the room like he was shot out of a cannon, landing in full grooming mode. He furiously rubbed his face on the carpeting, licking his paws and wiping nose, eyes and ears like he thought dog cooties would ruin his bad boy reputation among the garbage can trollers. The look on his face showed the full repugnance of what he had just endured. Grandma Dog quickly claimed the bright spotlight, lifting her face to the sun's rays in bliss.

Several minutes later, when Squeakers had calmed down, he recalled the first rule of cats: He who dies with the most dignity wins and if one can embarrass another, that loss of dignity transfers to his own. Squeakers felt he had a point to make; he had to put that ignorant little dog in her place once and for all. He puffed out to nearly double his size, laid his ears against his skull and with arched back and stiff legs, marched across the room.

Just when I thought I might need to step in to prevent the next St. Valentine's Day massacre, Grandma Dog handled the situation herself. She stretched her neck out and displayed just the tip of her little pink tongue. Squeakers reeled back, nearly retching in disgust and decided not to retreat, but in his catlike way, change plans and head to the easy chair at a safe distance. Ever after, all Grandma Dog had to do in order get her way was simply extend her tongue in Squeakers' general direction and he promptly remembered a terribly urgent appointment elsewhere.

Gratitude For Dogs
John J. Brugaletta

For Daisy

Thanks be to plenitude for dogs,
for St. Bernards, Chihuahuas and Great Danes;
Labrador Retrievers, black, yellow and chocolate;
for Poodles, Pomeranians and pugs;
Bassets, Bulldogs, Beagles and mutts;

For those who watch over homes,
for those who point or retrieve,
for those who love tennis balls and children.

Give thanks for those who learn our words:
sit, stay, toy, let's go for a walk.

For the dogs who follow at heel
or venture a quick sniff of an absent dog.
For those who come when called,
who watch over our cats.
who eat the same kibbles day after day,
who are always excited to see us,
who lie at our feet for our warmth,
or go with us undaunted to see bear damage.

Thanks be to repletion for all dogs
and for the wolves from which they came.

Guadalajara Bus Station
Cynthia Jacobi

In the path of the occasional passengers walking
along the wide sidewalk lay a yellow dog, mature
coyote size, dozing in a slant of sun. Regular breath
moved his ribs. His ears flickered. His top eyelid
opened and closed. Travelers passed the sprawling dog
taking care to not brush him with shoe or rolling suitcase.
The sun rose higher. The dog sighed, rolling over
to catch shifting sun beams. He was not a pup
nor was he old. He was a typical young
unemployed male, a good-for-nothing charmer.
Two people paused, murmuring endearments to him
deciding he might need food. The yellow dog stood,
stretched his hind legs one at a time, sniffed and
turned his head, refusing their offer of bread.
He lay down, stretching full length across the
sunny geographic middle of the walkway.
People continued to smile at his obstruction
while stepping around him.
He was perfectly capable of moving.
He was not begging for handouts.
He followed the sun.

Guten Morgan
John Bayley

It's early morning; the house is dark, and warm, and quiet. From the faint glow of a nightlight, a pair of dark, sleepy eyes looks up from the shadows to meet mine. As I turn on the light, I see a ruffled head of tan hair, large triangular ears, and two legs stretching off the night. I undo the latch and watch the dog; who is quickly taking on the shape of a bear cub, leave the comfort of his bed, and enter the day.

Then Morgan goes through his morning ritual; a bit of ear scratching, more stretching, and then a snake-like thing; done on his back, with all four legs and his very round belly pointed toward the ceiling. I will assume he does this to take care of an itchy back. A moment later his look tells me he's ready, and he leads me to the back door so we can do our business.

Morgan is forever exploring the yard. There is always something new to see, an interesting smell, a sound he hasn't heard, and something stinky to roll in. Then when the notion strikes him; which is almost every day, he makes a snack on God-only-knows-what he finds in the grass. Such is the life of our little shelter dog.

Then, for no apparent reason, Morgan decides to have a seat. I watch the wind ruffle his hair, his nose up, and eyes looking at nothing in particular, or at least nothing I can see. It's during these times of quiet solitude; when it's only Morgan and me, when there's nothing to distract him, I swear I've seen him breathe a sigh of relief.

It's during these quiet times that I sometimes catch Morgan looking at me over his shoulder. He looks like he has something to say, and I wonder what the little dog would tell me if he could. Then, when I see his head twitch and his body convulse, I'm not sure I want to know. Morgan was abused by his first owner and then spent years in and out of foster care.

Then he's up again, we take the first of his two daily walks before it's back to the house and into the morning.

Morgan enjoys being pampered; in fact, he expects it. He's also an astute observer of human behavior. He knows my morning ritual, and only once I've settled into my seat he then trots up and makes his request.

As I pet Morgan, I realize just how far we've come. Eight months ago, this contact would have been impossible. Mostly because I didn't understand my little shelter dog; he was and still is, afraid of everything. His natural reaction to that fear is to bite, which I blame on his abuser.

Now satisfied, I watch Morgan slowly walk away, pick up his favorite orange chew toy, take it into the family room, and begin to nibble. As I watch my little shelter dog, I am reminded of two things: First, that any relationship worth having requires understanding, forgiveness, patience, and love; lots of love. Second, the angry, dark side of human nature, and those with the propensity to lash out against helpless victims; women, children, and little dogs who cannot defend themselves, and why it cannot be allowed to go on.

Life with Morgan, our little shelter dog, is not easy, and it's a task a lot of people would not take on. When I see him happy, rested, and playing with his favorite chew toy, I know our efforts are worth it.

Hobbes And Calvin
Beth Stone

Our journey began on November 1st, 1993, when we had the opportunity to adopt a five month old mutt who had been banned from the apartment he was living in with his then owner. A neighbor two houses away knew we were looking for a dog to adopt and suggested we take a look at him. She warned us that the dog had separation anxiety and that he might be difficult to raise. "Nonsense," I thought as I marched over to her house to pick him up, along with his wire crate, toys, food and bowls. In my eyes, he was perfect!

I will never forget the call I then made to my husband asking him to guess what was walking around our kitchen. He guessed, of course, and when he got home, our new puppy met him in the driveway and barked at him. My husband barked back. We laughed and walked into house to begin a journey that we could never expect.

Hobbes was a collie/spaniel mix. He had reddish long hair and a beautiful face. And he absolutely had a separation problem. So much so, that when we would leave the house (we both worked at the time), we would put him in his crate in the basement and securely close the door to the stairs. It never failed to amaze us that this little dog would greet us at the door when we got home. To this day, we only have one explanation for how he could possibly escape the safety of his little crate and open the door, but you would need to believe that our house was also occupied by some friendly spirits who were probably not happy about all of the barking; but that story is for another essay. Suffice to say that he did not live in a crate for very long, but we did have to clean up several messes from soft items he would chew. We had no idea just how much stuffing was in one small couch pillow. But I digress.

On November 10th, nine days after we adopted Hobbes, we found out that we were expecting. We were thrilled beyond belief and could not wait to add to our family of three, but we knew that our house on a busy little street was probably not the safest place for a dog and a baby, so we sold our house and moved to a quiet neighborhood with plenty of room for Hobbes to run around outside. We knew that we had found the best place to raise our family, but this new house had more challenges for Hobbes and his separation anxiety. We never once thought that he was just a puppy and that puppies like to chew things; we thought he was being destructive and decided to seek out the help of a doggie behaviorist. We did a little research and found one who we hoped could help us understand our new dog and all of his nuances.

At our first and only meeting, we were ushered into a large living room, which allowed Hobbes to freely explore the new environment while we talked to the doctor about Hobbes' behaviors at home. I was about seven months pregnant at the time, which was more than obvious to anyone who looked at me, and after only fifteen minutes of observing Hobbes, this doctor informed us that Hobbes had a chemical brain problem, would most definitely harm our new baby and that the only way to help Hobbes was for him to have brain surgery. I was shocked and could not believe that this doctor could be so sure about this after only fifteen minutes of watching our now beloved dog, but this information gave us pause and we decided that the best thing to do was to return him to our neighbor in hopes that she could find him a home with plenty of love and plenty of room to run. I will never forget the look on Hobbes' face looking over my husband's shoulder as he was carried into her home and as we had to say goodbye. It was one of the saddest days of my life. And it was a decision that I would quickly regret, even though our neighbor assured us that Hobbes had been given to a family who owned a five hundred acre farm in a town an hour from us.

For the next two weeks I cried and cried and cried as I stared at the picture of Hobbes that was taped to our refrigerator. I begged my husband to get Hobbes back and told him to offer the new family $500. My husband held me as he also cried and told me that this was the best thing for Hobbes and for our soon to be born baby. I could not take the loneliness any longer and called the behaviorist doctor to see if they had a suitable dog we could adopt. His assistant, Mary, told me that they had a great dog for us to come see and we made plans to head over there the next day. Unfortunately (or to be more accurate - fortunately), Mary called that next day to tell me that the dog she wanted us to see had been given to another family. I hung up the phone believing in my heart that there was a reason for this. After dinner, I told my husband that we were going to go to the Humane Society that night to look for a dog to adopt. Without hesitation he said "okay" and off we went.

When we arrived we were taken to the area where there are rows of pens with beautiful dogs with beautiful eyes that beg to be looked at and adopted. I wanted all of them and forced myself not to cry as I made my way down the row. What I saw next was something that would be forever ingrained in my brain. HOBBES!

I stopped, stared, and then screamed. My husband and the employee he was talking to thought I was going crazy as I kept screaming for them to "get my dog out of the cage!" My husband ran over to me and was also shocked to see that Hobbes was indeed in a cage. Apparently our neighbor was not completely honest with us, but in her defense, she said she was trying to protect us from the sadness of what she had to do. Within minutes, we were walking out the door with Hobbes, and headed to the pet store to buy new equipment for him. In the Jewish religion, this is known as *bashert*, or "meant to be." It was meant to be that Hobbes be our dog.

In July of 1994 we welcomed our first daughter and Hobbes could not have been happier or more protective. Fifteen months later we welcomed our second daughter and Hobbes had an even bigger job of protecting his two sisters.

Over the next almost fifteen years, Hobbes was our "son." He brought us joy and love and after he died, he brought us our new dog, Calvin.

On March 30th, 2008, one day after we returned home from a vacation, Hobbes had a grand mal seizure and we knew that we had to be humane, and let him go. It was an awful day saying goodbye forever to this remarkable dog who we loved more than words can possibly say.

I spent the next week in bed crying and just could not believe that he was gone. I was a stay-at-home mom and Hobbes was my constant companion. We were always together and I felt as though a part of me had died. But, I also knew that I had so much love to give to another dog that we had to visit the Almost Home Shelter in Southfield, Michigan to look at a dog I had found online. Truth be told, I was drawn to this particular dog because he looked like Hobbes. We planned to go to the shelter on April 5th.

On April 4th, less than a week after saying our sad goodbyes to Hobbes, I had a dream that Hobbes brought me a white dog with a brown face. I had the image of that dog in my head as we entered the shelter to see the dog that reminded me of Hobbes.

It was clear after a few minutes of visiting, that the dog we came to see was not for us, and we decided to look around. In the meantime, our older daughter kept pointing to a dog who was very noisily trying to get our attention. I told her that I was not interested in "that" dog, but she insisted that I look at him.

I will never forget the feeling that came over me when I finally looked at him - a white dog with a brown face. The dog Hobbes showed me in a dream. Our dog. Our Calvin.

It has been almost six years since we adopted Calvin and we could not have made a better choice, or should I say Hobbes could not have made a better choice.

Holding Paw
A.J. Huffman

My Chihuahua is afraid of the rain.
Hide-under-blanket-full-on-body-shaking
terrified. A sight that triggers every nurturing-
motherly instinct I have into overdrive. I cuddle,
caudle, attempt to reassure in calming vocal tones –
all tragically useless. In the end,
I cave, break, crumble in pity till I am lying
on the floor next to his favorite dog bed, one
tiny forepaws cupped reassuringly
in each of my hands.

Home
Melissa Grunow

And never shall I forget
The trembling interest with which I heard
Her voice in a low thunder:
"You are safe here."
 ~William Carlos Williams, "Abroad"

Mexicantown, Detroit. We stand in front of a tri-story house that looks as if no one is home; in fact, it looks as though no one has been home for years.

"Are you sure this is it?" I look around and see nearly nothing except for an abandoned brick building across the street, and debris collecting in overgrown flower beds that are dreary and withered with the onset of winter.

"This is the address they gave me." Joe shrugs in his black leather jacket unzipped over a t-shirt, a baseball hat on his head, the brim pulled slightly to one side. It's warm, especially for the first of December. I'm not even a little cold in my black-and-white cardigan sweater, having forgotten my wool coat draped over the back of my office chair in my rush to leave.

I shrug my shoulders and lift my face to the windows, looking for light or movement, but the house is still and silent behind closed curtains. Instead, a white van pulls up next to the curb. A young woman with dark hair smiles at us and nods slightly as she passes through the gate and closes it behind her, disappearing into the backyard. I look over at Joe as if to say, "What now?" but his face is already saying it.

A moment later, the same woman returns, her arms wrapped around three squirming puppies, each just eight weeks old. She drops them to the ground and latches the fence behind her.

From the backyard we hear incessant barking, the mother wondering where her little ones have gone. The puppies respond in kind with high-pitched whimpering as they clamor at the gate, digging and scratching, desperate to return to the backyard.

It's Joe who wants to get a dog. Being that I'm the homeowner and he's the tenant, the decision to adopt ultimately is mine to make. We stand together and watch the puppies fumble over one another, two boys and a girl. Three days ago getting a dog wasn't even a consideration. Now leaving without one doesn't feel possible.

I bend over and scoop up the mongrel that has separated from the group. He's a mix of white and gray, with a solid black head, save for a white zigzag stripe between his eyes. The pup snuggles into me and sticks his nose in the crook of my neck.

Joe is grinning.

"But I wanted a girl." It's barely a protest.

Joe raises his eyebrows and smiles wider.

I look up at the woman. "A hundred dollars, right?"

She nods and sticks her hand out. She may not speak English, but she definitely speaks money.

****

It's August. I'm in the front seat because I'm a girl. Two of the guys got into the back before I could even object. A third is driving. We're riding in the cars with the windows down because the midnight air has cooled the sticky discomfort of the late summer day. I'm resting my head on the edge of the door; the wind sobering and soothing against my face.

I'm drunk. I wasn't, and then I was. Am. Everything is humming around me in pieces of moments. A moment in a bar. People I know. People who know the people I know, but I don't know them. Introductions, forgotten names. The bill was paid without me noticing, my drinks and salad on someone else's credit card now. My reality is a patchwork quilt, a compilation of pieces, ripped and cut and sewn, coming together to make some sense of how I ended up in a car with three men ten years younger than I, just barely old enough to drink themselves. My love affair with alcohol has left gaps in my memory and my ability to reason, the stitching coming undone, the fabric unraveling.

"Hey guys," I say. My great idea compels me to sit up and turn my head. "So, I'm too drunk to drive home, right? I was thinking we should stop at a liquor store and get some beer. I'll buy."

The one driving laughs. "You're going to drink beer while you sober up?" He slaps his hand against the steering wheel and adjusts the volume on the radio.

"Oh my God, Melissa, will you marry me?" In the backseat, one of them takes off his seatbelt and kneels on the floor. "Look, I got down on one knee and everything. Please say yes."

I respond by accepting the proposal with a smile and question. "So does that mean we're stopping for beer?"

The joke doesn't end that night, because within a few weeks, Joe—the backseat suitor— signs a lease to rent a room in my house. Almost immediately, our home takes on an air of domesticity, as though we actually are in a loveless, sexless marriage with little communication, but maintaining a household together nonetheless. We're two introverts who share silence and respect each other's privacy so much that we often find ourselves on different floors of the house and going days, weeks, without talking in person.

****

We put a blanket down in the backseat, but the puppy disregards it, preferring instead to run from one door to the other, pausing only long enough to put his paws up on the window, and twist his head back and forth while he watches a new world come to life through the glass.

"What are we going to name him?" Joe glances in the rearview mirror at the dog that has attacked the corner of the blanket and is scratching at it with his paws while pulling with his teeth.

A few half-hearted suggestions are shared back and forth, but none of them really stick. I think of the Doberman I had growing up named Princess, and Duchess, my dad's dachshund when he was a child. The husky in the back of Joe's car is the next in a long line of canine royalty.

"How about Duke?"

The pup jumps the distance to the front seat, scrambling to get his balance on the armrest between us before being nudged back.

"Duke," Joe says, trying it out. "I like Duke."

"I like Duke, too," I say, as his royal highness pounces on the seatbelt buckle, and then suddenly lies down with a sigh.

****

It's September. An hour before the tenth anniversary of my twenty-first birthday party, a storm rips through the city, relentless rains and winds that tear down tree limbs, shingles, and the utility pole in my backyard, leaving my street flooded for the night and without electricity for five days.

People show up for the party anyway. "You have free beer," someone tells me. "The party will go on."

And go on it does.

The downed power lines in the backyard push the smokers into the driveway, and as the night dries up, more and more party-goers move outside to escape the humidity building in the house. A few of us brought blankets to wrap around our shoulders, the combination of cool sidewalk beneath our jeans and iced beer bottles in our fists bringing on shivers.

Scott's eyes focus on Davey and Nick, who are propped up against the bumper of Joe's car, snuggling under a blanket. His jealousy appears as he starts shouting at the two of them, unable to mask his long-time love for Davey.

I stand up and let the blanket fall around me. I rest one hand in the palm of another. "Scott, you need to calm down."

"You don't understand! Davey only cares about Davey. Look at them. Right in front of my face! I should just go home."

I take a step closer to him, but he doesn't back away. I am within hitting distance, and I know it, but I worry about his shouting drawing attention from the neighbors. "You know you're in no condition to drive."

Scott's eyes are dark and glassy, and he leans slightly forward, swaying gently like the bow of a tree, the alcohol searing through his veins. "I've walked home before. Nobody cares, Davey doesn't care—" He looks down where Davey was sitting, but she and Nick have since relocated to the couch in the basement having witnessed Scott's drunken charades before.

My toes are practically touching his. I'm alone with this man who is known for violent outbursts when he's drunk, defending the integrity of a mutual friend who has abandoned me for the safety of my home.

"Hey man," I sense Joe just behind my right shoulder, literally backing me up, his voice low. "Relax. Come on. It's her birthday."

I close my eyes waiting for one of them to throw a fist, knowing full well that the only thing between them is me.

Instead, Joe continues to talk, his voice languid, his words leaving no room for dispute. Instead of getting punched, I find myself being hugged, while Scott is sobbing apologies against my ear. I turn and see Joe next to me. He's the first man who has ever come to my rescue in an escalating situation without actually rescuing me.

When Joe is arrested two weeks later for driving while intoxicated, the police officer is less amused, less impressed with his ability to handle himself under the influence. It's raining the morning I drive him to impound to pick up his car. My windshield wipers whine as they try to keep visibility, an overcast sky adding glare and distraction. He rarely speaks as it is, but his silence morphs into a new shape. It takes up its own space in the car between us, like steam from a screaming kettle that neither of us can remove from the fire.

We will get turned away twice before he can get his car. Once because he needs cash, the second time because the gas tank drained while the car sat running on the side of the road, Joe passed out drunk in the driver's seat, facing west on an eastbound road. He won't know this until he meets with a lawyer and gets a copy of the police report. He won't remember driving the car at all, passing the exit to our home and continuing on the freeway, getting further and further away while I slept, the night quiet outside my window.

We kneel together, side-by-side in my bathroom, our sleeves pushed up, massaging puppy shampoo into Duke's thick fur as he struggles in the water, scrambling and fighting, his nails clicking against the bottom of the bathtub. The lather piles up and catches dirt that has settled in deep from spending the first two months of his life living in a dusty backyard.

"He needs his nails trimmed," Joe remarks. I push a soapy finger into the tip of my nose as if to say, "Not it!" and Duke takes it as a cue to scramble out of the tub. We grab him together and wrestle him back down while I pour one cupful of water after another over his fur, dirty water splashing beneath him, and white fur emerging where it was before a light tan.

After Duke is fully rinsed, Joe lifts him out of the tub and we wrap him in a towel, rubbing him dry, while he lies still on the bathroom floor, panting and watching us.

Downstairs in the kitchen, I pour his over-sized bag of puppy food into a storage bin, the kibble a peaked mound as the bag empties. Duke sticks his nose into the bin, knocks some food to the floor and starts munching, the bin just a little shorter than he is.

"It's not a buffet," I tell him, but don't push him away.

After he's had his fill, Duke wanders into the crate he will outgrow in three months, circles twice, lies down, and falls asleep.

"We have a dog," Joe says, as we stand together and watch our puppy sleep, releasing sighs and snores while he dreams.

****

I'm packing. There are grocery bags sitting on the floor of my kitchen, and I'm filling them with items that belong to a man I'm trying to kick out of my life. A toothbrush, deodorant, pajama pants, a hand-made stuffed rabbit sewn together by an ex-girlfriend. Don't forget the blanket he brought over to wash and never took home, or the hoodie he always wore because I keep the thermostat low, even with winter approaching. I'm too angry to feel sad. Instead, determination and fury keep me moving, taking care to keep CDs from scratching, book pages from tearing. I may be angry, but I'm not destructive.

When I come home, Joe senses something has changed. He can see the emptiness left behind where a man once was. He's sitting at the dining table, playing music on his computer with the volume turned low. It's our sign, an invitation to talk. It's his way of saying, "I'm here to listen if you need me."

Joe's presence is a comfort but also a nagging reminder of what it means to be accountable to someone else, how easy it is to lose myself if people aren't ever present. He is to me what I want from a man who wants nothing from me.

I sit across from him, and put my head down, the tablecloth scratchy beneath my cheek. A series of text messages from the other man, and I throw my phone across the kitchen. When it lands, it breaks apart into four pieces that will never go back together the same way they had before.

"It's over," is all I say. I would say it again. The scene would replay with other men who would leave, or I would leave them, or we would abandon each other. Some I would let go of quickly, easily, one would disappear completely, never to be heard from again, and another would end the relationship without warning, leaving me in a spinning state of drunken depression that lasted for days.

One late and drunken night, very early on, the sun will appear on the horizon, and I will point an accusatory finger to Joe and say, "You weren't there for me when I needed you."

He will turn his head, and I will think I see tears. I'll kneel on the floor next to him and apologize, over and over; I'll apologize, because it's against everything in me to cause a grown man to cry.

He'll take my hand, whisper "Come here," and pull me onto his lap to get me up off the floor. I'll drape my arms across his shoulders, and he'll kiss me lightly on the cheeks and the forehead, then gently touch the tip of his nose to mine, his hand cupping the back of my neck.

"I'll take care of you," he'll say. "I promise."

I'll nod and expect him to lean in to kiss me for real, to take total advantage of my vulnerability and my need for comfort, but he won't. Instead, he'll lead me to my room, put me to bed, and stay with me until I fall asleep, promising, "I'm here for you. I'm here for you."

So many months later and someone would ask me, "Do you think on some level he loves you?"

I won't even have to pause. "I think he loves me on many levels," I will say. "But not the one where he is in love with me," but I won't relay the night he made his promise to me, a commitment even greater than the joking marriage proposal. No, that night I will keep to myself, holding it close to my heart like an injured bird.

****

Joe is on a restricted license and forbidden from consuming alcohol. I feel as though I'm wearing a mask all the time. Joe hides in the basement with the television. I stop eating and hide in the bottle.

"We should get a dog," he suggests when a friend of his adopts a husky puppy from a breeder in Mexicantown. We're both so terribly unhappy that we wear our contempt for the world like a badge.

"That's the craziest thing I've ever heard," I say. "We are *not*, under any circumstances, getting a dog."

"We should get a dog," he repeats.

Three days later, we bring home a dog. Together. Duke. *Our dog.*

****

Michelle's heart valves only open for Joe. Often I don't even know that she's spent the night until the next morning when I see her shoes by the front door. I learn who she is by the shoes that she wears: Tall black boots, yellow sandals, hand-painted canvas slip-ons, and the red flip-flops that Duke chews into so many pieces one morning that she has to go home barefoot, walking through the parking lot and into the residence hall building hoping no one will notice that her not-boyfriend's dog scattered her shame all over his not-wife's kitchen floor.

There are many nights where the three of us find ourselves seated around the dining kitchen table, talking. What is the truth of what's between us? Michelle and Joe sharing a bed. Joe and myself sharing a home and a dog. Michelle and I sharing a friendship. We are a Three's Company of contemporary America positioned in a Detroit suburb in a recovering economy that's on the fringe of hope and wantonness. We all love each other, but we're all too frightened by what that means to ever talk about it, no matter how much we drink.

Michelle often talks to me about Joe, speculating as women do, as to why he won't commit, why he won't make it official, because everything between them points to a relationship. But I don't bring it up with Joe. I hide behind the veil of respecting his privacy, but the truth is more so that I fear jeopardizing our relationship for the sake of preserving theirs. I need them both too much to risk losing either if they do happen to end up together. I can't sacrifice him for her happiness, and I can't watch her suffer because of his failure to commit to anyone but me.

****

Our puppy is growing. I can't carry him like a stack of books with one arm anymore. He learns how to go up the stairs, and finally gets the courage to go down them as well. He can jump on my bed without any assistance. He shares my bed the most, and develops his attachment to me more so than Joe, but Joe is the one who teaches him tricks. I teach him the practicalities of "sit" and "lie down," but Joe teaches Duke how to shake, fist bump, and catch a treat in the air. We send each other picture messages of Duke doing cute things, obnoxious things, I-love-our-dog things, your-dog-is-in-trouble things. Our communication, our lives, are centered almost entirely on the dog. I wonder if Joe knows that someday he will move out, and when he does, Duke will remain with me, and I will be the one with a dog's life of companionship. Joe will carry on. Alone.

****

There are six of us crammed into the extended cab of a pickup truck riding home from a dance club after celebrating Tony's twenty-first birthday. He barely makes it inside my home before he lifts the lid of the trashcan and throws up every fruity birthday shot we bought for him throughout the night.

I feel instantly sober, barking directions at my friends to get a washcloth, a towel, a glass of water. Duke whines in his crate and someone lets him outside. I throw Tony's clothes in the washing machine because they're covered in sweat or vomit or both.

Joe comes out of his room and a chorus of apologies rises up from the group for waking him. As the night wears on, Tony is barely conscious and everyone else has scattered to couches or mattresses throughout the house. Michelle brings a sleeping bag and a spare pillow from a closet, Austin wraps the pillow with a towel, and we put Tony to bed on the kitchen floor. He starts to vomit, but this time he doesn't wake up.

"He's going to choke in his sleep," I say.

More directions given, and I have a comforter and a pillow, then I'm on the floor next to Tony nodding off slowly, being pulled out of sleep every few minutes to prop him up and hold a bucket under his chin.

Everyone has gone to sleep except Joe, who is standing in the kitchen, leaning against the counter not saying a word.

"Where's Michelle?" I ask him.

"She's sleeping in your room."

I settle back down on the floor, grateful I had mopped it that afternoon. "What is your problem, anyway?" I ask him. "Why don't you just go for it with her?"

He doesn't say anything.

"This isn't one of those times where you can get away with not answering."

His voice is a whisper. "I'm afraid of screwing it up."

I close my eyes and rest my head on the pillow. When I open them again, Joe is still standing there, looking at the floor in front of him, but not at me. Not at me.

"You need to fix this, Joe," I tell him with my eyes closed. I know I'm slurring my words, but I also know I'm speaking the truth. He knows it, too. "She loves you. *Loves* you. And you treat her like crap."

Silence. Vacant nods. A clenched jaw.

"I don't interfere in your life very often. So when I do, it should count for something."

Thirty minutes later, I wake up to hold the bucket for Tony, and Joe is still standing there to make sure we're both okay. His loyalty to me mirrors Duke's. But just to me. Never to Michelle.

****

A new relationship. I spend the beginning of summer disappearing on the weekends, chasing love for hours on a freeway to a man who lives in another State. Joe will stay behind with the dog, and only ever ask me one question: "When are you coming home?"

This same man will shut down the relationship before things start to go wrong, providing explanations that don't make sense, reasons I can't process, so after a week of drinking my feelings, I take Duke to the lake by my parents' house and toss a tennis ball into the water. The dog who hates to be bathed lunges after it, paddling through the murk, scooping the ball up in his jaw and bringing it back to me. We play the game all afternoon while my brothers and nephews splash in the water together and my parents watch from a park bench. At sunset, my sister-in-law takes a picture of Duke and me in front of the water. The dog has replaced the man in my pictures and my life.

I'll return home, rest my head on the kitchen table, and look to Joe to explain what went wrong this time. He won't have an answer except to say, "You deserve better."

You deserve better. You deserve better. You deserve better.

But what does better look like?

****

Joe hands me a stack of twenties. "Here's November rent," he says. "And also my notice that I'll be moving out December first."

He tells me about his new apartment. It's a third-floor walk-up with a balcony and a hefty price tag.

"Aren't you going to miss your dog?" I ask. I'm trying to be supportive, but Joe has already slumped to a seated position on the kitchen floor, ready to hash this one out.

"Yeah," he says. "And you."

"This feels like a break-up," I say. "I feel like I got dumped." For once, I'm the one who doesn't want to talk. I go upstairs to my room and leave him behind on the cool tile.

I had a feeling this day was coming soon. I could tell he had been unhappy. Yet, I still don't know how to react except to pretend to be supportive and hope it turns into the truth.

"I have such mixed feelings," he says the next day. "I think that living alone is something I should experience, but I also don't want to leave you."

"Don't stay because you think I need you. Stay because I want you to."

"I know," he says.

But in the end, he doesn't stay.

****

Michelle is home with Duke. Joe and I are in the woods in Ohio with one hundred and eighty college-age men volunteering for EDGE—a leadership development program hosted by a national fraternity. I'm clutching medicine in a plastic bag we had just retrieved from a pharmacy for a participant who needed it. We run from cabin to cabin tracking him down, opening the doors and shouting, "Tommy!" as the name echoes off the cavernous walls.

We're a team. Over a year of living together, and it truly feels like a solid relationship, where we can move around each other without fumbling, anticipating how the other moves and turns. I knew it was the last time we would be together leading anything that matters, being a part of something bigger than our collective selves. We save seats for each other at meal times. Whenever I need help setting up for the next event, he is at my elbow offering his assistance. He is my go-to technical expert. He brings participant issues to my attention so we can resolve them together. Together. Together, we have built a sharper EDGE.

The last event of the weekend took place in the mess hall where all of the participants stood in one large circle stepped forward with statements that applied to them starting with "Cross the line if..."

Cross the line if you've cried in the past month.
Cross the line if you've been hurt by someone you love.
Cross the line if you've hurt someone you love.
Cross the line if you've ever been arrested.
Cross the line if ...

Joe is standing next to me, and it takes everything in me to not reach out and squeeze his hand when we step forward and reveal new things about each other. Even after a year, we don't know everything, but we are three weeks away from him moving out. I would never again be that close to him physically or emotionally. Together we had crossed our own line, and for us, there was no stepping back.

Hounded
Vivian McInerny

I'd cleared the supper table and was up to my elbows in dirty dishes when a taxi pulled up. My sister got out. She stood at the end of the driveway doing some kind of yoga stretch as the cab driver ran her credit card. Her flight wasn't even due to land for another ninety minutes.

"Mom," I called out. "Lizzie's here."

Mom couldn't hear a thing with the television blasting but the dog came skittering into the kitchen yapping, ears flapping. I shushed him. That got him more excited. Schnitzel orbited around my feet while I scrubbed furiously at a casserole dish. The scouring pad was useless, all gunked-up with baked-on cheese.

Lizzie reached her right hand behind her back to grasp her left. The cab driver popped the trunk. He struggled to pull a rolling suitcase from the back. It was small but apparently heavy because he half-dropped it onto the street. Lizzie held her pose. She was very flexible.

"Mom!" I shouted to be heard above Schnitzel's yips and *Wheel of Fortune*. "Lizzie is here early!"

I surrendered the casserole dish war and tossed the scrubber in the sink. Gray dishwater splashed the front of my good blouse.

"Damn it."

Dabbing at the spot with a towel only made it worse. A soapy, cheesy, smear spread across my boobs just as my sister walked through the back door.

"Hey," she said. "Looking good."

"You're early," I blurted out.

"I caught an earlier flight."

"We were going to pick you up."

"I took a cab," she said like a verbal shrug. "Business expense."

Lizzie rolled her suitcase into one corner and parked it. I pulled my blouse from my skin and tried to fan it dry. Lizzie checked her reflection in the little mirror in the hall. The dog's toenails clicked the linoleum in a nervous dance.

"Lizzie!" Mom squealed running to tackle-hug my sister. "You're here!"

The dog piddled on the floor. I grabbed a roll of paper towels.

"How was your flight? Did you get something to eat? What time is it over there?" Mom's questions came out all girly-giggly but her grip on Lizzie was fierce. "Can we get you anything?"

"A cup of coffee would be great," said Lizzie peeling Mom's arms from her neck.

"Peg will make us some coffee," Mom said "Won't you, honey."

They both looked at me mopping up the pee. For a miniature, the dog had a bladder.

"Isn't that thing housebroken yet?" Lizzie asked.

****

Mom led Lizzie to the living room like special company while I dealt with coffee and *that thing*. The dog was a gift from Lizzie three years earlier. She came home that time completely unannounced en route to Singapore. Mom opened the door expecting the mailman only to find my sister grinning with a tiny puppy in hand. Lizzie declared *happy belated birthday or early Christmas or something* and presented Mom with a mini Dachshund. He was black with tan markings so that his eyebrows looked posed in permanent surprise. Lizzie named him, *Schnitzel, because he's a wiener.* She said she bought him from some fancy breeder in New York and flew to Minneapolis with him in the cabin. First class, no doubt. The next day Lizzie continued onto Asia for a business meeting, Mom went into her post-Lizzie ritual mourning period, and I shopped for dog food, bowls and a bed for Schnitzel. I am a cat person.

"Regular or decaf," I called to Lizzie. Mom only drank decaf.

"I need a serious hit of caffeine."

Only my sister could make a cup of coffee sound like something sold illegally in dark alleys. I put a couple mugs of water in the microwave and punched start. I wasn't thirsty. I found some Folgers instant in the cupboard. It was decaf. Schnitzel circled around in his bed like a broken wind-up toy.

"Cream? Sugar?" I called out to Lizzie.

"Black."

The timer dinged and the dog and the microwave stopped spinning. I carried both mugs into the living room. Lizzie sat on one end of the new couch. Mom huddled next to her on the middle cushion, patting her arm. I handed Lizzie her cup. She took a sip.

"Oh. Instant." She held the mug in the air as though it were something vile and possibly contagious. "Do you have a coaster?" A coaster? Who did she think she was? Mom and I didn't own the kind of furniture that needed to be protected with coasters.

"No," I said. "No coasters."

"We don't have *any*, Peg?" Mom asked like I might be hoarding a secret stash in a backroom. "Are you sure?"

"I'm sure."

Lizzie set her mug down right on top of the latest issue of Time magazine that had the Pope on the cover. It left a ring like a wet halo around the head of his Holiness. I took a seat in one of the blue wingbacks.

"Are you here long?" I asked.

"Long enough," she said with a smile.

"It's never long enough," said Mom.

Lizzie launched into one of her fauxpologies that started with *I'm sorry* then went on to recount all the ways in which she was so terribly busy with her fabulous *career*, never a job, and how she was *slammed with meetings* here and *crammed with conferences* there. She was working on a project in Amsterdam. She had another in Hong Kong. She yammered on and on. What my sister actually did for a living was a mystery to me. In the past, when I asked, she gave smart aleck answers like, *I work corporate magic* or *I make CEOs weep*. My sister once handed me a business card with her official title printed in fancy script, and it still didn't mean a darned thing.

"Peg," Mom interrupted my thoughts with an exaggerated stage whisper. "I think the dog's got to do his business."

"Maybe he should make an appointment with Lizzie," I muttered as I got up to get the leash.

****

Less than ten yards from the house, Schnitzel lifted his leg on a bed of mums. I considered turning back. Instead, I zipped up my sweatshirt and kept going. We both could use some air. I walked him down the street, two blocks over, and through the gap in the hedge of the old church graveyard where the trees were tall. Outsiders might consider it morbid, but the seventeen-acre cemetery served as a kind of park for the neighborhood. During the week, elderly parishioners strolled the grounds for exercise. On Sundays, grandkids visiting from the burbs played history detectives in search of the oldest headstones. Leashed dogs were permitted as long as their owners showed respect and, of course, we did because we all had family six feet below. Besides, the groundskeeper lived on site.

Schnitzel stopped to smell the base of an old elm. Early evening light filtered through the branches. Already, some leaves showed the reds and yellows of the coming cold. They rustled in the breeze. As a kid, I'd imagined that sound was the whispering angels of the buried dead.

The dog walked his stubby front legs up the tree trunk and stretched his neck to the right to follow an imagined scent. A squirrel spiraled down and around the tree in the opposite direction. Schnitzel barked.

"Come on," I said tugging on his collar. "Don't be a chump."

He gave chase and the leash wrapped around the tree Maypole style. It made me think of childhood games of hide-and-seek in the graveyard with my sister. Once, I stayed hidden behind a headstone, my back pressed against the cool marble slab for what seemed like hours, so proud of myself for outsmarting her until I emerged to discover she'd abandoned me for other friends. Mom found me crying in my summer sundress, a huge letter 'S' pressed into the skin of my bare back from the Shaughnessy family crypt. Lizzie said it stood for stupid.

****

I couldn't have been gone more than twenty minutes, thirty tops; but when I turned the corner I saw the yellow taxi waiting out front. At first I thought the driver returned because Lizzie left something in the back of his cab. Then Mom stepped out onto the front porch and yelled.

"Come say goodbye to your sister!"

Lizzie squeezed past Mom and down the walkway pushing that stupid suitcase in front as if she were walking a wheeled dog.

"Hurry, Peg! Hurry! Lizzie is leaving!"

I cut across the neighbors' yards and stepped right into one of their dog's messes. *My sister comes home for less than an hour and my world goes to shit.* That's what I thought. I'm not prone to swearing aloud, or in my thoughts either, for that matter, but the situation just seemed to call for it.

"Shit. Shit. Shit," I said wiping my shoe on a clean spot of grass. "Shit."

Lizzie laughed. She left her suitcase on the curb for the driver and carefully picked her way across the front lawn toward me in the fading light. Mom stayed to supervise the cabby wrestling a retractable handle that wasn't living up to its name.

"I'm off," said Lizzie.

"That was fast."

"I had a three-hour layover but traffic here was a bitch. I don't want to risk my connection."

"Sure."

We both looked down at the dog. He looked up at me.

"Peg?"

"Yeah?"

"Thank-you."

"Thank-you for what? I didn't do anything. You were barely even here."

"No, I know. I mean, thank-you for everything, for taking care of the house, for taking care of Mom. I know it's not easy. Mom isn't easy."

"Mom is Mom."

"And I'm just so busy."

"Yeah."

"Yeah, well..."

We walked together to where the driver stood holding open the backdoor like a chauffeur. Mom bear-hugged Lizzie one last time before my sister managed to get into the car and close the door. Mom pressed her palms against the glass. The driver tapped the horn farewell as they drove off. Mom waved furiously at the rear windshield window, at the back of Lizzie's head. She didn't give up until the car turned the corner.

"She's gone," she said.

I nodded. The porch light came on in the twilight. Mom shuffled up the walkway to the house. Hummingbird moths came flitting around the azalea. The dog snapped at the air around them. He'd never caught one but he never stopped trying. Scooping up Schnitzel I buried my face in smooth fur that smelled of damp earth and leaves and dog.

House Sitting Nim
Susan Adams

The puppy curls into my leg bones,
bereft,
this simple harness tethers hope.
I stroke her lament
her yearning to belong
but my hand is a lie
the owners have gone for several weeks
and she has no way to know.

Soft tongue licks me like a love song
to make me bond.
I smile and smile to get her trust
but it's a trap,
I must leave also.

Forlorn has weight
we slow-suck our breath
wait for the other's move.
'Walk?'   is the break
she grabs her leash, I grab the key
and we are gone.

That night she snuggles into bed
harmed, fooled, warmed, calm.

I'm Actually A Cat Person
Jen Camilleri

    I paused for a moment to gather my hair in a ponytail and wipe the sweat from my face. I took a deep breath and looked into the face of Sophie, the large Stafford Terrier with the bad leg that my mom and I were trying to lift carefully into the back of my SUV. I still wasn't sure what had possessed me to sign my mom and me up to work a dog adoption event with Almost Home. I had been a volunteer with Almost Home for just about a month but had specified that I wanted to work with the cats. I had owned dogs before but I had become more of a cat person in the past ten or so years. Yet here I was in eighty-five degree weather trying to boost a dog bigger than me into my car. With one big heave, we loaded Sophie into my car and she rewarded me by licking my face.

    I waited for the last dog we were transporting and began to count down the time until I would be home again in my nice air conditioned house. I noticed one of the volunteers carrying a small, hairy, wriggling creature with four legs that was peeing all over with excitement. I said a silent prayer hoping that wasn't my final passenger. Clearly, I should have prayed a lot louder because the next thing I knew my mom and I were handed that crazy dog whose name was "Bryson". It took two of us to try to control him and calm him down enough to load him into his carrier in the back of my car.

    Within an hour we had arrived at the adoption event, helped set up and unloaded our canine passengers. After a while I was asked to let Bryson, the hairy ball of terror, out of his cage. I fastened his leash around him, let him out, and he immediately ran to my mom and jumped on her lap. While sitting there, he calmed down and allowed us to pet him. I noticed that when he sat there, he wasn't just a ball of fur. He was a very small dog, a Yorkie terrier mix with curly brown and gray hair covering his body. He was very affectionate and gave lots of kisses and wriggled with excitement whenever he was petted. By this time he was on my lap enjoying having his ears scratched. When I stopped, he turned around, put his paws on my chest and looked in my eyes. The feeling that came over me was indescribable. I felt as if this dog had just looked into my soul and understood everything about me.

I spent the rest of the event with Bryson out of his cage next to me. I wanted him to find a forever home yet at the same time; a nagging feeling inside me hoped he wouldn't be adopted that day. I had started volunteering at Almost Home in an effort to make me feel better about my life. I was working at a job I didn't like, I was suffering from depression, I had moved back home with my parents in an effort to save money and all of my friends were an hour away now. I loved the time I spent at the shelter and felt I was really making a difference with the cats. So why was this little dog having such an impact on me?

That night over dinner my mom filled my dad in on the adoption event. I was pretty quiet that night and went to bed early. I woke up in the middle of the night unable to fall asleep knowing that I had to adopt Bryson. I woke the next day and announced to my parents about my need to adopt this dog. My parents were very accommodating people as I had brought two cats with me when I moved back to their house, adding to the two cats they already had. They were not, however, accommodating about the thought of a dog in the house. It took about a week of begging, crying, and plotting to finally convince them that a dog would be a welcome addition to the home. I tried to tell them how this dog was able to see into my heart and soul and was sent to me for a reason. They were rather skeptical but agreed that I could adopt Bryson in hopes it would help bring me out of my depression.

I adopted Bryson the following Saturday. I felt like a proud parent as I took him to the pet store to buy food, toys, a bed and treats. On the way home I decided to change his name to Edison. After all, Bryson was the name of the four year old dog that was found wandering the streets until a nice policeman brought him to

Almost Home Shelter. Edison was the name of MY four year old dog whose new life was about to begin. Edison made himself right at home in our house and thought of the cats as his new playmates.

I'd like to say it was a smooth transition and there were no issues but that wasn't the case. It was obvious his previous owners had never trained him and had hit him when he misbehaved. He was aggressive around food and other dogs. My parents and I decided to enroll him in a very intense school that he absolutely loves. In the eight months we have had him he has made great strides. Now, he is potty trained, crate trained, knows how to sit, lie down, and stay. He loves to play and has a complete love of life (and treats). He is great to cuddle up with on the couch for a nap, even if a cat joins us. He has a silly sense of humor and sticks out his tongue when he is being playful. He is very expressive and loves to be the center of attention.

Since adopting Edison, I quit the job I was unhappy with and began to pursue what I was really passionate about. I've found that Edison has made me more active which in turn helped draw me out of my depression. Edison has become a hobby for both my parents as wel,l as we all try to help him with his training. He was given the title of "Most Improved" in his training class and has become good friends with three other dogs there. We couldn't be more excited about his progress.

As I sit here, writing this, I notice Edison sitting on the couch next to me. He is sticking his tongue out at me because he wants me to get up and play with him. When he looks into my eyes, I still know that he can see deep into my heart and soul. I'd like to write about how great I feel to know I saved a rescue dog. However that would be a lie. The truth is, my rescue dog saved me.

Josie the Wonder Dog
Elisabeth Ward

We wonder about our little Josie.

A black, medium-large dog with a pointer's head, cricked tail, and black-splotched white vest and paws, Josie is a rescue. Friendly and outgoing when we met, slightly prim at one and a half years, she took immediately to our large mature Weimaraner, greeted him like a long-lost friend and did not want to leave his side.

To those whose Weimaraners end up as rescues, yes, there is such a thing as a mature Weimaraner and it's worth the wait.

"Pointer mixed with what?" I asked the dog-savvy man attending Josie.

"They say Lab, but I don't really see it. She's still so new here she's pretty cautious. She's sweet and affectionate, but her personality hasn't expressed itself yet. She's not ready to play, but she likes the idea. She's more comfortable watching others."

Ah, I thought, *not overly excitable.*

He went on. "She'll want to sleep on the bed with you."

Okay. Our Weimaraner sleeps under the covers, as did his uncle.

"She's a counter hound."

That's doable. Nothing has the reach or problem-solving ability of a Weimaraner when it comes to food on a table—or high counter—or pantry shelf—or in a zipped suitcase.

"She'll need lots of exercise."

Got it. Five hours a day served the Weimaraners pretty well.

Full of confidence that Josie fit our lives and could fulfill her own on our small farm of four acres, all fenced to protect her, the Weimaraner and our cats from the road; we drove two days to her new home. Once there, Josie kept me in sight at all times, even tearing up and down along the pasture fence whenever I was with the horses, chickens and goats.

Our house is small due to its narrowness, but is long enough to be slightly jointed in the middle—like Josie's tail. We have a pet door in the bedroom half and magnetized screens in the middle of the house, just kitchen-side of that tail-crick.

Josie spent her first two days alternately zooming in circles around the yard or bumping open the screen to check on me in the kitchen. (Our sedate Weimaraner won't do that, but insists on calling us to open whatever door he wishes to use. So much for maturity.)

Come nightfall, Josie ducked in through the pet door to lie by the bed and let the Weimaraner take care of barking along the fence lines when coyotes howled. When my husband and I turned in, she slept between his head and mine, with the Weimaraner safely guarding the foot of the bed from his lair under the duvet. How did my husband adjust to this sleeping arrangement? One night several weeks after Josie's arrival I felt his hand on the back of my head and heard him whisper, "Hi, Cutie." I rolled over. His hand patted my face. "Oh that's *you*," he said.

Our son, daughter-in-law and their seven children aged eleven-and-under arrived for a visit on Josie's third day with us. Josie acted as though she'd been waiting for them. Although she jumps up to hug every adult she meets, she did not jump on the children. But she did run with them, play ball with them, play tug-of-war with them, follow them past that crick in the hallway, and curl up and sleep with them. When the youngest four splashed in our swimming pool's fairly large and very shallow end, Josie stood in their midst and vibrated with joy. The older children could not lure her into deeper waters.

Josie did not bark when anybody came to the house. She stood at the door, or gate, and pointed.

Almost painfully friendly, when leashed Josie became hysterical at the sight of another dog. Although others sometimes mistook this for aggression, it was her request for freedom to play. Fast enough to outrun any other dog, Josie was fearless in all canine interactions.

Off-leash when I rode horseback or hiked, Josie raced in circles—or straight lines if topography or trees commanded—with the constant whiz back-and-forth of a county fair shooting gallery. Although often out of sight, she was never far from me.

She was so easily distracted by a tennis ball we soon took to referring to it as her leash. We could take her around the neighborhood to visit so long as we had that ball, which she always returned to our hands with a simply stated *Give*.

Though quick to learn commands, and showing signs indicating previous training, Josie did not respond to *come!*—or any other harshly spoken command—but happily appeared by my side at a breezy *this way* so long as I kept moving. Whether in sight or not, to turn around was, as it had been for the Weimaraners, a signal to reverse course and follow me as surely as stopping told Josie to continue her chase. I don't know how they know, but they do.

My husband worried when we took her to the ocean. We were sure she'd get rolled over by a wave and pulled away by an undertow. Our Weimaraners had proven themselves to be strong swimmers, but generally waited for me to enter the water first.

Josie flew down the beach, just behind or just ahead of whatever shorebirds rose, then walked to the water's edge with thoughts of a drink; soaked her feet, tickled her nose with the salty sizzle, then tore up and down the beach again for the sheer joy of running. Her mouth opened, her tongue flapped, her eyes went wild, her lips curled back and she ran faster.

The Weimaraner grew sick of watching her and lay down in the shade.

When Josie got too hot she wallowed briefly in the wash after the waves broke. Then she ran again.

"What an easy dog!" we agreed. "Whatever she is, she's the perfect mix."

A word about her grasp of the English language:

One day, at a loss for something interesting to do, Josie went to our bookcase and selected a bird guide.

"No, Jos, don't chew books. Go find a bone to chew on."

Five minutes later she pulled down *The Rule of the Bone* by Russell Banks. Coincidence? One might think so, but...

Our thirteen-year old granddaughter, spending a week with us, had one assignment to complete during that week. I was anxious for her opinion on a Young Adult manuscript I was polishing. She'd already given her opinion in an off-hand way. She did not want to go upstairs to her room and finish reading it. But, House Rules: do what Grammy says.

She went upstairs to read. About fifteen or twenty minutes later we heard Josie scramble up the steps, and not long after, our granddaughter came down with a book and a big grin.

"Look what Josie brought me."

Yes, Josie had brought it. The dust jacket was outlined in Josie-mouth-sized slobber. The book was *How to Read and Why* by Harold Bloom. It had been on a high back shelf of the bookcase, not Josie's usual Oort Cloud of book selections.

As Weimaraner owners we have a pretty hefty collection of William Wegman's coffee table books. Knowing Josie's attachment to Weimaraners, it's no surprise she sometimes drags these forth. She will choose them carefully, but seldom chews them. And, as a hunting dog, it's not surprising she also brings down field guides.

Hardly enough to claim Wonder Dog, but certainly enough to make us wonder.

What would make a dog deposit the A.R. Ammons poetry collection *Garbage* at my feet when I returned to the house after running out to add something to the trash?

I finished reading, and was holding, Terry Tempest Williams's *When Women Were Birds* while my husband I discussed the book and TTW's writing.

"Josie," he said, looking across the room, "what have you got?"

He picked up the book she dropped and gave me a quizzical look. "Red? Does this mean anything to you?"

"By Terry Tempest Williams, right?"

Right.

Despite Josie's literary pursuits, her vocabulary is limited. It does not include the word *no*.

Whereas a Weimaraner will do anything for an eighth of a small dog biscuit, Josie's focus cannot be broken by any food held in front of her nose, or even stuck under lip. She's too hardwired to be attentive to anything but her chosen prey. In fact, the only food she has shown any interest in, other than her own meals, is salmon.

We're not sure where she'd previously been salmon fishing, but at our house she fishes for it in the kitchen sink or, in one absent-minded moment when I'd run to the barn, in my purse. The tennis ball on top of my wallet provided a hint of my slipup.

It dawned on us on our first road trip that Josie was wary of strange places. Returning home with us convinced her of our love. The more comfortable she became and the more trails she learned, the more trails she left to explore the surrounding brush and hillsides.

The nightly howl of the coyote would have called her across miles if not for our fence. Should she see one when I rode, she was off on the merriest of chases, joined by her protecting Weimaraner. But he always came back when called. (Okay. It took six years, but for a Weimaraner a lesson learned is a lesson remembered forever.) Josie kept up the chase even over or through holes in fences, only returning when I finally went home along that busy street I tried to avoid.

Yes, she was perfect in a strange place. But we can't move every year just to make the dog obey... Can we?

According to the website for English pointers, this is a "galloping breed" requiring space to run off-leash. They do not like to swim but will if pressed, though they prefer to stand belly-deep. "Affectionate and brave," "outgoing and friendly," "quick to learn" were other descriptions that went with the admonition that it will chase anything anywhere and take advantage of a lax, or even relaxed, owner. There was no mention about forward-facing whiskers that allow Josie to react instantaneously to anything coming toward her mouth. Nor did it mention a vibrating lower jaw and the soft *hiy-y-y-y,hiy-y-y-y* sound of her hind teeth clicking whenever she's excited, be it over prey, a tennis ball, the arrival of the grandchildren, or something as simple as breakfast. I kept hearing pointers weren't black. Yet there on the website was a black, white-bibbed dog so strongly resembling our Josie that my son and his children were convinced it was our Josie.

Then came the box of birds.

Toward the end of her first year with us we bought three new chickens, which were placed in our henhouse while we were away for the evening. When we returned, Josie ran to the closed henhouse door to sniff, whine, leap and pace for an hour or more. She got up at least three times during the night to stalk the henhouse. Come morning, it was all I could do to wash the crate they came in and leave it outside our gate. She stopped stalking the henhouse only when the chickens went into the pasture and she could run frantically along the fence.

We stopped wondering about her mix. We pictured the hunter who trained her giving up when she spent the day chasing birds away, and stopped wondering how she was left to wander a small town's snowy streets for a week before being picked up by a shelter worker. Now a solid, sleek and muscular fifty-five pounds, Josie weighed only forty-two when we met her.

We'd heard with our first Weimaraner that the breed mellows out at seven. Our younger one calmed down closer to six because he had a very dedicated teacher in the older dog. As a new, unsettled, extremely master-dependent breed, a Weimaraner becomes neurotic very easily. Once its rules are instilled in the owner, however, it's hard to find a better teammate for daily life—if your life is an active one. English pointers, according to Josie, are *never* neurotic. They do not brood over their mistakes. They don't make them. We do, but a pointer trusts we won't do it again— unlike our Weimaraner who chews his paw raw awaiting the moment we *will*. My husband and I picked up Josie's optimistic outlook and decided a pointer settles at three years, as did his Golden Retrievers and my sister's Labs.

We took Josie to Wyoming for her first winter visit when she'd been with us for six months. Our Weimaraners had easily learned to *stay on the trail* because we taught them in winter, when to leave the trail was to sink haunch-deep in snow. But Josie is half their weight and twice their speed and runs through snow as though it were confetti.

Does her galloping instinct make her front feet, which strike hard ground in normal fashion, point upward when she runs through powder? The heel strikes first and creates a snowshoe effect that keeps her running instead of plunging. It didn't take us long to discover a *trail* for Josie is the track *she* makes.

She ran her usual circles around our path, or did her back-and-forth devil-dog run with open mouth, peeled-back lips and wild eyes, but she was tractable. True, she got caught in an elk stampede, but that wasn't her fault.

She had run so fast up the trail ahead of us that the two-dozen elk never saw her, but jumped up from their beds on the far side of a river at the sight of a cross-country skier and large gray canid. In panic, they swam the river and fanned out directly in front of us, forcing us to turn around. We were cut off from Josie. I knew she'd turn when we did but be unable to reach us.

I heard the yelp of a dog in pain and hoped she hadn't been kicked in the head or back.

She'd make it to us on a broken leg. We turned at an angling trail in case she had to hobble the long way around and meet us across the river. But before we could go more than a half-mile I heard a clinking sound behind us. What could sound like Bo Derek in her *10* cornrows? Josie, covered in icicles! The yelp must have come when she hit that cold water, her only means of escape.

Once home again, Josie was so confident she tore wildly through neighboring yards we passed to reach our favorite Sunday-morning trailhead. One by one, trails began to close for us. Serious training was in order.

My husband begged me not to try the electronic collar I'd used with a modicum of success on our younger Weimaraner, whose only reaction to the buzz had been a jump, a squeak and continued forward progress toward whatever he was supposed to be ignoring. Eventually, the eighth of a small dog biscuit worked better. But he's not Josie.

We tried agility, which had brought our older Weimaraner, also a rescue, from the brink of euthanasia to hanging on my every word. Josie caught on in minutes. Ever attentive when enclosed, she acquired no ability to care when out in the open.

For some reason we're unable to recall, we retained our belief that Josie was calming on reaching the age of three, and happily packed off for our second Wyoming winter visit. We relaxed when our first day's pre-breakfast snowshoe, afternoon cross-country ski and evening walk were uneventful. Then again, we saw no wildlife. Josie may have. According to *her* trail she ran everywhere looking for it. Maybe after her escape from the elk Josie now felt ready for anything. We did not grasp her increased self-confidence until the second afternoon cross-country ski excursion when she dashed into willows some fifty yards off our path.

My husband and I watched in horror as a moose blasted from the brush, ran across the trail and disappeared into woods on the other side, Josie not only chasing but running circles of excitement around it. Our relief at seeing her turn toward us was short-lived. She was on her way back into the willows.

See previous paragraph.

See previous paragraph.

Yes, there were three moose, and now they were once again together. Josie ran up to us excited beyond measure. This was more fun than birds-in-a-box. The Weimaraner, whose reputation for chasing big things and grabbing and shaking little ones is well known to friends from coast to coast, proved to be angelic. Mellow might be spoiled, but it's trustworthy.

"Now do you think she's ready for a shock collar?" I asked my husband.

We juiced it up overnight. In the meantime, we put Josie in her old harness tied with a length of clothesline so she was free to range within our range but no farther.

Now, unless enclosed in our yard, Josie never goes outside without the collar and harness and clothesline. She looks like she's prepared to scale Mt. Everest. We only hope she'll attain the pinnacle of obedience because a trained dog is a happy dog.

Josie the Wonder Dog.

We wonder what Josie knows. We wonder what to do with her. We wonder if she'll ever get it.

I wonder if she's like our first Weimaraner. Although we underwent extensive training together, I realized he gave up his frightening behavior patterns not due to all that training, but because during it he grew to love me so deeply that nothing else mattered.

We wonder when Josie, using these training tools we've tied her to, will scale the heights of knowledge and learn *Come!* and *No!* And we wonder if, like that Weimaraner, eventually it will all depend on the magic of the word *love*.

Lonesome
Jeanette Perosa

Charles and I were walking down to the lake on a brilliant August afternoon. The sun streamed down like ribbons through the soft cotton clouds, washing us with its warmth. We walked along together, kicking gravel and stirring dust, fishing poles dangling over our shoulders. We passed the wheat fields near the trail to the lake. The tall, golden grass swayed in the warm breeze. Charles stopped for a moment, gazing out over the meadow, eyes bright.

"Is that your brother?" I said, putting my free hand to my brow.

"Yea, it's Josh," Charles replied as he continued down the path before stopping.

Joshua was hidden within the stalks. I could see the sunlight shimmering in his blonde hair, illuminating him. His eyes were bright and his smile stretched across his face. The tall wheat shuttered and moved, revealing an animal below.

"What's he doing?"

"It's probably that dog," Charles said as he started down the path again.

"What dog?"

"It wandered onto our property yesterday. Big, black one." Charles said as he tilted his ball cap.

I stood there for a moment watching the two of them move together through the tall grass, causing the wheat to seem like a wave.

"Is that dog limping?" I asked.

"Who knows? Leave it to Joshua to want to keep a broken dog." Charles shook his head as he twirled a stone between his fingertips.

They began to move towards the end of the field, closer to the road, and to me. The dog's coat was shiny black and his tongue hung from his mouth. Joshua's eyes searched for his brother and me— hesitating before his eyes meet mine. A smile broke across his face as his hand stroked the dog's black head. They both started towards me when the rock whirled past my head towards Joshua. His eyes went wide before turning to run, disappearing into the waving wheat.

I heard the dog give a yelp before limping away.

"What did you do that for?" I said.

"Don't want him following us. Aren't you coming?" Charles' voice called out as he stood by the trail that led to our fishing hole.

"Yea!" I replied, and then rushed to catch up.

The trail was overgrown and thick during that time of year. The thickets kept catching my legs, pricking them. Charles was way ahead of me. I spied him sitting on a large rock, a lit cigarette dangling from his lips.

"Thought you got lost. Maybe you're still a kid like my brother," Charles said, cigarette bouncing up and down from his lips.

"I ain't no kid."

I leaned my pole next to the rock. Charles offered me a cigarette.

"Damn thickets...cut me all up." I replied while taking a light.

"My brother didn't follow you, did he?"

"Nah... too busy with that old dog,"

"Kid can't follow me all his life. Dad says he's gotta be more independent now that I am going into high school," Charles said, his eyes clouding over as he drew in on the cigarette and then puffed out like a chimney.

"Know what ya mean."

"Hey, maybe Louise and her sister will be by! Maybe they'll even go swimming...naked!" Charles said, his face glowing.

I smiled back. The idea of seeing those girls made my stomach spin. I baited and tossed my line into the water, then drifted away in the bliss of that summer afternoon. Before long, the afternoon quickly turned to evening, and Mom was expecting me home for dinner.

I waved to Charles at the foot of his driveway before making my way home.   His father sat on the porch watching us, face ghost-white. His eyes looked like two holes in the snow. He held a flask in his hand, drinking it down before wiping his mouth with the back of his bony hand.

"Charles! Get here boy!" His voice crackled.

I raced away dragging my fishing pole behind me.

"Joshua got a dog," I blurted out over dinner to my family.

"Yea, I saw him walking down the road with a dog. Looks like a Lab, black one," my father responded between bites of fried chicken.

"Got a bad leg, though," I said.

"Might be what he needs. That boy hasn't said one word since Darlene left. So young not to have a mother," my mother said as she passed the basket of biscuits around.

"Gordon does what he can for those boys, Sally," my father said as he took a biscuit.

Mom rolled her eyes.

"Mr. Everett scares me," I whispered.

"He's had a rough time. It's hard for a man to raise two boys on his own. Charles is always in trouble, and Joshua, well, he's just not right," Mom shook her head, "very sad indeed."

"Charles says Mr. Everett took Joshua to a doctor. Doctor says he's retarded," I commented as I spooned peas into my mouth.

"Hank Breyer, that is an awful thing to say. Don't listen to that delinquent! That boy is as sweet as his Momma! He's a picture of her, too. She just couldn't seem to take care of him."

"What happened to their Mom anyway?"

Silence fell over the room. My parents gazed back and forth to one another as I waited for an answer. The air was filled with the glancing of eyes and the clanking of dinner plates. I frowned.

"I heard she left because Mr. Everett drinks too much and she liked another man," my sister blurted out between mouthfuls of biscuit.

"Emma," my mother said, mouth gaping open.

Pa shook his head and let his eyes meet mine.

"That's what Lindsey's mom said," Emma said shrugging her shoulders.

"Charles said that it was because of Joshua. Too much to handle," I said.

I pushed my peas into a pile.

"Well, that is just untrue. If any kid is too much it's Charles. Always getting in trouble. Why, I heard the police picked him up for stealing a bike," Ma's voice lowered to a whisper and her eyes were wide when she spoke.

"Is that true? Whose bike?" Emma said.

"Don't know. He's just trouble. You better not be hanging around with him, Hank Breyer. I mean it." Ma wagged her fork at me.

"Good dinner, Sally," my father quickly interjected, "that's enough talk about other people for one night. Tell me more about this dog, Hank," then he winked at my sister and me.

****

On one crisp December afternoon, Charles and I sat on the banks of the lake, skimming rocks. Charles laughed, tossing his black hair back with a flick of his head. His hands were shoved in the pockets of his worn coat, strings dangling from the sleeves like fringe, and his black Converse sneakers covered his feet.

"I should be getting into town. My Ma's gonna kill me if I don't go to the library."

Charles shrugged.

"Blow it off and hang out with me. You don't need no stupid book," Charles said.

"How come you haven't been to school?"

Charles twisted his face.

"Don't need school. I got all I need right here," Charles said as he patted the pocket of his jacket.

I tipped my head to see what he was talking about. He grinned and pulled out a small metal flask. His fingers fumbled with the top before pouring the contents into his mouth. His face turned bright red and his eyes widened. After wiping his mouth with the back of his hand, he extended the flask to me. I shook my head.

"Just take a swig. It'll warm you up," Charles said. The flask looked dull in the light, the rim shiny from the droplets of liquor that remained.

"My Pa will kill me if he smells that on me. I'm supposed to be at the library."

Charles pulled it back and twisted the lid back on.

"My old man is too drunk to know it's missing." Charles shoved the flask back in his pocket and tossed another stone across the water.

The sky wore a grey veil that usually preceded snow. I shivered as the wind pushed up against us. I spied Joshua and the dog across the lake, the dog's tail flagging high in the wind as Joshua waved a large stick over his head. In one motion he tossed the stick into the water and the black dog bounded after it, sending the cold water splashing out around him.

"What's that's dog's name, anyway?"

"What?" Charles said, scrunching his nose up.
"That old dog...the one that follows Josh. What's his name?"

"I don't know...I think Josh calls him Lonesome or something. Hard to figure out since Joshua barely talks," Charles replied as he released a stone to bounce along the mirrored water.

"Seems like a cool dog," I said, tossing a rock after Charles.

Charles' stare was as icy as the air. His eyes were two black stones in his head as he turned to scowl at me.

"You can't be serious?" Charles said.

My heart pounded. Charles seemed to stiffen. His eyes shrunk to slits.

"What's your problem with that dog?"

"No way! That thing is useless. It can't even walk right," Charles spat, then hurled a rock in their direction.

"Chill out, it's just a dog," I said.

"Whatever."

Joshua and Lonesome never noticed. They continued their game, even as the first snowflakes began swirling down from above. Not seeming to tire, the old dog repeated his task again and again. Joshua's laughter trickled across the lake ringing our ears. "That dog and my brother are both retarded. Only good thing is now he wants to be with that dog and not me!" Charles shouted over the lake in Joshua's direction.

"Calm down. I just like dogs," I said, looking towards my feet.

"I'm going home. Too cold." Charles said rushing up the embankment.

He left me sitting there, watching Josh toss the stick again and again as evening fell down around me.

****

The next morning the world had turned white. My breath frosted in front of me as I made my way down the snow-covered road, each footfall crunching below me.

"Hurry up, Hank!" Charles called to me.

He had heard that the Gibson sisters were down at the lake. Louise, the oldest, had called Charles that morning asking him to meet her. Charles' voice was wild and his eyes sparkled as he spoke about her.

"She's going skating! I bet she looks darn nice in one of those he fancy skating outfits," Charles said, eyes glimmering and smiles wide across his face.

I followed behind, arms wrapped around myself. The cold air hammered into my lungs, stinging them as I rushed to keep up with him.

"Slow down!" I shouted.

Charles whipped around, sending a cloud of snow puffing out into the air. I saw his eyes grow small and tight as his fists clenched into little balls. His gaze was sharp on something behind me.

"Go home, stop following me," Charles screamed.

I turned around to see Joshua and Lonesome trailing several feet behind us. The snow had revealed the sound of their footsteps. Snowballs whirled above me as Charles began an onslaught towards his little brother. I watched as Joshua protected his face with his mitten-covered hands and collapsed into a pile, snow pounding down upon him. Lonesome commenced barking frantically at the both of us, tail wagging.

"Shut up, mutt!" Charles said as he hit the old dog with a snowball.

Not once did the dog leave Joshua's side. He barked as he walked circles around the snowy mound, sniffing and checking his friend.   Charles left him there, crying.

"Let's go, Hank!" Charles said as he continued down the lane and disappeared into a wooded trail.

I looked back over my shoulder at Joshua. Lonesome whined as his brown eyes pleading with me. I took a step towards them. The dog wagged his tail. I stopped, hesitated, and then raced after Charles.

The lake was a sheet of frosted glass. Piles of snow dotted the shoreline like sand dunes.   We made our way through the bare branches and drifted snow to the banks below. The two girls swirled around like fairies, their dark, silky hair flying behind them. They had colorful scarves woven around their necks that fluttered like wings as they glided across the ice. Their laughter sprinkled the air and tickled my ears. They stopped when they saw us watching them, holding each other's hands. Their faces were flush and rosy, and just the sight of them made my stomach tickle and twirl. Charles nudged me with his elbow and nodded towards them.

"Told ya they would be here," he said.

"Hello ladies!" Charles shouted, waving his winter cap above his head.

Louise made her way closer to where we stood, her eyes inviting and pink lips smiling. I couldn't help thinking how good she must smell.

"Hey, Charlie….Hank." She smiled.

"That looks pretty easy!" Charles lowered himself down onto the ice, his shoulders back, hands shoved into his pockets.

The girls giggled and moved further out onto the ice. "Be careful!" They laughed.

I made my way closer to the ice as Charles almost lost his footing. He extended his arms out, balancing himself.

"Hey Louise, what's up with you and Tommy Harway?" Charles teased her. He continued to move forward, watching his every footfall.

I made it to the water's edge. The ice was thinner there. I could see small droplets seeping onto the snow, making it translucent in spots.

"Come on, Hank!" Charles called to me.

I shook my head. My feet were freezing. I rubbed my hands together and puffed my breath into them. Freezing... I was so cold. Charles continued to make his way out. Louise was circling him, smiling and laughing as he reached out to catch her. He jumped a little to try and grab her as she skated just out of his reach in a flurry of giggles.

I think I heard it first. It was a snap that was a light as a whisper. My ears perked up and listened. It came again, louder this time.

"Charles, did you hear that?" I shouted to him.

My call fell on deaf ears, as Louise mesmerized him. She dipped in and out, getting closer and closer to him, playfully. His laughter increased as he grabbed her scarf and twirled it around himself.

Something snapped again. Louder this time, more like a whip cracking. At the moment of realization, the world fell silent. My eyes fell to the ice below and began waving my arms. "Get off the ice," I shouted as a crack as loud as thunder opened the ice.

Charles turned towards me and his dark eyes met mine. His face turned ghostly white, before disappearing into a splash of water. The lake swallowed him. The girls flocked to each other like deer, rushing to the other side of the lake. My feet moved before I did, carrying me out onto the dangerous ice. My weight forced the lake to rumble and moan as it splintered everywhere underneath me. My foot fell through and water rushed into my pant leg, stabbing like knives. I pulled it out and made my way to the shore, breaking through the ice several times. I could hear Charles. His splashing and screams for help were deafening.

"Get help!" I shouted to the girls as they held each other. They fled up the road, their feet flashing as the sun caught the silver blades on their skates.

I reached the shoreline once more. My eyes darted around looking for a branch, rope, anything. My heart pounded hard within me, muffling Charles' cries. Then silence. The open mouth in the ice rippled and burped. I stood there, wide eyed.

I heard panting behind me, like a heavy train rushing down the embankment. It was Lonesome. His black fur shone in the sunlight. His legs moved beneath him, eyes bright. He whisked past me in a blur and burst out onto the ice. He lost his footing at first, but quickly regained it. He went right to task, his nose to the ice, sniffing. When he reached the opening he stopped. His eyes met mine for a moment before he plunged his head into the icy depths, tail flagging above him. His rear legs gripped to the ice as he began to reverse. Lonesome's head came out first, a rag held in his mouth. He pulled and pulled, working hard against the slippery surface. Charles bobbed up. Lonesome held his hood in his mouth and continued working. Charles' hands clawed at the ice as the dog nudged at him. They worked as a team, pulling and tugging until Charles lay on top of the ice. His soaked body lay limp. Lonesome shook himself free of water and began barking. He blanketed himself on top of Charles and barked like I'd never heard before.

"I'll be dammed. The dog pulled him out." I heard a man say as he rushed past me.

The rescuers came barreling down the hill. Rafts were launched, sirens roared, and people made their way down to see what had transpired.

"He's a good dog," a small voice said beside me.

"What?" I replied.

Joshua smiled up at me, his blue eyes singing.

"Just 'cause he limps people think he's no good. I knew he was the best dog ever."

"He is the best dog ever," I agreed, smiling back at him.

Lucky
Christopher Woods

I knock softly, then slowly open the door. Teddy goes before me, a short leash's length ahead of me. We enter another room for the dying. A man sleeps in one hospital bed, and in another, a woman is asleep. Single beds, I think to myself, and consider the irony. I take another step forward and see a woman, a sitter, in a chair around the corner nearest to the bed where the woman sleeps. The sitter is keeping watch for Mr. and Mrs. Carington, an elderly married couple who are, unusually enough, in hospice together.

Sometimes hospice patients hear us enter and wake. If they do, we make small talk. If they are able, they reach out to pet Teddy. He will then move closer to them, getting their scent, enjoying the attention. If they remain asleep, we linger for a moment, a kind of silent tribute perhaps, before making our exit.

Teddy is a huge, completely white Great Pyrenees. He is also a therapy dog. My wife and I adopted him two years ago. He is four years old, and as is often the case with rescue dogs, his earlier life was not the easiest. He was kept crated for many hours each day, so much so that his bottom teeth are pretty much gone. He kept gnawing on the crate door, but no one would let him out.

Now he has a purpose. Great Pyrenees are often protectors of livestock. Sheep, goats, cows, horses, and even geese, are their charges. My wife Linda and I do not have livestock, so we decided to train Teddy to become a therapy dog. Pyrs like to have a job, and being a therapy dog seems to agree with Teddy.

Neither Mr. or Mrs. Carington awaken. I make small talk with the sitter. I tell her that I remember the Carington's from the year before, when they both lived on the Alzheimer's unit in this same retirement community between Austin and Houston in rural

Texas. We own a small farmhouse nearby. I remember that, when first seeing Teddy then, Mr. Carrington called to his wife Mary to come see the dog. Teddy is something of a spectacle and this is not so unusual. But Mr. Carrington exclaimed, "The dog's tail is like a white bedsheet!" An odd visual description, but this is why I remembered this couple. On that day, Mrs. Carington emerged from their room in the Alzheimer's unit to take a look. She smiled, apparently agreeing with her husband.

Now, Teddy and I leave the Carrington's room, and I have the same thought I often do when visiting these people. I may not see them again. They will be gone. But I also know that someone else will soon take their places. There is a rhythm in this.

As Teddy and I walk down the hall toward another room, to the next person on my list, I think about the Carrington's. Death is a sad thing, yes, but there must be some kind of tender solace in departing life with your partner, your spouse, your husband or wife. Together. Such a strange thing, in fact, and I have not experienced such a thing before in any of our visits.

I look for my own wife, Linda, in the long hallway of disappearing lives. I do not see her, but I know she is with another person who also has a therapy dog. They are visiting someone else. Alone with Teddy, I think about our own lives. We have been married over forty years, but there have been times when I doubted if we would continue. Six years ago, Linda was diagnosed with breast cancer. In addition to the surgery for that, it was also discovered that she had a thymoma, a tumor lodged between one lung and her heart. That required another surgery prior to the scheduled chemotherapy and radiation treatments. At the time, I had many doubts, as did Linda. What would happen next? What would become of us? But things worked out over the months that followed. Then, when Linda finished her last radiation treatment, I fell ill. I was so weak I was almost falling over. That was when I was diagnosed with colon cancer. Several operations later, I too began chemotherapy. Months later, I finished with it and we both moved forward. Then, a year or so later, our beloved Golden Retriever was diagnosed with lymphoma. River was gone in five weeks.

When we said goodbye to River, I think we were also saying goodbye to our personal cancer era. We decided to adopt a new dog, a different breed. We chose Teddy, and he has been a true blessing. A therapy dog, he takes us places we would never have ventured before.

I come to the next room, but before I knock softly on the door, I think of the Carington's again. I think of Linda and I. How on so many nights, we each watched the other suffer. We wondered what we would possibly do if the other departed early. I never considered how time and circumstances might change things, how we might depart together. The odds of this happening are very rare indeed. So in a way I envy the Carrington's. Very few of us will be so lucky.

Mamaloi
Diane Ludlam

Back in 1974 or 1975, my mother was driving down a side street in our neighborhood when a Doberman mix puppy ran into the street. She promptly stopped her car, rolled down her window, and yelled to a man doing yard work to watch his dog. "It's not my dog, it's been running around here the past few days." With that, the car door opened, and the story of Mamaloi begins.

The dog had not eaten for what appeared to be several days, so the first thing my mother did was provide the pup with limitless food, not knowing that a gradual amount would have been better for her. She ate so much that she bloated, and almost passed out. The next thing she did was call my sixteen-year-old brother, to ask him if he would like the dog, it would be his responsibility to take care of her. He took the offer.

Now, this pup was a Doberman/Sheppard mix. She LOOKED like a Doberman, perfect markings, but was built wide like a German Sheppard. She was rather goofy looking until her ears and tail were cropped, then she looked VERY intimidating, especially when she would stare at you.

To back up just a bit, we already had several animals at our house. We had a dog named Sheba, she was about three, two cats (one of which had a litter), a lame pigeon that we had for several years named Charlie; hermit crabs; mice; toads; and hamsters. We have always had animals. Our father worked for the railroad, so he would be gone sometimes two or three days at a time.

A few days later, my dad came home from work. When he opened the gate to the yard, he was greeted by Sheba and Mamaloi. "Hey, come on, outta the yard, you don't live here" I heard him say. "Come on, get out!"

I ran to the window and hollered, "She's ours!"

"OH NO SHE'S NOT!" he replied.

"She is too! Mom found her, she doesn't have a home." With that he entered the yard, greeted Sheba, looked at Mamaloi, and came in the house shaking his head. I was not privy to the conversation he had with my mom later.

She grew to be a large dog, she was very beautiful. She was goofy, sweet, and full of mischief. My brother would sometimes snap a kitchen towel in the air, and she would know it was time to play. She would run into the room, take a broad stance, and do the Doberman "snap" back at him. We all thought it was cute, and funny to see her try to be so tough, when we knew her as nothing but a big lap dog.

We had new neighbors that had moved in across the alley, a pregnant woman, and her Marine husband. Not long after they moved in, the woman was outside hanging laundry on the clothesline. Now, when you hang laundry outside, you generally take it out of the basket, snap it a few times to remove wrinkles, and clip it to the line. You guessed it! Mamaloi thought the lady wanted to play. She jumped the fence out of our yard, and the fence into theirs and took her stance. She frightened this poor woman terribly. Her husband came over to talk to us that night.

Another time my dad was working in the garage. He heard the dogs a few yards over barking sharply. They were small dogs, poodle mix. He looked out in the alley to see what they were barking at. There were two boys from down the street, thirteen or fourteen years old, teasing the dogs with a stick on the fence. My dad grabbed Mamaloi by the collar, and took her out in the alley.

"You want a dog to tease?" he asked.

The boys looked at him, shrugged and said "Turn her loose."

Now, Mamaloi was usually a very obedient dog. In my dad's mind, she would surely stay if he told her too. He let go of her collar and said stay. The boys took off running home, and Mamaloi was on their tail. He called her to no avail, she was on a mission. My dad took off after her. The boys ran into their yard and closed the gate, Mamaloi hopped the fence with ease. By the time my dad got down there, the boys were in their house, and Mamaloi was sitting at their back door. This thank goodness, ended with no one hurt.

Another summer afternoon, I was in the living room watching TV, and there was a knock at the door. There was a gentleman on the porch who notified me that my dog hit his car. MY HEART SANK! He could see that I was upset and quickly said... "No, no, no, she's okay! She is back in your yard, that's how I found you, but she damaged my car."

What? I looked in the driveway, and his quarter panel was caved in. I went to the stairs and called up to my brother, she was HIS dog after all. The conversation went something like, "Hey, Mamaloi hit a car, SHE'S OKAY, she's in the backyard, but the driver is on the porch." He raced down the stairs and went straight to the yard. Mamaloi was standing there wagging her stub of a tail.

He then went to get some information from the driver. He stated that she was chasing a squirrel, and ran into his car, turned around, and jumped the three fences to get home. My brother took Mamaloi to the vet to get her checked out, and she was fine. The vet said she may have a headache for a few days, but other than that, she was okay. I remember listening to my dad reporting the accident to our homeowners agent, and several other people they transferred him to. The conversation went, "my dog hit a car... no, no, the dog is fine, but will my homeowners cover the damages to the car?" Then he would chuckle.

She lived to be eleven years old, and was one of the most loved dogs in the world, even though she could be challenging at times!

Man's Best Friend
Jon Moray

"The dog is loose again," my son stammered, as he barged into the house via the sliding glass door from the back porch. "Did you see where he went?" I huffed.

"He went out towards the woods," he screamed, teary eyed.

"I guess I'd better go find him," I said, long tired of the dog's escape charade.

The escapee is a beagle named Gunner. The original owners gave him that name because he is a hunting dog. I suggested "Gonna" since I felt he was gonna drive the whole family crazy. We got him about a month ago after his owners had to give him up because a new baby and a high strung beagle was a recipe for chaos.

Everyone loves Gunner. Everyone except me. All he does is get in my way when I am preparing meals to eat. I trip over him every morning when I leave for work and I always end up taking him for walks, which means having to pick up his crap. And he is called man's best friend?

I threw on my coat, grabbed the leash and half-heartedly headed towards the woods to retrieve Gunner. It was a cold January afternoon and I had about a half hour to find him before darkness set in. I called his name several times, without acknowledgment. I crept into the woods, dodging tree branches that scratched my face, as the dirt began to feel swampy with each step that suctioned into the ground. Not wanting to go any further, I made one last call, to no avail.

Why am I going through the trouble? I don't even like this dog, I wondered, while I pondered aborting the impromptu search.

But suddenly, as if by illusion, a double charcoal hued, cast iron gate appeared about twenty feet away. The gate was about six feet in width and eight feet in height. What I found odd was there wasn't a fence on either side. It was just a gate in the middle of the woods. I convinced myself to go as far as the gate and then head back; the evening beckoned and the sun was not about to stick around. I cautiously stepped forward, wary of snakes, raccoons and other creatures that might cross my path. As I inched closer, I heard one of the doors creak slowly back and forth. I froze as I heard rapid ruffling in the trees to my left. I waited out the sound as sweat beaded my forehead, and continued toward the fenceless gate. I reached the entry and called out for Gunner, without reply. I surveyed the gate with my hands and peeled away some of the rust along the bars. I gently pushed open the door on the right and stepped through. Immediately, the winds picked up as tree branches swayed and leaves swirled in a vortex rotation.

A booming theatrical voice off in the distance called, "Welcome, welcome, step lively, hurry. I know why you are here."

As I neared, a man, with snow white hair, wearing round bifocals and dressed like a royal guardsman without the bearskin tall fur cap, waved me over.

Who are you and what's with the gate?"

"What gate?" he asked, massaging the tip of his thin, bicycle handle mustache.

I looked behind and pointed, only to be hit with the shock of the gate no longer there. "I walked through a pair of gates about twenty feet behind me," I exclaimed, shaking a fist.

"I must certainly agree, my good man. There was a gate there until you penetrated it. It's disappearance signifies the beginning of your journey."

"My journey? What the heck are you talking about?"

"You are here to retrieve your pet? Your beagle, I presume."

"That's right."

"Well, you are certainly on the right track," he said, excitedly. "Your dog ventured through the disappearing gates a minute before your arrival. The mysterious gates you have entered through represent a portal to a realm full of fantasy and adventure. You can retrieve your dog but adversity awaits in the form of foes reserved for a person's imagination and are not of this Earth."

"You mean I am going to fight ogres and hobbits? You don't know me very well. I don't even like this dog. My family wanted a pet and I sacrificed for their happiness. You can keep the dog. I'll just go home and put up lost dog signs and secretly hope he never returns."

Suddenly, Gunner was heard whimpering off in the distance. I looked all around in the now thick misty fog and could not distinguish what direction his yelp was coming from. The close proximity of his call and the sense of urgency concerned even me, as I began to grow curious of this journey the man was proposing. "Explain this journey you speak of," I said.

"Ah, I can tell your sporting blood is flowing with eagerness. In your mission to retrieve your pet you will encounter several adversaries in the form of a ninja robot, a cyborg samurai and a flying lizard man. Your dog's bark will direct you in what direction to travel. You will know when your journey is complete when you see your pet at the reappearing gate. Any questions?"

"Robots? Samurais? Lizard men? These freaks are probably not only powerful but armed too. Am I right?"

"Perhaps," The mysterious man said, with a nodding smile and arms folded in a comfortable, satisfied fashion.

"And here I am with nothing more than a dog leash. That sounds fair," I said, facetiously.

"Oh, you won't need the leash," he beamed, and then suddenly the leash I was holding was in his possession. "The leash will be hanging on the gate when your journey is complete... if you make it, of course."

"This is getting stranger by the moment. This is just plum crazy."

"You underestimate my thoughtfulness. I would never let anyone enter a dangerous situation unarmed." He suddenly unsnapped two gold buttons, reached into his red coat and pulled out a shiny purple yo-yo.

"A yo-yo? You expect me to ward off the enemy with toy trick entertainment?"

"Again, you underestimate me. Here, give it a whirl."
I reluctantly snatched the toy out of his stubby fingers and twirled it toward the ground with natural ease.

"So?' I asked, with a shrug.

"Now aim it at that snake beside me."

I ho-hummed and conceded to his request. I twirled the yo-yo toward the curled asp and when it reached the end of the string, a powerful lightning bolt emitted from the toy and fried the snake where it laid. "Now you got my attention," I expressed, as a distinct sizzle emanated from the dead serpent.

"I will be shadowing you every step of the way and will offer warnings as I see fit. You can stop at any time by just saying the word 'quit'. The gate will reappear and you will be able to exit. Of course if you do, it will be without your dog."

"Why are you doing this? Why don't you just let me have my dog back?"

"Let's just say we are testing the theory of a dog being man's best friend. Are you game or do you want to go home and bear the sad news to your family?"

"I guess I should give it a try. Just say 'quit' and the game is over, right?"

"Correct. And now, follow the sound of your dog's bark." He flailed his left arm outward like a game show host revealing a jackpot prize, and then I heard Gunner wail.

I cautiously encroached toward the sound of my hound and then suddenly a mechanical moving ninja dropped in front of me from a limb of an oak tree. The ninja displayed an impressive array of gymnastics as he went into instant attack mode. Just as he was about to dive on me, I wielded the yo-yo and flung it between his eyes. The flash of lightning partially blinded me, but when my eyesight returned the ninja lay lifeless on the leaf littered terrain.

"Good show, ol' chap," the man commented, with applause.

"That wasn't too bad. Hopefully they all go this easy."

"My advice to you is to be wary of your next adversary. He's known to cause stabbing pain. I nodded and crept towards my dog's bark. It should've been dark by now but this fantasyland kept the daylight despite the thick London-type fog.

I trudged through the heavily wooded area for a short while, when suddenly, the forewarned samurai appeared. He was clad entirely in satin blue metal with ruby swords protruding from his chest plate. His arms, all six of them, were holding crescent shaped swords that glimmered through the fog. My plan of attack was to wait until he got within my yo-yo's range, and then strike.

The cyborg samurai twirled and rotated the swords with such speed that I would've gotten dizzy if I were to try to follow one by eye. I focused on his chest plate as he neared. When he got within striking distance, I twirled out my dynamic yo-yo. The samurai reacted by slashing through the string, leaving the toy to lie harmlessly at his feet, emitting a low spark. The samurai laughed in a creaky steel grinding tone as the word 'quit' tickled the tip of my tongue.

I looked around for the man but he was nowhere to be found. I backed away slowly as the samurai was about to mount his attack. Suddenly, Gunner appeared from behind the cyborg and nipped at the inside of his knee joint causing the samurai to stumble to the ground and onto the yo-yo. Suddenly, the toy re-energized and sent powerful electric bolts through the samurai's metal armor. Smoke permeated from the cyborg as he met his ill fate. Gunner howled once and disappeared.

The man reappeared with raving accolades towards my dog. The pooch saved my butt. Maybe he isn't so bad after all. But, it was his stubbornness that got us into this mess in the first place. There is still more work to be done. Hopefully not much because I am now without a weapon.

"Sir, do I get a replacement?"

The man looked puzzled for a moment and then it hit him, "oh, you mean your disabled yo-yo. I'm afraid it's one to a customer. Good luck."

The perturbed glare I set upon him was interrupted by my dog's wail ahead and to the east. I regained my focus and headed towards his sounds with my head on a swivel. I picked up a jagged fallen tree branch for protection and treaded about a quarter of a mile when I was blindsided by a beast that shoved me to the ground and pounced on me. I somehow managed to get turned around to see my assailant. It was the flying lizard man grappling with me. Its strength was too much for me to overcome as he began to head butt me into unconsciousness. As my vision blurred, Gunner pounced on him from behind and began to chomp at its neck. The lizard man used its powerful tail to knock my dog free, catapulting him into a tree and rendering him disabled on impact.

Amid the scuffle, Gunner's collar was knocked free and within arms distance of me. I managed to reach it as the lizard man returned its focus on me. My reflexes enabled me to grab the collar and wrap it around the lizard's neck in one fluid motion. I tightened my choke hold and held on for dear life as it struggled for air. Its short arms were its weakness but still it was strong enough to inflict damaging shots to my midsection. Still, I held my choke hold, when suddenly, my dog Gunner reappeared with teeth clenched on the lizard man's tail. The teamwork between me and my pet overwhelmed the enemy and moments later, the lizard man collapsed on top of me. I desperately pushed the reptile aside and panted on the ground, struggling to regain my senses.

I began to crawl away and then heard Gunner bark to the south of me. I turned and saw him sit before the reappearing gate, with his tail in a Ferris wheel type motion. I gathered myself, picked up the collar and stumbled over to him. I then heard shuffling in the leaves and to my relief, it was the quirky host scampering towards me.

"What do you think of man's best friend now, my good man?"

I pondered his question and then looked over at my dog, "I think we definitely created a bond, me and my furry creature."

"Just a bond?"

"Well, he did do a lot of things on this journey that only a best friend would do. I'll keep him and go home."

"Ah, another satisfied customer. It brings joyful tears to these eyes of mine."

"What's going to happen once I cross the gate?"

"The gate will disappear as will every creature you encountered, including yours truly, as if it were only a memory."

"Only a memory? Was this just a fabrication in my mind?"

"Only you know, my friend. Cheerio," he said, and playfully pushed me towards the gate. I leashed Gunner, pushed the door open, and exited. I turned around and the old man and the gate were gone. I knelt down to Gunner's level and he lovingly licked my face. I massaged his nape and looked into his brown marble eyes, wondering what it's like being him.

"C'mon, my friend, it's time to go home," I said, as we walked side by side, man and man's best friend.

Maxine's Story: The Dog That Changed My Life
Stephanie Commyn

I began volunteering at Almost Home Animal Rescue in Southfield, Michigan, in the summer of 2009. I had no idea what to expect, but I never imagined that I'd end up meeting a dog that would change my life. She came into my family's life at a time when I think we all needed a little saving. There are a lot of skeptics of fate, but I'm a believer.

Shortly after I began volunteering, I told my mom she should start coming with me and she did. Both dog lovers, it broke our hearts to see so many little faces behind the cages each week. So many of the dogs are so misunderstood, with people passing them by, not willing to give them a chance. But, we always believe that each dog has a kind spirit in their heart, they've just had it damaged by humans that never deserved them.

One day in the summer, the Southfield Animal Control brought in a dog. To be completely honest, she wasn't the most attractive one in the world. She was mangy, dirty, her nails were so long they were curled around her paws; her fur was so long you could barely see her eyes, and she was skin and bones. My mom was there when she came out of the animal control car - she was one of the first people she saw. She walked out of the van, on a leash no problem. Although we know she was terrified, she didn't act as timid as you would think towards my mom and she definitely wasn't aggressive in any way. The rescue named her Maxine.

My mom sat with her that warm, sunny day on the lawn outside the shelter - just petting her and talking to her, providing her with the kindness that she had been lacking for so long. They trimmed her nails down and got her a bath. She was groomed up and fixed up. The way she responded to my mom that day was amazing - like they were long lost friends who finally found each other again.

Maxine was the reason we kept coming back - even more diligently now. The shelter volunteers told us that she was so quiet and shy towards everyone; she wouldn't eat, and refused to come out of her cage - unless my mom was there. As soon as she saw my mom, she instantly perked up, tail wagging, and excited to go outside. We knew there was a special connection there that we just couldn't walk away from.

Maxine needed surgery, and the shelter really didn't want her to recover in a cage. My mom and I knew we had to bring her home. It broke our hearts every time we left the shelter, walking away seeing her sad little eyes. Now, we just had to convince my dad. We said that we would just foster her, while she recovered, until somebody else was willing to adopt her. He finally conceded and came to the shelter to meet her. He had never been inside one before, so the experience itself was shocking enough. We took her outside in the yard and the two met. He will never admit it, but I know he fell in love with her that day.

The next step was introducing her to our other dog, a Golden Retriever named Mickey. Now, Mickey got along with everyone - but Maxine we weren't so sure about. She had become very protective of my mom. We brought Mickey to the shelter, and to the other side of the outside gate where Maxine was. He was all excited - a new friend to play with! Her initial reaction - she growled at him. Him being the adorable dope, he was so confused. The reaction made me nervous. Mickey was my baby, and I didn't want anything to happen to him. They sniffed noses a little more on opposite sides of the gate - and we took a chance.

We brought Maxine home, and it soon became clear that we were never letting her go. Her short; little, stubby legs, and fresh surgery scars kept her from going up the stairs. She set up camp in our living room. Despite her initial reaction, it didn't take long for her and Mickey to bond. He loved having another dog around and she soon came to adore him - to look up to him like he was her big brother. Anything Mickey did, she had to do. Anything Mickey sniffed, she had to sniff. *Mickey likes it, so it has to be good.* She followed him around, as the saying goes... like a puppy dog.

She didn't seem to know how to play, so we worked on that with her. Except every new toy she got, she wouldn't actually play with for a while. She just liked to carry it around, like she was showing it off, but also letting everybody know it is hers and they better not take it. And soon enough, the two dogs were best friends. She was a lot shorter than him, so most of their play involved her biting his legs, and then the chasing around started, and always lots of barking. They went on walks, walking side-by-side. Maxine loved her walks. She could never make it onto the couch, so she lay right below it - right below Mickey. She always had to be by his side - whether they were sleeping or chewing their bones (some as big as she was)- she always had to be near him.

When he would leave to go play with the puppies at daycare, she would wander around looking for him - feeling lost without her best friend. When he would come home, she would greet him - so excited and kissing all over his face. She soon joined him at daycare, and while she never played with the other dogs the way he did, she made some friends and enjoyed the companionship. When they stayed overnight, they always had to be either in the same cage or right beside each other to sleep. All the workers fell in love with her too, wanting to adopt her as their own.

But, Maxine was picky when it came to who she liked. She was very protective over her new family - including Mickey. She was always nervous around new people. She was also an older dog, although no one knows for sure her exact age, so we believe she also had vision problems. After seeing someone a few times, she warmed up to them. She loved, loved my brother's friends - which was surprising because she wasn't that fond of males. But, she adored them, although she didn't always show it - with her nips at their ankles. If you were kind to her, she liked you. She just had to make sure of it first.

With busy schedules, she was often home at dinnertime with my dad. They soon bonded more than I ever thought they would. He was so against the idea of bringing her home at first. But, it was, and is still, very clear that she softened him. She worked her way into his heart in a way that I have never seen before - she changed him, too.

They began to have a ritual - sitting outside on the deck and then having dinner together. First, he would make a large bowl of food for her (we were trying to fatten her up at the beginning) and then he would always share some off his plate. Soon, she began to be able to go up and down stairs, and she would join him in the basement anytime he had any sort of food (or she thought he did). It was clear they both came to enjoy these nights alone together.

About a year later, she was beginning to have some problems. It was more difficult for her to walk and she always seemed to be injuring a leg. Sometimes she would fake limp, when she didn't want my mom to leave. But, it appeared to be something more. We took her to the vet and he had a couple of possibilities. He said she would need surgery - that would cost $2,500. We didn't know what to do. We had no idea how old she was, so we were worried she wouldn't even survive the surgery. I instantly said, "I don't care. I'll pay for it." I was willing to empty my savings if it meant that we would have her in our lives one more year, one more month, even one more day.

We had some time to spare, to think it over. But, in the end, Maxine made the decision for us. My mom and I were going up to my aunt's lake house for a few days and we decided to take Maxine with us. She was fine the whole car ride up, but after we got there, she started deteriorating really quickly. We began to take turns sleeping next to her after the vet's diagnosis – making her a makeshift bed full of pillows and blankets. It was comforting to be next to her, but I also got the sense that I wouldn't have that feeling much longer. If you've never witnessed it, watching an animal you love slowly die is the most heart-wrenching thing in the world. The image will never leave you. We took her to a vet that was nearby, and before he even spoke, I burst into tears because I knew what he was going to say.

Our vet back home didn't have a clue what was really going on with her. She didn't have anything wrong with her leg. Her organs were beginning to fail her and she was bleeding internally. This vet up north said he thought she was a lot older than previously predicted - she was an elderly dog. There wasn't really anything he could do for her, except provide pills to numb her pain. So, we took her back to the cabin and made phone calls to my dad and brother that were back home. It was only a matter of time.

I watched her take her last breath as I screamed and cried for her to hold on, to stay with me. But she had no more fight left in her. And, who could blame her - for all we know she had fought her whole life before we rescued her. My only regret is that everybody didn't have a chance to say goodbye, including her beloved Mickey. My only relief is that I got that chance.

The rest of the night and the ride home is a blur. I was frozen in emotion and cried hysterically every fifteen minutes. Mickey was so confused when we got home. He came running out to the car looking for her. The only thing that breaks your heart more than losing a pet; is seeing your other pet feel that same loss. He was depressed for weeks - just sitting on the couch, looking around for her. Whoever would have thought at the beginning that the two would love each other so much?

There isn't a day that goes by that I don't miss her and her spunky little personality. I think about her all the time and the enormous amount of pictures I took of her are still placed around the house, which some days brings me smiles and other days brings me tears.

I was telling my boyfriend the other day about a dog that I had met that I fell in love with and wished I could bring home from Almost Home, she was also on the older side. I told him that if he's gonna be with me, he's gonna have to deal with my bringing home many rescues over the years - some that I adopt and some that I foster back to health and pass on to a different forever home. He asked me, "Why do you pick the older dogs? How can you deal with that? When they die, it's so sad." My response was: he's right; it is incredibly sad and extremely painful. But, this way I know they are happy and safe. That's why I do it: so that the few good years that they have left are spent in a warm, safe home with a family that loves and cares for them.

I did it so that Maxine died happy, knowing that there were people in this world that loved her more than words can express.

Every dog deserves nothing less than that.

We can't blame the dogs for the things that humans created in them. Every dog deserves love - no matter their breed, their temperament or their past.

So volunteer at a shelter or rescue. Foster a dog. Adopt a dog. Rescue a dog. Donate any spare money. Donate supplies. Help save a life. If nothing else, help make a life better.

I promise you it will be the greatest, most rewarding thing that you ever do. You think you're not making a difference those few hours a week or month that you volunteer. But, you are. Because, for those few minutes or hours, you are making them feel happy, safe, and loved - something they otherwise wouldn't be feeling if you weren't there. It does make a difference - to them.

Maybe one day, a dog will change your life the way Maxine changed my family's. Maybe one already has. I know that I am definitely a better person because of her. She has inspired us all to continue to help fight for these animals and to rescue our future dogs. I changed her life, but I think the real reason our paths met, was so that she could change mine.

In loving memory of my Maxy - our beloved rescued dog, who actually rescued us.

In support of Almost Home Animal Rescue (Southfield, Michigan) – whose tireless volunteers continue to do amazing work saving the lives of animals and who brought us Maxine, for which we will forever be grateful. Thank you.

Miley
Daniel Barbare

Oh Miley, looking from the inside
out, how she barks but
only wishes to wag her tail
to be petted like any other
dog. She smiles when she is
showing her teeth. Like
someone else I know. If only
she could see from outside in
as if comfortable in her own skin.

Miley In Summer
Daniel Barbare

I put her bowl of water
on the foyer step,
so she can stretch on the tile
and cool her belly.
And feel the air from the little fan.
But in her eyes
she still seems to yearn
for the green grass and the sun.
So I put her back in the yard
as she wags her tail.

Miracles Do Come True
Theresa Nielsen

Outside the sun was shining bright, but it was a very cold day. Louise was busy washing walls for one of her customers when the phone rang. "Oh no, you've got to be kidding. I'll try to find help and call you back," said Jenna into the phone. Louise stood by listening, wondering what was going on. When Jenna finally hung up, she couldn't help noticing the worried look on her face.

"Louise, how is the cleaning coming along?"

"Fine, but forget that for a minute. Was that bad news on the phone?"

"Yes, I'm afraid so. Mary over at the Northside shelter got a distress call to take in three newborn pups but, she doesn't have the space. Besides that they need twenty-four hour care."

"Oh no, now what?" Louise said concerned for them. "You heard me tell her that I would try to help, but we don't have the space here either."

"Wait, I can help," Louise told her.

"I only have two cats and Barney won't mind. He's a good dog."

"Well, Barney wasn't who I was thinking would have cared, what about Harry?" asked Jenna scratching her forehead.

"Oh yeah, him. Well he's never home anyway. Besides I'll be the one taking care of them."

"Right, but he is your husband. Don't take it for granted that he'll be happy about it."

"The way I see it, we both have issues but this is important. Look at it this way, I'll foster them for six or eight weeks and they'll be ready for adoption. He can certainly handle that time-frame I'm sure."

"Whatever you say, here is the number to call. Her name is Sheila. And good luck."

Louise and Jenna had been good friends for a long time. After Louise lost her job at the bank she had been doing odd jobs for Jenna around the house to make ends meet. Louise and Harry had been married for ten years but lately, it was a battle for them to stay together.

****

Early the next morning, Louise was up and dressed, she put on a bright red sweater with her favorite blue jeans. She pulled her hair back with a clip and even put on a little makeup. She was sure the pups didn't care, but she would rather not scare this person she had never met.

The car had been packed right after she got off the phone with Sheila, there were newspapers, some boxes, blankets and an extra flashlight just in case. She poured hot coffee into her mug, gave Barney a big hug and was out the door.

Thankfully, at eight o'clock in the morning the expressway was still clear of snow and the traffic was light. Louise thought of the pups as she drove, who would abandon puppies who didn't even ask to be born. Sheila had explained to her that there had been a fire, the mother became frightened and ran off. When the owner managed to rescue her, she was too traumatized and wouldn't let the pups nurse. So the owner had just dropped them off at the door with a note.

Louise glanced at the map on the passenger seat. The shelter was just up the road on the left side, Baxter Street. As she turned into the parking lot a blonde-haired woman was flagging her down.

"Hi, you must be Louise. It's nice to meet you, I'm Sheila. I was out looking for you, afraid you had changed your mind."

"No, I couldn't do that to you," said Louise as she followed her up the steps into the shelter. Once inside they went down the hall into a small room. There were dog crates stacked up in rows, every one of them with a dog inside. Louise tried her best not to linger on any one of their faces too long for fear she would leave with all of them.

Sheila was standing near a box on the counter, Louise gasped when she looked down in the box. "Oh my goodness, look at you." Louise reached down and felt the warmth of their little bodies as they snuggled together.

"The owner was kind enough to tell us that the pups had some difficulty being born so you will need to watch them closely in case they have trouble breathing. But I think they will be fine."

"I have a heating pad to keep them warm on the way home, what do you think?"

"Great idea, and I'll give you some small syringes to feed them since they don't know how to suck." Sheila reached into the box and took out one of the pups handing it to Louise. "They are all females, as sweet as any puppy could be. You will need to feed them around the clock like a new baby. It's also how the mother would feed them if she were able. I'm sending you home with puppy formula and later, you can supplement it with cereal," Sheila told her.

"Thanks for all the tips, I'm anxious to fill in as dog mom."

"No; thank you for giving your time to help out. I don't know what I would have done if you had not stepped up."

Sheila wrapped the pups up together in the blankets Louise had brought and laid them carefully in the carrier. Once everything was loaded, Louise was ready to take her new part time family home.

The two women stood by the car now looking at one another, once strangers and now friends united by the pups.

"I guess this is goodbye for now," said Sheila, giving Louise a hug.

"You have my number; call me if you have any questions at all."

"I sure will," said Louise. "Talk to you soon."

Now that everyone was settled, the puppies secure on the back seat, Louise waved goodbye and headed for home. It was a smooth drive with little traffic; John Denver was playing on the radio. Louise sang along, "take me home country roads." As she pulled into the driveway it was now after seven, she was glad she had left some lights on in the house. Barney didn't like the dark, her two cats Tillie and Maddy never seem to mind, but Louise always hated coming home to a dark house. That was a sore spot between she and Harry because he never remembered to leave any lights on and Louise was easily annoyed by it.

She hurried into the house to say "Hi" to Barney. Her neighbor Jo had come over to sit with him for a while and give him and the cats dinner. Louise didn't want anyone upset when she came home with new friends. She then went back to the car to bring in the pups and their supplies. She poked her head inside the carrier, "Wait until Harry sees you, it will be love at first sight. The phone rang breaking the silence, "Oh speak of the devil, Hi Harry," she said.

"You home yet?" He asked.

"Yes, I just got here."

"Oh, don't wait dinner. I'm gonna grab a burger with the boys," Harry said.

"Alright then, Louise told him. Have fun."

Louise set the phone down. She knew he was doing that just to spite her for having taken in the pups. She had already prepared them a spot on the old changing table she had saved. The side compartments were filled with wet ones, pads, towels and diapers to catch their dribbles.

Louise lay each of them on the table and took a picture of them. "How adorable you all are." After mixing their food, she began to feed them one at a time, little feet kicking this way and that eager to receive a warm meal. Now that they were fed and dry, she had them all tucked in and warm.

The teapot whistled; a cup of tea was just what this new mom needed. She sat down with her calendar and notebook she had purchased to keep notes and important information on the pups. She would track their progress daily and record how much they weighed. The pups were five days old, the day and date were entered on the calendar.

Barney was sleeping at the end of the couch when he first heard the pups cry. He dragged himself off the couch to see where that tiny little noise had come from.

"Barney these are your new friends, they will be staying here. You'll have to wait until they grow a bit before you can play with them." Louise put the carrier down where he could sniff them. He licked her hand as if to say, "great Mom." He followed Louise into the spare room and watched as she placed each one on the changing table.

Each little pup looked exactly like its mate, with the exception of one with a white tip at the end of its tail. Louise was just wrapping them back up when Barney jumped off the chair. That meant Harry was home.

"Hey Lou, where you at," he called out.

"I'm in the back bedroom Harry, how are you?"

Seeing his face after a long day away, she smiled up at him. "Glad you're home, I hope you ate something to go with those beers you had." His breath was a dead give-away even from across the room.

"Of course, but I'm not going to haggle with you," he said, leaving the room in a huff.

Louise knew by now to leave him be, no use dealing with him when he was in a mood and tipsy. She wrote down some notes about the pups and the time. There was time for one more feeding before she turned in for the night, she thought of calling Jenna to fill her in, but decided to wait until morning. After all, it had been a long day and she was tired too. She helped herself to a second cup of tea and sat in her favorite chair to do some stitching on the quilt she had started earlier that month.

Quilting had been a part of her life since forever; she loved piecing the quilts, picking out the colors, doing her own thing and then hand quilting them. She knew so many women who preferred machine quilting but it was not for her. As a young girl, she watched her mother and grandmother quilt and she knew that one day she would continue the tradition. And so it was.

Louise heard the puppies stir; she went to check on them, everyone must have decided to soil the bedding all at once. So now they were both hungry and wet. "Oh my, you girls sure know how to make a momma feel blessed. This brings back memories for me."

As she talked and changed the pups there sat Barney again, taking it all in. It was after midnight when Louise finally fell into the bed, she set the alarm for four, at which time the pups should be hungry. When she woke to feed them, she heard Harry's voice, she moved closer to the room. He was telling them how lucky they were to be safe and warm with Lou for a mom. She smiled up at him; he was holding one of them close, smiling back at her.

It was no surprise when she woke again to feed them first thing in the morning that he was already gone for the day. Fresh coffee had brewed, and a danish was waiting for her, too.

The little charges were now fed, cleaned and tucked away in their bed sound asleep.

"My goodness, it looks like I'll have to wash some laundry, it looks as if more than three puppies live here, doesn't it Barney?" Louise took the basket of soiled laundry down the hall, being careful not to use too much detergent for fear it would harm them.

"Whew, Barney. They stink too."

Louise sat down on the floor and snuggled Barney close. "I love you Barn. You're such a good dog to share your Mom with these pups."

Now that everyone was fed, the cats had a treat, Louise poured another cup of coffee and sat down to read the mail. Harry must have brought it in when he came home. There was a reminder card about the annual birthday party at church.

"Oh dear, I can't let them down, its my turn to bake the cake. "What will I do, Barney?" Louise made a call to Dee at the church. She agreed to bake the cake and deliver it, but wouldn't stay long because of the pups. She told Dee she would make it up to them the next month.

By then, the pups would be older and need fewer feedings. She gathered her quilt up in her lap and continued stitching where she had left off the night before. It would be finished soon; it was going to be raffled at the quilt show in the spring. By then, the puppies would be ready for adoption. *To think, they just got here*, Louise thought to herself.

****

The little pups were now fourteen days old, their eyes were open and they were trying to move around more. Their feedings had now changed to every five to six hours and they were messy, it was a chore to keep them clean. Jenna had stopped over to see them once she got back from her vacation. "Lou, I hope you took lots of pictures, I want to see how much they have grown."

"Oh you will. I'm going to do an album. Barney has taken a real liking to them and I've got one of him sitting with them that is very sweet. The cats are jealous, but that is to be expected."

"So what about Harry, what does he think?" Jenna wanted to know.

"Really, he hasn't said much, but then he hasn't been around either. I guess he needs his space. Luckily for me, I have my own job and friends, I don't dwell on him. He will come around when he's ready, or not."

"Aren't you worried he may not come back at all?" Jenna said.

"To be honest, no. After losing my Mom last year and then taking in these puppies has made me realize life's too short for the nonsense. If he loves me and I make him happy then he will find his way back to me, but if not then it is what it is."

"Sure hope you know what you're doing, Lou. He's a good man."

"I know that, but I'm tired of putting everyone else first, I took care of my mom when my family wouldn't lift a finger to help, but I got through it. In their short time here, the pups have taught me a lot."

Jenna nodded her head. "You are a smart woman, I envy that about you."

"Don't sell yourself short, Jen. You've come a long way too; finally got rid of that bum you were supporting, we've got a decent business together now. We still have work to do but we're making it."

"You are right, and on that note I've got to go and meet Walt about the carpeting. I'll talk to you soon."

Louise finished feeding the pups and then checked her list of ingredients for the cake she was baking for the party. She added corn oil and baking soda to her shopping list. For this party she was also going to bake a cake for the young boy who had recently moved to Monroe with his family. His name is Timmy. Louise had met him in church one Sunday and she was so taken by him and his family. He would be seven and would celebrate his birthday this month. She thought it would be a nice way for his family to feel welcome. Timmy was a special needs boy with a big heart. Louise was going to bake his cake in the shape of a car. Excited, she grabbed her purse and headed out the door to go shopping.

After the shopping was done, she still had a few minutes to stop at the craft shop to purchase her favorite quilting thread, as she didn't have quite enough to finish the quilt. She hurried back to the car so fast she almost knocked someone down.

She knew the puppies were fine, she just didn't like being away from them too long. They were growing and she didn't want to miss any of it. Louise had asked Jo if she would come and sit with them while she was at the party, although she wouldn't be long. She was hoping to get a chance to talk to Timmy's family.

****

Louise woke refreshed the next day, the puppies were sleeping through the night and she was getting lots of rest. Once they were fed, she set about to bake the cake. This was going to be a great day. The cake was in the oven; Louise grabbed her things and jumped in the shower. For a moment she thought she heard a voice, but Harry had not been home in a few days.

Louise chose a soft pastel blue sweater with navy slacks and low black pumps. She would feed the pups just before she left. She spent less time feeding them these days and more time just staring at them and watching them play and amuse one another.

Then there was Barney, he loved them all. He would just lay there on the floor while they crawled all over him. In fact, Louise had noticed Barney and the pups were bonding, which made her pause to think about when it was time for the pups to go. Even she didn't want that day to come.

****

The party was a huge hit and so was the special cake for Timmy. He and his parents were so grateful that Louise had taken the time. Louise sat down at the table next to Timmy's mom. They were happy they had made the move to Monroe; hopefully more doors would open for their son.

"Timmy, are you having fun? Louise asked.

"Yes I am. Thank you for my cake. Maybe next time you will make me a dog cake," he said.

"Timmy," said his mom. "Be nice."

"It's okay. Timmy, do you like dogs?" Louise wanted to know.

"I love dogs Miss Louise. Do you have a dog?" he asked.

"I do, his name is Barney. Would you like to meet him someday?"

"Could I Mom, could I?" he asked.

"If it's okay with Miss Louise, then someday." Timmy was excited, he stood and with his cane in hand hobbled away. Louise watched him go over to see the other kids. His parents shared with Louise that he had wanted a puppy for his birthday but they were still getting settled in their home, getting Timmy into school and other things, there was no time to think about a puppy. But that maybe one day they would get one for him.

****

At five weeks, the puppies were really growing. Louise need only look at the progress notes to see how far they had come. They each had their own little personalities, she loved them all. But Barney liked one in particular, the one Louise referred to as her little miracle. She was smaller than the other two, but proved herself to be just as tough as the others. It would soon be time to take the pups for adoption and Louise was nervous and reluctant to let them go. They were her morning routine, her lunch time affair and the end to her day. She knew it would be hard, this would hurt too. But she knew that it would happen. She lay in bed at night with Barney at her side thinking how it would be if she kept them all. She had the space, they were almost potty trained, but she wasn't being practical. She did know that she wanted to keep at least one. She would probably keep the one Barney liked. She definitely had room in her home and in her heart for a puppy. She knew Jenna would question her choice, but she didn't care anymore about what Harry would think. She made her own choices with or without Harry around. In that moment laying there in bed, Louise made another decision; she was going to let Timmy and his family adopt one of the pups. It would be wonderful for Timmy, he could grow up with the pup at his side, and labs were great with kids.

"Well Barney, it's settled, I'm going to check on the pups and then get some sleep."

The next morning when Louise crawled out of bed, it was half past seven. The little whimper of the pups got louder as she got closer to the room. "Somebody must be hungry, I'm coming. To her surprise they were all running around, they had figured out how to jump out of the box. "Oh my goodness, look at you," she said.

The pups had just turned six weeks old; Louise felt her heart racing as she put food in the bowls for each of them. "I know my Barney has his favorite but I love you all," she whispered. "This is going to be very hard letting you go, but it will be for the best. After all, I've given you a great start, and the truth is, I must get back to my work. I've been asked to create a wall mural for the library, but do it in a quilt. What do you all think of that?"

"I think it's marvelous," said Harry.

Louise, startled by his voice, nearly jumped out of her skin.

"Harry what are you doing here?" she asked.

"Well I do still live here don't I?" he said as if he were questioning her.

"Of course, but where have you been? I haven't seen you in several days, weeks even."

"I know and I thought it was best, I've been selfish. You didn't need me; we were both going in different directions. So I just made the choice to leave, I hope you understand." He looked rugged and unshaven but the sparkle in his eyes that drew her to him all those years ago still remained.

"I don't think I do understand; you see, problems don't get solved by running away Harry but I'm happy you're back."

"Would you mind taking these girls out to the yard for a little exercise, and I'm sure to potty. I'll put the coffee on so we can talk, is that okay with you?"

"Yes, Lou. I missed your coffee."

As he walked out of the room, the pups close at his feet, he turned around and winked at her.

This time her heart did more than race, it was flip-flopping inside her chest the way it did when she first saw him at the conference so many years ago. Harry came into the kitchen where she was standing at the sink. He walked up behind her and nuzzled his face against her neck. "I really missed you, and I'm sorry."

She turned around to face him, touching the scruffy beard. "Are you going to shave this, or trim it at least?"

He pulled her close to him, they shared a brief kiss. "I guess I'll have to if I want to be close to you, and be able to do more of this." He tried to kiss her again but she pushed him away. "I'll be back."

After Harry left the room, Louise fed Barney and the cats. She poured her first cup of coffee and sat down with her calendar.

Today was a new day, and more good news was right in her lap. Harry was home to stay, Barney was getting a little sister pup, and Timmy was going to get his first puppy. Louise knew the right person would come along for the remaining pup but there was plenty of time for that. Until then, she had a nice warm home with people who loved her. When she looked up from her calendar, there stood Harry. His face was free of beard and there again, was the sparkle. "Miracles really do happen, don't they?"

Miss Pretty
Ellen Woods

Miss Pretty was a blue-eyed demon. An Alaskan Husky, she was known to bite and had been to doggy jail in the past year. She was a fixture inside the iron-gate surrounding the yard and the driveway, which I traversed daily outside my apartment. My daughter and I lived in the upper rear of a massive red Victorian, and shared a deck with four students who lived in the upper front apartment. Below us reigned our landlady, Slim, living alone in a multi-room flat filled with mismatched furniture and piles of empty boxes left over from incomplete projects.

Like Miss Pretty, Slim had a quick temper and a sarcasm that often manifested as a poison pen. Scathing epistles typed in twenty-four point caps appeared intermittently on my door for all to see. In them she found fault with my personality, my tone of voice, my parenting skills, and any planter that I placed on the deck. (She seemed envious that I had a green thumb while her plants turned brown and were left to die.) Though we rarely talked, she disliked the fact that I stayed on, while other tenants, mostly students, left their apartments after a year or two, allowing her to raise the rent. I was protected by rent control, so the rent went up one to two percent per year. As the years progressed she became more hostile, hissing "Watch out" or "Run" when I walked down the driveway. I looked straight ahead and said nothing, but had to hire a lawyer from time to time, to make sure any problem was resolved.

When my daughter was in high school, Slim threatened to evict us and move in a family member, but by then I was sixty and had over a ten-year tenancy, which made me a protected class by rent control standards. I loved my Victorian apartment with its bay windows, hardwood floors and twelve-foot ceilings, and I had no intention of leaving. I planned to retire and begin a new life as a writer in my cozy apartment.

In my mind I was an ideal tenant, a quiet minimalist who paid my rent ahead of time, got along with my neighbors, and recycled all my trash. Slim, however, saw it differently. She knew she had control over what was necessary to me: my home and my security. She never failed to remind me of her belief that she could snatch it all away, or drive me out by her bad behavior.

As a student of meditation, I sat every day on my cushion and faced the demons of fear and anger evoked by her toxic behavior. I focused myself with this meditation poem: *In, out/deep, slow/calm, ease/mind, release /present moment, wonderful moment.* Each time the negative feelings arose, I tried to remember to breathe and affirm that I was more than my emotions. It was a slow process, but I kept at it.

Slim sometimes swore at me as I walked down the driveway, where she stood hosing the lawn, dressed in her sweat pants and faded flannel shirt. Her grey hair and lined face were a testament to her fifty years of woe. Her moods were soon ignored by the neighbors, though Miss Pretty remained at her side, a captive audience. We tenants were holding our collective breath awaiting Slim's response if Miss Pretty got hit with a second strike, removing her from society for good. In the doggy world, the death penalty prevails.

One spring morning I heard a scream outside the window and ran to my deck overlooking the yard and street below. A sobbing young girl was being pulled down the sidewalk by her mother. I heard Miss Pretty yelping as I saw her tail disappear into Slim's apartment. The door slammed and Slim yelled, "Bad dog, Miss Pretty, bad dog."

Had the inevitable occurred? A call from the next-door neighbor confirmed that her six-year-old niece had been bitten by Miss Pretty. Slim had warned the frightened child that if she told the police, Miss Pretty would be killed. The girl was inconsolable when, at the emergency room, the doctor said he was legally bound to report the attack to Animal Control. The mother immediately wrote a letter to Animal Control asking for a stay if Slim would put up additional dog-proof fencing around the yard. The case was continued for six months.

Miss Pretty was all Slim had. When I first rented the apartment, my daughter Lulu was six years old. Slim's son Julep had graduated high school that year and had moved out shortly after we'd moved in. He stayed away. That was when Slim got Miss Pretty, saying it was too hard to live alone. Various boyfriends moved in and out, but Miss Pretty always stayed.

Miss Pretty had always been friendly to me, and was particularly fond of Lulu, for whom she would roll on her back, feet in the air, demanding a tummy rub, which Lulu would provide with pleasure. Miss Pretty seemed to consider us family. Having known us since she was a puppy, she never growled or snapped at us, as she did at strangers. And Lulu had a special gift with animals, a fun-loving warmth that brought them to her seeking love that spilled from her heart like a waterfall. It was amazing to watch. Miss Pretty would bound up to Lulu as soon as she entered the gate after school, and Lulu would drop her pack in the driveway and wrestle with Miss Pretty, who never bared her teeth. Soon they were chasing the soccer ball that lay idle in the yard, until Miss Pretty plopped down for the tummy rub.

Apparently, Miss Pretty bit people who reached through the fence to pet her as she sat sunning by the gate. She was very appealing, with ice blue eyes, a long fluffy grey and white coat, and a curved mouth that looked to be perpetually smiling. Slim had posted *Beware of Dog* signs, but they didn't stop most people, especially neighborhood folks. I had heard from a man who had known Slim for years that he was passing the gate when Miss Pretty approached him, wagging her tail. He bent down to her level, pooched his lips in a kiss, and she lunged at his mouth, tearing his lip. That was the first strike, again because the ER had to report. "I almost didn't go, but my lip was torn and blood was everywhere" was how he justified it.

Slim had made a special effort to reconnect with her son. He was committing to his life partner and had invited Slim to drive him down the grassy aisle of his outdoor ceremony in Golden Gate Park. Slim painted her 1964 VW bug mint green, put the top down and filled the back seat with baby pink roses. Julep rode shotgun in the parade that ended at a knoll where his partner awaited. A neighbor who attended reported that something went wrong. Before the reception Slim jumped in the car and drove off without explanation. I never saw Julep visit his mother after that day, and Slim was left alone with Miss Pretty. I found myself worrying about what would happen if Miss Pretty were put down, and I wondered whether there was anything I could do to prevent her demise.

I have never been responsible for anyone's death, but had carried for many years a fear of death for those I loved. A wise therapist helped me to see that my fear was rooted in a sense of responsibility that I had adopted due to a rare illness my mother suffered when I was young. As a child of six, I wondered if I had caused her illness, and if I could prevent further occurrences and potential death by being a better girl. My mother lived into her eighties and I was finally able to release that guilt. That is, until Miss Pretty evoked my childhood anguish.

After the potential second strike, Miss Pretty and Slim kept a low profile for weeks and eventually reappeared in the yard. Slim greeted me with her usual invectives and left occasional toxic notes on my door. Within a few months, Miss Pretty disappeared. The rumor was that she had committed another crime, though no one knew for sure, and Slim wasn't talking. It remained an unsolved mystery, and in time was forgotten.

****

Years later, still in the same apartment, I awake at dawn, having dreamt about Miss Pretty. In the dream, she is stretched out on a white velvet bed. With feet serenely raised, she looks like a dog who only wants love, but even in a dream-like state I see all too clearly the harm she can inflict. I see her beautiful silver and black coat shiver as they place the alcohol swab on her neck. I feel my nose sting as the needle is injected and the sharp medicinal smell permeates the room. Slim stands nearby, stoic, eyes closed, repeating the words *I'm sorry.* I feel compassion for her pain and sense our connection.

Miss Pretty goes quickly, her black lips open in a smile, her white teeth gleaming. When her breath stops, I see her spirit rise like smoke, disappearing into the air. I take a deep breath and find myself in the presence of a warm and embracing energy, and hear myself say *I forgive me*. I feel as if a weight has been lifted and I gratefully release it.

****

There is the familiar clatter of glass on glass in the recycling bin. Slim is yelling, probably to the homeless woman who collects bottles early on pick-up day. "You box of rocks, that's for paper!" Hearing her voice reminds me of the dream, as well as the compassion I felt for Slim. It's painful to think about the hurt she inflicts on others, and it's unsettling to accept that she may never change. Like Miss Pretty, she is a victim of her animal instincts.

Nigel
Michele Theisen

When our senior dog Maddie passed away in October it left a huge hole in our hearts. Even though we have three other dogs, she was special. She was our senior dog. My husband and I have been volunteering at Almost Home Animal Haven in Southfield since April and it has been an incredibly rewarding experience. They truly are the epitome of a sanctuary because they do not under any circumstances put an animal down. In our experiences we've seen some very beaten down animals that have truly gone through some terrible times in life. Almost Home is always right there picking up the pieces of a wounded and battered life and putting these precious animals back together physically and emotionally. They truly do protect animals from further abuse and neglect.

In November, another senior dog came in to the shelter. They named him Nigel. His story was that he was found as a stray and brought in by the police. Upon seeing him we thought for sure someone would come for him. He was a beautiful Rottweiler but you could see age in his face. His fur was black except for his face which was speckled with white. My husband saw him first and when he took him for a walk, Nigel lost his balance and fell. My husband was pretty upset because it reminded him of our Maddie. He told me we couldn't let Nigel spend the rest of his life at the shelter. I hadn't met him yet but when I did, my experience was very similar to my husband's. We both felt very strongly that we should foster him. We weren't over the shock of losing Maddie but people don't automatically step up to adopt a senior dog. So we filled out the paperwork and brought him home with us.

It took a while for the other dogs to adjust (two other males and a female) but our attitude is, once you're in our home, you're here to stay. Everyone was just going to have to get along. One thing we learned about him that no one at the shelter would have known-we live in a subdivision in the country, across from a county gun range and he's terrified of hearing gunshots. Needless-to-say, he doesn't like to go outside when he hears the noise. We are slowly working around this problem but it's going to take some time. He is now a member of our family, sleeps on the side of our bed, plays with our female dog and just wants to be loved, and that's something we've got a lot to give.

October Ground
Jay Dardes

"She seems stiff," Noah said to Debra as he watched Maggie walk out of the Vari-Kennel where she slept at night in their bedroom. "Her gait seems a little funny."

Debra continued putting on her makeup, "Probably just slept too long," she said.

As Noah walked Maggie out the garage door to pee, he found himself agreeing with his wife's opinion. A worrier, a glass-half-empty person, the kind of guy who got his car keys out when he was still a block and a half from the vehicle, Debra's cheerful positive view of life often seemed like denial to him. But this time, she was no doubt right: no big deal. When Maggie was done, he brought her back inside and filled her dish with kibble. Maggie very slowly ate only a couple of pieces. Noah's concern returned then: at just over nineteen pounds, Maggie was large for a Miniature Schnauzer, all massive muscle and no fat, but she always gulped all her food as soon as it was presented. *Something is wrong*, Noah thought. He went back into the bedroom and Maggie followed listlessly.

"She didn't eat," he told Debra.

A brief frown creased her brow. "Hmmm. Well, we'll keep an eye on her."

It was Noah who kept an eye on her over the next couple of hours while Debra busied herself with household tasks. He couldn't take his eyes away, in fact, noting every nuance as she stood in a frozen position, walked just a little around the living room, or lay on the floor. He saw the increasing weakness in her left legs, saw her progressively tilting that direction, and moving rather drunkenly. Finally he said, "She's got to go to the vet... now." Debra looked at the Schnauzer carefully and nodded. Noah suspected that she had been observing the dog more than was obvious.

Debra got into the passenger seat with Maggie in her lap and Noah backed the small SUV out of the garage. The vet was about twenty minutes away and when they got there, Noah was very relieved to see that out of numerous doctors who worked in the low, modern building, the one they would be seeing was Tex. Not "Tex" really, but Doctor William Lombard; "Tex" was a nickname Noah and Debra used in private for him because of his east Texas drawl and his degree from Texas A&M School of Veterinary Medicine. Tall and lanky, he had been the doctor who had provided most of Maggie's care over her fourteen years. He examined her quickly and thoroughly, asking Noah and Debra lots of questions. He said he couldn't be sure. It could be an inner ear thing and he could arrange it so they could take Maggie over to Minneapolis to have this checked out. More likely, it could be a stroke, in which case it would either get better or worse soon. They both shook their heads at the idea of going to Minneapolis; they knew a stroke when they saw one, so they opted to take Maggie back home and keep an eye on her. Tex told them to bring her back in a week or call in the interim if it became necessary. He discussed the possibility of euthanasia if it came to that. They were quiet on the way home except Debra said, "Maybe she'll get better."

Noah said "maybe" but the tone of his voice showed he was not as optimistic.

They talked some that evening, sitting on the couch with the TV on but ignored. They talked about feeling sorry for Maggie, this strong, active, dominant dog now diminished. They talked about the big role she had had in their lives over the last fourteen years, all the more because they had elected from the first not to have children and how Maggie had filled that need in many ways, ways they found, truth be told, to be preferable to having a child. They talked about what life would be like without her if this turned out badly. Then Debra went to bed and Noah sat up alone, staring at the TV but not seeing it.

The next day they were up early. They anxiously checked Maggie's kennel, then pulled her out. She gave little sign of recognition. Her left paws weren't working at all and, had they not helped her, she would probably have fallen over. As it was, Debra got her outside by looping a bath towel under her chest and pulling up on it so she could stand, however awkwardly. Still, she did not pee nor eat, make any sound, or interact with them. She maintained what in human soldiers would be termed, a "thousand yard stare." This lack of expressiveness contrasted with her normal vivaciousness.

Noah finally said, without emotion, "We'll have to put her down," and Debra did not disagree. They called the vet and were offered a time in the morning and one in the afternoon. Debra elected for the afternoon and Noah called into work for the second time in two days; his boss, Kathy, a dog lover, expressed her sympathy and, on a practical note, said, "You can take sick days for a family member. She's a family member. Don't worry about it." All morning Debra sat with Maggie on her lap, stroking her over and over, sometimes talking to her in a low voice.

Their house was built on twenty acres of forested land and they decided to bury her in the yard under a shady sycamore tree. While Debra stayed inside with Maggie, Noah dug the hole. The ground, in October, was cold but not frozen yet, even here. Normally digging here would mean being plagued by heavy roots and many rocks but it seemed to go smoothly, despite his wish for the earth to resist, and soon he was finished.

Too soon it was time to go. Debra spent some time fishing in her huge, denim purse for the car keys and handed them to Noah. She sat in the passenger seat with Maggie wrapped in a blanket on her lap while he drove slowly to the clinic.

They checked in at the reception desk and Noah noted the sympathetic looks from the four female staff members. They took seats in the waiting room but a vet tech immediately called them in to an operatory where Tex was waiting. He made some comments about how hard this was to do and then asked if they wanted to be present or not. Yes, they did. He explained that he would run an IV and would first give Maggie a shot that would knock her out, she would not be experiencing pain or fear, just sleeping when he gave her a second shot which would stop her heart. There would not be any observable trauma. He then took Maggie out the back door of the operatory and returned promptly with the IV inserted in her leg.

With the first shot she finally looked peaceful again, sleeping. As he loaded the second shot, he talked to Maggie, telling her what a good girl she had been and how much he had always liked her. Noah thought he recognized the somber tone Tex had used with them today. He was reminded of the funeral director back home who had buried his grandmother, father, mother, and aunt. That man had always spoken with a soft and mournful voice; in fact, Noah had never heard him speak otherwise. He realized it wasn't authentic but he tolerated it because it was the best the poor bastard could do and it did fit the occasion. As much as he admired Tex, he thought this was his "euthanasia voice" for bereaved pet owners. After all, how many dogs and other animals did this guy put down; and how could he get caught up in the sorrow? So if he had to fake a little sympathy that was okay. But Tex's words to Maggie did seem to have personal meaning and Noah glanced up at him. He was shocked to see the big man, loading the needle, had tears rolling down his cheeks. Noah, amazed, found a new level of respect for this animal doctor.

Debra stroked Maggie's head as Tex administered the second shot. She was crying too. Noah kept his head down, watching Maggie but otherwise avoiding eye contact for fear he might break out sobbing himself. Not that it was unmanly (at times in the past he had seen tearful guys bringing in their dogs to be put down) but… well, he was a control freak, uncomfortable in letting his feelings show in a dramatic way.

Maggie remained still. Tex checked her three, four, five times with his stethoscope. "She's gone," he said, gently.

Noah pulled the car around to the back of the building and they took her to the car wrapped in the blanket. Debra held her and neither of them spoke the whole way home.

At the house again, Noah lowered the dog into the hole. He didn't like setting her on the bare ground, almost felt as if she should keep the blanket. He looked at Debra, who was holding the plush person-shaped squeaky toy that had been Maggie's favorite since she was a pup, the only one she never destroyed. "Aren't you going to put it in?" he asked. Firmly, almost coldly, she shook her head no. That's the thing about denial, Noah thought, when you can't pretend things are okay, then you're really up against it. Whereas gloomy people like him always assumed the worst, saw it coming even when it wasn't and weren't caught so off guard by it. Hesitantly, he tossed a small shovel of dirt into the grave. It hit Maggie midsection, dry brown earth over her still shiny black fur.

Oh shit. Oh shit. Oh shit, he thought. *This isn't right to be doing to her.* He felt as if he would vomit, not just the contents of his stomach but all his internal organs would heave up and into the ground with Maggie. But slowly, he kept shoveling and his pet gradually disappeared under the earth.

After the grave was filled and tamped down, Debra brought over a garden ornament, a three-foot antiqued metal pole with a metal hummingbird on top and pushed it into the soft earth. "A memorial," she explained.

"It'll fall over," he worried.

"Just for now. When the ground hardens up we can push it in deeper."

It was over. They stood by the grave silently, looking down. The honking of some Canadian Geese flying overhead was the only sound. They didn't speak. Debra clutched at the toy, Noah leaned on the shovel. Finally she turned and slowly walked into the house. Noah went to the garage and put the shovel in its proper place then idly began straightening and adjusting the other tools on their hangers.

Our Guard Dog
Daniel Barbare

Miley
barks.

I
can
just
see
her

white
as
the
moon,
nocturnal
as
big
eyes

sitting

watching
over
the
yard.

Our Little Girl
Nickolas Frank

The day Tillie came into our lives seemed like any other day but, little did we know, it would change our lives forever. She didn't look like that little doggy in the pet shop window begging to come home. She looked out through the bars at Almost Home with a kind of indifference towards the caring faces looking back at her. Even though she had a bald spot on her tail from weeks of stressful nibbling and one floppy ear that didn't quite stand up like the other, there was something special about her that no one could deny. So she came home and life truly began.

From the very start, she loved to cuddle up under a warm blanket and simply be next to you. As she started to accept her new family, the hair on her tail grew in because she no longer had to worry about where she might call home. She let the cuddle bug that she has inside come out more and more. It didn't take long before everyone fell in love with her. She has always had the ability to capture the attention of everyone, whether it be on the street or at home with her family and friends. Maybe it is the playful way she greets you with her one ear flopping almost like a wave or how she is so quick to give affection even during the first time meeting her, but something about her makes everyone fall for her charm.

One thing is certain; her family loves her more than anything and is so grateful to have her.

Peyton And Bailey
Robert Perlaki

This is the story of Peyton and Bailey. Peyton was a rescue dog, a lab-mastiff mix, she weighed about one hundred and thirty pounds, she was my girlfriend's dog. Bailey is a long haired Chihuahua, weighing all of six pounds, and she belonged to me. Their friendship was like no other. Although Peyton had one hundred and twenty-five pounds, and four years on Bailey, Bailey was definitely the boss! Bailey would eat first, while Peyton sat and whined, worried that there would be no food left for her.

One sunny October afternoon in 2009, we decided to take our girls for a nice autumn walk at a local State Park before we went out for dinner. My girlfriend and I walked the trails with them on their leashes, all the way to the dam, Peyton was ready for a swim, but we didn't allow it. Once we crossed the bridge, we were on trails that aren't traveled often. So, I decided to take off the leashes, and let them enjoy some freedom, chase leaves, have fun.

They were very happy, running up ahead, turning around and running back, running ahead, stopping to wait for us, and running ahead again. Everything was fine. We were watching the dogs, enjoying conversation. The dogs ran around a bend in the trail... and DISAPPEARED, VANISHED! We rounded the bend and looked down the trail, and they weren't there. We called and called, and there was nothing but silence, no barking, no rustle of leaves, nothing. This State Park is 4,700 acres... and we didn't hear a thing.

We were concerned about Bailey, there are marshes, and wild animals bigger than her, snakes. We continued along the trails, calling them, whistling, asking the few people that were out there if they had seen them. After about thirty minutes, we decided to split up and see if we could find them. When we met up again, it was starting to get dark. I told my girlfriend I was not leaving without our dogs. The temperature was starting to drop; I sent her home to get supplies, (flashlight, jacket, gloves, protein bar, Gatorade).

When she got home, there were several messages on voicemail with their whereabouts in the park, of course that was hours ago. "We had Peyton, and we got your number off her tags, she was with a little dog, when we tried to catch the little one, she ran off, and Peyton got away. I really hope you find them, please call us and let us know if you find them." And, "Hey, we saw your dog near the nature center, we live right by there, we tried to get them in our yard, but the little one wanted nothing to do with us, so we let Peyton go."

I was waiting for my girlfriend in the parking area to bring me the supplies so I could hike back out to the woods. It seemed like it was taking forever, it was dark now, and I was so worried. Finally, I see headlights heading into the lot. I walked over to the driver's side door, while I put on my jacket and gloves, I was told about the messages that were left for us. As we were setting up a game plan, we heard a familiar "jingle" of Peyton's tags on her collar. I let out a whistle, and THERE THEY WERE! Peyton was running towards us with Bailey behind her. WHAT A RELIEF! They were as happy to see us, as we were to see them.

They were gone on their adventure for almost four hours. We greeted them only to realize that they were soaked, we think they swam across the lake to get back. Peyton got her swim. We loaded the wet muddy mutts into the van for the ride home. It didn't take us long to realize that they apparently had rolled over every dead animal they came across on their adventure. THEY STUNK!

I looked back at them before we pulled out of the lot and said (in a fatherly manner) "I have half a mind to bring you two back here tomorrow and do it again to see if you have learned your lesson."

My girlfriend said, "No, I think we learned ours!"

Needless to say, we didn't go out that night, we were too busy bathing dogs.

To this day, we argue about whose dog was the "bad influence" on the other. I guess we will never know. If only dogs could speak.

Peyton passed away in 2012, and I swear Bailey still misses her to this day. I know we do.

Questions I Can't Ask My Dog
Elisabeth Ward

What do you hear now,
Now that you can't hear me?

Is your life dense and thick,
        mysterious
As muffled feathers on a grouse
Silently stalked through snowy forests?

Is it hollow, empty and hovering,
        curious;
A vapor carried toward a rising moon?

Or is your world encased in noise,
        whirring;
A spring wind blasting through open meadows
Forever ahead of your eager mouth?

Is your day defined by scent
        or sense?
Sleeping until you feel a stirring
You used to hear, you raise your head,
        search
For those you think no longer speak.

Your thoughts are now your own,
Where once you hung on every word
        I uttered.

I am but an echo rolling ever fainter,
        ever farther...

Until you catch me weeping.

Ralph
Jane Sloven

I'm still not sure what captured my heart – the black snout surrounded by gray, the dark eyes overhung by white brows, the forlorn expression, or the heart-rending description, *Distinguished elderly gentleman seeks home.* Ralph, an eleven-year-old lab mix, in the West Kennebunk Shelter, surrendered by his owners, along with his long-time littermate.

Ralph's bio said he had lived with cats, which was a pre-requisite for joining our family. My husband and I already shared our home with two elderly felines rescued from the same shelter six years before. I'd been having dog-longing for years, but with allergies, adopting a dog was a bit tricky. The poodles and poodle-mixes at the pound always seemed to go very quickly into other adoptive homes.

Scanning photos and dog descriptions from all the shelters in Maine had become a ritual for me, the seeking and stopping an on-going activity until that Sunday, three weeks after I had first seen Ralph's photo and description. There he was on the website – still – an eleven year old *distinguished elderly gentleman*. His litter mate had been adopted.

My husband and I walked throughout the neighborhood, discussing the pros and cons of up-ending our lives by adopting a dog. *Could we really do it? Were we ready to do it?* By the time we returned home, it was too late to get to the shelter. Ambivalence reigned for me, but my husband stopped at the shelter the next morning on his way to work. He called me from the car.

"If you don't absolutely love this dog, then I'll have to say I don't know the woman I've been married to for the past twenty-three years," he said. "You have to come down to meet him before they'll let us bring him home."

Though I wasn't able to get there that day, I called the shelter to say I would be there first thing the following morning. Then I phoned a dog-wise friend who arranged to meet me there. We caught up with each other in the parking lot of the shelter and the volunteers brought Ralph into a special room to meet us.

It was immediately clear that Ralph would make a perfect match for me – an older guy who would love to take leisurely walks and hang around the house with me when I wasn't working. He didn't make eye contact easily, but he came around for pats and wagged his tail.

My friend reassured me. "He will be a great dog," she said. "And I know dogs."

There was no reason not to trust her judgment, nor my husband's judgment, nor my own, but I felt nervous. Ralph and I both descended into panic attacks on the drive home. *Was it crazy to change my life in my mid-fifties, bringing a mongrel – a brindle-colored lab-mix with a whole history I couldn't fathom – into my home, to join my husband and two cats?*

It took Ralph time to become comfortable with us. The poor guy remained frightened, traumatized, we thought, by the loss of his family and his littermate, as well as a month or more at the shelter. And I cannot say that our bonding was instant. Ralph couldn't sleep and made it impossible for us to sleep. He had diarrhea in the middle of the night, every night. Two weeks of sleeplessness and cleaning up after him led me to reconsider – to go so far as to call my friend and discuss returning him. She made clear that would be a death-sentence for Ralph. So we persevered. We cooked special meals for Ralph – rice, meat and vegetables, enhanced by various vitamin concoctions. Despite the ups and downs, we got used to each other. We took multiple walks every day. Ralph walked wonderfully on a leash, leading proudly. When I spoke to him as he sauntered, he wagged his tail. He liked to sniff everything, and acted surprised when everyone we passed did not want to stop to say hello to him.

At first, Ralph checked out every car, scanned the neighborhood as we walked. It seemed as if he was still seeking his original family. But eventually that stopped. We could tell that we had become his people, and he had become our dog.

Ralph would not let any man approach me without his protection. If he didn't know the man, he would jump between us, not aggressively – just enough to make sure they knew he was taking care of me. Ralph was also hyper-vigilant to raised voices, especially in our home. If my husband and I argued, we had to do so quietly. My husband said Ralph was a *Bodhisattva*, bringing peace and harmony into our household, reminding us to speak thoughtfully, to be gentle with each other.

After one of our cats passed, our black cat began to nose Ralph in greeting, and Ralph nosed him back. When Ralph barked, our cat joined in with his own chattering, as if they were barking in unison. Ralph developed his own form of purring. The two of them often stretched out full length on the floor in parallel positions, paws crossed in front of them, eyes closed.

Our lives became richer, fuller, and more complete with Ralph. He enlarged the loving circle of our family, and I know it was a kind of divine intervention that led us to each other. I fell in love. My husband fell in love. Ralph fell in love. We became Ralph's people, and he became our dog. He shared his life with us for five wonderful years and turned us back into dog people.

Rascal
Jane Sloven

"It'll be alright," Matt said. "I promise." His eyes darted back and forth, back and forth, settling briefly on hers, alighting like a dragonfly and taking off again. She couldn't help but notice. His arms enfolded her, drew her close.

She rested her head against his shoulder but there was no rest there. Not now. Not any longer. She moved her head, pushed off his embrace. "Let me go Matt."

He stepped back so quickly she stumbled, unprepared for the force of his release.

"You said you'd forgive me. You said we could start over." He swept his hand across the stubble on his chin. "Didn't you? Didn't you say that?"

She looked past him, to the dunes, to the long expanse of beach, to the horizon, the endless ocean. "I did. I did say that." Her own hands brushed curls back from her face, gathered her hair in a ponytail, and twisted it up. One hand held it there while the other faltered, like her speech.

"I can't though. I can't forgive you. I don't want to be here, with you. Not anymore." Her eyes caught his, held them steady. "I can't do it Matt. I can't."

"What? You're forever going to hold it against me?"

"I don't know. I hope I can forget. Forget Rascal, forget what happened, and forget you."

"He was a dog, Sally, just a dog."

"There is no *just* in that sentence, Matt. He was a *being, a living being.* He was *my* dog. He was *your* dog. He was *our* dog when there was an *us.*"

"I made a mistake. Do I have to beg your forgiveness? Do I have to get on my knees, sob, shake, what? What's going to do it for you, Sally? What?" Matt sank to a bench on the boardwalk.

"Nothing's going to do it for me, Matt. Nothing. You left our dog in the car in eighty-five degree heat with the windows only part-way open so you could sit at a damn bar with your friends and toss back a few cold ones. You killed him."

Matt held his head in his hands and started to sob. His sobs became loud, almost frightening. His breath sounded ragged between sobs, sounded, Sally thought, almost like asphyxiation.

Sally thought of Rascal, alone in the hot car, waiting for Matt, asphyxiating in the heat. It had been eighty-five degrees that day, and the temperature inside the car could have reached one hundred and two degrees within ten minutes. Sally had read that on a website, *Trips with Pets.com.* It said that at one hundred ten degrees, pets were in danger of heatstroke. She imagined Rascal, panting, poking his nose out the partially opened window, waiting helplessly for Matt. The website said that on hot, humid days, the temperature could spike thirty degrees in a minute – thirty degrees every minute – if a car was parked in direct sunlight. In only fifteen minutes, Rascal would have had brain and organ damage. Sally couldn't get the statistics out of her mind, like she couldn't get those images of Rascal, dying alone in that hot car, out of her mind. She couldn't get over losing Rascal.

She looked at Matt and felt pity and love and hate for him all at once. "You'll have to figure out how to live with yourself. I won't be living with you ever again." She patted his head the way she used to pat Rascal's head, tenderly, before she walked down the steps into the sand. She kept walking, towards the water.

Sally slipped off her dress and adjusted the straps of her swimsuit. She stepped out of her sandals and plunged into the sea where her own tears could be met by a larger, more encompassing force, where she could bid goodbye to Rascal, to Matt, to innocence and ignorance.

The waves tossed her out and she dove back, wondering how to make something good come from something so horrifying. She thought of making posters and putting them on every car in every supermarket lot to warn people not to leave their dogs in their cars.

The waves crashed over her head, threw her out onto the sand but she dove in again and again, crying, thinking, planning – until exhausted, she lay atop a rock to dry.

Sally knew she'd eventually adopt another dog. Maybe two. Not that Rascal was replaceable. No pet was just replaceable. She'd take time to mourn Rascal. But eventually, she'd save a dog. She'd save a dog and the dog just might save her.

http://www.tripswithpets.com/twp-blog/pet-friendly-travel-pets-in-parked-car; Leaving Pets in Parked Car Can be a Deadly Mistake

Reading Berryman To The Dog
Wendy Taylor Carlisle

Some people maintain dogs have souls, I believe
they're bloodthirsty as generals. The new Rottweiler
one hundred pounds plus, treasures dried pig ears,

hoards them like a recruit. At night, I can hear
him in the garage shattering them, chewing. The dog
flew in on American with my sweaty tee shirt

in his crate for the smell. Still, we were strangers
when the front-end loader set him down on the tarmac,
strangers when I had to touch him first

and the day went slick in my hand. I grubbed
in my pocket for a Ken'l Bone, crooned a safe-dog song.
Years after Tet, I loved a tall Marine

who seldom spoke about the war. In Asia he had
friends and enemies he couldn't tell apart. In my bed,
he dreamed of napalm and demolished sleep.

Not at home yet, the new dog noses the furniture. Uneasy
as a heathen at morning mass, he measures the cat's intent
with a long stare. The manual says his breed is fond

of small animals. They will however, kill rabbits.
After a decade the soldier phoned. His words made a fist
sound. The receiver slid in my palm. I listened

to his familiar voice, didn't hang up. Since then, he
calls sometime. Sometimes I answer. If I happen to cry,
the dog stands close, waits for the all-clear sign and if he whines,

I ache for him, take him out to the porch let him rest his sad head
on my foot. And read to him from Berryman—the Opus Dei,
the Dreamsongs, the prayers—until he can finally sleep.

Reading Berryman Again
Wendy Taylor Carlisle

When we divined it was his time to die, we got the poison
and I read to him, again his big head on my lap
as it had been six years ago when he came,
huge and frightening, crated from the plane.
The symmetry at first and last was Berryman. And death
was slow enough for more Dreamsongs after # 14
and then to bring the family in to hear how at the end,
he mourned the clumsiness of men. He keened.
We all stood, dumb. It took too long. Our heads hung,
like the Judases we were, each one of us ashamed.
Not worth a hind paw of the hound
who wouldn't leave us here without a fight,
who knew our need and how it filled our human hearts.

Rescuing Vixen
Nicole Koppin

"Don't even think about going to the shelter! You're too young, you don't have enough time! What makes you think you need a dog!? How will you feed it? How will you train it? You have had family dogs before but never one of your own! You can't afford it. This is a life decision. You are making a big mistake!" Remarks from my family fell upon deaf ears.

You know that feeling you get when something in your life is missing? That's exactly how I felt. Wake up in the morning, go to work. Come home at night, cook, watch TV, and then go to bed. Same story every day. Life shouldn't be repetitive, boring, and lifeless. It's called life for a reason, but I definitely wasn't living!

I was sitting at home one night after a long day at work, staring at Facebook, waiting for an interesting post to pop up. Suddenly, one of those annoying advertisements that pop up on the side of your news feed caught my eye. It was an ad about adoption. "Adopt a shelter pet, save a life!" read the banner on the side of my screen. It reminded me of those commercials you see on TV from the ASPCA that make you want to curl in a ball and cry your eyes out for those poor animals who are suffering without a home! I thought about it for a minute then went to Google and searched Michigan Humane Society.

They have so many pets and looking through the pages at all their wanting faces nearly made me cry. I saw one dog on the website that really caught my eye. Her name was Vanessa and she had this mischievous fox face to her that was absolutely adorable! I decided then that the very next day I was going to the shelter and I was going to save a life.

Right after work I went to the shelter in Westland, Michigan. I was nervous and wondering how I would be able to pick only one dog to rescue. I walked in and the staff directed me to the dog kennels. Walking through was like walking down death row. Many dogs had a potential family in front of their kennels but the ones that didn't pulled at my heart. I just wanted to take them all! I heard a family talking in front of a kennel about a dog. The children really wanted to take her home but I heard the parents say how hyper and ill-behaved the dog was. They walked away and I looked, it was Vanessa.

Seeing her in person was so much different than seeing her online. She stopped jumping at the door for a minute and looked up at me and wagged her tail. It was in that moment my heart completely melted and that was it, I was hers. I took her paperwork and practically ran up to the desk eager to take her home. They asked me a few questions and I filled out the adoption application and that was it. I was approved. I went and spent an hour in one of the play rooms with her. She was the sweetest dog I had ever met. First thing she did when they brought her in the room was jump up on my lap and start giving me kisses. She was a wiggly little thing, too big to be a lap dog, but she didn't care! She had endless energy and was so happy to be in my company, she must have known that I was going to take her home.

One of the staff members came into the room and let me know that they were closing. They were going to take her to get her shots, and the next day she would be spayed. I really didn't want to wait that long but it allowed me time to buy things for her and prepare my apartment. I said goodbye and they put her on a leash and began to take her away. I walked back towards the exit and turned to look at her as they took her away. She was standing on her hind legs straining at the leash to follow me, the staff members were trying to get her to go with them but she didn't want to, she wanted to follow me! I told her I would see her soon and then they took her away into the vet office.

I was so excited to get my apartment ready. After leaving the shelter, I went straight to Petsmart and bought all the supplies I would need for her. Crate, toys, food bowls, food, leash, collar, dog bed, etc. I went and talked to the apartment about her and got everything set up and ready. I could barely sleep. I couldn't wait to have my puppy home!

My mom came with me to pick her up and I decided to change her name. I didn't like Vanessa; it was too boring for her cute personality, so I named her Vixen. I lived on the third floor of my apartment building and since she was just spayed, I had a few weeks of carrying her up and down stairs, it was a good thing she only weighed nineteen pounds! Within a few days it was apparent she had never been house trained. She never asked to go outside and would wet in the apartment, apparently not knowing it was wrong. It took three weeks to successfully house train her; I was impressed with how smart she was! Crate training really helped, soon she knew right when I got home, and first thing in the morning, it was time to go outside!

Daily walks became both of our favorite times of the day! I was able to explore the city and Vixen got to smell all the smells and see all the little critters around the apartment complex. She loved to watch the swans and geese, but I would never let her get too close!

When it came time to try the stairs, Vixen was too afraid to even walk to the edge of the staircase. It took about a week but between myself, my friend Christy, and my mom, we were able to teach her that stairs aren't the enemy and it was okay, and fun even, to run up and down them. Her favorite way to climb and descend the stairs was at a sprint. There were a few mornings she almost pulled me down the stairs when I was in a sleepy morning stupor.

I was sitting at home one night after work, playing fetch with Vixen. She can't get enough of those squeaky tennis balls! It struck me that my life was no longer boring! Vixen was exactly what was missing! Her spunky personality, her puppy kisses, how she loves to cuddle right before sleep, my life was now anything but boring.

It has been just over a year since I adopted Vixen. We have since moved to a house with a fenced-in backyard and boy, does she love to run in it! This is her second winter with me and she sure loves the snow! She can't get enough play dates with my brother's black lab Jake, and daily walks are still our favorite activity. She no longer needs to be crated; she's the smartest and cutest dog I know! She is my protector, always warning me when people or squirrels are in the front yard. My travel buddy, she loves car rides and gets excited when she sees me start packing the car because she knows it's time for another adventure. Best of all, she's my companion, always eager to please, she's at my side the second she senses I'm feeling down, she lays at my feet and sleeps next to my bed. I don't know where I would be without my Vixen! One thing is for sure, they say I rescued her but really, it's Vixen who rescued me!

Rufus
Jane Sloven

Everything was fine until Harry walked through the door, stubble shadowing his face, mud splattering his Bean boots, his ears so bright red from the cold they almost matched his wool jacket.

"Damn that dog," he said, tossing the leash like a lasso up and onto the wooden peg on the mudroom wall. "Had me chasing his tail all the way to the river, must've seen a fox or something."

"Where is he?" I said, alarm burning a trail through my chest. "You found him, didn't you? You didn't leave him out there? Not with the storm approaching."

"Don't know where he is and I don't give a damn either," Harry spat. "I tripped over so many tree limbs hidden under the snow I near busted a leg."

"You let him off leash, didn't you? I told you he's not to be trusted." The frustration that lay coiled like a snake in my gut raised its head and hissed. "For once in your life you just might try listening to me. Now I'll have to go out and find him." I yanked my down jacket off a hook and pulled a wool hat over my ears, muttering a string of curses.

"Leave him be. He'll get cold and hungry and head home soon enough."

"He doesn't know the land yet, Harry. We've only had him three days. If we get a foot of snow like they're predicting, he'll be a dead dog, and I'm not living with that." I set one of my fiercest glares loose on Harry. "Christine's due home tonight. How'd you like to tell her that her Christmas present is a rescue dog you lost in the woods?" A flush swept up my face and set it afire.

"All right, all right," Harry muttered, hoping to forestall a greater eruption, one he knew all too well. "Come'on, we'll take the whistle and some dried salmon sticks. He seems to smell those from a distance."

I opened the back door to see the sky already darkening, snowflakes descending in a slow dance, an interlude before the winds whipped up and the blizzard set upon us. I hoped Christine would get home soon. Harry grabbed a flashlight while I strapped on a headlamp and stepped out, into the icy air.

The ground, pockmarked with the imprint of boots and deer hooves, was slick with old snow melded to ice from daytime thaws and the black freeze of night. As we rounded the barn, my foot slipped and I nearly landed, splat, on my bad hip, but Harry caught me. Leaning against the barn wall to steady myself, I yelled again for Rufus.

Damned if that dog didn't barrel around the corner and make a beeline right for me. All eighty pounds of him leapt up, and I braced for his weight, but when his paws landed on my shoulders they settled gently, as if he knew I couldn't take the whole weight of him. We stared into each other's eyes, and before I could do a thing about it Rufus planted a big wet one right on my lips.

When I stopped laughing, I said to Harry. "Good thing we bought Christine a whole pile of presents, cause she sure isn't getting this dog."

Shelter Roof, Bloody Floor
Jennifer Koch

Thanks Mike and Diana for making writing so amusing!

Daniella shielded her eyes as she stepped across the Animals Welcome threshold and out into the strange and incessantly sunny winter's day. The last two patron visits hadn't amounted to much except the usual promises to 'think about it', and she was beginning to wonder if today would follow the trend of the last few, ending with only one or two dogs finding their forever homes. As another family came and went, without a wagging tail following close behind, Daniella slumped back against the doorframe and sighed, trying to expel some of her frustration with the cold breath that appeared in the chilled air before her.

"Still caring too much, after all this time?" Mark asked from his spot behind the counter.

"Always," she said, smiling at his continued allowance of her need for a daily dose of Harry Potter fun.

"Well, everybody got their medicine and food so that's done. Only thing left to do is clean up the big kennel out back, you want to flip for it?"

"What makes you think I, the front desk clerk for the day, am going to help you clean up a kennel that you got messy in the first place with your grand birthday party for Boris here?" Daniella asked as she stepped back around the counter and scratched Boris, their watch poodle, under the chin.

"Because I'm your boss, and I made you front desk clerk for the day," Mark grinned as he pulled out a quarter from the nearby cash register.

Daniella raised her hands in defeat and called heads as the quarter sailed through the air. Just when Mark caught it and flipped it up onto the back of his other hand, the bells above the main door jangled, and they both looked over to see a pleasant looking Indian man enter in from the cold. Mark placed the quarter, unread, on the counter and raised his hand to shake with the man as he approached the counter and removed his gloves. "Welcome to the Animals Welcome Shelter sir, how can we help you today?" Daniella asked in her most chipper demeanor.

"Hello, my name is Arjun Shah. I was wondering if you accept hard to control dogs?"

Mark and Daniella looked at each other. "What do you mean hard to control?" Mark asked.

"Perhaps like from a fighting ring or something?" Daniella added what he would have asked next.

"No, nothing like that," Arjun said, waving his hands as if the suggestion was ignominious. "However, they are quite dangerous; I can no longer control them. They are precious to me, but something has changed them."

"Could they be sick?" Daniella questioned, wondering if perhaps the dogs had gotten mange or some other disease that made them frustrated and their owner crazy. It wouldn't be the first time that someone dropped an animal on their doorstep simply because they didn't want to or couldn't pay the vet bills.

"Perhaps, I am not a doctor, so I do not know what it might be," Arjun said.

"Well, let's have a look and see what's what," Mark offered, but Arjun waved his hands again.

"I appreciate the trouble, but I think I have reached the point that I simply can no longer handle the burden. Is it possible to simply surrender them?" he asked.

Daniella looked over to Mark and could tell he was frustrated at the idea, but he brought out the paperwork just the same. Arjun quickly signed. Leading them out to his car, Arjun waved his hands to silence the dogs that growled from his backseat as they approached. He then asked if they had a cart to carry the two large cages the dogs were held in, saying he was not comfortable in letting them out.

Daniella turned around and quickly walked to the rear of the building to grab their roller cart. Only moments after grabbing the cold handle and cursing about forgetting her gloves, she spun back around when a loud yelp of pain rang out - clearly human. "What happened?" she asked when she got back and saw Arjun holding one of his gloved hands.

"Nothing, I will be fine, it's just my glove," Arjun said, and Daniella figured he had probably been nipped by one of the unhappy dogs that now whimpered over the idea of causing their master pain. "They are just upset and scared. It's nothing."

Arjun then lifted the two cages, each holding a medium sized and rather strange looking dog, onto the cart. He shook Mark's hand again before saying goodbye. Daniella noticed the dogs had moved from whimpering to barking as Arjun climbed into his car, and they were in full yowl by the time the car had rolled to the end of the drive.

"Well, that was definitely the most interesting customer of the day," Mark joked, feeling Arjun clearly won their daily lottery of strange and unusual patrons.

"The day has just begun young grasshopper," Daniella countered.

Mark cracked a broad smile and then helped her push the cart back towards the kennels. As they reached the main gate, Mark's arm crossed over the cages when he reached to unlock it. The dogs immediately jumped up and tried to attack it.

"Well, they're definitely violent. Probably not adoptable without some serious training," Mark said, not really flinching over something that was all too common with dogs when they first crossed through their kennel gates. Usually it was out of fear or stress, but these two seemed to have a genuine desire to tear a chuck out of him.

"You think that's even possible?" Daniella asked as the dogs continued to growl. She grimaced, and then growled back.

Mark pushed the gate opened and made note of the other dogs backing away inside their cages. "Well, it doesn't seem like they're going to make a lot of friends here," he said.

As they looked around to see where to place their newest arrivals, Daniella heard the bells on the front door ring. Someone was waiting for them up front. She looked over at Mark, and he waved her off to go take care of it. She wasn't entirely comfortable leaving him alone with such strange and violent dogs, but she really didn't have a choice in the matter as she heard someone call out from the main waiting room to see if anyone was in the office.

"Coming!" she yelled back and disappeared into the front of the building.

****

"How..."

Blood had mixed with the saliva on their jowls and turned into a frothy, strawberry jelly-like mixture with small bits of ripped flesh and sharp, jagged teeth in between. Two dogs had come in, yet four stood before her now. Daniella couldn't quite manage to comprehend what was happening and whatever she had meant to ask originally was forgotten, replaced with a strong feeling of annoyance towards the man who had gotten them into this mess. "What the heck did he expect us to do with them?" she cried. Her high-pitched yell caused several of the dogs in the kennel to howl, which was in part a welcome change from their continual low growling ever since the two new dogs had entered.

Mark didn't answer her. He was focused so intently on what he was doing that he was almost unaware of her presence. In his large dog wrangler suit, he looked almost twice his size as he attempted to get the four deranged mutts into the large, empty kennel near the end of the strip. He had made the mistake of trying to do too much at once and somehow the original two dogs had gotten out. Somehow, they had started a fight...

Upon hearing the pandemonium, he had grabbed his suit and successfully got the two original mutts into the cage. It was only afterwards that he found the two dogs they had overwhelmed were starting to get up and move around, displaying similar behaviors as the two before. He had been wrestling with the last of the four when Daniella returned to see what all the commotion was about.

"Well, we can't adopt them out, that's for sure," Mark said, finally locking the cage door and falling to the floor a safe distance away.

"But, we can't kill them either!" Daniella's exasperated mood gave out with a sigh and she rubbed her temples as Mark counted all his fingers and toes, making sure he was still in one piece, and that the blood that covered him wasn't his.

"Another option is to let them loose to roam the countryside and start an apocalypse."

Daniella looked at Mark with a face that wanted to be incredulous but only made him laugh. Her jaw hung open, ready to respond but saying nothing, and he imagined the same froth around the dog's mouth on her. It was certainly amusing to him, but he didn't dare tell her about it.

"Be logical," she finally said, trying to avoid the situation in front of her. It was easier for her to believe that it was all some freak magical occurrence rather than something wholly and truly possible in the realm of reality. She mused that they must have been digging up the bones in an Indian burial ground, or chewing on the leg bone of a lynched African, or maybe they had found some tasty meat still attached to the arm bone of some affluent murdered mistress to some upscale New York gentlemen... yes, it had to be something like that. It had to be, the only other option was not even an option at all.

When Mark had finally climbed out of his suit and washed himself off, he took to the Internet and began to look up any information that he could. He later confronted her with the news that at least two different research experiments, one in 1940's Russia and another in 2005 in America, had resulted in zombie dog-ification, but she refused to listen.

"It's not possible..." she stammered.

"Well, what are we going to feed them?" Mark asked, clearly accepting the idea like it was just another day at the office.

"Oh, don't even..." Daniella started. Mark held up his hands in defense and backed away.

After a few moments though, she continued, "You know, this would be a great punishment for all those evil people who abuse animals..."

"What sort of logic is that? We're a no-kill shelter for animals yet somehow humans are expendable?"

"Their bad people," Daniella said in defense. "I think it would be a good plan. Even if they don't get hurt, it sure would scare them straight."

"Sure, just try explaining that to a lawyer."

Daniella looked at him, knowing he was right, but still not wanting to give in. "Why do you always have to be right all the time?" she asked.

"Because I'm the boss," he smiled.

Daniella rolled her eyes, "Funny. Okay, boss, then what do you plan to do about this?"

"Well, isn't the whole point of a zombie that they're already dead? So, it's not like we're killing them right?"

Daniella stared at him, speechless because she hadn't thought about that first. "Besides," Mark continued, "not many people know this, but no-kill shelters can euthanize animals when they are considered 'unadoptable' or 'non-rehabilitatable'. I think this would be the ultimate definition of that."

"So, what? Is that like the death penalty for animals or something?" Daniella asked, not comfortable with the idea.

"Yes, I suppose. And, I know you don't like it, Daniella, but we can't save them all. We save as many as we can and that has to be enough."

"The world won't end if we do this, besides they're already dead anyways," Daniella said, mostly to herself for reassurance. "And, we'd be saving so many more if we stop this nonsense here and now... Okay, fine! Let's send them to their forever home."

****

Jamie, arriving for her weekly volunteering, showed up to an empty office and a quiet kennel. She peered around a few corners and eventually found Mark and Daniella near the back of the cages, cleaning up an unidentifiable mess with strange, red looking water. "What happened?" she asked.

"Zombie dogs," Mark said. Jamie just blinked, confused, unsure if he was joking with her or being serious.

"You know," Daniella said, leaning on the mop handle. "Sometimes animals are just a real pain in the ass."

"Wait, did one bite you?" Mark asked, only partly feigning concern.

"Not funny Mark."

Dedication: While this piece is meant to be both darkly funny and absurd (although still containing bits of truth), it is dedicated to all the hard-luck dogs in the world and the wonderful and dedicated people who spend their time rehabilitating them. A zombie dog might not be able to be saved, but no real dog is beyond redemption.

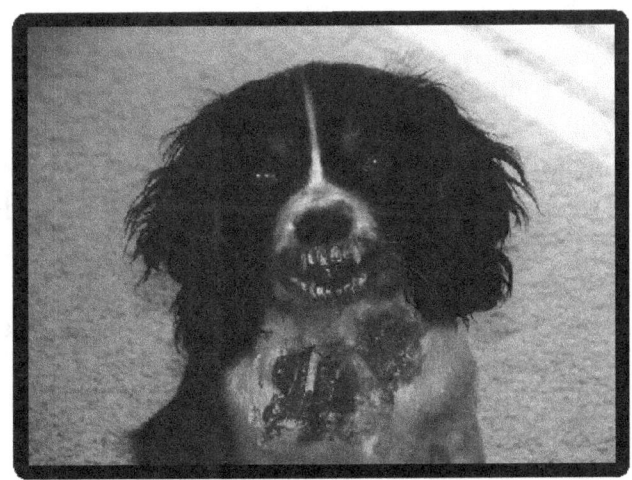

She's No Chloe
Mark Jeross

Our first dog, Kibbitz, is a "pure-bred" Shiba Inu. I put the pure-bred in quotes because for a dog with such lineage, you would never expect that he would be so difficult. In fact when he turned a year old, something snapped in his brain and he became so aggressive that we had to send him away to boot camp for nine weeks. That was the most painful decision we had ever had to make but when the alternative was to have him put down, it became a no-brainer.

When my wife decided that at four years old he "needed" a sibling, I was more than skeptical. I was always resistant to getting a second dog and I would tell her that he would not behave well with another dog in the house. She didn't believe me. However, when she brought home a basset hound puppy it was a disaster, and I felt that the conversation was over. Later that year, after countless hours of combing the Petfinder website, she came across another dog, Chloe, who was housed at the Almost Home Shelter. My wife was determined to try again. She kept threatening to bring home another dog, and she even made a deal with me that if we got another dog, I would not have to buy her a birthday, anniversary, or Chanukah present as long as the dog was alive. That is a hard deal to pass up!!

First, she went to see her at the shelter and took her for a walk around the grounds. Then, the following Sunday, my wife convinced me to come along to meet her and see what I thought. This dog was so timid, and skittish that you could not help but feel sorry for her. She was also a mess. Her fur was long, kind of dirty, she was scrawny, and I told my wife that she is not a Chloe, but more of a Shmutz (which is Yiddish for dirt). We were also told that she had been adopted but the woman returned her as she was too difficult (can you say, "HUGE RED FLAG!"). At this point, I was not too optimistic about her prospects with us.

My wife spoke to our trainer and he gave her some pointers to introduce "Shmutz" to Kibbitz on neutral ground and even how to bring them into the house correctly so that Kibbitz would not feel threatened or be aggressive towards his new sister. After a four-plus hour appointment at the groomers, she looked almost cute enough to keep, but the final decision was going to lie with her "new big brother."

They seemed to hit it off right away, and had a pretty good rapport with one another. It was even comical that on the first day we left them home together, when my wife came to let them out at lunchtime, Shmutz was out of the crate and sitting on the floor in the front hallway. The crate was still locked and there were no signs of escape. It was like the two dogs were in cahoots.

It took quite some time (about six months) for Shmutz to figure out how to play with toys (the noises scared her initially). Feeding time was also a challenge. We had to figure out how to get her to eat without her feeling intimidated by her brother. She loves to eat, and has put on quite a few pounds, but she is not fat, so says her mother.

Shmutz has a "caregiver" quality about her. One Sunday when we were getting ready to leave for a party, we noticed that she was incessantly licking her brother's eye. It turned out that he had an eye infection and she was trying to make him feel better. Also, one day at daycare, my wife noticed that she was lying next to another dog who was crated (she had just had surgery, but couldn't stay home). The person at daycare explained that the dog in the crate was one of Shmutz's best friends and she had just had surgery so she couldn't play, so Shmutz just laid next to her to keep her company.

Our two dogs may be complete opposites, but they do complement each other in many ways. Where Kibbitz will walk around puddles on rainy days, Shmutz will splash right through them without a care! Don't think that you can pet Kibbitz without Shmutz bullying her way into the fray for attention. Every night before we go to sleep, we watch television in bed. Shmutz decided that time is her cue for "daddy-daughter" time. She jumps on the bed and lays on me while I pet her. When I tell her it is time to go to sleep, she gets up without hesitation and goes to her bed.

Thinking of all the dogs in area shelters that are stuck without a home, it is really difficult to not to feel sympathy and a responsibility towards these innocent animals. I realize that we did a nice thing by bringing Shmutz home and giving her a stable home environment and she has a pretty good life with people and other dogs who love her. It is so important to give these animals good homes. They pay you back tenfold in love, devotion, and companionship.

Shining Starr
Shelly Migora

I lost my dog Lucky on January 28, 2011. It was the worst day of my life. After many strokes and seizures, we had to send our baby to the Rainbow Bridge. He was seventeen years old. I vowed to never own another dog again because the pain of losing a fur baby was just too much to bear. I couldn't go through the heartbreak.

Even though I said I could never own another dog, I would find myself perusing animal rescue sites. Deep in my heart, I longed for the love and companionship of another dog. I absolutely adore dogs and really wanted one again someday. One cold winter afternoon, on February 28, 2011, one month after my Lucky passed, I came across Petfinder.com. I saw a picture of this little white, fluffy dog named Muffincake. He was a terrier mix. There was something so special about this little ball of fluff. I thought he was absolutely adorable, but there was something else about him. I couldn't see his whole face, but in the picture, someone was petting him and he was looking back at his tail. I found out Muffincake was located at Almost Home-No Kill Shelter. I knew I had to meet him, but I was also scared. I was scared that I would have to go through the pain and suffering of knowing eventually something bad could happen to this dog and it would be unbearable yet again.

So, I did it! I went to Almost Home with my mom. I did not call before I went there, so I wasn't sure that Muffincake would even be there. I thought maybe he was in a foster home and I may lose my chance to meet him. Almost Home had some information about Muffincake's past. They informed me that he was a stray and he was taken to a high kill shelter. Almost Home saved him and he went to a foster home for a couple of weeks. I can't imagine my sweet boy being on the street with no food to eat. I can't even bear the thought of what would have happened if Almost Home did not save him!

I was so anxious to meet this precious angel. They brought him out of his kennel and into the lobby to greet us. As tears rolled down my face, I knew he was the one. He reminded me of my Lucky, as he was cream and white just like him. He was so excited and jumping for joy and I looked into his big, beautiful, brown, copper eyes and said, "This is my dog!" I brought him home that day to meet my husband and we decided to change his name to Ringo Starr!

Ringo has brought us so much love and joy to our family. He is the best dog in the world. I can't imagine our lives without him. Not only did I rescue him, but he rescued me. One has to continue to love or one cannot be loved. I am so glad that I opened my heart to this homeless animal. Also, I am so glad that I decided to love again. If I never rescued him, I wouldn't know the joy that he has brought us.

I am so excited to go on this journey with Ringo. He has a spunky, fun and gentle demeanor. He enjoys plenty of walks with Grandma and me, jogging with his Dad, playing fetch, chasing birds and squirrels, playing with his dog pals and most of all, snuggling with his Mom, Dad, Grandma and Grandpa. We love our Ringo Starr to pieces!!!

Please rescue, donate or foster an animal. Don't shop, adopt!!!! They will love you for it!!!

Thank you Almost Home for saving our boy and for all you do for homeless animals!!!

Simba
Courtney Theisen

Four years ago I talked with my mom about wanting to adopt a dog. At the time we already had two dogs, Roxy and Remy, but they belonged to Allison, my older sister. At that time, I had been following online this shelter called Last Days Dog Rescue and really wanted to adopt a dog. So my parents and I talked about it and they told me I could adopt. The dog I chose was a lab mix named Simba. He was brought to our house on a Sunday evening by a rescuer/transporter who was bringing him from a high-kill shelter in Ohio. Because he had no tags and was not an owner surrender, he was set to be euthanized on Tuesday. When she brought him in and we had a meet and greet with him, he started to sniff around the house and something in his behavior made her (the rescuer) say to us, "I think he knows you saved his life."

We started to adjust to life with Simba, Roxy, and Remy. It was going to take some getting used to. The dogs were finding their way around each other.

One day my mom was cleaning the glass on the coffee table in our front room and noticed there were small dry water splotches all over the top of it. She cleaned it off and at dinner that night, mentioned it. Little did she know that Simba was using the coffee table as a bed; for some reason that table was a comfort to him. At that point, I started corralling him at night and bringing him up to my room where he would sleep in my bed. He is a very gentle soul that loves to have belly rubs.

I am a nurse working midnights and when I'm having a bad night, I come home and snuggle next to my dog. He is my best friend. When I move out in the spring Simba will be coming with me. My parents will be very sad but; they know he is my dog and I wouldn't want to be without him. I told my mom, "everyone says I've saved a dog from a shelter; but in reality; he's saved me."

Some Animals Are More Equal Than Others
Michael Kitchen

Trevor Aldabra stood outside his office. "Ginger," he said to his secretary who sat at her desk in the lobby behind him, "What is this dog doing in my office?"

"What dog?" she said. The young woman rose from her chair and approached.

"THAT dog," he said pointing.

"There's nothing there, Trevor." He looked. She was right.

"I could swear..." They entered his office together. He made his way around the space between the thick mahogany desk and the wall of bookshelves heavy with legal tomes, looking between it and the window to locate the hiding animal. Ginger circled the front of the desk.

"What kind of dog was it?" she said.

"A large mutt of some sort," he said. "All white, furry, with long legs and short ears."

"Did you have your coffee this morning?" she asked. He looked at her with raised eyebrow. "There he is!" he said, pointing towards the doorway. "He got by us and ran into the lobby." Aldabra strode out the door, Ginger close behind. There was no escape from the small lobby. The front door was closed and the animal was not small so it wouldn't be able to hide beneath the chairs. Scanning the room he found only himself and his secretary.

"You saw it, didn't you?" he asked. She shook her head. He folded his arms, frustrated. He knew what he saw.

"Maybe it's one of your special friends," Ginger said. Her back was to the window, which overlooked the parking lot from their fourth floor office. Movement beyond the window pane caught his eye.

"You may be right. Do I have any appointments this morning?" he asked, looking beyond her. Ginger started to turn to see what captured his attention, but he held his hand up for her not to move.

"Mrs. Sanderson has a ten o'clock about her will, Mr. Johnson an eleven o'clock about his divorce, and you have to be in court for an arraignment of Mr. Boynton in the afternoon."

"I'll be right back," he said. He grabbed his long black coat and maroon scarf. "If I'm late for Sanderson and Johnson, tell them an emergency came up."

****

Aldabra drove, but it wasn't far enough to get the interior of his car warm. The dog revealed itself to him for brief moments, long enough to get his attention and far enough ahead of him on the road that Aldabra easily followed. He passed through the gates of Memorial Gardens Cemetery and wound through the curvy cement path of the grounds. He slowed the vehicle. The dog sat beside a gravestone. Aldabra exited his car and approached the burial site, his black dress shoes scrunching the wet orange and red leaves. The shiny granite gravestone reflected the morning sun. He created a visor with his hand and read:

Muriel Capra
January 12, 1970 - November 15, 2013

Just last week, Aldabra thought reviewing the date at the end of the dash.

"Tragic, isn't?" He turned his head to see the woman standing next to him. "Was she someone you knew?" An attractive woman in her forties, adorned in a navy blue dress looked at him with a frown on her face. Her long dark hair unmoved by the autumn breeze. He looked down at her bare feet and noticed nature's debris beneath them undisturbed.

"No. Did you?"

"I don't know. I'm really not sure who I am."

"Do you know the dog?"

"What dog?"

He nodded in the direction over her shoulder and she turned her head. The dog sat next to a wreath mounted on a wire frame a few yards behind.

"Snowball!" she said and squat. The dog came running, tail wagging. "It has been a long time since I've seen you, boy."

"How long?"

"Oh, a few months. Snowball died and..." Her demeanor changed and she rose. She looked at him. "If he's dead, then I'm..." Aldabra nodded. "Then you must be..."

"Trevor Aldabra."

"Trevor Aldabra," she said. "I was told I should seek you out."

"Snowball led me to you. Let's talk, shall we?"

****

Aldabra parked in the street in front of the home in Farmington Hills. He ascended the steps of the porch, pulled open the screen door and knocked. The hard wood front door refused to give with each wrap of his black glove-covered fist.

"Who are you?" the woman said standing in the entranceway. Her tall muscular presence made him step back.

"My name is Trevor Aldabra. Are you Helen Napoleon?"

"What of it?"

"Ms. Napoleon, a friend of yours indicated that you could use my assistance."

"What do you do, Trevor Aldabra?"

"I'm an attorney." She folded her muscularly defined arms in front of her. She was dressed in a t-shirt and sweatpants despite the chill. "What do I need an attorney for? And who sent you?"

"I've been told that you have a couple of issues. First, that your friend, Muriel Capra, lost her life suddenly, and the prosecutor's investigation is targeting you as a suspect."

"What? I told that needle-nosed man that I could have been killed too, but Muriel insisted in getting in the blind, first."

"Indeed," Aldabra said. "Nonetheless, we need to talk this through, so you'll be prepared for the police when they come to make an arrest."

"Oh, I'm prepared for the police," she said. "The question is will they be prepared for me?" Her smile was one welcoming a battle.

"Or, through conversation and evidence, I can show why you should not be a suspect in Muriel's death, so the police never have to arrive."

"You are beginning to bore me, Trevor Aldabra. Who's the wise ass that sent you to me?"

Aldabra looked into the desert brown eyes of the woman. He braced himself for her response.

"Your friend for forever and a day."

Her eyes widened. "Why did you say that?"

"Muriel led me to you. She shared that with me."

"How could you..."

"May I come in so that we may talk?"

Helen Napoleon stared at him. She took a deep breath. She stepped back from the doorway and he walked past her into the house.

The main room was decorated in dark wood and hunter green. A fireplace filled the room with warmth and the sound of crackling wood. Mounted on the wall above the mantel was the bust of a buck with a fourteen-point rack.

"Have a seat, Trevor Aldabra. Would you like something to drink?"

"Some water would be fine," he said. He took off his gloves, scarf and coat. "And you can call me Trevor."

"You look like a man who can handle more than water, Trevor. A beer perhaps? Our bar is well stocked."

"A beer is fine," he said. He sat in a leather recliner, leaving the footrest down. She returned with a can and popped it open.

"Here you go," she said handing the cold aluminum container to him. "You can call me Hel." She sat at the end of a couch next to an end table. A beer can sat on a cork coaster. She picked it up and took a long swallow then looked at him. "So how did you know Muriel?"

"To be honest with you, Helen, she sought me out."

"When?"

"Yesterday morning."

Helen coughed. She stared at him fiercely. "What are you trying to pull, Trevor."

"I'm not trying to pull anything. She came to me because she thought you were in trouble both with the nature of her death and with her family."

"What do you know about her family?"

"I know that they want to take possession of all her things, including everything you two shared... like this house."

"How do you know this?"

"It is difficult to explain, Helen, but people, or spirits, are referred to me to handle legal issues."

"Are you like one of those flaky mediums I've seen on TV that ghosts talk to?"

"I know it is hard to believe, but spirits will present themselves to me. Muriel is concerned about you."

Helen sat back on the couch and put her hand to her mouth. She took a couple slow breaths, closed her eyes. He sensed that her soul absorbed his every word. She took another drink of her beer then asked, "What do you need to know?"

"Let's start with what happened that day."

"We were at The Pointer Lodge and Hunting Club, northeast of Frankenmuth, for the opening of deer season. There are twenty of us in the club. Muriel wasn't a member but they allow for spouses to stay there as well. There are five cabins and a lodge that has twenty single rooms. Muriel and I rented a cabin. I'm fourth in seniority in the club, which gives me priority in renting a cabin or room in the lodge.

"Muriel and I woke up early, before everyone else, and went to our blind. There are about forty blinds scattered about the couple hundred acres of land the club owns. The day before, we secured the one we always use, stocking it with provisions for the day. I was in it, getting things organized while she was out taking pictures with her camera. When we got to the blind the day of the hunt, she wanted to go in first. It was moments before sunrise, and the opening faced east. She wanted to capture a photo of the sunrise as it came over the clearing. She climbed the ladder and entered. The next thing I heard was the loud explosion over my head, and the rain of wood that descended upon me. Bits of Muriel amongst it."

Aldabra sipped his beer. "Then what did you do?"

"I called the lodge to have them call the police. Ian was going to ring every room in the place to warn them of what happened, but the blast was loud enough that the other hunters were awakened by it."

"How long have you known Muriel?"

"Almost a decade. It was love at first sight. I worked at a fitness center, and she was this bubbly little brunette that was clueless around the machines. I familiarized her with the facility. I was astonished and flattered. She kept coming back during my hours, and she made the first move."

"Obviously, you have nothing to gain by killing her. There is no motive here, unless there is an insurance policy you'll be collecting on."

"None."

Aldabra sipped his beer. "So who would have reason to kill her? What did she do for a living?"

"She was part-owner of a shelter in Detroit."

"Women's shelter?"

"No. Animal shelter. They don't believe in killing and help abandoned or abused animals find homes or live out their lives."

"And she would deer hunt with you?"

"No. She would go, but she would hunt with her camera. It was a little competition we had. She'd shoot photos and I'd shoot bullets. Whoever 'shot' the most won. I'd bag my first kill then stop. It would provide enough venison to last me several months. She was vegan, so I didn't have to share. But it was amazing to see how many different deer she shot with her camera each time. Where I'd kill a single deer, she'd have photographed six or seven that were within view of her camera from the blind."

"What kind of camera?"

"I don't know. It's a digital, I know that much. I shoot with guns."

"Do you still have it?"

She shook her head. "Blown to bits."

Aldabra looked at the buck mounted above the mantel. "Did you kill that one?"

"Yes," Helen said. "I have more trophies in the basement. When we bought this house, I made the payments but her name is on the title because her credit rating was better which got us a better interest rate. She wouldn't have my trophies on the main floor, except this one because it is so beautiful."

"But dead nonetheless," he said. "Let me see if I understand this. Muriel was a vegan who worked at a no-kill shelter for animals. Yet she lived with you, a carnivorous woman who hunted and killed animals for sport. Some animals are more equal than others, eh?"

"It is against our nature, Trevor, to not kill animals and consume them. We have canine teeth which predisposes us to the eating of meat."

"That was not her belief, though. I am amazed that you two were able to live together for so long with that fundamental difference."

"We did more than live together, Trevor. We were married."

"And that's what your second problem is," he said. "The house is in Muriel's name. Her parents and more importantly, the State of Michigan does not recognize you as her spouse."

****

"You know, it's probably not a good idea bringing me," Ginger said. "I love animals."

"I need your intuition. Someone rigged the blind to blow up and kill either Muriel, Helen, or both."

"Well, I hope all the animals are ugly so I don't want one or two or five," she said.

They entered the building, greeted by a symphony of barking and squawking. A young woman sat behind a desk, talking on the telephone, with a tabby in her lap. She held up a finger and mouthed the words 'I'll be with you in one moment.' They walked over to a cage containing a white cockatiel. Ginger touched the cage. The bird barked.

"Okay," Ginger said. "I won't disturb your home, Fido."

"Can I help you?" the woman asked, drawing their attention.

"Yes. We're here to see Eve Major."

"I'm Eve," she said.

"I'm Trevor Aldabra. This is my assistant Ginger Desjardins."

"Pleased to meet you."

"That's a nice cat," Ginger said.

"Max? He's had a hard life. An animal hoarder had him amongst two dozen other cats in an eight hundred square foot apartment. It was pretty nasty. Some of the poor creatures were put down before we could get to them."

"Do you only take in dogs and cats?" Ginger asked.

"And birds that think they're dogs?" Aldabra said.

"We take in all animals. Would you like to see?"

"Can we?" Ginger directed her question to Aldabra. He nodded.

Eve led them through a door taking them to the back. Along the left side were small pens for cats and small dogs. To the right were tanks housing hamsters and guinea pigs; lizards and tortoises. A string of bird cages lined the back. It looked like a pet store.

"What brings you to see me, Mr. Aldabra? Are you seeking to adopt one of our friends? We have some large dogs in the kennel out back."

"Is that where Snowball was?"

Eve stepped back. "How do you know Snowball?"

"He was Muriel's dog, right?"

"Yes," she said.

"How did Snowball end up here?"

"Snowball was an Argentine Mastiff. He was trained by the Macomb County Sheriff to be a bomb-sniffing dog, however after a couple years of false positives they decided to get rid of him. One of our volunteers' cousin works at the county jail and heard about the dog. Because of the false hits, no one really liked him, so he ended up here. Muriel fell in love with him, and took him in for herself. He died back in April."

"Ms. Major, I'm an attorney. My client is concerned about her spouse and has retained me to help her."

"How can I help?"

"My client was the owner of this establishment and suggested I talk to you."

"Mr. Aldabra, I don't know who you've been talking to. I'm the owner of this shelter."

"Today, that is correct. Prior to Muriel Capra's death, you were only a co-owner."

"Are you saying that Muriel's your client?" He nodded. "That's ludicrous. She died a couple weeks ago."

"Eve," Aldabra said. "One thing Muriel asked me to check on was whether Daisy's heart surgery was successful and if Boris and Natasha were getting along."

Eve stared at him. Only the humans were silent. She walked to a cage occupied by three long-haired dachshunds. "That's Daisy," she pointed to the only one laying on a dog matt. "It was touch and go, but she's recovering." Eve then walked over to the encased cages. There were two tortoises in separate aquariums. "Boris was still biting Natasha. Even punctured her left front leg. I've tried to put them back together, but he keeps attacking her. Then, we had this new tortoise come in just the other day. It belonged to an older man who passed, and his children didn't want to care for the tortoise. They think he's about fifteen years old. I haven't named him yet, and I haven't decided if I can keep him with either Natasha or Boris."

"He looks sweet," Ginger said. "What kind of tortoises are these?"

"Russian. So how can I help Muriel?"

"It's Muriel's spouse, Helen, that she's concerned about," Aldabra said. "The police are looking at her as a possible murder suspect in Muriel's death."

"I wouldn't be surprised," Eve said. "The woman kills everything."

"We're not sure she's guilty. Neither is Muriel and that's why she contacted me."

"Are you a vegan?" Ginger asked.

"Yes," Eve said. "That's how Muriel and I first met. We worked at a vegetarian cafe. She came into some money when her grandmother died and wanted to open a no-kill shelter. We went in together on it. But how she fell in with that carnivore I'll never know."

"Were you in love with Muriel?" Aldabra asked.

"No. I don't swing that way. My boyfriend and I have lived together for about five years now. There's no common law marriage in Michigan, is there Mr. Aldabra?"

"No," he said. "So you saw Muriel every day?"

"I saw her more than Rambitch did," she said.

"Did she have any enemies?"

"Muriel? Heavens no. Everyone loved her. All the animals loved her. It was the saddest day in this community when she died. Even some of the animals here expressed grief. Animals know these things. There were so many vegans at her funeral that there were two separate post-funeral meals - one for the carnivores and one for us."

"You don't think it's a denial of man's nature as a carnivore with canine teeth to hunt and eat wild animals?"

"Mr. Aldabra. We are human beings, not animals. We have a consciousness. Has any animal composed a symphony? Written a novel? Invented a transportation vehicle? Performed surgery on another of its kind to save its life? With a higher consciousness, we are above base animal instincts. We have the intelligence and consciousness to develop a diet that is free from killing animals"

"I agree," Ginger said. They both looked at her. "What? Didn't you know I was vegan?"

"The only person that might have a motive would be that Rambitch she lived with. Maybe there was a lover's spat. Maybe she was tired of Muriel and had another lover on the side. A carnivore. I don't know. If the police think Muriel was murdered, that bitch should be their number one suspect."

****

"Sorry, we're temporarily closed," the portly senior citizen wearing an orange hunter's jacket said. Aldabra and Ginger had not yet reached the clubhouse. He was walking towards them, a rifle resting against his shoulder.

"Are you Mr. Pilkington?" Aldabra said.

"I am. And I said we are closed. No hunting here for a while."

"That's what I'm here to talk to you about," Aldabra said. He introduced himself and Ginger. "I'm here on behalf of Helen Napoleon."

"Has she been charged?"

"Not yet. But I have some questions and would like to see the site, if I may. If she is charged, I will be defending her."

"Let's go in the lodge. It's warmer there."

They went inside the large building. A fire was crackling in the lobby's fireplace. "Get ya something to warm up? A coffee? Hot chocolate? Something a mite bit stronger?"

"A hot chocolate sounds good, Mr. Pilkington," Aldabra said.

"Make that two," Ginger added.

"Call me Ian. Marshmallows?" They both nodded. "Have a seat and I'll be right back." Within minutes, Aldabra and Ginger were warming their hands and insides with mugs topped with frothy melting marshmallows.

"Damn shame about Muriel," Ian said. "Lovely woman."

"Do you think Helen had something to do with it?"

"Hell no. Helen's a very good hunter. And she loved Muriel. You could see it."

"How long have you known Helen?"

"Oh Jesus. She's been a member of the club for years. She'd come as a kid, with her father, God rest his soul. A fine hunter he was."

"What do you think happened?"

"Haven't got a clue. After the blind exploded, I closed the lodge down. No hunting. No one, 'cept the cops that went out in the field."

"Has anyone been to any of the other blinds?"

"Well..." Ian squirmed in the leather chair he sat in. "I wasn't about to let the season go without getting out there. I've been in a couple of blinds and nothing happened to me."

"Were they in proximity to the one Muriel was in?"

"Heavens no. They were to the south of the lodge. I went west. I always find deer on the western acreage."

"Can you take us to where Muriel died?"

"Sure. We've got time before it gets dark. But bundle up. It's getting darn right chilly out there."

Ian Pilkington led them through the woods south of the lodge. Fifteen minutes of walking, they came upon the splinters of the blind in a clearing.

"There she is," Ian said. "What a bloody mess, eh?"

Yellow caution tape encircled a mass of splintered wood and charred ground. Aldabra looked in the field. He could see Snowball standing and panting.

"Let's go that way."

For the five minute walk it was to the next blind, Snowball appeared briefly ahead of them along the way. Only Aldabra saw him. The dog appeared briefly near a standing blind. "Let's check this one out," Aldabra said. Snowball was barking viciously at it. Ian and Ginger approached it, not hearing the dog's warning.

"Wait!" Aldabra called out. "Don't go in it!" They stopped and he cautiously approached. He looked up inside it. Snowball appeared standing within, blocking entry, his attention facing the corner. Aldabra scanned the opening and the ladder leading up. "Ginger, call 911 and request the bomb squad. I think there's something dangerous inside this blind."

****

"No shit," Helen said. "Thank you for getting me off the hook."

Aldabra sat across from her, in the chair he sat in on his first visit to her home. "That's what Muriel wanted. But that doesn't address who would rig five of the blinds with dynamite."

"That's how many they found?"

He nodded. "And the police took their time and examined every one of them. Good or bad, it's lucky that only one was detonated. If all the hunters had gone out together, there could have been more killed. I'm trying to think about who would do such a thing. Did anyone have a gripe with the lodge, in general, or Ian Pilkington, specifically?"

"The lodge is private, so if anyone had a gripe with it, we'd have a good idea who it would be. But no one I know has. And everyone likes Ian."

"There are those enviro-animal rights societies that use terrorism to free animals being experimented on. They've taken on puppy mills, cosmetic firms, and universities. I suppose they'd target hunters, but it would be the first I've heard of it."

"You said I could help," she said, sipping her coffee. "How so?"

"Muriel's camera."

"Blown to bits."

"Yes. But I thought about it and wondered about what you said. The day before she was taking photos. Would she have downloaded the photos from the camera onto her computer, and start the next day with a clean memory?"

"Maybe. Come to think of it, I remember her doing that at the cabin at night. She showed me some of the photos she took that day."

"Where is her computer?"

"Upstairs in the office." Helen led him up the stairs in what was the house's second bedroom. They had converted it into an office with book shelves, a dented grey filing cabinet, and a desk. Atop the desk rest a laptop computer and printer. There were animals mounted on the walls in the room, however they were images matted in oak frames. Helen sat down at the desk and fired up the computer.

"Is that Muriel?" Aldabra asked, pointing to a photo on the desk.

"Yeah. That's her and Eve when they opened the shelter."

"That's Eve? Didn't recognize her wearing that cap and hoody."

"It was a cold day. Muriel's cheeks were not normally that red." The login display appeared on the screen. Two separate icons appeared. "Muriel was the computer geek. She had this set up where we could both operate the computer, but had divided access so that she had her personal space and I had mine."

"Why was that?"

"When she wasn't rescuing animals, she was writing about them. She had also kept a computer journal for years and wanted it to remain private."

"I won't look at the journal," Aldabra said. "I'm only interested in the photos."

"Why not? Maybe it will have a clue to her killer."

"Her death was a random act. She was not a target. The hunters or the lodge was the target."

"Oh." Helen stared at the screen. "It requires her password, and I don't know it. I don't suppose..."

"Snowball2003," he said.

Helen transcribed then tapped the enter key. She looked up at him. "Do I want to know how you knew that?" Aldabra remained silent. She returned her attention to the computer and found the file containing her photos. She found the folder containing the photos from the day before Muriel's death and opened the first photo. It covered the screen. She rose from the chair. "Here, I'll let you drive."

Aldabra slowly clicked through the photos, examining every pixel of them. At a photo well in the middle of the file he stopped. He advanced through the next three or four, and then backtracked to the photo.

"Do you see anything here?" he asked Helen. She leaned over his shoulder and squinted at the screen. "On the edge of the woods."

"It looks like trees to me... no, wait. There's something odd sticking from that tree."

"Let me zoom in. There. It's a bit fuzzy."

"It's definitely something."

"And as you'll see, it's not in any of the photos taken in the same general area in the preceding or following shots."

"What is that?"

"I have an idea. But there's something else. What's the status of the Muriel's property?"

Helen sighed. "Her parents are taking it to probate and gave me an eviction notice. I've got thirty days to find a new home."

"Are you prepared to fight it?"

"What's to fight? My name's not on the house."

"What if I said you have a strong case for keeping the house?"

"In this State? Are you kidding me? Look, if you need the work to cover your annual dues at the country club, I'm not going to be that client. I'm a fighter. But I also know when I'm beat."

Aldabra looked up at her and smiled. "What if you have a weapon?" She scrunched her nose in disgust. "Where is her key ring?"

Helen left the room. He continued through the photos. A metal ring of a half dozen keys crashed on the desk next to him. He picked the ring up, located the car key with its thick black cover and buttons which unlocked its doors. He held up the first key next to it. "What is this key for?"

"That's the house key," she said. He then singled out the key on the other side of the car key and held it up. "I don't know. Maybe one of the keys for the cages at the shelter."

"You need to take this key to the bank where you have your joint checking account with Muriel, and use that to access the free safety deposit box the two of you share. Your weapon is in there."

****

Aldabra sat at his desk in his office. The door was closed and he had just ended a phone call with the prosecutor. He had assured her that he was not retained by Eve Major, and to do so would be a conflict of interest.

There was a knock at the door and he verbally granted entry. Ginger peered from behind the open door. "How's it going?"

"Good." He raised his eyebrow. "Is everything okay with you?"

"Oh. Of course! I was just checking in to see if you need anything."

"No. I'm good. Helen hasn't arrived yet, has she?"

"No. But you stay put and I'll give you a call when she does."

Ginger closed the door behind her. Aldabra sat back in his chair, wondering why his secretary was acting a little weirder than some of his clients. He opened a document on his computer - a brief he was working on to dismiss charges against a young man charged with drug possession while being a passenger in another's car. The phone rang on his desk. He answered it, hung up, and then waited.

"Hello Helen," he said, standing. "Have a seat."

"I don't know how you did that," she said. It was the first time he saw her subdued.

"I didn't do anything. It was all Muriel and Snowball."

"I still can't believe it. Eve Major, Muriel's best friend. I was shocked to hear that."

"I know. Apparently she is a member of LEAP."

"What's LEAP?"

"Liberators of Environmental and Animal Prisoners."

"Never heard of them."

"Not a lot of people have. It's a small group of radical environment defenders and animal rights activists that take direct action - mostly illegal and destructive - against those that they deem enemies of the planet."

Helen sighed. "So, the half-owner of a no-kill shelter killed her partner. Some animals are more equal than others, eh?"

Aldabra chuckled. "Well, to be fair, she wasn't trying to kill anyone. Just damage the blinds to prevent the killing of animals. The glitch was that she didn't set the timer on the explosives properly, and it was the contact Muriel made with the bomb that detonated it."

"So what happens to the shelter?"

"I've had my clerk, Ginger, working on that. She's been in contact with other no-kill shelters, finding homes for the animals."

"That's sweet."

"Did you bring the contents of the safety deposit box?"

Helen opened her purse and withdrew an envelope. Aldabra had two copies of the retainer agreement out and ready for her. "What should we do first?"

"Let me look at what you've got. If it meets all the requirements, this should be an easy case and we'll go over the retainer agreement. If it doesn't, then I'll have to assess whether we have a case or not."

He looked over the document. "Very good," he said. "This meets all the requirements of a legal will. A will that turns all of Muriel's possessions over to you."

Helen smiled with a tear leaking from her eye. They went over the retainer agreement, signed them, and she wrote a check.

"I can't believe this is really happening," Helen said rising to her feet. "Muriel was always prepared. For everything. I wish I had been a better spouse to her."

"That was the final thing," Aldabra said. "She wanted me to tell you that you're the best, and Tally Ho!" Tears burst the damn Helen had been fortifying. Aldabra's muscles tightened.

"Unbelievable," she said, regaining control. "Tally Ho!, eh? That was our code. We'd say that whenever there was some obstacle or something bad that happened and we needed to remember to carry on despite it."

****

Aldabra exited his office and looked at his redesigned lobby. "What is this?"

"I thought I'd just change things up," Ginger said. "Do you like?"

Aldabra walked over to the new aquarium set up against the near wall, opposite the guest chairs. He opened the lid, reached in and lifted the creature that resided within.

"And who is this?" He supported the tortoise's underbelly, and rubbed the top of the shell, trying to coax the critter retracted within.

"I'm naming him Trevor Junior," she said. "You know that Aldabra is a species of tortoise."

"No, I didn't."

"Big tortoises. No way could we keep one here. But a little guy like this? Can we keep him?"

"Couldn't find a home for him, eh?" She shook her head. "I suppose."

"Awesome," Ginger said. The phone rang and she stepped over to the desk to answer it. Aldabra put the tortoise back in its home and closed the lid. He looked towards the corner and saw the apparition of Snowball. The dog sat, his mouth open, panting.

"This is your doing, isn't it," Aldabra said. Panting, Snowball's head bobbed. The dog slowly vanished.

Spot
Hal O'Leary

All fathers love their sons a lot.
I'm no exception. No I'm not.
And when he was a little tot,
My good son Sean, or so I thought,
Would be of ties, a real ascot.
I beamed with all the joy he brought,
For he was everything I'd sought
To be the genius I was not.
Although in math he wasn't hot,
He showed that language was his slot.
At six, he read of Camelot,
And of his hero Lancelot.

So as reward for this I bought
A beagle pup for his mascot,
And he should name him, should he not?
I told him just to take a shot.
I knew it as I watched him squat
And knowing that his mind was fraught
With names like Good Sir Lancelot,
For the exotic he would opt.
I waited wondering just what.

But then I trembled, quite distraught,
When looking up, the little snot
Said, Dad, I know, I'll call him...SPOT.

So, Spot it was, and what it brought
Was one good lesson I'd been taught.
At first I thought, What hath God Wrought?
It wasn't quite what I had sought,

But Sean was six and I was not.
I was the one who had been caught
In what I knew was naught but rot.
For when I'd had a second thought,
Of course, with Sean, it should be Spot.

Through thirteen years, the two would trot,
And watching him, from just a tot,
Grow to a man, the man I sought.
I realized from all we got,
How much of it we owed to Spot.

Stray
Samuel K. Wilkes

The intoxicating smell of a Sweetgum tree filled my nostrils. I remember thinking, if *only I could chew on that smell all day, but something so right would probably kill me.* I still tried to make the tree mine.

"Back off! Outta my yard!" Mallory barked from his porch.

"Oh, hush," I huffed under my breath. "Keep your Sweetgum, I can find another."

Squirrels! Squirrels were everywhere, sprinting in the yards, cracking acorns, their bushy tails twitching on the trees; taunting me because I cannot climb. Not like Cleo—my old roommate—she was light on her feet, flying up trunks and branches as if the large oaks were her second home.

I needed a second home. I needed a first home. But then again, I was just recently freed and off the grid. No identification, no parents, no tether held me back. There was only one downside to such freedom—continuously avoiding a return to that concrete hell of death row; the cold bars, the cold floor, the echoing cries and shouts of others, the mysterious back room.

I couldn't go back, I wouldn't go back, I repeated like a mantra in my head.

Then a slight breeze off the bay sent the familiar smell of Ada my way. I pictured her long blonde hair and shapely behind. I quickly realized why: her house sat a block from where I stood. I knew there was a reason for taking this route; as if by instinct and fate, the unseen workings of the world were pulling me in her direction. Thoughts of that cold cage and cumbersome muzzle left my mind. I only pictured Ada now, sitting on her back porch amongst the sounds of the bay lapping against the shore; her lust filled thoughts transmitting through the ether, wondering where I went that last time I inexplicably disappeared.

"Oh Ada, it wasn't my fault. It was the man! I'm coming now!"

"Watch it, pretty boy!" a black pussy hissed from her driveway.

"I don't want you! It's Ada I seek! You know Ada?"

"Best believe I'm watching you, boy," she leaned her back against the car.

I ran away from the pussy towards Ada, past the houses, my mouth open to the elements, my tongue flapping like a love-sick fool. Squirrels darted from my path like birds taking to the wind, but I knew I mustn't stray from my mission. And there it was: the white brick house with the black door. I checked the markings on the large oak in the front yard—yes, it was still mine.

"Ada!"

I wondered if she still waited in the back yard for me. I then saw her roommate in the window holding something black to her ear.

"Ada!"

Her roommate pointed in my direction. *She must be telling Ada I'm here,* I naively thought. The same romantic narrative ran through my head like last time: the bad boy from the block had broken free from prison and was returning to see his bitch; we will chase the wind and I will mount her.

Just then a white van pulled into the driveway with black and white markings that seemed familiar.

Is that Ada's? I turned in my head, knowing I had seen that van before.

Almost simultaneously, Ada's roommate opened the front door of the house. She looked at the van in the driveway and pointed to me.

"Yes, it's me! Please tell Ada I've returned," I yelled as I circled in place.

The man from the van approached slowly and grabbed my neck, "Let's see ol' boy, you got any identification on you."

It all seemed eerily familiar. And now I know why. That was my last day on the outside. I tell myself this story so that next time I break free I will not forget and lose focus. Next time I will not go astray. Bitches provide nothing but a distraction.

Telltale
Ruth Sabath Rosenthal

Up-
right,
it wags
side to side.
Life's fine
where a good
master abides.
Earlier, barks
emerged from
its opposite end.
It hung, prompting
the giving of a
tasty tidbit,
guaranteed
to pop it up
swinging
(an expression
of gladness
like singing),
its position ruled
by disposition,
lows & highs
dependent on
attention paid to
the whines & whims
of the particular canine.
Play & bellyfuls of
kibbles & love
keep it wagging
& make for a dog-
gone good life.
So, on behalf
of canines, far
and wide, please
don't' fail to
heed this
(not) far-
fetched
tale

The Canine And The Cans
Mark Hudson

Keith Sanderson got his pet
and to this day he has no regret.
Sanderson had a stroke and cancer,
but getting his dog Max was the answer.
He went to the kennel with his wife,
at a very sad point of his life.
Cats were being viewed by his daughter,
but he saw a dog that made his eyes water.
He saw a black lab, sad and alone,
and he knew he needed a happy home.
He filled out the adoption forms
at the shelter, Orphans of the Storm.
He wanted to keep the dog strong,
so he'd go for walks and take Max along.
Soon, Max the dog retrieved recyclables
and suddenly, he'd become very likable!
He became a hero as a recycling dog,
clearing the path for people who jog.
Bottles and cans were recycled because
Max the pooch simply does what he does.
Americans spend billions cleaning up trash,
wouldn't you say that's a lot of cash?
Max the dog could've been put to sleep,
but Sanderson found him and took him to keep.
We all have purposes, one and all,
even creatures little and small.
Max was given to a human being
to serve and keep up neighborhood cleaning!

(Source for Idea; Tails magazine)

The Challenge: Greta
Tricia Carey

My adopted German Shepherd mix, Sally, came from a rescue group. She knew me better than anyone, and I liked her better than anyone. When she was eleven it hit me that she wouldn't be around forever and that I would be an emotional wreck when she left. So, I found a no-kill animal rescue group "Almost Home Animal Rescue League". They were a foster –only group at the time and I set out to find a puppy.

The foster home I visited had a mother dog and her six or seven lab, pit-mix puppies and two more tiny puppies from another litter. The mother of the tiny puppies was not in the home. She was rescued from a high-kill shelter, but was too ill to care for her litter. She'd had five puppies originally, but only these two survived. Their caregivers were hoping these orphan puppies would bond with the other litter. When I watched them all together, the others were all so big and these puppies were so small that they just seemed intimidated.

I saw one of the orphaned, tiny puppies curled up, laying all by herself and trying to sleep. She was fidgeting, trying to get comfortable and looked cold. I picked her up and she relaxed and fell asleep quickly in my arms. It's pretty hard to let go at that point.

When I first got her home, she was afraid of everything; the yard, her food bowl, her collar, her tags, bike riders... I literally mean everything. After my older dog passed, she began to get growly and stealing my things and guarding them. She looked and acted like she wanted to kill me. I thought briefly about returning her, but I knew that no one else would want this dog and she would sit in a cage for the rest of her life or be euthanized. I couldn't live with myself with either option.

We've worked with several trainers over the years. The one who assessed her as aggressive made her worse and she became frightened of me for a long time. The one who looked at her and said "She's afraid" was my savior. From that point on her training consisted of firm, calm tones, treats and love and she responded immediately in small, positive ways.

She and I have gone through a lot of trouble over the last eight years on a never-ending quest to get her relaxed and comfortable in different situations. Most often, with time and patience, I am successful. She learns quickly and is really smart. She also has a mind of her own and is hilarious, quirky and trusts me completely. I love her not because she's perfect, but because I stayed loyal to her and she became unfailingly loyal to me. That is my Greta.

The Dog That Won My Heart
Frank Evola

This is the story about a female Lab/Mastiff mix named Peyton who was brought into my home one day without warning. I thought my family was going shopping. I had no clue they were shopping at "Meet your Best Friend at the Zoo" and this animal was actually being brought into our home to be our dog.

My family thought they were rescuing a dog that was perhaps abused or homeless. They found out after the papers were signed that that was not the case. The rescue gave them a tote to take home, inside were her toys, her bowls, her medical records, and a note from her former owners about her likes, dislikes, habits. Seems they were an older couple, and Peyton had just gotten too much for them to handle. So, they had "rescued" a two-year-old spoiled dog!

We already had two beloved cats named Foley and Haley, and Haley was my favorite. Why on earth did we need a dog! I thought our home was entirely too small to adequately house a dog of her size and that we were perfectly fine with just our cats. When they brought her home, Peyton came storming into our house like a wild stallion. What a nightmare! Both cats were terrified and traumatized by her shrill bark and her size. I'll never forget how upset I was to see our cats cowering in fear on top of the kitchen cupboards.

Peyton also seemed to have issue with me and stood and barked at me relentlessly for the first few weeks. We later surmised that she, for whatever reason, took issue with the baseball cap I wore. She even eventually chewed up the cap, and the bonding began!

It took me quite a while to accept that Peyton was now a permanent member of our home, but I in fact, did indeed, eventually accept it. Our cats were relegated to the upstairs portion of the home because Peyton owned the main floor and the cats knew it.

Over the course of time, I took Peyton for walks regularly and through these walks I began developing a close bond with her. When I came home from work, she greeted me at the door with a bone in her mouth and her tail wagging with so much excitement her entire torso shook! She became my girl.

One day, we came across the documents from her adoption which included the phone number of her previous owners. I felt like Peyton was so special they needed to know she had a very loving home and received lots of affection and attention. I called her former owners, and spoke to the husband. "Hello, you don't know me, but we adopted Peyton, and I just want you to know she is safe and loved by our family." He relayed the news to his wife who cried with joy that she had a good home. During the conversation, they asked for our address, which I willingly shared.

About a week later, a package arrived addressed to... Peyton. Inside the package were cookies for her favorite Kong. Then, a few weeks later, another package with Bacon treats. My wife sent them a thank you card from "Peyton", and included a few photos of Peyton playing with the kids, sleeping on the bed, etc. The last package that came arrived with a note from her former owners, saying how happy they were she had kids! And they, in return, sent Peyton's puppy pictures to us.

Peyton became very special to me and I couldn't imagine our home without her. She won my heart and will always be the best pet I have ever had the pleasure of sharing my life and home with.

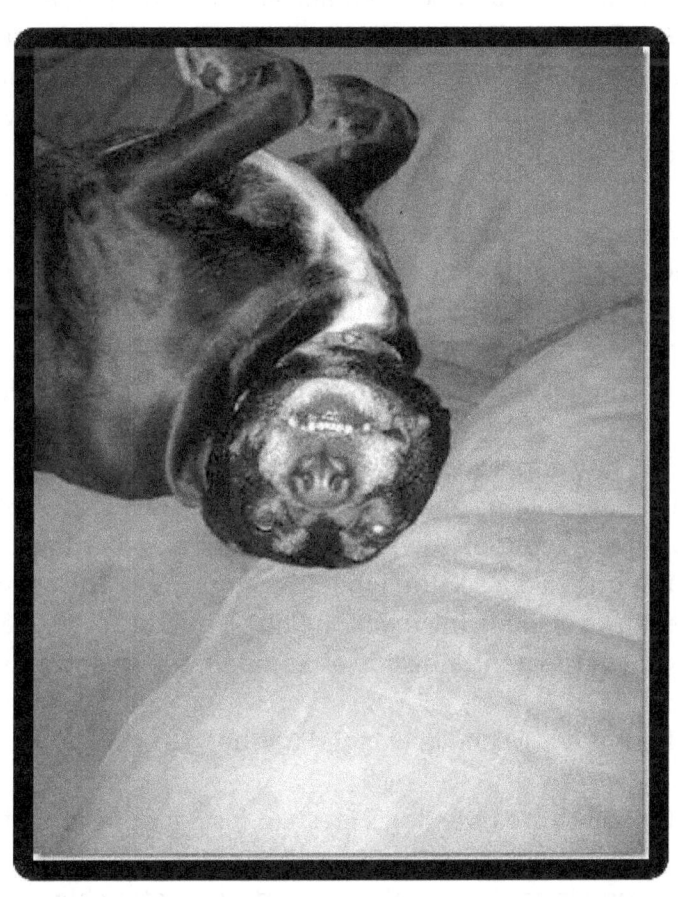

The Dog Widower
Matt McGee

He was always there.

There was Chris with his Boxer, Michelle and her wolf, Jack with his Aussie mutt, and occasionally Frank with the full-blooded St. Bernard that ate all his paychecks. Then there was the guy on the bench. He had no dog. But he was always beside the entrance, petting the dogs as they arrived and greeting their owners with a simple *good morning* or *hello*.

Most people assumed he had a dog running around somewhere and thought nothing more of him. Others figured he was just an old man hanging around the park like any other. Jack, however, counting the dogs in the place, realized he was just kind of around, and decided to sit down and get to talking one day.

"The guy adopted a Shepard with the same physical malady as himself," Jack told us one windy morning. "They were both epileptic. They even took the same medication and dosage. Then one day the dog had a seizure while the guy was at work and died. So he went into a shell. Still owns the dog's bowls. Its last cans of food are still in the pantry beside an unopened bag of treats.

"Poor guy," Michelle wagged her head.

"He still carries the dog's leash in his coat pocket," said Jack. We all got the weight of this, but also the sympathy; it's hard to judge someone in mourning. We all started greeting him after that, though no one knew his name. We just called him the Dog Widower.

I'd had my Shepard-Retriever mix almost eleven years at this point. Somewhere in the back of my brain I knew our dog park days would have to end at some point, but that seemed far off. She was still a runner, headstrong and fast.

We were leaving the dog park one afternoon and the previous visitor hadn't latched the gate for us. The Shepard-mix saw the opening and bolted straight out, toward home, toward the road. The brown station wagon lazily passing by wasn't equipped with the kind of brakes that could stop in time.

Two weeks later I brought her ashes into a moonlit dog park to scatter with the breeze. By the third week the shock began to dull and the first real pangs of loneliness stabbed through. Finally, I went to the dog park for consolation, but it was the middle of the afternoon and Jack wasn't there, nor Chris and his boxer or Michelle and her wolf.

But there on the bench, as always, was the Dog Widower. I took a seat beside him; we nodded each other's way and exchanged the kind of muffled hellos that men being held hostage might make when talking through a sock. We looked into the open field where dogs and owners romped about, outsiders for the moment, each of us feeling the leash we'd brought tucked in a coat pocket.

That lasted only ten days. A best friend is never forgotten, but I found something else out soon enough on the afternoon my phone rang. I was on the bench beside the Dog Widower, enjoying the afternoon when the cell went off.

"Hello."

"Hey!" a female voice exploded. "Guess what today is?"

I waited but the voice didn't register. "It's... 'National Guess Who's Calling Day?'"

"It's Veronica, dope!"

Right, now it registered. My ex-roommate. "What's up, roomie? Still working at the fire department?"

"Yep, got my big yellow pants and everything. But on weekends I volunteer at the animal shelter."

I nodded. Then I realized she couldn't see it so I said "uhhuh, cool."

"Yeah. You busy?"

I looked at the Dog Widower. "Nothing I can't get out of."

"Good. You might be familiar with Black Friday?"

"Is that when the stock market crashed?"

"No dope, it's when those of us who buy new clothes once in a while go bargain hunting."

I nodded to myself again. "Yeah, wouldn't know anything about that."

"No you wouldn't, you're probably wearing that same floppy blue and green flannel right now."

I covered up the blue and green material on my chest. "Veronica is there a point to this call?"

"I'm down at the shelter now," she said. "Since everyone's having Black Friday sales, we decided to have one too."

"Yeah?"

"Yep. There are some friends of mine down here I'd like you to meet."

I may not understand everything but I know when a sign is thrown my way. I stood up.

"See you over there."

"Okay!" she shouted. We hung up.

I slipped the phone in my pocket and looked down at the Dog Widower. He looked up at me. Then, he nodded. It may have been a 'have a nice day' nod, it may have been an affirmation, having overheard the conversation. I moved toward the gate and lifted the latch, feeling a little more free, thinking of all the other cages that might be opened that day.

The Fall
A.J. Huffman

My Chihuahua, named Icarus, loved to lay in the sun. It was his god, his guide. He followed it from room to room, sliding comfortably into whatever projected shape of warming rays. I watched him smile, sigh with content, never worrying about sunburn or skin cancer. His fur was a protective blanket from such hazards.

One day he followed the golden embrace to the top of the couch, stretched himself long, arms and legs splayed like wings in attempt, I guess, to warm his belly. But complacency is a quiet killer. He got so wrapped up in his own comfort he slipped, crashed to the ground, got stuck in the crawlspace between sofa and wall. I rushed to his aid, moving mountainous furniture as if it were wicker. I quickly assessed back, legs and head. All still intact. He survived, uninjured, but sadly was never quite the same.

From that moment on he became a creature of shadows, tucking himself in nooks of chairs, folds of blankets. Gone was the puppy that frolicked in the light. It was sad to watch his wax wings melt, to see how quickly he lost his desire to fly.

The Lost Daughter Saloon
Nancy Cole Silverman

"Hey Charlie, it's Cate. Look, I've gotta pull off. The wind and sand are blowin' somethin' fierce and I'm getting' pushed all over the place. Can't see beyond the jeep's hood and ol' blue eyes's actin' weird." Cate reached across the seat and scratched the big dog behind the ears. "It's okay, boy, it's just the wind," she whispered. "Look, I'll give ya a call back when I can get back up on the road. Tell mom I'm sorry. I'm trying, but it looks like I'll be late. Let her know I love her. Damn, I hope you're getting this. Cell reception's crap! Charlie?"

Cate white knuckled the steering wheel of the '98 Jeep Renegade as the fierce desert winds buffeted the Jeep's side, threatening to rip the ragged soft top off its frame and take the car airborne. Ahead a momentary break in the blinding blur of desert sand and tumbling sage revealed a large a billboard - a welcome sign to the *Lost Daughter Saloon and Quartzsite's Annual Gem Show*, exit one half mile.

Blue Eyes growled as Cate pulled off the Quartzsite exit and crossed over the freeway. In front of her stood the Lost Daughter Saloon, a local watering hole turned curio-antique shop, direct from the 1880's, complete with a weathered storefront of stressed timber and supported by a lopsided wood framed porch crammed with stuff; wagon wheels, branding irons, copper pots, and a life sized cigar store Indian. The type of things guaranteed to attract the growing number of senior trekkers who visited Quartzsite each year in their RV's, caravanning across the desert from hot spot to hot spot in search of the latest collectable.

Gathering the dog's leash, Cate pushed against the saloon's splintered door and coaxed the dog inside.

"Can't bring that critter in here," a cowboy standing behind an antique brass cash register at the end of the bar leered at her as she entered, his eyes running up and down her body.

"And I can't leave him in the Jeep! Not with this wind." She snapped back at him, sizing him up and deciding the old dude behind the cash register was less of problem than the severe wind that threatened to push her off the road. "Please, just 'til the storm passes. The wind's freakin' him out." She turned away slightly and taking off her baseball cap, let her long, tangled, amber locks fall freely over her face, and smiled, a move she counted on to win the favor of men, particularly older men for whom, from time to time, she found she might be *difficult*.

"Jist keep 'im on the leash," The cowboy ordered, his voice nearly drowned out by the wind's unmerciful howling as the door banged behind her, and he walked over to secure it. "Have to say, wasn't expecting the likes of you. Don' look much like you belong with the RV-ers."

"Slim, stop! Don't bother the girl. You know darn well she's not with us." From the other end of the bar, a group of four seniors sat beneath the dim golden light of a flickering hurricane lamp. "Don't mind him none, honey. The dog's just fine. Slim here's got nothing better to do with his time."

The thin, high pitched voice came from a small, bent grey haired woman who shuffled forward on her cane, and leaning into Cate's face, introduced herself.

"My name's Roberta, Roberta Rose and that there," she said pointing her cane back in the direction of the bar, "that's my husband Rob. People round here call us the Travelin' Roses, and sitting next to my husband, that's Goldie and Herb Snyder. We're what you call Quartzsite regulars; make the gem show every year."

Roberta extended her hand, "So, what's your name and where you from, darlin'?"

"Name's Cate. From LA. I'm headed to Phoenix."

"Must be an important trip to venture out alone 'cross the desert with these winds."

"Wasn't windy when I left."

"I 'spose not. Important trip then?" The old woman dropped Cate's hand and turning, nodded to the three caravaners sitting at the bar.

"Come on. Join us for a drink." Herb stood up and waved for Cate to join them.

Outside the wind howled again, its forces causing the building to shudder, while inside, a cold draft pushed the girl forward towards the bar. Even in the bar's dim light it was impossible for the four caravaners not to notice the similarity; the gentle line of her profile, how just like her mother, the girl crossed her legs as she sat at the bar, then laced her long fingers together, her thumb impatiently tapping her hand as she waited.

"Just like 'er." Herb whispered into Goldie's ear as he nodded to Roberta.

"Shush!" Goldie gently placed a finger across her husband's lips, then leaned closer to Cate. "So, why are you driving, honey? Pretty girl like you shouldn't be out solo in the desert, particularly on a night like this."

"Faster to fly," Herb said, pushing a mason jar of cold beer in her direction.

" 'Fraid I didn't have the cash for the airlines. Trying to make it home in time for my mother's birthday." Cate tipped her beer in the direction of the caravaners. "It's a surprise or was 'sposed to be anyway. Looks like I get to disappoint her, again! Always been pretty much of a drifter myself. Kinda like yourselves. What'd you say? Rambling Roses?"

Roberta smiled, her eyes flashing in the direction of each of the three carvaners, who silently nodded in agreement. "I doubt she'd be disappointed."

"I donno. I think I've pretty much been a letdown, never kept to a job, settled down or got married. Can't even seem to make it to her birthday party in time. 'Stead I'm stuck in some outta the way saloon in the middle of a wind storm."

"Maybe it's no accident." Roberta shifted her small frame onto the barstool. "You ever been here before?"

"You mean here? The Saloon?" Cate shook her head. "First time. Mostly just drive by, stopped for gas once. But I don't 'member the saloon. How 'bout you folks? Coming here long?"

"Sweetheart," Goldie placed her thin hand atop of Cate's and gave it a squeeze. "If I told you how long we'd been coming out to the desert you wouldn't believe it."

The caravaners laughed awkwardly, exchanging looks before Herb spoke up. "Actually we all met here, the Roses and us, when we came for the gem show some years back."

Rose interrupted. "Can't say 'xactly when it was, but it's not important. Just that we all started to find ourselves looking over some of the same old stuff from one of those long tables there." She pointed a shaky finger in the direction of the collectables: old clothes, pot and pans, mostly odds-and-ends piled high, like they might be at a flea market.

"Started talking as we mused through some of the items, 'til we came upon a pair of little girl's lace-up boots. Rose found one of 'em first, then I found the second and both of us had the same vision, came to us, 'bout the same time."

"Vision?" Cate asked, looking back and forth the between the two women.

"That the shoes belonged to a little girl…" Goldie said.

"Now you're gonna have to tell 'er the story?" Slim left his post by the front door where he had bolted it shut and stood like a sentry. The dog tucked closer between Cate's legs, his blue eyes following the cowboy's pointed boots. He growled as Slim placed a candle on the bar, casting an eerie shadow on the walls around the caravaners. "Go ahead, tell her how the Lost Daughter Saloon got its name. Bet she might find that interestin'."

Roberta tapped Robert on the shoulder. "Get the shoes from my bag." She pointed to a large canvas bag beneath her husband's feet. "It's quite a story. Dates back a few years after the Civil War, say 'bout 1868."

"Quartzsite was barely on the map back then," Robert said, searching through his wife's bag for a small, white pair of little girl's lace-up shoes. " 'Nothin' more than a pit stop cross this barren stretch of scorched desert full of cacti and rattlesnakes. Trading post for some lonesome miners 'tween here and Phoenix." Then finding the shoes, one at a time from deep inside the bag, Robert placed them on the bar. "These here belonged to Kathryn, least that's what we believe."

"See we found 'em when we came for the gem show maybe ten years ago. That's 'bout the time we all bumped into one 'nother. Thought then it was a total accident," Roberta said.

"But then, there was something 'bout the shoes. Just couldn't be an accident." Goldie said, "We just couldn't put them down. Then Roberta and I started to tease each other 'bout their history. First we thought we were just making it up. Started to finish each other's sentences, like it was real. Came to believe these shoes really did belong to this little girl who'd come..."

"Who'd come with us!" Herb interrupted and the four caravaners all stopped talking at once and looked at Cate.

"With us?" Cate's eyes clicked back and forth between the caravaners. "You mean with you? Here? Nearly what? One hundred and fifty years ago?"

"Can't start with the girl," the cowboy said checking the door and moving closer to the bar. "Gotta tell her 'bout the town and the preacher first. That's where it all began..."

"You're right," Roberta said, "but I think you should tell her that part."

The cowboy stood at the end of bar, smiled at the group and pored himself a beer, and then began.

"Story goes, one day this itinerate preacher comes to town. He'd been visiting Quartzsite regular, but back then we didn't have a church of our own. Weren't 'nough people to justify that type of thing. So he comes to town in a buggy 'long with his wife. Usually he comes alone, but this time he's got the wife with him. She's all dressed in black and sitting beside him. Real mystery. Must have been in mourning or something, 'cuz of the way she's dressed, but whatever, she was never popular with the women folk. Rumor was the preacher's wife was a barren woman, who bore her childless state bitterly, and the women in town, while obliged to offer them room and board when they came to call, found her chilly and unresponsive to their hospitality. Anyways you can see 'em coming for miles, this black carriage with this dusty haze kicking up all 'round him. Even then, the road in and out of Quartzsite was just a long slim stretch in the dessert. Nothin' more than a set of wagon wheel ruts for as far as the eye could see, with cactus and dry rolling hills on either side. And in the distance, always in the distance, a mirage, teasing us into believing somethin's there when it's nothing but an illusion, just beyond our reach, leaving us with an unquenchable thirst for the unknown."

"Stick to the story Slim..." Herb nodded to the others, smiling politely. The cowboy looked away from caravaners, returning his attention to Cate, and continued.

"See, behind the preacher, traveling in a wagon was a group of Holies, non-denominational types, part of what then was called the Holiness Movement. People coming from all over, who believed their purpose was to save the souls of sinners, and rid a world rife with evil by coming together at revival meetings. They hoped to bring about a new millennium of righteousness. And they came with their tent and bibles and planned to do one of them revival meetings right here in Quartzsite with the good preacher the next day."

Outside the wind pitched a rusted wagon wheel cross the saloon's old porch, banging it against the wall causing a great scraping sound and interrupting the cowboy. "Aw yes, the wind. I mustn't forget to tell you how the wind was blowin' that day. You see all of nature was part of the story, particularly the wind, but mind you, that comes later."

"First, the preacher man needed to visit with the Indian tribes in the area. See, right after the Civil War, President Grant decided it might be better to have a man of the cloth calling on the tribes to check things out rather than some government official. Figured a preacher-man might oversee things and maybe even teach a little Christianity to the Indians. Called it a 'civilization policy' aimed at getting the tribes better prepared for citizenship."

"You can imagine how well that worked," Herb laughed.

"'Bout as well as you might expect, but none-the-less, the preacher was a man of his word, and after dropping his wife with some of the families in the area, he headed out to the reservation to make his calls on the Indians. But 'fore he gets there, he's met by a young brave, who comes ridin' up bareback on his white horse all painted with war paint and feathers woven into his mane. Told the preacher he was no longer welcome on the reservation. Seems last time the preacher came to call he baptized couple of the Indians, and not long after several members of the tribe got sick and died, including the chief's daughter. The chief believed the Indian gods wanted to punish them for abandoning their Indian ways and he forbade the preacher to come near his people. Truth be told, those Indians probably died as a result of diseases brought west by the settlers and not some baptism, but try as the preacher did, he could not persuade the young brave that the girl's death was not a punishment by the Indian god spirit. He asked to speak to the chief, but the brave refused. He told him a pack of wolves had come to the area. The tribe considered the wolves a sign of protection to separate the Indians from white men, and any who tried to approach them would be taken by the wolves. The brave also said he had seen a sign, an evil omen, an owl's nest resting above the trading post, and warned the preacher an owl resting so close to the town's trading post was a sign of death and bad times."

The cowboy paused as though for affects, and Cate noticed how the room, now dark with only the light from the small flickering candle cast a ghostly shadow across the faces of the caravaners.

"After a while," Roberta said, "we started to the share what vision we each were getting from not only the shoe, but also from being here, in Quartzsite."

"It was as though we'd been here before," Goldie said.

"It was, what'd ya call it, Herb? A para-natural experience?" Robert asked.

"Paranormal," Herb answered. "Experiences that lie outside the normal range of things we know to be true every day."

"Like time travel!" Roberta said, grabbing the shoe and holding it to her chest, "Like traveling back in time and finding the answer to something you thought you lost long ago."

Cate looked at Herb, her eyes wide in disbelief. She waited for someone to tell her they were joking.

"Actually," Herb said, "science knows that time and space are infinite and at some point space folds back over upon itself, and under the right circumstances, there are those who believe it's possible to travel back in time. We've never proved it. I think perhaps what we have here is some sort of genetic memory, perhaps from some previous generation that's been passed down to us, and for lack of a better term, it 'haunts us,' compelling us to complete some unfinished mission."

"So when we started to compare notes, talking about what it was about this coincidence that brought us here to Quartzsite and the strange feelings we had about the shoes, we started to believe that maybe we'd been here before."

"You see," the cowboy said, "even back then, the Roses here and their friends, Herb and Goldie, were part of a traveling caravan. Only then, rather than trekking for gemstones an' such these caravans were wagonloads of Holies that followed behind the preacher that day. They'd come to be part of a big revival meetin'."

"And traveling with us, was our daughter Kathryn." Rose said, "Pretty little girl, just four years old. We'd lost her sister to a cholera epidemic the year before and I was still mournin' her loss, but we came just this same. Wanted to be a part of this movement to the new millennium."

"So after a while the preacher returns from meeting with the young Indian brave." The cowboy stood up and returned to the front of the bar, and looked at the caravaners. "We all knew from the way he's acting that things hadn't gone well with the Ingins' but nobody talked 'bout it, cuz they needed the tent set-up and ready for the revival meetin' next day. But fact of the matter was, the preacher was worried 'bout things 'tween the Ingins and people gathered for the revival meeting. He felt something was up and wasn't sure what it might be."

"All I know, is we were all very excited. I remember telling Kathryn how important that night's meeting was going to be, but she was excited 'bout something else, long with the rest of the kids that day."

"Right you are," Robert said, smiling. "Somebody in town had a camel and kids were all keyed up 'bout going to see it. Seems like Quartzsite had a hero living in their midst back then. A retired camel jockey, an Arab hired by the US Government some thirty years earlier to drive camels 'cross the desert from Texas to California, but the darn critters so scared the horses and mules the entire experiment went bust. But this Hi Jolly guy, that's his name, b'lieve that? He comes here with a couple of his camels, hoping to bring mining supplies from the Colorado River to some of the miners in the area and the kids couldn't wait to see a camel up close."

"Maybe that's why we didn't pay a lot of attention to where the kids were. Families back then always looked after 'ch-others children." Roberta sighed.

"It wasn't 'til the next day and we were all inside the tent and the preacher was speaking, when suddenly, like out of nowhere the wind picked up. Just like tonight." Goldie reached over and took Roberta's hand.

"I thought Kathryn was with the kids up front by the preacher," Roberta looked at Cate and back at her husband, "I just didn't think…"

"None of us did. And then there was no time." Robert stood up his hands above his head, mimicking how the wind lifted the sides of the tent nearly off its posts. "It came gushing though the tent, whipping the sides up and over the top, tearing at the canvass, and people started to grab their kids and run out."

"I looked everywhere, called her name! Kathryn! I yelled. But we couldn't find her. Not anywhere." Roberta closed her eyes.

"It's why we come back, every year." Goldie reached across Roberta for one of the little girl's shoes. "Once we understood that we each knew the same story we realized we had to come back."

"We just had to find out what happened to Kathryn." Roberta leaned closer to Cate, almost pleading with her. "You see after the wind came and knocked the tent down, and blew everything in all directions, it got real quiet and all you could hear was the sound of the wolves howling at the moon in the distance. The preacher knew the Indians believed it was wolves protecting them against the white men and he's too concerned for the sake of his flock to send them into the desert to look for the girl. And so they sat and prayed and the next day, the wind just kinda kept humming in the background, a kinda low soft murmur, blowing tumbleweeds with the start-up of little dust devils in the sand, but no matter how long and hard they prayed, my little girl, she just didn't come home. Not that night. Not never."

Goldie put her hand on Rose's shoulder. "Some people figured the Indians come took her, swapped her life for that of the Indian chief's daughter maybe. Others even thought perhaps the preacher maybe even made the story up 'bout the Indians and the wolves coming to protect 'em. Believed he and his wife might of bundled the girl up and hid her in their carriage; the preacher's wife being barren and all, not having any children of her own, and some thought perhaps Kathryn had just wandered off, went to look at the camel and got lost. Or maybe the wolves got her. My husband says there're stories where wolves have been known to take a child and raise it in the wild. Kids like that they never come home. Always restless and wild-like."

"But try as we have all these years to figure out the mystery, we never have. "Til tonight, when you walked in."

"Me?"

"Yes, you." The cowboy looked at her and wandered back to the front door, checking the bolt. "It was obvious the moment you walked in, you and your dog here ain't no caravaner, and why a young gal like yourself was out on the road alone at night. Just had to be. You even said it. Called yourself a 'drifter.' Kinda free-floating through life. No attachments."

"So you think I'm Kathryn?" Cate shook her head.

"Please, just take the shoes." Roberta thrust the shoes into Cate's hands. "Hold them. Tell me what you feel when you hold them in your hands. Tell me what happened to my daughter. I was never able to say goodbye. I just need to say goodbye."

"Please," Cate pulled back, "I'm sorry. I'm uncomfortable with... "

Robert stepped forward, and placed his arms around Cate before she could complete the sentence. "You're uncomfortable, but not because of this." He paused and looked into her eyes.

Cate closed her eyes and concentrated on the shoes. "You're right. The shoes... they didn't fit. They were tight."

Roberta smiled, tears in her eyes as reached out to touch Cate. "Settlers' kids didn't wear shoes, 'cept on Sunday and these shoes..."

"Belonged to her sister." Cate looked up at Robert and Roberta, "they didn't fit, they pinched and she didn't want to wear them. She took them off and placed them beneath the bench then went outside."

The caravaners looked to one another, then grabbed each other's hands and circled Cate.

"Yes!" yelled Roberta. "That's what we've all felt too. You have gotten the same reading. It's no coincidence."

Cate stepped back, looked at shoes in her hands and gently passed them back to Roberta. "I don't know what happened to your daughter after that, only that she was happy. That much I can feel; a child's overwhelming sense of wonder as she walked out of the tent that night."

The lights flickered again and the cowboy unbolted the front door, and then hollered back inside to her. ""Hey, the wind's died down, miss. If you're planning on going, you should leave now."

Cate smiled at the caravaners, leaned forward and kissed Roberta on the cheek, then looked down at the dog, his big blue eyes met hers, and she smiled, "Time to go."

The cowboy called to her as she walked out the door. "Hey, what'd you say the name that dog was?"

"I didn't. Nicknamed him Blue Eyes. Not many wolves keep the blue eyes they're born with, but he's different. Been my guide for years now.

The cowboy smiled and tipped his hat as she passed through the door. "You travel safe now, ya hear?"

Cate waved her hand over her head as she skipped back to the car and allowed the dog to jump into the seat beside her. Putting the car in reverse, she headed out of the parking lot and glanced in the rearview mirror, the scene behind her faded like a mirage in the desert. Stopping the car, she turned and looked over her shoulder in the direction of The Lost Daughter. It was gone, vaporized in the desert heat along with her story, and replaced by a mirage shimmering, just like the cowboy said, *"always just beyond our reach, leaving us with an unquenchable thirst for the unknown."*

The Man And The Dog
Dennis Klotz

The man was old, the dog older in dog years. *It would be hard to get the dog out in this weather, but we might as well enjoy the nice last days of autumn before the winter chill,* the man thought. He grabbed the leash, donned his coat and hat and signaled the dog to the door. He would take the route through the park, where the runners would be out starting their day in the early blue light of dawn. From there he would go on the outskirts of the neighborhood, to walk the dog in the alleys behind the shops. Most of them were still closed at that hour, save for the bakery. The smell of the bread warmed him whenever he walked past it, but the dog seemed to no longer notice it.

The walking of the dog had become a daily ritual after the passing of his wife, although now it was more semi daily. The dog enjoyed the walk, but it tired him and he slept most of the day. The dog was graying, and his dark thick coat even showed a few white hairs. The man had grayed many years before.

During the evening, when the dusk began to creep through the curtains, the man would rest in his large leather chair, his feet resting on a stool with the dog beside him as he sat in quiet reflection with his cup of tea and his paper. Pictures set in frames the man had made himself stood on a mantelpiece that he made sure to dust daily. They did not face the window for he did not want the sunlight to fade what the frames enclosed. Pictures of a wife, a son, and a family he had had long ago. Helen, Anthony and himself when they were young and happy and had more in front of them than they did behind them.

He had been good to her when they were first married and the man remembered that excited look on her face when he surprised her with the mink coat. An anniversary gift marking their first year as young newlyweds. That was before Anthony. All of it was a very long time ago. They had purchased a small house in the countryside, a warm splendid home back before the city had been built up, back when there was nothing but the fields and the main road that ran through the town. If you had a dog you could take it with you to the fields or the forest beyond to hunt. Things were different now. There was no more hunting in the city, and one had to travel far north to hunt. But the man was too old to hunt and he never had a dog to hunt with when he could have hunted freely.

The house was simple now, but the man made sure to keep it in pristine condition as best he could. He cleaned it frequently, and he paid the neighborhood boys to take care of the seasonal upkeep. He paid them well and he admired them, for they always did a fine job cutting the grass in the summer and raking the leaves in the fall. Soon he'd need them to shovel snow. He enjoyed them, but he wondered how anyone could bring a child into this world. He had had one, and that was enough. Anthony brought him joy at one point, but not the joy that Helen had for Anthony. The man remembered when the doctors let him in to see Anthony when he was first born. Helen held him close to her breast, and there was light in her eyes when she looked upon the new infant. He inspected the newborn like he would a car, making sure everything was to his expectation, checking for any flaws. He felt no emotion but Helen's look stayed with him. She did not look the same to him after Anthony. She never looked like anything much after that, and the risky birth ensured that she would never bear children again. This was one thing the man had never forgiven Anthony for.

Anthony was not the son a man would want, not a man like him. The man sensed this from Anthony's youth and as the boy grew older the man saw more and more faults with him. He did not enjoy things like football or horse races or fights. The boy was passive and never grew out of his shell, no matter how much the man pushed him to. There was a cowardice the man saw in Anthony and it sickened him. This was not the legacy he had hoped would carry on his name. When Anthony grew old enough to leave, the man gave him a sizable chunk of money he had made from his stocks and his good job in the city. He told Anthony to live his life, but to no longer think of the man as his father, for he was no son to him. Anthony did not cry, or plead, or do anything the man expected. Anthony had looked him dead in the eye and said nothing. It was the only real sign of strength the man had ever witnessed from him.

Helen grew very withdrawn at the man's decision but the man didn't care. She was less of a wife to him than she had ever been by that point and there were other women in the city who took care of his needs. His business, his stocks, his resentments all took precedence over Helen or her feelings. "Let her find the boy if she loves him so much", the man would tell his friends after a few cocktails. They all knew of his affairs, his marriage, and his son but they said nothing; for the man would not listen to anyone but himself.

The resentment festered in him and he grew more and more bitter as the years went on. He put up with Helen and he knew she would never leave him. There was a weakness in her too, and he often thought that's what she had birthed in Anthony.

As they slipped into the quiet afternoon of life, they received a letter from a man in a uniform. The officer gave them a flag that the man locked in a drawer and forgot about, and news that broke whatever was left of Helen's heart. After Anthony's death, Helen had leaned on the man for emotional support for she knew that despite his flaws, he could be counted on to be strong. The man again felt nothing. He spent his time tending to things. He sorted out Anthony's few possessions, giving most of them away to charity, took care of the paperwork, picked out the casket and arranged for the burial. When going to Anthony's small apartment, he found waiting for him a small miniature dachshund. He took it back with him to the house until he could take it to the pound, but when he put the dog in his pickup truck to cart him off, Helen had stopped him. She implored him to keep it. They had never had a dog before. The next day he drove it down to the vet to have the dog checked, but the dog was fine. Anthony had taken care of everything. After that, he returned to his day-to-day affairs. The weekly Thursday night poker games, the opening and closing of the markets, the paper -and the dog.

Helen loved the dog, and the dog loved her. When she grew sick the dog would not leave her side, and the night she passed, the dog whimpered and cried. Again the man took care of everything, even paying for a funeral he did not attend.

As the years wore on, the man stopped counting birthdays for it was a reminder to him that should he have a cake, it would have more candles on it than he had people he could genuinely call his friends. The few remaining friends who had not passed on, he saw less and less of. Some were bedridden, and others could not remember the man's name for more than a few minutes.

But the man had himself. He had his routines, what was left of his strength, and the dog. The man was content with that. He felt the days getting colder. Soon it would be too cold to walk the dog. He shouldn't be out in the cold himself in his condition.

A month passed and on the first snowfall of the year, the man could barely get out of bed. His cough had worsened and he knew that the walk would be too harsh for the dog and himself. When the night came and he sat in his chair with his tea, he looked out at the snow blanketing the view outside. He coughed again and felt for the first time in his life that his strength was behind him just as everything else was behind him. The man looked at the dog, and at the picture on the mantle again. He let out another aching cough as he stood and made his way to the mantle.

Oh Helen! Oh Anthony! The man held the frame in his wrinkled hand. He felt his old body quiver and he let out a few trembling sobs.

The dog was on the couch now. He was asleep, his old body rising and falling with each breath as he slumbered. The man did not want to wake him. He whispered the dog's name faintly, but he knew that his voice was old too and it did not have the depth or the warmth of his younger prime. He knew the dog could barely hear anymore, too. He went to the couch, resting himself softly on the cushion so as not to wake the dog. He petted him but the dog did not wake or move, only wagged his tail. He let out an aching whimper, an almost human like breath of sound. The man sat there stroking the dog's coat softly, his wrinkled hand finally petting him on the head as the dog groaned once more. *Sometimes perhaps it's best*, the old man thought to himself, *perhaps it's best to let sleeping dogs lie.*

The Pauper And The Poodle
Mark Hudson

A man who would dine on ramen noodles,
decided to purchase himself a poodle.
He knew his budget was tight,
but a poodle would make things right.
He counted up the cash that he owned,
he didn't have much, and he groaned.
"A poodle is not in my budget."
So off to the shelter he trudged it.
As he looked into at the eyes of the canines,
he saw all their wonderful designs.
Creatures that were part of God's plan,
destined to be the sidekick of man.
He looked for a poodle but saw none,
the wealthy had every single one.
Perhaps, he'd take one of these
because the price tag was perfect: free.
The dogs all barked for attention,
they begged for divine intervention.
They wished for a warm place to sleep,
and a shelter where their home wasn't cheap.
The pauper settled on a greyhound
who looked like the last to be found.
The dog looked at him with eyes droopy,
it was as if he was adopting "Snoopy."
The man still remains rather poor,
but with the dog he doesn't need more.

The Pit Bull
By D.T. Wine

I slip my chain and collar-
Out to the road to meet new people.
I amble, tongue lolling.
I happily greet my new friends.
Yet all I see is fear.
Mothers grab their children- they hide.
People run- arms flailing.
I'm caught on my reign of terror.
To the home- back inside.
I lay down with a whimper.
Missing people

The Prayer Lists And One Bad Dog
Tricia Carey

One of the first statements I said to my therapists – both of them – was, "I never thought that I'd be this age and not be married and not have a family." Kelly, the second and permanent therapist, assured me that this was normal for a woman in my position, and at my age, forty-six. The problem is that I don't fit the typical demographic profiled in articles and on women's television.

I've never been that career oriented, working woman only interested in getting ahead. I've gotten opportunities because I'm a hard worker, trustworthy and dependable. I have wonderful life-long friendships with a lot of really great people; men and women. I've been in several long term relationships, including one marriage; admittedly, most of those should've been short-term, but I don't regret the relationships per se. I've always wanted children, but I couldn't imagine becoming a mother on my own - on purpose. After my divorce, I could've married at least one of the men I'd dated. Officially, I didn't actually hear him propose, I frantically cut him off and made him get up when he got down on one knee. Weirdly, I don't regret major personal decisions; my marriage, my divorce, buying my home, adopting my dogs, or committing many years to a gravely ill boyfriend who wasn't able to commit to me. I'm left to wonder, how could I feel as if I've made the right decisions, yet also feel as if I've ended up with the wrong life?

I'm fortunate to have had only had a couple of panicky, self-evaluation crisis moments in my life. The first was when I got laid off from a job, and again, recently, after my mom died. She passed away in February of 2010, and even months later my gloominess seemed to be getting worse and not better. I'd find myself sitting at work and suddenly realize that the page I was reading was getting wet. I seemed to be crying randomly when I wasn't particularly sad or while my mind was occupied with other things. Time did not seem to be healing these wounds, as everyone promised, and that's when I began therapy. I still feel incredibly selfish with the discovery that my feelings of loss had become more about me and less about missing my mom.

When I was back home in Minnesota for my mom's funeral, we discovered that she had prayer lists around her house. These were hand-written cards that were primarily filled with the names of sick friends and family. My name was also on these lists, despite the fact that I've never been seriously sick or injured, in jail, on drugs or homeless. It was really funny, at the time, reading the list that began "All babies," then "Tricia," followed by the names of fifteen or twenty sick friends and relatives. My brother-in-law, Steve, discovered that she was also praying for me in the bathroom. On that card, tucked into a book on sports trivia, I was at the top of the list with "All babies," being much further down. The three-by-five note card was protected with packing tape making it, essentially, laminated. Laminated? Apparently, there was no hope that I would ever have a status change. We laughed until we cried. I took the cards with me, but a week later back in my own Michigan home, alone, and without the dark, Irish humor of my family to protect me, the cards just made me introspective and deeply sad.

My mom valued her faith, marriage and children more than anything. I have neither marriage nor children and I've all but stopped attending church. At my age, my mom was nearly twenty-five years married and had ten children ranging from age three to age twenty-two. I have one unsuccessful marriage that ended thirteen years ago and two adopted dogs. I imagine that by her standards my life seemed solitary and unfulfilling. I'm so grateful to her for praying in silence and never expressing this to me in person. Naively, I always thought that my mom was proud of me for making good and decent decisions and having an ability to take care of myself. You don't get included on a laminated prayer list because of pride though; she was clearly worried.

I've been asked by my therapists – both of them – if I've had suicidal thoughts. I'm speculating that phrases like, "my life feels meaningless," or, "there's no point to my existence," and, "no one would know for days if I've died," can be interpreted as red-flag statements. I'm not suicidal and never can be. I know this because I have one bad dog. Really, I have two dogs; one dreamboat, perfect, never have to worry about dog, Nigel, and then the other one, Greta. I love her deeply and she's endlessly hilarious, but she is an acquired taste, to put it mildly. When I leave town, the place where I board them gives me "Pawgress" report evaluations from their stay. Nigel's are typically, "Nigel was a perfect gentleman," or, "Nigel had a great time and loves everyone." Greta's are artfully crafted by select staff and begin, "Greta has her own special personality..." or, "Greta didn't always feel like making friends..."

Often, she returns home with no voice. The boarding staff have never expressed this, or complained, but I'm certain it's due to days of endless barking or whining. Greta gets crabby when she's tired, she steals and guards my things, she's fearful and growly, and I can't entirely trust her alone with children and un-savvy adults. I joke that in my will, I could offer Nigel with my burned out oven mitts and he would be snatched up in a second. Greta, on the other hand, would have to come with a binding contract that she not be euthanized, dumped in the woods, or put in a shelter and in return, I would offer up every penny from every investment that I've ever had. And it would still be a hard sell. Greta is slowly improving over time with seemingly endless positive training, but my job here is not done. As the one person in this world who understands her quirks and loves her unconditionally, she needs me and I worry about what would happen to her if I were not here.

So, that's what mom and I shared – worry. I'm not completely delusional, I understand that there is a difference between humans and animals; however, the *feeling* of worry is the same no matter what the target. I would venture to guess that the worry is much more intense with a mother for her daughter, than me for my dog. In fairness to me, however, my mom never had to worry that I may be euthanized if I were to get out of the yard, be rescued, and then snap at my savior out of fear. It's why I keep an extra clip on my gate latch and also why Greta wears a special tag that states, "Please be gentle, I growl when I'm afraid." I'm thinking of adding another which would read, "If you are a stranger, my mom is worried sick." This, I suppose, is something that my mom would've liked to have created on a brooch in tiny, pastel cross-stitch and pinned on me.

Once I had the "worry epiphany," the prayer lists no longer made me cry or feel empty and pathetic. When I look at them now, I feel much closer to the memory of my mom. I'm comforted by the fact that I shared something real and, more importantly, something maternal with her. Nonetheless, if what defines a family involves only the physical structure then I still may be as irrelevant as I'd proclaimed – I have no husband and no children. My therapist has been trying to convince me, though, that I can't judge my life by the standards of my mom and that I need to stop thinking and saying that my dogs are just a fake substitute for a real family.

So what if I allow myself to see the true character of a family as not what you have, but what you feel or what you give? What if family is really found in the love you offer, the care and comfort you provide, your unquestioned commitment and financial support or even the everlasting worry of a laminated prayer list or custom dog tag? Well, if that's the case, then I'm closer than I thought to the life I've always wanted. I should invest in a better vacuum cleaner.

The Return
Judith Gille

Friends and dog lovers who hear Nacho's story often ask if it was difficult to bring a dog into the United States from Mexico. What we discovered was that it is infinitely easier for a Mexican dog to immigrate to the United States than a Mexican human. All we needed was a certificate from the veterinarian verifying he was current on his rabies and distemper vaccines, and a letter stating he was in good health. Finding a crate in which to ship him home on the airplane was by far the hardest part. We finally found one at a Costco outside of Puerto Vallarta while on a weeklong search for warmer temperatures that winter.

The day Hannah and I were to travel with Nacho back to Seattle, I picked up some tranquilizers from the vet. Paul had already left, since he was traveling back through Texas to visit more family. My daughter and I plastered the dog crate with signs that read *"Por favor, no ponga nada encima de la caja,"* in hopes that the Mexicans would not place anything heavy on top of our cheap, collapsible Costco crate and crush our new dog.

At the airport in León, I gave Nacho half a tablet of Calmivet, a Valium-like drug for dogs. In two hours we'd be in Dallas where—we were informed by the agent at American Airlines—we were to pick him up as we passed through customs. I planned on giving him another tablet of tranquilizer before transferring him to the five-hour flight home to Seattle.

We cleared customs in the Dallas airport, but when our luggage arrived, Nacho was not with it. I inquired with an agent, who directed us to a special area of the airport where animals were processed.

"He's already been transferred to the Seattle flight," a perfunctory uniformed customs officer informed me. I panicked, afraid that traveling untranquilized on a thunderous jetliner for five hours might be more than our luckless Mexican street dog could endure.

When we arrived in Seattle, Hannah and I were relieved to see the crate waiting for us at the baggage claim. We rushed over and opened the door, but when I reached in and pulled him out, poor Nacho was catatonic. His body was stiff and unyielding. He had a wild, distant look in his eyes.

Not knowing what else to do, I piled our luggage on a cart and whisked him outside, where I searched in vain for a patch of grass where he might relax and go pee. I finally put him down on a corner of the concrete sidewalk, but he didn't move. He just stood there, frozen with fear.

I tucked his rigid body under one arm and with the other helped Hannah push the luggage cart onto an elevator.

In the elevator, Nacho finally came back to life, and along with his decision to live came a sudden need to urinate. Pee began spraying out of him like water from a pressurized hose. I screamed and held him away from me, pointing him first in one direction and then in the other, trying to avoid getting Hannah and our luggage soaked. But by the time the elevator's doors finally glided open, the walls were thoroughly rinsed in the urine of a Mexican street dog with a new lease on life.

The Reward: Nigel
Tricia Carey

I adopted my dog, Greta, from "Almost Home Animal Rescue League" they are a no-kill rescue and do wonderful work. Almost Home teamed up with a city in my area and began running a no-kill shelter. I volunteered shortly after they opened.

One evening, the police brought in four puppies and two adult dogs that had been seized from a yard where the owners had moved. The police were called, not because they were abandoned, but because a young neighbor had jumped the fence and was beating one of the puppies with a baseball bat. They were all brought in and the beaten puppy was rushed to an emergency clinic and survived. They named her Faith.

The rest of the puppies were put in the typical, gated pen of a shelter. They separated the adults; clearly no one was spayed or neutered. The three healthy puppies were held together. I loved going into the puppy pen, it was far messier to clean, but I enjoyed wrestling and playing with them. When I would squat down, one puppy would climb on my lap and sit calmly as if he belonged there. He did this every time I entered.

It took a while for this group to become adoptable. The "owners" were claiming they were still caring for the dogs despite having moved, leaving a yard full of dogs behind. The police and lawyers got involved, but eventually the shelter received rightful ownership.

On my typical Wednesday evening shift, I came in to volunteer and saw one of the puppies on the shoulder of a woman as she completed the paperwork for the adoption. I panicked and ran back to the other puppies. There was one puppy left in the pen and I went in. I squatted down and he climbed up in my lap and sat calmly as if he belonged there. I closed my eyes, hugged him gratefully and didn't let go all night. I cleaned and swept with one arm until the shelter closed.

I am a planner and what I decided to do that night was a complete out-of-character impulse move. I had no intention of adopting another dog; I had my hands full with my very nervous terrier-mix, Greta. I took him home that night to "foster." It took about ten minutes before they began to chase and play and that was that. They became instantly inseparable. I called the shelter about an hour later and left a message letting them know that he was staying. He is the calmest, easiest going dog I've ever met; he loves everyone and everyone loves him. He is completely confident in every situation and is afraid of nothing. He is yin to Greta's yang. I often read stories about how a shelter animal will pick you. To me, it always sounded like typical rescue cliché, but now I know it can happen. That is my Nigel.

The Story Of Wilson Originally Known As Henry
Angela C. Arnott

I adopted Henry from Almost Home back in 2003. I wasn't planning on it at all. I went to the adoption event intending to maybe adopt a small fluffy dog as a friend for my current dog, Freight Train, but Gail begged me to foster Henry because she could hide the small fluffy dog at her house and would have to board Henry. See this was before Almost Home had a shelter so they had some of their dogs in foster homes and others were boarded. I just couldn't say no to Gail or Henry so I agreed to foster him.

He was so scared in the back seat of my car. But I got him to my home, and Freight Train and he were fast friends. They played and cuddled. He just fit right in. I did keep taking him to adoption events like a good foster should but he kept coming back. Since I lived in an apartment and he was a very active boy I felt he needed a home with a back yard to romp in. He even got adopted at least once but was returned and I fostered him again.

Finally, there was another family extremely interested in him and when I looked at him after all of these months I couldn't go through with it. Freight Train and Henry (I changed his name to Wilson) were brothers and I couldn't bear to separate them. So I called Gail and asked if I could just officially adopt him; she said yes. My Wilson was such a character. He was always making me laugh. Unfortunately, in 2008 Wilson became very ill. I did everything in my power to get him well. He went through so many procedures, blood transfusions, surgeries. He was a trooper but no one could figure out exactly what was going on. He was usually happy and wagging his tail when he would go back for his testing but one day he looked at me and I could just tell he had had enough. He didn't want to poked or prodded anymore. He just wanted to live out what was left of his special life in peace at home with me and Freight Train.

I spoke to his specialist and they said they were running out of options and he wasn't going to last much longer. I decided it was enough and he should just enjoy his remaining time having fun. Wilson did really enjoy the last few weeks he was with me. He treed a possum, went on lots of walks and ate whatever he wanted. I noticed that he was becoming weaker. One fateful day, I came home from work and he didn't get up and greet me like normal. In fact he could barely lift his head. I carried him outside and he was so weak that he could barely stand and he ended up urinating all over himself. I knew it was time. I called my vet and they stayed open late just for us. I carried my baby Wilson in to the office and he didn't move much. The music that was playing in the background was the theme song from the movie Titanic, *My Heart Will Go On*. I held him until he took his last breath. He seemed to be at peace. I was so upset that my vet offered to drive me home but I declined. I just wanted to be alone.

The next day I had to go to work although I probably should have called in. I was walking out in the court yard and all of a sudden there was this tiny little bird right in front of me on the ground. I thought it was injured and that was all I needed was another death. But I went down and got really close to it. It looked me in the eye and then fluttered away. I think in some way that was Wilson trying to let me know that he was okay. I know that sounds strange but I could feel his presence and I was comforted. Even though it has been a few years, I still miss that sweet boy so much! He was very special to me and will always have a place in my heart.

The Sun And The Stars To Me
Ruth Sabath Rosenthal

Clown-like
Happiest on your back
Feet to the stars
Galactic capacity
To immerse in sensation
Stare into space
Entranced
As my fingers traverse
Your length and breadth
Your breath imperceptible
As though
Heaven bound
Till I stop stroking you
My precious dog

The Touch
Charlotte Mielziner

Touch carries an unexplainable magic of life. Lovers, babies, dreamers and the dying, drowning in a pool of lost opportunities all crave touch. That electrical, wonderful connection from one to another says we are no longer alone in the darkness. With a simple contact, we join with another and become part of a whole, a universe that is greater than either of us were before. I was privileged to witness this miracle drift through a lonely man's hospital room and settle it's gentle presence via a small, but wise old soul.

My mother was chief of nursing in a local nursing home. It was years before therapy dogs were celebrated in such places for their ability to draw out the lonely and calm the anxious. On occasion, she'd ask me to bring my dachshund to visit the residents. Barely through the wide front doors, arms would reach out, not for me, but my little red dog. Holding her like the now grown babies that once rested in their arms, she would gaze into the wrinkled faces above her and read the story of their lives.

One late winter day, Mom called and asked me to bring Grandma Dog for a visit. This was Gretchen, my fifteen pound dachshund with the empathic skills and insight given only to old souls. She spent her days on self-appointed tasks, keeping her routines so predictably, we decided she was like living with a little old lady. The nickname fit her so well, all who knew her called her Grandma Dog.

"Little Mr. Lehrer needs her." Mom referred to all of the residents as her "little people." The concern in her voice was the same soft tone she used when death was imminent. It was as if she announced "Little" Mr. Lehrer had just passed.

In fact, Mr Lehrer's family had dropped him off at what they declared was the Cadillac of old folk's homes, signed each paper placed in front of them, dropped a generous check on the director's desk, begged her to take sterling care of their precious father and left. That was three weeks ago. No one had heard from them since.

Filled with anger, shock, and the pain of abandonment, Mr. Lehrer refused to cooperate with the day to day routines of a nursing home. He would not come to the cafeteria and shouted at any who tried to welcome him. He fought back at any attempt to care for him with clenched fists and curses. In three weeks, no one had yet seen him open his eyes. There was nothing Mr. Lehrer wanted to see.

Mom took Grandma Dog from me before we entered his room. She paused a moment, like she was gathering herself and quietly opened the door. "Mr. Lehrer, there is someone here to see you," she said.

"Well, there's nobody I want to see," his voice was raspy and weak.

There, in the bed was an emaciated old man, scrubby white beard hairs, poking at all angles. His eyes were screwed up tight and fists raised, ready to strike. Mom walked to the side of his bed and laid my beloved dachshund across his lap. I held my breath, hoping my mother could intervene before he had a chance to hurt Grandma Dog.

For a long moment, no one moved. Slowly, Mr. Lehrer began to relax. "Whose this?" He whispered. Mom gently took one of his small, clenched fists in both her hands and lowered it to Grandma Dog's back. She stroked the back of his hand and the gnarled fingers opened. His other hand lowered and found the leathery ears.

For the first time in three weeks, this stubborn, angry old man opened his eyes. "Well, look at you!" he said.

Grandma Dog raised her head and held his gaze; her large brown eyes looked deep into the pool of his watery blue ones. The chasm between alone and together closed in that moment. She touched this man in a way no one else could. Without a word, this dog took his burden on her own small shoulders and gave him rest.

I brought Grandma Dog as often as I could in the next weeks. Mr Lehrer allowed the aides to bathe and shave him. Trays of food were no longer shoved to the floor and residents still determined to be friendly were allowed in. As he stroked my little girl's long back, Mr. Lehrer told me stories of his life. With each tale, he'd glance down at Grandma dog and say, "isn't that so?" As if she were beside him so many years before and agreed on the details.

He was fading, as they say of nursing home residents not long for this world. One afternoon, after only a brief visit, Grandma Dog crawled up his chest, licked his chin and turned to me to leave.

"She says it's time," he said, softly.

"You mean time for us to go?" I asked glancing at the clock.

"No... it's time. Goodbye and thank you," he said, pulling up his covers.

I was a little concerned, but left for home. Mom called the next morning. Mr. Lehrer was right, it was time. Putting the phone down, I turned to Grandma Dog and saw his echo in her eyes. She knew. I picked her up and buried my face against her neck. The acrid smell of old man was still on her and for a brief moment, I felt the touch of arthritic fingers brush my cheek.

The Wheel Box
Cate Caldwell

I run. The tall grass, much taller than me, parts as I pass. I feel it whip across my fur, and a couple times I must close my eyes. I love the feel of the wind rippling through the short hair on my face as I increase my speed. The field is exploding with scents. All kinds of flowers, small critters I don't know, and other dogs who have been here not long ago. Young dogs, old dogs, healthy dogs. One sick one, who hasn't got much time left.

I feel the sting of an object hitting my face, above my bad eye. I yelp awake.

"Stupid dog, even barks in its sleep," the ugly one says. He's huge in an unhealthy way, with pasty white skin, almost green, and an ill-scent about him. Not as much physically sick, though a little bit of that, too, but deeper. He reeks of something nasty deep within.

"Get the hell out," he yells, opening the door. I run before he can kick me. He kicked me once, in the face. That's why my eye is bad. That was the only time she made him leave. I thought she was done with him, but he came back. My eye hasn't been right since, and sometimes my head hurts. My sense of smell is still good, though. Enough to know he smells bad, anyway.

My little friend is walking past with her human companion. That one smells okay. I speed over to say hi. *Still healthy? Still happy?* I inquire. She is. *Your poor eye*, she responds, licking it through the fence. I'm glad for it, since I can't lick my own eye to help it heal.

"Shut up, shut up, you stupid dog! Get the hell in here!" I don't want to go in, because I haven't gone to the bathroom yet, but he keeps yelling, so I slink off. I smell sympathy from my friend and her companion.

It's not long before I need to go out again. I stand by the door. It starts to get worse. I scratch, even whine a little, though I hate whining. Finally, I bark. Only once. He throws something at me.

I don't know what to do. I'm dying. I can't go. I can't hold it. Finally, I can't help it, anymore. I go on the floor. I'm sick with humiliation. I want to hide, but don't know where. She comes. I look up at her miserably. *Forgive me? I forgive you. I love you, anyway, despite anything. Even him.*

"Oh, Jesus, Inky. Bad dog. Bad, bad dog," she says, smacking me with the paper towels. It doesn't physically hurt, but I'm miserable because I've disappointed her, again.

"Is Stinky at it again?" he says. "Worthless animal."

I want to bite him so much. But he's bigger and meaner. I wish I was a big, super scary dog like the one across the street. His human companion calls him Leroy Brown. I wish I was Leroy Brown. I would bite the pasty-faced troll so hard.

I don't want her to think I'm a worthless animal, though. I look up at her. *Is that what you think?* I implore. But she just gives me a mean look and pushes me outside.

I'm scared she's right, that I'm no good. But there's a little voice inside of me crying, *I am a good dog! I am worthy!*

I partly believe that voice, and partly the other one.

I am out here so long they forget about me. I don't mind so much. At least they don't yell and throw things at me. But it's a little hot and I'm hungry. And thirsty. I sometimes eat the grass, but it makes me throw up.

I wish she would get into the wheel-box and go back to the old one, who was good and kind. My companion took better care of me, then. There was always food and she always remembered to take me outside. I get sad when I think that she'll never love me again.

They get in the wheel-box and they go, but they don't bring me with them. That's okay, I don't want to go if he goes. They are gone a long time. So long the sun rises and sets more than once. I'm so hungry it feels like a thousand thousand birds in my stomach frantically flapping their wings trying to get out.

I look and I look, but there's no food, only grass. *I am a mighty hunter*, I think. I try to catch a rabbit or a squirrel, but the rabbits are too fast and the squirrels can climb. I try to get out through the gate. I dig and I dig, but I can't dig enough. I begin to despair. I am abandoned and unloved. Worthless, says the bad voice. The other voice only howls in pain.

I hear and smell my friend's companion, and another human, but not my friend. I don't bark. I don't feel like it. I am not sure I want to go over to say hi, but I can't bear to be alone any longer. I am a dog. I belong in a community. I limp over to the fence and give a slight wag.

The human I don't know squats down and puts his finger through the gate. "Hey, buddy," he says. I smell him. I don't smell anything bad, just good intentions. And ice cream. I lick his finger and wag my tail.

He turns to the other, my friend's companion. "Would you look at this dog? He's skin and bones."

"I told you," she responds.

He turns back to me. "What's wrong with your eye, buddy? Uh oh. Yeah, that's not good. Think we might need a trip to the vet."

She comes down. "Jesus! Why do people like this have dogs?"

"Well, they aren't going to have this one any longer."

"We can't just steal him," she says.

"Oh, yes we can," he says.

"And then what?"

"And then I leave a note that says, 'hey, douchebag. I stole your dog. If you do anything about it, I'm filing a police report, so suck it.'"

"Brian!" She exclaims.

"Angela!" He mimics.

"Maybe we should sick Leroy Brown on him," says Angela.

"I think we should get a whole pack of armored dogs. Panzer hounds," Brian says, scratching my ears. I like that.

"He wagged his tail at that, did you see?" says Angela.

"Is that what you are buddy? A Panzer dog? That's what I'm going to name him. Panzer."

She laughs. "A ten pound shih-tzu?"

"Yup. Panzer. Paaaan-zerrrrr," Brian says, still scratching my ears.

"Well, if we're going to do this, we'd better be quick," Angela says. She climbs the fence and jumps over to my side. I'm a little nervous, but I let her pick me up. My legs go stiff and I make a little yelp. I don't want to bite her, though, so I shut my mouth tight.

She hands me off to Brian who musses my fur. Headlights are coming down the street.

"Uh oh. Run," Angela says. Brian runs, holding me tight, until we jump into a wheel-box and speed off.

I run. I run with joy in the wild, riotous wind. They take me to the field every day. They throw the ball, or sometimes not. They feed me and cuddle me and tell me what a good dog I am. I still can't see out of my eye, but they fixed it so it doesn't hurt, anymore.

When I get old and sick and then die, I want to send a spirit to tell them how grateful I am that they saved me that day. Brian and Angela not only saved my life, but made me feel worthwhile, again.

I am Dog. I am loyalty, nobility, and sincerity. Those who have known me know love.

Till Winter
Michelle Cacho-Negrete

It was barely dawn when Maggie's scratching at the door woke Leah who reached over to poke Doc and touched empty space instead. One month. She rolled over to press her face into his pillowcase, still unwashed; imagining some faint scent of him lingered, and ran her hand over the mattress as though some residual warmth had been retained. Leah had been certain that she'd die without Doc's soft, even breathing to set the pace of each day; she didn't. Life happened all around her, dragging her into it. The sun still rose, the dog still needed to go out, the shopping and laundry and bill paying still had to be done.

The faint sound ocean waves, usually masked by passing cars, indicated it was early, although she didn't know how early. Doc took a particular pride in his innate sense of time, outlawing a bedroom clock. He insisted he had "a handle on time." Not Leah. Since his death, time had shifted crazily out of control, night when it should be day, three in the morning instead of six, a month suddenly gone; she needed to become her own timekeeper and somehow put the hours right. She should buy a clock, but this simple act gave her pause; if she woke in the morning to its ticking, she'd lose those few precious, groggy moments when he was still alive for her.

Leah stared out the window at a strip of rosy sky wedged between treetops and black clouds. There was a density to the day, to the heavy salty air that warned of rain or maybe snow showers. Maggie's scratching grew more frantic and she sighed, sat up, slid her feet into her shoes not bothering to change the socks she'd slept in, then pulled on sweatshirt and pants and made for the kitchen. It was what she'd wear all day. Doc always told her how pretty she looked; now it no longer mattered. She ran a brush through her hair, and in an childish fit of anger left the bed unmade, something she and Doc had sworn to never do, because both enjoyed plumped pillows, smoothed sheets, turned down blanket. The clock in the kitchen said five thirty. Maggie's tail thumped furiously as she ran back and forth between Leah and the front door, her eyes dark coals in the faint morning light.

"Okay," Leah said, her body lethargic, demanding coffee and more time to awaken. She put on her jacket and leaned over to leash Maggie. The dog's eyes swung to the bedroom and she began to whimper, suddenly refusing to move. Inhaling sharply with frustration, Leah jerked at the leash, pulling the dog to her side and opened the door.

Outside, the air was damp and chilled, trees motionless and glistening with moisture, sun buried behind a layer of grey clouds. The pearly gleam of a few minutes ago was gone. It was a cold New England morning rich with the dark scent of moist earth and pine needles. Crows cawed loudly overhead and settled into the oaks on the front lawn to watch her pass. The dog looked back at the closed door behind them. Leah felt a surge of anger and yanked hard on the leash again, immediately sorry at the dog's yelp. She took a deep breath.

"He's gone, Maggie," she said. "Can't you get that through your thick head?" She leaned down to scratch the dog behind the ears and whispered, "I'm sorry girl, for both of us."

****

Although early September, Doc had fired up the wood stove. Leah was grateful for the pungent smoky smell as she washed the dishes, enjoying the warm water running over her hands and the feel of the smooth wet surface of the china. Some memory of the crackling bark and deep rich smell of wood burning made Doc impatient for the first fire of the season, so that each year he lit it earlier than the year before. She imagined the first men crouched around a fire, holding back the night with its red-fingered warmth.

Something of that primordial sense of safety and comfort must exist in memory, easing the way into the cold and dark of winter. Foggy columns of smoke, visible, through the window over the sink, blew across the road and spiraled up over the pines until they were lost in a sky darkening into the early autumn night. She wrung out the sponge, wiped her hands on the dishtowel, hung it up and went to join him; the same routine most nights. After forty-two years of marriage, she'd been twenty-two when they married, Doc twenty-three, nothing was new, everything a ritual grown comfortable and reassuring.

Doc was in his chair, newspaper spread across his lap, a path of yellow light slicing his body from the floor lamp behind him. He'd moved her loom and the basket of wool closer to the stove as he did each autumn. Maggie lay stretched in front of him, one paw delicately resting over her muzzle, legs extended behind her and twitching in the midst of some dream. He smiled up at Leah, newspaper rustling as he shook it, prepared to offer her a section, and then all at once he stopped still, head cocked as though listening to something. A puzzled look passed over his face, and he put his hand over his chest, leaning back so that she saw his eyes fill with pain.

Doc said faintly, "Call the ambulance, Leah," then coughed and slid forward in the chair. She'd moved swiftly to help him, heart thumping wildly, and he whispered, "Now, Leah, call now," but something in his eyes was already drifting far away. The dog sprang up, lowering her head onto his knees, her eyes fixed on his face, hidden from Leah as his shoulders contracted and his head fell forward. Doc reached out, his fingers curling slowly over Maggie's skull as Leah dialed 911 and paced impatiently, shoulders rigid with fear. She stared out the window at leaves whipping through the air in a frenzied scarlet spiral as the autumn wind lifted them, listened for Doc's breathing, willing him to hold on.

"It's ringing," she said. "It'll be okay." *Just a moment more*, she told herself; then, just as emergency services picked up, the dog began to howl, and she knew. She thought, then, that she must sink to the floor on all fours beside Maggie, the two of them with heads lifted to the unrelenting sky, howling in an ancient, visceral, frantic acknowledgement of death. Instead, with a steady voice, she answered, "My husband is having a heart attack," gave the address and asked them to hurry, even though the dog had told her there was no need.

They sat together beside Doc while they waited, the dog whimpering and Leah silent. She held Doc's hand in one of hers and smoothed back the thin white hair with the other, checking to be sure his shirt was clean and buttoned up, a last tribute to his sense of order.

****

The dog wouldn't eat. Every night Leah emptied out most of the food she'd put in Maggie's dish. She tried to tempt the dog by giving her the leftovers of her own untouched meals, but Maggie wouldn't even eat that, the same food she begged for during the whole thirteen years she'd been with them. It was as if the sole purpose of eating had been the nightly game of Doc slipping food to her under the table while Leah pretended she didn't notice. "Not hungry?" She scratched the dog, smoothing the thick fur as Maggie looked up at her with dulled eyes. "Me neither."

The phone rang and she hesitated, not certain if she wanted to pick it up. It would be Ana's nightly call. If she didn't answer, Ana would be worried and probably drive over. She reached for the phone and felt that inexplicable sensation of falling she always felt at Ana's voice.

"Hi, what are you doing?" Then, as if Ana had witnessed the previous few minutes she said, "Maggie not eating yet."

"No." She hesitated then, with a catch in her voice, said "I guess neither one of us is very hungry."

Ana, always sensitive to Leah's moods after their fifty plus years of friendship, was silent a moment then asked, " Do you want me to come over for a while?"

Leah thought about Ana coming, silently noting the unmade bed, the clothes, the dark circles beneath her eye, and answered, "No. I was just about to put on some TV and I'll probably fall asleep in front of it. I'll see you tomorrow for lunch," cutting the conversation off.

Ana hesitated a moment then said, "Okay, see you then."

"Yes." Leah hung up.

Ana and Leah had been best friends since high school, crying together over boyfriends, bad grades, parental injustices, pimples, weight gains, celebrating all the rest. Ana had been with her when she met Doc. They were both in their last year of college and inspired by an unusually warm day, decided skip their class and picnic in a nearby park, transferring wine into a juice container and feeling very bold and reckless. Leah remembered, with a pang, how young they'd been, how sure of themselves. Doc, passing them on his way to a class, asked if he could join them and sat down without waiting for an answer. She'd taken it for granted that it was Ana he'd be interested in; Ana with her soft brown hair and long body, but he wasn't. He'd directed most of his attention to Leah and she liked the sound of his soft voice, something both magnetic and gentle about this man as he shared the history of the park and explaining that he wanted to work with plants in some way. There was a certain awkwardness about him, as though he wasn't sure he could pull this off, could make himself interesting enough to elicit a *yes* when he asked her for dinner, that she found charming.

"Well," Ana said when he walked away. She brushed Leah's hair back from her face with tender fingers and Leah blushed. "Now do you believe me when I tell you are every bit as pretty as I say you are." Ana, to whom grades and dates came so effortlessly never failed to compliment Leah's intelligence, her long-lashed hazel eyes and the sweetness of her freckles, but Leah was never quite convinced.

Ana had been maid of honor at her wedding, staying over the night before, the two of them sharing wine, ridiculous jokes and memories from high school and college. They'd gotten pretty drunk and Leah had fallen over onto the bed, whacking Ana on the way down leaving them both hysterical with laughter. It had been then that what had seemed inevitable had finally happened, Ana kissed her, gently touching her face and hair. Something had shattered inside Leah then, the breadth of something new and yet familiar, something utterly dangerous. Leah returned the kiss, she couldn't help herself and then they began to unzip, unbutton, pull shirts over their heads, they couldn't stop, but Leah knew this was it, only this one time, only now. The following morning neither had said anything, nor had either of them been embarrassed; something pent up and waiting had been given rein, and that freedom had somehow been enough. A year later, Leah had been maid of honor at Ana and Joshua's wedding.

****

It was late-October, but whenever they began their walk, the dog turned and looked back toward the house, her ears pointed and listening for a voice she'd never hear again. It was the same each morning, as if she now doubted her own baying pronouncement of Doc's death, only giving up once they were out of sight of the house. Leah took the same route Doc always took, along the road that hugged the coast, despite the relentless wind. A squirrel clutching an acorn took to a tree at the sight of Maggie as they passed; turning to chatter angrily down at them, but the dog ignored it, nuzzling along the grass. Leah turned onto the gravel road that ran along the rocky beach where the smooth red globes of rose hips hung from the stubby branches like Christmas ornaments. The wind was brisker here and she felt salt spray on her lips as she stood watching the sun-glowing ocean. The white foam heads of waves reminded her of the curved backs of dolphins breaking the surface. It was low tide and seagulls dived crazily at water's edge, looking for clams and crabs exposed by the receding water. One lifted a heavy clam and flew close to the ground, followed by a shrieking chorus of gulls attempting to steal it. She laughed, and then picked her way over the sharp grey boulders. The path dipped in a tight curve down around a dune and for a minute they were out of the wind and roar of the waves. All that was visible was the sky and thick green bushes and then the path rose up again and the ocean came slowly into view. It was then that Leah saw the man coming toward them from the opposite end of the beach. His head was down against the wind. His heavy plaid wool jacket and the cap he held tightly onto his head were like Doc's, a common occurrence in this part of Maine where most dressed for comfort. One hand was jammed in his pocket and edges of thin gray hair peeked out over his ears. The dog began to whine again, tugging frantically against the leash, tail fanning back and forth rapidly. For a moment Leah's heart surged wildly as though the dog knew something she didn't, and she allowed Maggie to drag her along until they reached him. He looked up, sparse hair blown around his cap like drying grass, offered a stranger's smile, said, "What a wind," then continued past them. Leah felt a sharp stab of disappointment that left her feeling angry and stupid.

"Foolish girl," she said to the dog whose tail sank between her legs, then bent to smooth the fur along her neck before they continued on their way.

****

The low respectful mummer of a crowd as Leah entered the funeral hall warned her of how many people had come to pay their respects to Doc. There were not only friends, but customers from the nursery, grateful to Doc for shoots and cuttings freely given, along with advice. She'd been a little dizzy at the fluorescent light and nauseous at the thickly sweet odor of the flowers everywhere, despite Leah's request for contributions to The Sierra Club instead; she supposed some people did both, but in the end it was probably fitting that he was surrounded with burst of color and leaves in death, since he'd been surrounded by them in life. She'd thought of taking Maggie with her when she left the house earlier in the day, dressed in Doc's favorite blue dress rather than the traditional black, a color he hated. The elderly dog came stiffly to her feet as if she'd read Leah's mind and stood looking at her, rigid and alert. Leah leaned over and cupped the dog's muzzle in her hands, certain the crowds would be too much for her. "I'll be home soon."

Ana had insisted she and Joshua would pick Leah up, but Leah had refused. She wanted to postpone the looks of compassion and symbols of support as long as possible. In truth, she wanted to mourn and bury Doc alone, closely holding her grief to her like a shawl. She brushed her hair noting how much chestnut still remained and applied a pale lipstick. Her eyes were shadowed with resignation, her face gaunt from the last few days when she'd only picked at her food. She sighed, grabbed the car keys, gave Maggie a final pat, put on the outside light, and left.

At the funeral home the name on the door of the room, Richard Willis White, momentarily confused her. She looked around for the right door, even thinking for one crazy moment that it was all a mistake and she could go home and find Doc sitting in his chair. He'd been called Doc for most of his adult life, because he could heal any ailing plant brought to Green Forays, the nursery he'd opened. Leah understood, then, that the same formality that announced a birth closed the circle at death. Doc was Richard Willis White again. She opened the door to a crowd already there and steeled herself to the hugs and commiserations of their friends. Ana, across the room, met her eyes over the small group around her and she felt comforted by the love she saw there.

Leah made her way to the open coffin and looked down, as she had yesterday by herself, into the face of a stranger. The stiff impassive features reflected none of the amiable intelligence and compassion that marked her husband, the mouth she remembered curved in kindness, was tight and crooked, and the cheeks hollow. Death had obliterated Doc, replacing him with Richard Willis White, a different man than the one people had come to honor. Doc existed now only in the words she would hear from their friends, in the quick flashes of memory, like old movies they'd loved and would cease to exist, they were gone. She didn't want others to see this stranger, to honor him as the man they'd known, that man was gone. She leaned over then and closed the coffin, struggling with the heavy lid, lowering it as quietly as possible, warning off the disconcerted director of the funeral parlor, holding one hand up in the air as he hastily stepped forward.

"It's okay," she told him and then fumbled in her purse until she found a small photograph of Doc taken long ago that she always carried with her, and placed it on top of the coffin. He was speaking to a customer, smiling quizzically, his hand resting on the slender trunk of a mountain ash.

"I nearly brought Maggie," she whispered to Ana who came to sit beside her, holding her hand. *We're old now*, she thought, grateful that they settled into this profound relationship, those long ago feelings by now comfortable and treasured. Doc and Joshua had been the rock in both of their lives and neither of them regretted it. They'd seen each other nearly every day. Ana's two daughters regarded Leah as an aunt and she and Doc had taken them home for a week many times to allow Ana and Josh time alone.

"You should have brought her," Ana whispered.

****

Leah and Doc had never thought of getting a dog, not only were their lives too busy, but they were certain the pet would be considered a replacement for the children they'd never been able to have. After her third miscarriage they'd decided enough, the hope and consequent sorrow was too much for them. They made their peace with being childless after a brief consideration of adopting, adored Ana's daughters, and their lives were good. But then, unexpectedly, there was Maggie. Doc had found her one night, abandoned in a dumpster, and with a tight face had brought her home, weak and dirty. Her matted fur smelling of rancid fruit had nauseated Leah. He'd gone right to the sink and put the whimpering puppy in and gently washed her, soaping the dirty fur and carefully cleaning her eyes.

"She can't be more than a month old," he said angrily, as he gently dried her.

Leah heated up some milk and crumpled bread and broke an egg into it. Later they'd fixed up a box, lining it with an old soft wool blanket, but the dog followed Doc to the bedroom and slept on the floor by his side of the bed. In the morning she was asleep on the bed by his feet, half-hidden under the blanket. From the beginning Maggie was Doc's dog. She waited for him at the door every night, protesting when Leah tried to take her out for a walk, so that even with pneumonia, Doc had gotten up, despite Leah's protests, to take her out for her regular walk along the beach.

****

After their morning walk, Leah put on the kettle for tea and offered Maggie a dog treat, but the dog ignored it, settling into the place in front of the door where she'd spent nearly every waking moment since Doc's death, her nose resting on her paws, her tail unmoving. Leah shook her head. "You've got to accept it, girl," she said to the dog. The kettle whistled and she made herself a mug of blackberry tea with honey, and turned, mug in hand, to her loom. She'd taken an order for ten shawls to be delivered by Thanksgiving that she should work on, but instead, seeing the envelopes strewn over the table, she decided to answer the cards she'd received in the mail and pulled from the flowers sent by friends to the funeral home. She sat down, cup of tea in front of her, and reached for the pen.

You're old, Leah told herself, as she realized she'd drifted off again, and turned her attention back to the table. There must have been a hundred cards and notes. She wrote, folded, addressed and stamped the envelopes until she was almost finished. All at once she recognized by the light it was late afternoon. Massaging her hand and twisting her shoulders as she sealed one of the last envelopes, she absently called, "Doc, would you bring me a glass of water?" The dog was immediately on her feet, whining, and Leah, felt a welling-up inside her.

"Stop," she told the dog in a choked voice and stood up to get something to drink. She looked at her reflection in the window over the sink; "Get over it," she told herself angrily.

****

Leah stopped walking Maggie along the beach, going instead through the near-by woods. It had been a warm autumn, their favorite season, this period between summer and winter when everything seemed to stand still for a brief period and hold its breath and despite it being November the vivid colors had lingered. Geese flew honking overhead, black V's in long geometric formations against a flat blue sky and drifting clouds. Coppery bracken ferns, long gold pine needles fallen over the muddy path, comforting smell of sweet-fern, and blazing trees arching against a restless sky made her ache with longing, sending her hurrying back to her weaving. She'd accepted far more orders than she could reasonably fill, but she was grateful to be busy.

A few days later, when Leah was lost in the meditative monotony of throwing a shuttle, working the treadles rhythmically with her feet, Maggie leaped up suddenly and stood pawing the door. It was growing dark and Leah realized that she'd skipped lunch again. The dog was keening softly and Leah sat staring at her, confused by her sudden agitation. Then she heard footsteps on the sidewalk outside, and recognized something familiar in the cadence of the stride. Her stomach churned and she felt faint. The dog was pacing frantically now, whining sharply, twisting back and forth between door and Leah as the footsteps grew closer.

Did they pause? "Doc?" Leah whispered, then the footsteps went past the gate and Maggie sank suddenly to the floor with a whimper. Leah swallowed hard, closing her eyes tightly against the tears that threatened, and for a second rested her forehead against a trembling hand, then turned to the dog who lay motionless now. "Dumb, dumb, dumb," she hissed, suddenly angry, "He's dead. Grow up."

The final week of November, she woke to frost coating the window. The sun through the silver-etched glass was bright and birds fluttered rapidly around the feeder in a storm of colored feathers and piercing cries. The thermometer said twenty-eight degrees and the grass was white crystal that crackled as she and Maggie walked through the woods, taking care not to slip on the icy leaves carpeting the ground. Overhead the thick clouds covering the sun glowed like the dying embers of a fire.

Ana called that day as she'd done every Saturday to ask how Leah was and if she was sleeping and if she should come over. "Yes, I'm sleeping" Leah brusquely lied, not wanting to reveal the troubled short bursts of sleeping and waking she experienced through a long dark night. She was afraid to see Ana too often, afraid that some dam of strength she'd built around Doc's death would burst and there'd be no way to live with the sorrow.

Something in her voice alerted Ana. "You could speak to the doctor about taking something if you are having a problem," she suggested. "It's natural to have a problem sleeping after somebody you've lived with for forty-eight years dies."

"Dying is natural, too and we should be used to it by our age," Leah snapped. A knot at the base of her stomach moved up until her chest felt as though it would explode. She swallowed hard, and apologized.

"And Maggie?"

"She hasn't got it through her head yet that he's gone. She keeps leaping up at every sound," she said and thought of the footsteps outside the door, coming closer, then away, thought of her own heart leaping up at the sight of the man on the beach. "It'll probably be till winter stuck in the house, just the two of us, when she finally accepts it."

"It takes time, Leah," Ana said and hearing the sympathy in her friend's voice Leah found an excuse to quickly hang up.

The house, now, seemed that of a stranger's, each room familiar, yet lacking familiarity. Never had she lived there alone and each item, the wood carrier by the stove, the dishes shiny with the patina of use through her and Doc's long marriage, the chair with the indentation still of his weight, all seemed things she knew but that belonged to somebody else. It was almost as though the very air had been pulled out of each room. Often, she felt smothered and peculiarly breathless and buried herself in her weaving. She heard her voice, as she wove, absent-mindedly speaking with him the way she used to, discussing the color and textures of the wool, the price that she paid, who the order was going to, and needed to bring herself up short with remembering. And each time she said his name Maggie would spring up, nose against the door, duplicating her own merciful memory lapse.

As Christmas drew near, Ana grew persistent that Leah and Maggie come Christmas Eve and stay overnight, but Leah put her friend off. It was as though leaving the house would be a betrayal, almost as though she needed to be there in case he returned. She shook her head again and again to clear it of this nonsense.

The week before Christmas a snowstorm blew in full and fast from the north during the night, the wind waking her as it hammered the wet flakes fiercely against the window. Leah snuggled down deeply into the blankets, feeling the deep cold of winter that had invaded the room and wished that she'd lit the wood stove the night before, a job Doc had claimed. He loved piling the kindling over old newspaper, making the small teepee of thinly split logs, striking the match and watching the red flames leap up in the sudden rush of crackling fire devouring the wood. She hadn't gotten around to firing up the stove since his death, relying on the oil heat instead.

Maggie began to whimper frantically, her body trembling as she raised up on hind legs and pushed her nose against the drapes trying to part them. Leah listened closely and through the howling wind she thought she could hear a vague whistling, high and sharp. She felt a chill course through her that the warmth of the blankets couldn't dispel.

"It's the wind," she muttered to the dog, but Maggie wouldn't be quiet, wouldn't fall back to the hooked rug she'd slept on since Doc died. She howled then a strange eerie cry so high and peculiar that Leah felt a sudden tug of fear.

"There's nobody out there, Maggie," she said, listening to the wildly blowing cold wind. *Nobody could tolerate that swirling white mass for long,* she thought, and then, *what are you thinking?* "What is it Maggie?" she asked and despite herself felt an explosive burst of hope that she couldn't understand, unreasonable but dauntless in its insistence.

"Okay," she whispered and stood up, pulling her shawl around her against the sharp bite of the winter air. She crossed the braided rug slowly to the window, chiding herself the whole time for what she was doing. The room was dark; she'd pulled the drapes tight against the night, and she felt like a child lost in a grown-up's world. The dog turned and pushed herself against Leah, insistently begging, then stretched up again, paws on the windowsill, nose tucked between the drapes. Leah took a deep breath, whispering in a voice she didn't recognize, "Doc?" and with a trembling hand flung the drapes open and screamed, although there was nothing but white fists of snow smashing against the window and desperate tree branches like dark arms blowing in a thick curtain of movement that took her breath away.

She caught her breath, her heart pounding painfully in her chest and began to tremble uncontrollably. She looked down at the dog, standing quietly now beside her leg. There was a strange luminous glow from the pale snow-filled night outside the window and the heavy plaid wool blankets on the bed were clearly illuminated.

"He's dead, Maggie. He's dead," she said and some waiting anticipation that she hadn't realized she felt, that had filled the hollowness of his absence was suddenly gone and she felt for a moment as though she was floating, looking down at her bed at the braided rug, the worn rocking chair and then she drifted back into herself and the room was suddenly familiar for the first time in months. She felt calmer, despite the tension that lingered in her body. The dog, after a moment, leaped onto the foot of the bed, circled in the blanket and was still. Leah felt the fluttering inside her refuse to quiet, although her mind seemed still and exact, and thought of making a cup of tea or lighting the wood stove. Instead, aware of a profound weariness, she climbed beneath the covers and listened to the storm violently flooding the night, watching the shifting white night through the window.

The next morning Leah woke all at once to the dog's nails scratching at the door. Silence had fallen with the snow all around the house and it seemed to Leah as if the world had stopped breathing. She realized that she hadn't pulled the drapes closed and strong clear sunlight tinged with blue filled the room.

"All right, all right," she told Maggie, "I'm coming." She stood shivering in the still, cold air, and looked out. Branches were heavy with snow, tiny green points of needles poking through. The tracks of birds and squirrels hatch-marked the white like the stitching of a quilt. The overhead sky was palely frosted, ground hidden, and everywhere nothing but white.   There must have been eight inches at least. She'd have to snow-blow after she walked the dog. She put the kettle on and made herself a cup of coffee, telling Maggie she'd have to wait. Then she dragged on heavy wool pants, a flannel shirt and thick sweater, two pairs of socks and her boots.

Drinking the coffee she thought about building a fire and assessed the wood piled before the stove. She decided to haul in at least two more loads when they came back. She realized that the snow would be too soft and deep in the woods now, and perhaps for the rest of the winter to walk her there and decided to take the path leading to the water. Maggie followed her around the kitchen whining urgently and Leah soothed her as she got ready.   She put a wind-breaker on, then her mittens and took the leash down, prepared for the usual struggle with the dog, but Maggie ran to the door immediately and looked up at her without looking behind. As soon as Leah snapped the leash on, Maggie was pushing at the door, eager to go.

Leah slowly turned to the bedroom and looked at the unmade bed and the drapes flung wide, but the dog was anxious and pulled at her arm. A heaviness that made it hard to breathe hammered at her chest then gave way little by little, till it finally collapsed under the weight of itself, and she accepted the truth of the coming winter; the streets and highways iced over and sometimes impassable, that truth of being left forever without him.

Her love for Doc that informed each breath she took, would, on each breath's exhale, disperse through the large empty house till the rooms were flooded, loss but also love reverberating endlessly, an echo that she would never stop hearing. She looked out the frozen window at the world, colorless and buried in the avalanche of snow.

She leashed Maggie who began tugging; pulling her forward and she open the door, knowing it was time to move on.

Tour of Duty
Elizabeth Ward

After reading a daily newspaper wire service story.

Lassie,
Sleek and able collie,
Courier of black and white messages in
Wartime movies,
Warned of bomb attacks and snipers;
Later,
Barking from a 7-inch TV screen,
Announced, "Timmy's in trouble!"

"Lassie"
Was but one of 4900 wartime service dogs who
Scaled walls, swam rivers;
Guarded the wounded,
Brought the morphine.
Trained not only to carry messages,
Service dogs prevented enemy couriers
From reaching their appointed rounds;
Attacked on command, wrested weapons.
Unrested themselves, they were fed
Only enough to survive.

These days, police take bomb- and drug- sniffing dogs
Through colorful public places.
Service dogs protect the innocent,
Perform search and rescue,
Guide the infirm,
Help children read,
Keep the peace.
At day's end these dogs play.

Those 4900 military canines
Were not trained for peacetime.
War's end deemed only 240
Adaptable to civilian life.
Others,
Not adoptable, were not sent to shelters,
Were not themselves rescued,
But euthanized.

Tour of duty over.

Training Toby
Gillian Lee

"Toby, come!" called Dad,
His voice loud and clear.
Toby just stood,
No move to come near.

"Come, now!" tried Mum,
Sounding all of a flutter.
"He just doesn't get it,"
Toby heard Dad mutter.

"Let's try with a treat,"
He heard them agree.
"Now they get it," he thought.
"They're listening to me."

So they offered the snack.
He came at a run.
His tail wagging hard,
"This training is fun!"

Tyrone Power
Allen Kopp

When he knocked on the door, Minneola answered it. She wore an immaculate gingham dress and a frilly apron. Her skin was shiny, the color of chocolate.

"Cletus, is that you?" she said.

"Yes, ma'am."

"What you want?"

"I came to see Miss Beezer."

"Miss Beezer dead, honey."

"I know. I brought her these." He held up a small bouquet of marigolds.

"Well, come on in, then," she said. "Nobody here but the sisters."

She took him into the "parlor" where Miss Beezer was "laid out." Two old ladies, not as old as Miss Beezer but still old, were sitting in dining room chairs. They looked at him as if he was a penguin that had just walked into the room.

"Who is this?" one of the old ladies asked.

"This a Cletus Duff, a neighbor boy. He want to pay his respects to Miss Beezer."

"Well, come on in, then, boy. Nobody's going to bite you."

They were Eula Watson and Zeddie Pulliam, sisters of Miss Beezer. Eula was fat with rolls of flesh hanging from her chin. She wore lots of face powder and a perpetual scowl to let the world know how much she disapproved. Zeddie was skinny with a sharp nose and sharp chin like a witch. She had deep-set eyes, strangely black.

Cletus stood there awkwardly; nobody had asked him to sit down. He didn't know what to do with the marigolds, since the person he had brought them to couldn't take them from him.

"Here, honey," Minneola said. "I'll put those in water." She went into the kitchen and came back with the marigolds in a glass. She set the glass on the closed half of the casket, near the opened half.

"Now she can see them," she said.

"Figuratively speaking," Zeddie said.

The casket was sleek and shiny like a guided missile. He approached it and looked in at Miss Beezer. She was all dressed up in a black dress with a high collar. Her bony hands with the huge blue veins were folded over her stomach. Pitzarrelli the undertaker had put rouge on her cheeks and lipstick on her lips, making her look like somebody other than Miss Beezer.

"How come you to know my sister?" Eula asked him as he turned from the casket.

"We were friends," he said.

"That's a mighty peculiar friendship between a nine-year-old boy and a ninety-year-old woman."

"I walk Tyrone Power for her."

"Oh, yes. That silly-looking black dog. As soon as the funeral's over, I'm going to put him in the car and take him downtown and have him euthanized."

"Maybe Cletus could take him off your hands for you," Minneola said. "It seems a shame to... do what you said."

"Don't you be telling me what to do, you! I've already made up my mind. Don't you have some work to do in the kitchen?"

"Was your mama an Anderson before she married your papa?" Zeddie asked him.

"No, ma'am."

"Did my sister pay you to walk her dog?" Eula asked.

"No, I did it for free."

"Then what did you get out of it?"

"Nothing. I like doing it."

"Nobody does anything for nothing."

"Well, I do."

"Don't you use that tone of voice with me, little boy! Hasn't your mother ever taught you to have respect?"

"Well, I really ought to be going now," he said.

"Yes, you do that little thing," Eula said. "It was awfully nice meeting you."

"Oh, my," Zeddie said, snuffling into a handkerchief. "I will be glad when the funeral is over and I can go back home. All of this is very trying for me."

"Stop that whining!" Eula said. "You won't get any sympathy from me!"

As he was going out the door, Minneola was right behind him with Tyrone Power's leash. She stepped out onto the porch and closed the door so the sisters couldn't hear what she said.

"I just can't stand to see her put that poor little dog to sleep when he's so healthy and loves life so much," Minneola said, holding back tears.

"Is that what that means?"

"You go quiet-like around to the back yard and put his leash on him and take him home with you. He's not mine to give but I'm givin' him to you. Tie him up in your yard so he won't come back here where he thinks he needs to come to get his food."

"I've got a good place for him!"

"Those two old scarecrows will fly off on they broomsticks as soon as the funeral's over. They'll forget all about Tyrone Power."

"Thanks!"

"Now you take good care of him and love him and give him a good home."

"I will."

"And thank you for comin' to see Miss Beezer and thank you for bringin' them mar'golds. I know she would have appreciated it."

When he got home, he tied Tyrone Power to a tree in the backyard temporarily and went into the house and told his mother they had just acquired a new dog. He knew she would protest at first but would soften as soon as he acquainted her with the word "euthanize" and the terrible thing that it means.

Victorious Victor!
Vicki Robertson

Hi, I'm Victor and have I got a story to tell you!

I am a five-year-old Shit Zhu mix that was found in a drainage ditch five feet deep in Ohio. Why didn't I climb out you ask? Well you see, I couldn't. Somehow, my back was injured and I was paralyzed in the back legs. I was so scared and was crying and losing hope of anybody finding me when a miracle happened! Someone heard my cries!

I was a matted mess when they found me and was in need of a bath big time! The man took me to a place with lots of other dogs and had a doctor look me over. The doctor didn't see much hope for me and recommended that I be put down (whatever that is, but it doesn't sound like anything I am interested in). A nice person there saw my potential and called around to different rescues to see if anyone was interested in taking me in and giving me a chance. That is when I met Gail and Lauren and all the others at Almost Home Rescue in Southfield, Michigan. They said they would gladly take me and see what could be done.

Gail and Lauren took me to some new doctors who said the same as the other one, but they weren't going to take that answer. They took me to a Neurologist who specializes in animals like me and he said that maybe with some physical therapy I might be able to walk again. You see I continually try to walk, but I just can't seem to get my rear end up off the floor, but that doesn't stop me from getting around. No sir! I just drag it along and move on my powerful front legs. I am not going to let a little thing like that stop me. I have too much of a positive attitude for that!

Gail and Lauren put my picture up on their website and said they were looking for someone to foster me. This is where my Mom and Grandma come in. Mom saw my picture (you see they already adopted one of my sister's from Almost Home earlier this year), and something about me said that I should come to live there, at least for a little while (maybe it was because our names are so similar and we both have issues with our legs).

Mom and Grandma came and got me and brought me to their home where I now have two sisters! They turned me loose to play in the house with them and boy, did we play! My littlest sister Ellie really likes to play rough with me even though she is half my size and I like it. My sister Daisy is a little shy, but I think I can change that.

That first week there was not a good start. I came down with pneumonia, but Mom and Grandma took me immediately to MSU emergency and got me help. I had to spend two days there with oxygen, but I responded well and was glad to go home as soon as I could. It didn't take long and I was back to my old self.

Mom got the phone number from Gail and set me up with physical therapy. Mom and Grandma took me to a nice place where the doctor looked at me and gave Mom and Grandma some exercises for me to do at home. The most amazing thing is the best physical therapy that I had received up until then, was playing with Ellie. The more I played and was taken outside, the more I started to use my back legs! It wasn't long and I was trying to walk, and I am succeeding! I don't walk quite like my sisters, but I am walking.

Guess what? Mom and Grandma have decided that I am staying here with them forever! They have adopted me. I am glad. They take such good care of me and I love them, too. I like it here with my family and everyone I meet. They all tell me I am such a good boy and so handsome. I try to be a good boy.

****

It is now four months later, and I can keep up with my sister's just fine. I still walk and run differently than they do, but I don't care. We have a big yard to play in and a nice house, with lots of toys and things for us. Mom and Grandma even take us on trips, and sometimes some kids stop by to play with us! We all like the kids a lot and it is hard to keep our excitement under control. I am so thankful that Gail and Lauren at Almost Home Rescue saw my potential and gave me to my Mom and Grandma. I am one happy dog!

Write To Woof

Contributing Authors

A.J. Huffman

Where are you from?
Ormond Beach, FL

Describe in one or two sentences how being friends with a dog has enriched your life.

My dog, Icarus, keeps me sane. He sits at my feet when I am working, and seems to know when I'm stressing. He puts his head on my feet to remind me that he's there, and that he loves me, no matter what. Makes whatever issue I'm dealing with seem much less draining.

Do you have any other pets; if so, what are their breeds and names?

My sister also has a dog, named Bumper. My sister and Bumper moved in last year and now the two dogs are inseparable. You'd think they were from the same litter.

If you are a writer (either by trade or compulsion) what first drew you to the craft? If you're not a writer, why did you choose to write a piece for this anthology?

I started writing in grade school. It's just something I've always done, but I did not decide on it as a career until I was in college. It was the only thing I could see myself doing for the rest of my life.

Allen Kopp

Where are you from?
Saint Louis, Missouri, USA

Describe in one or two sentences how being friends with a dog has enriched your life.
A love for animals always enriches your life because you receive in return a non-judgmental love without complications. If you ever feel unloved, a dog or a cat will love you when people don't.

Do you have any other pets; if so, what are their breeds and names?
I have two beloved cats. Tuffy is a Balinese (long-haired Siamese) and Cody is a Siamese.

If you are a writer (either by trade or compulsion) what first drew you to the craft? If you're not a writer, why did you choose to write a piece for this anthology?
In school I was good at English and interested in writing. A writer is the only thing I ever really wanted to be, although I've been forced by circumstances to do many other things along the way.

Angela Arnott

Where are you from?
I currently live in Pontiac, Michigan.

Describe in one or two sentences how being friends with a dog has enriched your life.
Being friends with my dogs has enriched my life by them showing me unconditional love, loyalty, joy, courage, determination and forgiveness on a daily basis without question. I only hope that I am able to demonstrate these qualities to others.

Do you have any other pets; if so, what are their breeds and names?
I have two dogs, Buddy, a Dachshund & Buster, a Hound mix.

If you are a writer (either by trade or compulsion) what first drew you to the craft? If you're not a writer, why did you choose to write a piece for this anthology?
I choose to write a piece for this anthology to support Almost Home and the great work that they do.

Beth Ford Roth

Where are you from?
I was born, raised, and educated in Southern California.

Describe in one or two sentences how being friends with a dog has enriched your life.
My husband and I have three rescue dogs, and they are truly the Antiques Roadshow of creatures. They bring endless joy, affection, humor, and companionship to my life. And yet, all three were discarded at some point in their young lives by human beings who had no idea of their worth.

Do you have any other pets; if so, what are their breeds and names?
Our pets are Bodhi, a nine-year-old pit-shepherd mix; Dino, a five-year-old terrier mix; and Frida, a seven-year-old Chihuahua mix. We also have a 17 year old calico cat named Friendly, who was also a rescue.

If you are a writer (either by trade or compulsion) what first drew you to the craft? If you're not a writer, why did you choose to write a piece for this anthology?
I started writing for enjoyment as almost as soon as I learned to read. I wrote plays for my sisters and I to perform for our parents. I wrote short stories when we had free time in school, or when I was grounded and couldn't watch TV. I now make my living as a journalist, and get paid to write, which is a dream come true.

Beth Ford Roth is the writer and curator for Home Post, one of NPR's 12 inaugural Argo Network blogs. Home Post is about military family life and culture, and has often garnered an audience of more than 100,000 unique page views per month. Home Post has been mentioned by name in news organizations as varied as the New York Times, Fox News, BBC, and Huffington Post.

Beth Stone

Where are you from?
West Bloomfield, Michigan

Describe in one or two sentences how being friends with a dog has enriched your life.
One or two sentences? At the risk of sounding cliché, my dogs have given me the gift of unconditional love. Hobbes was my first dog. He grew up with our daughters and when he died, a part of us died, too. Calvin came into our lives and rescued us! How these animals wind their way into our hearts is beyond me.

Do you have any other pets; if so, what are their breeds and names?
Does a fish count? Until a few weeks ago, we had two, Ricky and Lucy. Now we have one. Ricky. Or maybe Lucy. I also watch our neighbor's dog, Loki. She is an Australian Shepherd.

If you are a writer (either by trade or compulsion) what first drew you to the craft? If you're not a writer, why did you choose to write a piece for this anthology?
I have been writing for years, both personally and professionally. I am the author of several articles and two how-to books on the art of seed bead work - *Seed Bead Stitching* and *More Seed Bead Stitching* - all published by Kalmbach Publishing. I love to express myself with the written word. Somehow my spoken word comes out all jumbled and emotional. I hope my writing brings the reader into a piece of my heart.

Cate Caldwell

Where are you from?
Detroit, MI

Describe in one or two sentences how being friends with a dog has enriched your life.
I had two little dogs, Miles and Bunchie, who are both now deceased. Miles was not only my hiking buddy and my roommate, but when I would cry, he would lick my eyes. It might have just been for the salt, but I like to think that he was trying to cheer me up.

Do you have any other pets; if so, what are their breeds and names?
My husband and I have four cats. Zathras, Friday, Hermione, and Pogo.

If you are a writer (either by trade or compulsion) what first drew you to the craft? If you're not a writer, why did you choose to write a piece for this anthology?
Ever since I can remember, I made things up and wrote them down. I never really wanted to do anything else.

Catherine Grow

Where are you from?
I am from Scotland, Connecticut, a very rural town of about 1700 people located in the northeastern part of the state known as "The Quiet Corner."

Describe in one or two sentences how being friends with a dog has enriched your life.
Our dog's exuberance and joy is so infectious that my husband and I are reminded not to take life overly seriously but take time for play and goofiness. His puppy-licks are heart-melting, and his constant love and companionship would see us through almost anything.

Do you have any other pets; if so, what are their breeds and names?
At present, we only have Maxwell, our gorgeous golden retriever rescue doggy. We are, however seriously considering getting him a "brother" sometime within this next year.

If you are a writer (either by trade or compulsion) what first drew you to the craft? If you're not a writer, why did you choose to write a piece for this anthology?
I've always loved to write and grew up inventing stories for myself and my younger brothers and sister to act out. Over the decades, such play developed into a passionate and serious writing regime that has yielded—and, hopefully, will continue to yield—a variety of published work. For me, writing is a necessity. It continues to be the most natural and honest way to express myself, whether I'm putting together a formal piece or jotting thoughts in a journal.

My work has appeared in a variety of online and print journals, news magazines, anthologies, and college-level texts, including *Common Ties*; *The Labletter*; *The Christian Science Monitor*; *Chicken Soup for the Soul*, and others.

Charolotte Mielziner

Where are you from?
Rural St. Charles County Missouri is well noted for Daniel Boone's home, but a bit less so for my own.

Describe in one or two sentences how being friends with a dog has enriched your life.
Even though each dog affects us in their own way, all good dog people have had a life changing dog. The one that has brought out the best in us; made us want to be a better person, just by gazing into that dog's eyes. I've been so fortunate to have been shaped by more than one silent partner in growth.

Do you have any other pets; if so, what are their breeds and names?
Currently, the dogs number three, Willow d'Wisp: Australian Shepard and fun police of the family; Fez: Border Collie with a brain the size of a planet; and Lily: a Samoyed of typical and eternal happiness. We also have two elderly quarter horses, Major and Bud, who are truly the equine odd couple and a typically serene and self-contained little Tabby cat, Hope.

If you are a writer (either by trade or compulsion) what first drew you to the craft? If you're not a writer, why did you choose to write a piece for this anthology?
Grey Wolfe Publishing's mission and energy is inspiring. I've been kicking the many adventures of Grandma Dog around for years; she was such a little character. When I read of the upcoming anthology, it seemed the perfect fit.

Christopher Woods

Where are you from?
Texas.

Describe in one or two sentences how being friends with a dog has enriched your life.
Teddy, a rescue Great Pyrenees, works as a therapy dog. We visit hospitals, nursing homes and schools. Teddy takes my wife and I to places we would not have gone before.

Do you have any other pets; if so, what are their breeds and names?
No other pets, just Teddy.

If you are a writer (either by trade or compulsion) what first drew you to the craft? If you're not a writer, why did you choose to write a piece for this anthology?
Christopher Woods is a writer, teacher and photographer who lives in Texas with his wife Linda and their rescue Great Pyrenees, Teddy. Among his published books are a novel, *The Dream Patch*, a prose collection, *Under A Riverbed Sky*, and a book of stage monologues for actors, *Heart Speak*. His photographs can be seen in his gallery at **http://christopherwoods.zenfolio.com/**

Clyde Liffey

Where are you from?
Brooklyn, New York.

Describe in one or two sentences how being friends with a dog has enriched your life.
It's always good to feel loved.

Do you have any other pets; if so, what are their breeds and names?
No other pets.

If you are a writer (either by trade or compulsion) what first drew you to the craft? If you're not a writer, why did you choose to write a piece for this anthology?
Reading and a desire to contribute to the reading and writing community.

Cynthia Jacobi

Cynthia lives on the edge of the Oregon coast. The wild beauty provides endless prompts for poems.

Several family dachshunds provided constant companionship in her childhood. They always listened, kept her secrets and loved her back.

After retiring from a career in health care, she began to write poems with the encouragement of her writing friends. Her goal is to be aware and observant. Her poems have been published in *North Coast Squid, Bohemia, Elohi Gadugi, and Verseweavers.*

D.T. Wine

Where are you from?
I am from the Shenandoah Valley. I was born in Harrisonburg on January 20, 1992, and raised in Broadway, a small town a few miles north of Harrisonburg.

When and why did you begin writing?
I began writing poetry my freshman year of high school. It started off as an exercise, but evolved into self-expression. Eventually I found a purpose, to deliver emotion through concision and simplicity. I want the reader to feel an experience from my work.

What would you say is your most interesting writing quirk?
I revise my poems constantly. I've deemed some finished, but later returned to and overhauled the entire piece. I doubt any of my poems will ever be safe from revision.

What do you like to do when you are not writing?
I enjoy watching movies, reading, following sports, and experiencing video games in my spare time.

As a child, what did you want to do when you grew up?
I always wanted to be a historian as a child.

Daniel Barbare

Where are you from?
Danny P. Barbare is from the Upstate of the Carolinas.

Describe in one or two sentences how being friends with a dog has enriched your life.
Miley shows me unconditional love. I can be silly or just act crazy and she doesn't care.

Do you have any other pets; if so, what are their breeds and names?
No other pets.

If you are a writer (either by trade or compulsion) what first drew you to the craft? If you're not a writer, why did you choose to write a piece for this anthology?
Danny P. Barbare has been writing poetry off and on for thirty-two years. He first began writing as a therapy after suffering from depression.

Danny P. Barbare has been published recently in **Blood and Thunder**, University of Oklahoma College of Medicine; **Doxa**, Nebraska Community College; and **Assisi Online Journal**, Saint Francis College. He works as a janitor at a local YMCA in Simpsonville, SC. He has been writing poetry off and on for 32 years.

Dennis Klotz

Where are you from?
The mean streets of Dearborn Heights, MI.

Describe in one or two sentences how being friends with a dog has enriched your life.
Whatever mood I'm in, be it happy or sad, a dog will always be there for me. Their loyalty and their love is something I'll always carry with me.

Do you have any other pets; if so, what are their breeds and names?
Just Pepper, my Miniature Dachshund who inspired the story.

If you are a writer (either by trade or compulsion) what first drew you to the craft? If you're not a writer, why did you choose to write a piece for this anthology?
I've always been a voracious reader and the short story really inspired me to write. It's a challenging form that when done well, can pack quite a powerful punch.

Diana Ludlam

Where are you from?
I was born and raised in Detroit, MI. I am currently a resident of Wixom, MI.

Describe in one or two sentences how being friends with a dog has enriched your life.
I have ALWAYS had a dog in my life. They are truly Man's Best Friend, and they are always there for you to make you laugh. No matter what mood you are in, they are there for you.

Do you have any other pets; if so, what are their breeds and names?
Currently, I have a cat named Foley, and I am fostering a Shitzu for Almost Home. When the time is right he will be mine.

If you are a writer (either by trade or compulsion) what first drew you to the craft? If you're not a writer, why did you choose to write a piece for this anthology?
I decided to submit a story because the topic is one I can relate with. My daughter works at Almost Home, and this is just a way of showing them support.

Edward Ahern

Where are you from?
A dangerous question to ask someone who's seventy one. In consecutive order: Illinois, Rhode Island, Washington, D.C., Germany, Japan, Connecticut, England, and Connecticut again.

Describe in one or two sentences how being friends with a dog has enriched your life.
The dog Shadow in my story was real and is described without embellishment. I was closer to him than a great many humans I know.

Do you have any other pets; if so, what are their breeds and names?
We've kept company with three dogs, Musti, a poodle; Shadow who looked exactly like a Belgian Sheppard but was bought out of the local pound and could have been anything, and Shlomo, our current dog, an amiable mongrel acquired from a shelter.

If you are a writer (either by trade or compulsion) what first drew you to the craft? If you're not a writer, why did you choose to write a piece for this anthology?
Resumed writing after forty odd years in foreign intelligence and international sales. Always wanted to be a tale teller, and now have enough time and money to do that. Forty-two stories accepted thus far.

Elisabeth Ward

Where are you from?
Now I live in rural southern California, but I lived in New York State for forty years as an adult, and grew up in the midwest.

Describe in one or two sentences how being friends with a dog has enriched your life.
We help dogs live in our modern world, but they bring understanding of an ancient and natural world to us. Which works faster and more efficiently - our amazing brains or their amazing noses? We complement and need each other.

Do you have any other pets; if so, what are their breeds and names?
I've always had cats. My adult life has also been blessed with horses, including our current three Icelandics, plus goats and chickens. They all have names but are too numerous to list here.

If you are a writer (either by trade or compulsion) what first drew you to the craft? If you're not a writer, why did you choose to write a piece for this anthology?
I need to write for the same reason I need animals: the opening of other worlds to better understand ours. Eradication of animal overpopulation and the resultant euthanasia will only be accomplished through awareness and understanding.

Ellen Woods

Where are you from?
I am a California Bay Area transplant since 1967 originally from the Midwest.

Describe in one or two sentences how being friends with a dog has enriched your life.
Since childhood I have considered dogs to be some of my best friends and greatest teachers.

Do you have any other pets; if so, what are their breeds and names?
No.

If you are a writer (either by trade or compulsion) what first drew you to the craft? If you're not a writer, why did you choose to write a piece for this anthology?
As an English major turned social worker, I rediscovered writing in the twenty-first century when I realized I had many stories to tell. My work appeared in numerous literary publications in 2013, including Inquiring Mind, Halfway Down the Stairs, Blood and Thunder, and Skive Magazine. I won awards in 2012 and 2013 at the Keats Soulmaking National Literary Competition, and at the 2012 Mendocino Coast Writing Contest.

Frank Evola

Where are you from?
Roseville, Michigan USA

Describe in one or two sentences how being friends with a dog has enriched your life.
Being friends with Peyton has been like being friends with a Guardian Angel.

Do you have any other pets; if so, what are their breeds and names?
I have a five year old male Orange Tabby cat named "Moose"

If you are a writer (either by trade or compulsion) what first drew you to the craft? If you're not a writer, why did you choose to write a piece for this anthology?
I'm not a writer but I chose to write the piece as a legacy for Peyton who passed away three years ago.

Gary Beck

Where are you from?
I live in N.Y.C., cultural and doggie capital of the U.S.

Describe in one or two sentences how being friends with a dog has enriched your life.
I had two dogs, one as a boy, one as an adult. They were the best dogs a boy or man could have, honest, Devoted and always a pleasure to be with.

Do you have any other pets; if so, what are their breeds and names?
When my daughter was young we had c. 200 gerbils, two cats, one dog and three alligators: Mr. and Mrs. Totus, and baby Totus.

If you are a writer (either by trade or compulsion) what first drew you to the craft? If you're not a writer, why did you choose to write a piece for this anthology?
I started writing poetry at the age of sixteen, influenced by Byron, Keats and Shelley. Many years later, among other writings, I wrote a batch of doggie stories, some of them zany.

Gay Pawlak

Where are you from?
South Lyon, Michigan

Describe in one or two sentences how being friends with a dog has enriched your life.
It' very simple, every time I look at a dog, a smile comes across my face and I always feel better. Can you imagine how many people miss out on smiling more and feeling better because they don't have a dog? They have taught me how to love more just by being a themselves and they aren't even aware they do it, nor care to take credit for it, but they do just the same. That's the thing about dogs, it truly is unconditional, and most people still don't know the definition of unconditional.

Do you have any other pets; if so, what are their breeds and names?
My little dogs, Daisy, Coco and Mimi (Shih Tzu) and two cats Misty and Lilly.

If you are a writer (either by trade or compulsion) what first drew you to the craft? If you're not a writer, why did you choose to write a piece for this anthology?
I am not a writer. The reason I submitted this piece was to help out the shelter I am a volunteer at, Almost Home Animal Haven in Southfield, Michigan and to say what a great thing it is to help out a little animal in need. Humans can help themselves but domesticated animals cannot. They are like a child but people really don't get that. You should never allow your domesticated animal to go anywhere, be with anyone, or give them anything that you would not give your 3 year old child. In dog world, they only get to be about two years old in human thinking. So they need our protection every minute of every day.

Gillian Lee

Where are you from?
I am from the heart of England.

Describe in one or two sentences how being friends with a dog has enriched your life.
My dog is one of the friendliest I have ever met. We "greet" every person and pet that we meet. He puts smiles on many faces every day.

Do you have any other pets; if so, what are their breeds and names?
No

If you are a writer (either by trade or compulsion) what first drew you to the craft? If you're not a writer, why did you choose to write a piece for this anthology?
I am a writer by compulsion. It is fun to make people smile.

Hal O'Leary

Where are you from?
I was born, raised and with the exception of a three year stint in the US Army (WWII), have spent my life in Wheeling, WV.

Describe in one or two sentences how being friends with a dog has enriched your life.
Being friends with a dog has made me realize the beauty, and yes, the necessity for an unconditional love in one's life.

Do you have any other pets; if so, what are their breeds and names?
We are the privileged companions of Hershey Chihuahua/Dachshund) and Itty Bit (Domestic Shorthair).

If you are a writer (either by trade or compulsion) what first drew you to the craft? If you're not a writer, why did you choose to write a piece for this anthology?
I was drawn to writing in retirement as a reward for and an appreciation of the poetry I've encountered in a long and eventful life.

Heather Moser

Where are you from?
I grew up in Carrollton, Ohio but currently live in Louisville, Ohio.

Describe in one or two sentences how being friends with a dog has enriched your life.
My first taste of responsibility and caring for others came from owning dogs during my youth. I cannot express enough how important their unyielding companionship has meant to not only my family, particularly my mother, but any other dog owner I have encountered. The love and the happiness they add to a family cannot be matched.

Do you have any other pets; if so, what are their breeds and names?
My husband and I own five cats; all are rescues. Blacky, Arod, Murphy, Stir Fry, Rocky.

If you are a writer (either by trade or compulsion) what first drew you to the craft? If you're not a writer, why did you choose to write a piece for this anthology?
My father writes love poems to my mother. I always thought that was so romantic. As a teenager struggling with all types of emotion, I turned to poetry as an outlet, hoping his skill of wording was passed down to me.

Jane Panich

Where are you from?
Hazel Park, MI

Describe in one or two sentences how being friends with a dog has enriched your life.
Being a proud owner of two rescued pit bull terriers, I have learned a lot about patience, determination, and unconditional love. "Jack" and "Atlas" are such a huge part of my life and I could not imagine life without them. They are family.

Do you have any other pets; if so, what are their breeds and names?
"Suzee Kitty"- age: 10yrs, breed: Fat Cat and "Bucki"-age: 20yrs, breed: Blue and Gold Macaw (parrot).

If you are a writer (either by trade or compulsion) what first drew you to the craft? If you're not a writer, why did you choose to write a piece for this anthology?
For me, writing has always come pretty natural and is something that I enjoy. I chose to write this piece because I saw an opportunity to write about something I am passionate about and I took it.

Janet Sloven

Where are you from?
I live in Portland, Maine.

Describe in one or two sentences how being friends with a dog has enriched your life.
The dogs in my life have been companions, dear friends, and beloved family members. My life has been enriched by their love and compassion, as well as by their irrepressible curiosity and excitement about life.

Do you have any other pets; if so, what are their breeds and names?
My husband and I have had many cat companions over the years, but at the moment our house is more than filled by Benji, the Yorkie-Jack Russell mix we adopted three years ago.

If you are a writer (either by trade or compulsion) what first drew you to the craft? If you're not a writer, why did you choose to write a piece for this anthology?
I love to write – and writing has always been part of my life. In the past few years the honing of the craft has been my focus – with classes, workshops, and writing groups. I believe my fiction, like my life, is enriched by the presence of dogs.

Jay Dardes

Where are you from?
I live in rural northwest Pennsylvania, two roads away from a paved highway, on twenty-two wooded acres. I live with my wife, Elaine, and my dog, Gretel.

Describe in one or two sentences how being friends with a dog has enriched your life.
She brings out my softer side, makes me laugh when people can't, and teaches me about living in the present. She's my kid.

Do you have any other pets; if so, what are their breeds and names?
No.

If you are a writer (either by trade or compulsion) what first drew you to the craft? If you're not a writer, why did you choose to write a piece for this anthology?
My father was a free-lance writer and I started writing after I retired from doing psychotherapy.

Jen Camilleri

Where are you from?
I am from Highland, MI

Describe in one or two sentences how being friends with a dog has enriched your life.
It's always nice to have someone who listens to my problems and concerns and responds by licking my face. The unconditional love that a dog has cannot be compared to any other relationship on this planet.

Do you have any other pets; if so, what are their breeds and names?
I have four formerly stray cats named Finnegan, Foster, Sophie and Truman. Plus there are assorted kittens that I foster from time to time. I am not the crazy cat lady yet, but defiantly hovering on the border.

If you are a writer (either by trade or compulsion) what first drew you to the craft? If you're not a writer, why did you choose to write a piece for this anthology?
I have always loved to write and consider myself a freelance writer. Writing is my way to release tension, to explore creativity and to make myself feel accomplished. It also gives me a reason to avoid doing laundry.

Jennifer Koch

Where are you from?
Lake Orion, MI

Describe in one or two sentences how being friends with a dog has enriched your life.
Dogs and cats bring a special kind of love into people's lives, and I know I wouldn't have made it through a lot of times without my dear furry family members to cuddle with!

Do you have any other pets; if so, what are their breeds and names?
I have two cats: Rhea (Ray-a) is a shy brown tiger/ calico mix and Mabine (May-bin) is a trouble making black cat.

If you are a writer (either by trade or compulsion) what first drew you to the craft? If you're not a writer, why did you choose to write a piece for this anthology?
I've been writing since I was a child, I don't know why but I know I haven't been able to stop yet!

John Aylesworth

Where are you from?
Athens, Ohio

Describe in one or two sentences how being friends with a dog has enriched your life.
I've never had as close a relationship with a dog (and many people) as I have with my Golden Doodle "Wally". He will probably be my last big dog and we will grow old together.

Do you have any other pets; if so, what are their breeds and names?
We have a rescue dog named Sophie and a month ago we lost our eighteen year old cat named Lucy.

If you are a writer (either by trade or compulsion) what first drew you to the craft? If you're not a writer, why did you choose to write a piece for this anthology?
Writing is in me and I learned early in high school that when it's working I'm simply along for the ride. I love words.

John Bayley

Where are you from?
I live in White Lake, Michigan with my wife Adele and our son Austin, a senior at Michigan State University.

Describe in one or two sentences how being friends with a dog has enriched your life.
We've cared for, and adopted a lot of dogs. My most satisfying moment is when you bond; when the dog knows that you love and care for them, and they don't have to be afraid anymore.

Do you have any other pets; if so, what are their breeds and names?
Morgan has two brothers; Toby, a brindle colored Cairn Terrier, and Albert a Black Lab mix. We also have two cats Doodles and Lily.

If you are a writer (either by trade or compulsion) what first drew you to the craft? If you're not a writer, why did you choose to write a piece for this anthology?
I've been writing for more than twenty years in the mystery and young adult genres. What first drew me to writing was the escape from everyday life, and the freedom to send my characters to wherever and whenever I chose. I wanted to tell Morgan's story. There are a lot of dogs that need a home, and they're not going to be perfect. But with time and caring, they will be.

John Brugaletta

Where are you from?
The Northern California coast.

When and why did you begin writing?
I've always preferred meaningful talk over small talk, and there isn't always another introvert around when you need one.

What would you say is your most interesting writing quirk?
I usually write in bed.

What do you like to do when you're not writing?
Eat my wife's cooking, call friends, throw a tennis ball for my dog.

As a child, what did you want to do when you grew up?
Heal people.

Jon Moray

Where are you from?
Kissimmee, Florida

Describe in one or two sentences how being friends with a dog has enriched your life.
I wasn't crazy about dogs before my beagle, Gunner, came along. Since then, this creature on four legs has dug a place in my heart and I now know that I will be a dog owner for as long as I live.

Do you have any other pets; if so, what are their breeds and names?
I have no other pets. Another dog for Gunner to sniff is not totally out of the question though.

If you are a writer (either by trade or compulsion) what first drew you to the craft? If you're not a writer, why did you choose to write a piece for this anthology?
I was drawn to writing by marveling at the stories from old Twilight Zone episodes. I have read stories written by Rod Serling and other talented authors that wrote for the show and was inspired to embark on a literary journey into a wondrous land whose boundaries are that of imagination.

Judith Gille

Where are you from?
Seattle, Washington.

Describe in one or two sentences how being friends with a dog has enriched your life.
For my son's eighth Christmas we finally got him the dog he'd been asking for even since he'd learned to talk: a Golden Retriever. I remember him sleeping in the crate with Katy the first night and ever since dogs have been an important part of our family.

Do you have any other pets; if so, what are their breeds and names?
Two more dogs: Max (a Lab/Husky mix) and Teddy the Schnoodle.

If you are a writer (either by trade or compulsion) what first drew you to the craft? If you're not a writer, why did you choose to write a piece for this anthology?
I'm drawn to writing because it helps me understand the world and my place in it. (I do write professionally.)

Kathy Ewing

Where are you from?
I live in Cleveland Heights, Ohio, and have lived in Northeast Ohio all my life.

Describe in one or two sentences how being friends with a dog has enriched your life.
Pretty much all the dogs in my life have enriched my life with their friendly affection and quirky personalities. I dearly loved my smart and funny childhood dog, Abbie. Our family dog Shucks, the dog in the poem, was a sweet, undemanding member of our family and is very much missed.

Do you have any other pets; if so, what are their breeds and names?
No.

If you are a writer (either by trade or compulsion) what first drew you to the craft? If you're not a writer, why did you choose to write a piece for this anthology?
My dad was a newspaperman, and my older sister loved to write. I began my imitating them. Since then, writing has provided me with opportunities to meet interesting people, communicate my thoughts and feelings, and supplement (in a very small way) my income as a Latin teacher.

Kevin Theisen

Where are you from?
Brownstown, Michigan.

Describe in one or two sentences how being friends with a dog has enriched your life.
A dog's love and devotion are unconditional. To have friends (four-legged) like that are truly a blessing. They are a big part of your life but you are their life.

Do you have any other pets; if so, what are their breeds and names?
Nigel, a Rottweiler; Simba, a staffy/Lab/Shibunu; Abby, a Lab mix.

If you are a writer (either by trade or compulsion) what first drew you to the craft? If you're not a writer, why did you choose to write a piece for this anthology?
Because of my love for animals and my dedication to Almost Home and the staff.

Mark Burgh

Where are you from?

I was born in Trenton, NJ during a blizzard and since I've lived all over the US. Currently, I live in Fort Smith, AR.

Describe in one or two sentences how being friends with a dog has enriched your life.

Dogs have been an important part of my life, providing companionship and protection. As a teacher, I often proved the adage "you can't teach an old dog new tricks" wrong by teaching several dogs over the age of ten to speak. Spike (RIP) took it to a new level, answering the question "Who is the president?" with "Barch". Close enough.

Do you have any other pets; if so, what are their breeds and names?

Big Dog – a mix of who knows what; Jasper, an orange tabby, and Junti, ad Siamese.

If you are a writer (either by trade or compulsion) what first drew you to the craft? If you're not a writer, why did you choose to write a piece for this anthology?

I have always been a writer.

Mark Hudson

Where are you from?
Evanston, Illinois.

Describe in one or two sentences how being friends with a dog has enriched your life.
Growing up, my sister wanted a dog and my one year she got one as a gift. When my sister went off to school, I become the care taker of the dog.

Do you have any other pets; if so, what are their breeds and names?
I have a Guiana pig named Willow. She is white with red eyes. I love her.

If you are a writer (either by trade or compulsion) what first drew you to the craft? If you're not a writer, why did you choose to write a piece for this anthology?
I wrote for this book because I love Grey Wolfe books. I believe it is a professional company and thought this was a worthy cause.

Mark Jeross

Where are you from?
I live in Huntington Woods,
Michigan with my wife and
our two dogs, Kibbitz and
Shmutz.

**Describe in one or two
sentences how being friends
with a dog has enriched your
life.**
I have had a dog since childhood. They really just put things in
perspective. One of the best parts of the day is picking them up
from daycare. You would think that you hadn't seen them in two
years. They are genuinely excited to see you!

**Do you have any other pets; if so, what are their breeds and
names?**
No.

**If you are a writer (either by trade or compulsion) what first drew
you to the craft? If you're not a writer, why did you choose to
write a piece for this anthology?**
To show my gratitude to my wife for bringing Shmutz into our
family, and to Almost Home, from where we got her.

Matt McGee

Where are you from?
Thousand Oaks, CA. I pretty much live in the local library. I carry a sandwich in my coat pocket like a hobo and drink Vitamin Water from the vending machine.

Describe in one or two sentences how being friends with a dog has enriched your life.
It's easy for me to climb inside my head and live there a while - not always the healthiest lifestyle. So long as there's a snout nudging my elbow to go outside and run around, I'll be okay.

Do you have any other pets; if so, what are their breeds and names?
Currently have a rabbit. I think she's part cat. She doesn't much care for anyone else.

If you are a writer (either by trade or compulsion) what first drew you to the craft? If you're not a writer, why did you choose to write a piece for this anthology?
Some kids played army, some kids played house – I'd sit in a leaf pile and play writer, typing away at the maple leaves.

Mel Dion

Where are you from?
Santa Cruze, California.

Describe in one or two sentences how being friends with a dog has enriched your life.
Dogs get me out of the house, make great walking partners, they are fun to travel with, and I'm never lonely.

Do you have any other pets; if so, what are their breeds and names?
Brody – Border Collie; Scout – Border Collie; Pubk – Terrier mix; two cats, Mimi and Tommy; and eight chickens.

If you are a writer (either by trade or compulsion) what first drew you to the craft? If you're not a writer, why did you choose to write a piece for this anthology?
I chose to write this piece to honor Brody.

Melissa Grunow

Where are you from?
Ferndale, MI.

Describe in one or two sentences how being friends with a dog has enriched your life.
My husky, Duke, has improved my sense of contentment, my physical health, and my overall outlook on life. He has also helped to establish and strengthen my relationships with other people, which is evidenced in my essay, "home."

Do you have any other pets; if so, what are their breeds and names?
I have four cats: Ani, Lola, Broadway, and Phantom.

If you are a writer (either by trade or compulsion) what first drew you to the craft? If you're not a writer, why did you choose to write a piece for this anthology?
I've been writing as long as I can remember. I was an avid reader as a kid, often choosing books over social events with friends. I started writing as soon as I felt I had a story to tell. It wasn't until late 2011, though, that I started to have some success with writing and publishing.

Michael Kamrath

Where are you from?
I'm a life-long resident of California, currently living in Forestville with my wife Lynn and our fifteen-year-old daughter, Kira.

Describe in one or two sentences how being friends with a dog has enriched your life.
Having a dog in my life makes me a more humble person.

Do you have any other pets; if so, what are their breeds and names?
Angus, a tabby cat; and Bella, a Labrador.

If you are a writer (either by trade or compulsion) what first drew you to the craft? If you're not a writer, why did you choose to write a piece for this anthology?
I write because I have to write to feel complete. I have published poems in various chapbooks and was a featured poet on the website *Poets Against The War*. I love sharing my observations on the world with others. The poem I chose for this anthology reflect, I think, the beauty and mystery of dogs.

Michael Kitchen

Where are you from?
Raised in Plymouth, Michigan. Currently living in Macomb County.

Describe in one or two sentences how being friends with a dog has enriched your life.
I work out of my home office, and having Zen, our Cavalier King Charles Spaniel around provides cute companionship.

Do you have any other pets; if so, what are their breeds and names?
I have a Cavalier King Charles Spaniel named Zen, a cat named Sam (short for Samurai), and two Russian Tortoises, Uma and Mariska.

If you are a writer (either by trade or compulsion) what first drew you to the craft? If you're not a writer, why did you choose to write a piece for this anthology?
An English Composition professor my freshman year at college encouraged me.

Michele Theisen

Where are you from?
I live in Brownstown, MI with my husband, three children, and four dogs. I have another daughter that is married and has a child; my only grandson, Jack.

Describe in one or two sentences how being friends with a dog has enriched your life.
My dogs are very comforting. They give love unconditionally. I couldn't imagine my life without them and I hope I've made a difference in theirs.

Do you have any other pets; if so, what are their breeds and names?
Abby is a lab mix, Simba is a lab/Staffy mix, Dyson is an Staffordshire terrier/American Bull Terrier, and Nigel is a Rottweiler.

If you are a writer (either by trade or compulsion) what first drew you to the craft? If you're not a writer, why did you choose to write a piece for this anthology?
Almost Home is a wonderful safe haven for animals. I wanted to support them.

Michelle Cacho-Negrete

Where are you from?
Portland, Maine by way of Brooklyn New York. Back then we couldn't imagine anything past New York, but here I am and quite happy here.

Describe in one or two sentences how being friends with a dog has enriched your life.
I grew up with dogs, but my mother had a little yorkie for eighteen years. It was her constant companion as she grew old and illustrated the possibility of unconditional love, or at least with a pet.

Do you have any other pets; if so, what are their breeds and names?
Because my husband and I travel a lot we decided that a pet was out of the question.

If you are a writer (either by trade or compulsion) what first drew you to the craft? If you're not a writer, why did you choose to write a piece for this anthology?
I grew up in absolute poverty and I wanted to make a difference by illuminating "third world America." The bulk of my work, mostly based on my life, has a strong political undertone. I have had three essays selected for the *100 Most Notable*, six *Pushcart* nominations, am in the *Norton Anthology* and *Thoreau's Legacy* through the Union of Concerned Scientists, as well as five other anthologies. UTNE magazine called my essay, *In My House*, about George Bush and global climate change, "an example of great writing". My essay on domestic violence, *In The Lion's Den*, won the *Hope Award*. I've been in a number of literary magazines, with the bulk of my work in *The Sun*. I edit/read for *Solstice* literary magazine.

M.K. Sukach

Where are you from?
Hebron, Connecticut.

Describe in one or two sentences how being friends with a dog has enriched your life.
All the dogs I've known in my life have been stoics. So, beyond how to love, I've learned how pain is often concealed for the sake of another—which in itself often seems to me a deeply tragic way of loving.

Do you have any other pets; if so, what are their breeds and names?
"Hobe" is a very young Corgi. We rescued her after "Syrah," a Terrier mix, died this Christmas Eve.

If you are a writer (either by trade or compulsion) what first drew you to the craft? If you're not a writer, why did you choose to write a piece for this anthology?
I think as a species we've always been writers because we're by nature story tellers. I'm simply participating in that ancient craft because it is the first and will likely be the last thing we ever do.

A Day In The Life first appeared in *Switched-on Gutenberg*, Issue 19, 2013 and *At the Poetry Reading Where I Imagine Dogs* first appeared in *The Bicycle Review*, Issue 20, 2013. M. K. Sukach's fiction and poetry appears or is forthcoming in a number of journals to include *JMWW, The Hamilton Stone Review, Connotation Press, Spoon River Poetry Review, Construction Magazine, Yemassee,* and others. **http://www.mksukach.com**

Molly Tamulevich

Where are you from?
Ann Arbor, Michigan.

Describe in one or two sentences how being friends with a dog has enriched your life.
My work with homeless dogs has profoundly changed the direction of my life-my career, priorities, ethics and education. I have loved and lost many dogs, and I was changed by every single one.

Do you have any other pets; if so, what are their breeds and names?
Two rats-Marla and Nova and two guinea pigs-Paul and Rosie.

If you are a writer (either by trade or compulsion) what first drew you to the craft? If you're not a writer, why did you choose to write a piece for this anthology?
I chose to write this piece because so many people have started wearing fur again, which I consider to be cruel, selfish and tacky, especially in a country where we claim to care about animal welfare.

Nancy Cole Silverman

Where are you from?

I was born in Seattle, Washington, one of the wettest regions of the country and grew up in Phoenix, Arizona, one of the sunniest. I suspect that why I always have a smile on my face. I've got sunshine in my soul.

Describe in one or two sentences how being friends with a dog has enriched your life.

My dogs are my training wheels! They keep me balanced, I keep them fed and happy and in return my life is sweeter and full of rewards.

Do you have any other pets; if so, what are their breeds and names?

Off and on in my life I have had the opportunity to know and own horses. They are also wonderful teaching companions and one in fact inspired my first novel, The Centaur's Promise.

If you are a writer (either by trade or compulsion) what first drew you to the craft? If you're not a writer, why did you choose to write a piece for this anthology?

I always felt the story picks the writer, not the other way around. The more I write the more stories seem to find me. I'm merely a vessel.

I have to credit my 25 years in radio for helping me to develop an ear for storytelling. In 2001 Currently I have three audio books with *MindWings Audio*. My first novel, *The Centaur's Promise*, was published by Eloquent Press in 2010 and since that time I have completed two additional manuscripts including my newest novel, *When in Doubt, Don't!* **www.nancycolesilverman.com**

Nikolas Frank

Where are you from?
We are from Saint Clair Shores Michigan

Describe in one or two sentences how being friends with a dog has enriched your life.
Our dog is not simply a friend but instead, a member of the family. She gives never ending love and affection and provides that bright spot in each day, no matter how good or bad it may have been.

Do you have any other pets; if so, what are their breeds and names?
We have no other pets at this time but are planning on adopting another rescue dog as some point.

If you are a writer (either by trade or compulsion) what first drew you to the craft? If you're not a writer, why did you choose to write a piece for this anthology?
Even though I am not a writer by trade, I wanted to share why we like to think that our dog is quite special. Even though she isn't a pure bred multi thousand dollar animal, she is priceless to us. Being able to save her from a shelter and give her a home has helped to create what our home is today and what it wouldn't be without her.

Nicole Koppin

Where are you from?
Madison Heights,
Michigan

**Describe in one or two
sentences how being
friends with a dog has
enriched your life.**
Vixen has brightened my life in all aspects. She has made my
gloomy days more cheerful, my boring days entertaining, and my
good days even better!

**Do you have any other pets; if so, what are their breeds and
names?**
Vixen is my only dog currently. She is a German Spitz mix, I also
have two cats, Lynx a domestic shorthair and Phira a domestic
long-haired cat.

**If you are a writer (either by trade or compulsion) what first drew
you to the craft? If you're not a writer, why did you choose to
write a piece for this anthology?**
While I have always written short stories and poems for fun I have
never been published. I wanted to submit a piece for this anthology
because I am an animal lover and wish to help save shelter dogs.

Renee Moxlow

Where are you from?
Grosse Ile, Michigan. I live on an island where the Detroit River meets Lake Erie.

Describe in one or two sentences how being friends with a dog has enriched your life.
Every day, dogs teach me unconditional love, support and loyalty. My rescue dogs know the value of gratefulness and they show it.

Do you have any other pets; if so, what are their breeds and names?
Oakley and Anniken are eleven-year-old Golden Retrievers and Sadie is a five-year-old Chocolate Lab.

If you are a writer (either by trade or compulsion) what first drew you to the craft? If you're not a writer, why did you choose to write a piece for this anthology?
I run an animal shelter and help with an organization called C.H.A.I.N.E.D. in the Detroit area. Rescues are my calling now.

Robert Bickmeyer

Where are you from?
Originally New York, NY; but the last thirty-five years I've been a resident of Troy Michigan. I was relocated by General Motors from New York to Detroit in 1978.

Describe in one or two sentences how being friends with a dog has enriched your life.
A man's dog gives him unconditional love. This has taught me to return such love, whether it be to a dog or my family. Further, when your heart is filled with love it aids you in having good health.

Do you have any other pets; if so, what are their breeds and names?
I currently enjoy and love our Cavalier King Charles Spaniel named Oliver.

If you are a writer (either by trade or compulsion) what first drew you to the craft? If you're not a writer, why did you choose to write a piece for this anthology?
I wrote for General Motors and love to write on any subject; politics, issues, sports, religion, etc. I currently am a contributor to *Military Magazine* published in Sacramento, California; for the *Think Club* and other local newspapers.

Robert Perlaki

Where are you from?
I am from Highland, Michigan.

Describe in one or two sentences how being friends with a dog has enriched your life.
I was raised with dogs, and have always had a dog in my life. I cannot imagine life without one. What they mean to me cannot be put into words.

Do you have any other pets; if so, what are their breeds and names?
No, I just have Bailey.

If you are a writer (either by trade or compulsion) what first drew you to the craft? If you're not a writer, why did you choose to write a piece for this anthology?
I decided that this story was perfect for this cause, and I hope readers enjoyed it.

Ruth Sabath Rosenthal

Where are you from?
Originally from Philadelphia, Pa. Have been living in Manhattan New York for decades.

When and why did you begin writing?
I began writing in 1999, when I got my first computer and, concurrently, signed up for my first poetry class. I selected poetry because I remembered how fond my mother was of one particular poem by Leigh Hunt "Abu Ben Adhem" and that inspired me to learn about poetry, in general.

What would you say is your most interesting writing quirk?
I can only write via a computer, as my longhand is atrocious and reading back more than a sentence or two would be a real challenge.

What do you like to do when you're not writing?
I love reading poetry, watching movies in the comfort of home on TV, dining out and spending time with friends and family.

Ruth Sabath Rosenthal is a New York poet, well published in literary journals and poetry anthologies throughout the U.S. and also in Canada, France, India, Israel, Italy, Romania, and the U.K. In 2006, Ruth's poem *On Yet Another Birthday* was nominated for a *Pushcart* prize. Ruth has authored three books of poetry: *Facing Home and Beyond*; *little, but by no means small*; *Food: Nature vs Nurture*. **www.ruthsabathrosenthal.moonfruit.com** and **www.poetryvlog.com/ruthsabathrosenthal**

Samuel K. Wilkes

Where are you from?
Fairhope, Alabama

Describe in one or two sentences how being friends with a dog has enriched your life.
Refines my ability to love and communicate without spoken words. Provides an example of unconditional love every day.

Do you have any other pets; if so, what are their breeds and names?
Gus a standard Dachshund.

If you are a writer (either by trade or compulsion) what first drew you to the craft? If you're not a writer, why did you choose to write a piece for this anthology?
The ability to create your own worlds and (hopefully) invoke universal thoughts with a mere pen and paper.

Shelley Kahn

Where are you from?
I live in Springfield Virginia, a suburb of Washington, D.C., but spend a good deal of time on the Delaware Coast.

Describe in one or two sentences how being friends with a dog has enriched your life.
My dogs have enriched my life in so many ways, they have been constant companions to our family in both good times and bad. My teenage children and my husband and I appreciate their silent non-judgmental acceptance and love. Our French bulldog, Corleen, has truly been a blessing in the last year as we have been grieving for multiple parents and other relatives who have passed. She is a tremendous comfort and joy to us all.

Do you have any other pets; if so, what are their breeds and names?
Not presently. We lost our much beloved English bulldog, Cleo, two years ago.

If you are a writer (either by trade or compulsion) what first drew you to the craft? If you're not a writer, why did you choose to write a piece for this anthology?
I have always been drawn to reading and writing. Both offer me an escape from the daily cares and challenges we all face in life. I have been writing poetry since childhood and in my legal career as a government attorney, I currently edit the written work of others. My poetry has recently been featured in publications such as *Melancholy Hyperbole, From the Depths Quarterly, and Moon Magazine.*

Shelly Migora

Where are you from?
I am originally from Detroit, MI and currently reside outside of metro Detroit.

Describe in one or two sentences how being friends with a dog has enriched your life.
My Ringo is my baby, pal and forever best friend. He has enriched my life by showing me what unconditional love is. No other being on the planet is capable of this kind of love. He is there for me every day whether I am happy, sad, or angry. I cherish every moment we spend together. He has truly taught me how to love again and to not be afraid. It's truly wonderful to wake up next to my dog every day! He will be part of our family forever!

Do you have any other pets; if so, what are their breeds and names?
Only my Ringo who is a terrier mix.

If you are a writer (either by trade or compulsion) what first drew you to the craft? If you're not a writer, why did you choose to write a piece for this anthology?
I am an occasional blogger and I love to write because it is relaxing and allows me to express my creative side. I contributed a piece to this anthology because when I heard the proceeds were going to save animals from death row and be donated to Almost Home, I was so excited to share my dog's rescue story and contribute to this wonderful cause!!! We rescued him from Almost Home! Almost Home does so many wonderful things for animals and I am so grateful they saved my baby!
http://shellylynneinmylife.blogspot.com

Stefanie Freele

Where are you from?
Wisconsin

Describe in one or two sentences how being friends with a dog has enriched your life.
I think my piece, *Blessed By The* Dog explains most. Having someone so loyal, so attuned, always watching out for you, is an honor.

Do you have any other pets; if so, what are their breeds and names?
Two cats: Señor (an old black cat born on my lap 17 years ago) and Sprig (a young tabby wish a sense of humor)

If you are a writer (either by trade or compulsion) what first drew you to the craft? If you're not a writer, why did you choose to write a piece for this anthology?
A love of books drew me to a love of writing.

Stefanie Freele is the author of two short story collections, *Feeding Strays*, with Lost Horse Press and **Surrounded by Water**, with Press 53 which includes the winning story of the *Glimmer Train Fiction Award*. Stefanie's published and forthcoming work can be found in *Witness, Mid-American Review, Wigleaf, Western Humanities Review, Sou'wester, Chattahoochee Review, The Florida Review, Quarterly West,* and *American Literary Review*.

Stephanie Commyn

Where are you from?
I grew up in Walled Lake, Michigan, but now reside in Birmingham.

Describe in one or two sentences how being friends with a dog has enriched your life.
Because of my relationships with dogs, I have learned what it feels like to give and receive true, unconditional love.

Do you have any other pets; if so, what are their breeds and names?
Yes. I have a five- year-old basset hound/ corgi mix named Dahlia that we rescued after she had & lost her puppies.

If you are a writer (either by trade or compulsion) what first drew you to the craft? If you're not a writer, why did you choose to write a piece for this anthology?
I chose to write my piece for two reasons: 1) to help Almost Home Animal Rescue and 2) to have a story of Maxine memories that I can reference forever.

Susan Adams

Where are you from?
I was born in New Zealand, and I'm now living in Australia.

Describe in one or two sentences how being friends with a dog has enriched your life.
My dog was trusting and loyal and always wanted to be with me. To be needed has harmony and happiness.

Do you have any other pets; if so, what are their breeds and names?
No.

If you are a writer (either by trade or compulsion) what first drew you to the craft? If you're not a writer, why did you choose to write a piece for this anthology?
To be able to use words like color to a canvas.

Terri Simon

Where are you from?
Laurel, Maryland, originally from Mount Vernon, New York

Describe in one or two sentences how being friends with a dog has enriched your life.
With a dog, you are never really alone. Mine are definitely my furry children. They teach me to live in the now and that the important things are snuggles and hugs. They know when someone isn't feeling well and do their best to fix it.

Do you have any other pets; if so, what are their breeds and names?
Annie is a German Shepherd-Hound dog mix. Tia is a Border Collie-Husky mix. Both are rescues.

If you are a writer (either by trade or compulsion) what first drew you to the craft? If you're not a writer, why did you choose to write a piece for this anthology?
I wrote my first poem when I was six or seven years old. I think nursery rhymes inspired me at first, but an appreciation for language grew by reading Poe, Cummings, Whitman, etc.

Theresa Nielsen

Where are you from?
Royal Oak, Michigan.

Describe in one or two sentences how being friends with a dog has enriched your life.
My dogs are my family, they make life complete.

Do you have any other pets; if so, what are their breeds and names?
Tillie, Maddie and Mama Kitty are my cats. I have birds, too, which are going to have their own book.

If you are a writer (either by trade or compulsion) what first drew you to the craft? If you're not a writer, why did you choose to write a piece for this anthology?
I have been a writer for many years; I have so many stories to share.

Tricia Carey

Where are you from?
Royal Oak, Michigan

Describe in one or two sentences how being friends with a dog has enriched your life.
I never realized that what you get from a dog would depend on what you're willing to learn. Each has taught me something different; from nursing skills to endless patience. It's all been useful.

Do you have any other pets; if so, what are their breeds and names?
Just two dogs; Greta – a terrier-mix and Nigel – a retriever mix.

If you are a writer (either by trade or compulsion) what first drew you to the craft? If you're not a writer, why did you choose to write a piece for this anthology?
I'm very passionate about no-kill rescue work and admire anyone with the tenacity to be involved. Since both of my dogs came from Almost Home, a wonderful no-kill rescue, I wanted to share our stories.

Vicki Robertson

Where are you from?
Howell, Michigan

Describe in one or two sentences how being friends with a dog has enriched your life.
It has taught me how to persevere and love unconditionally.

Do you have any other pets; if so, what are their breeds and names?
We have two other Miniature Poodles by the names of Ellie and Daisy who are also rescues that we got in 2013.

If you are a writer (either by trade or compulsion) what first drew you to the craft? If you're not a writer, why did you choose to write a piece for this anthology?
Victor's story just had to be told.

Vivian McInerny

Where are you from?
Portland, Oregon.

Describe in one or two sentences how being friends with a dog has enriched your life.
A cold nose and a tail wag makes every day better.

Do you have any other pets; if so, what are their breeds and names?
No.

If you are a writer (either by trade or compulsion) what first drew you to the craft? If you're not a writer, why did you choose to write a piece for this anthology?
When I was a child, a priest from Denmark read to my third grade class, *The Snow Queen*, and *The Little Mermaid* by Hans Christian Anderson and I felt transported into those worlds.

Wendy Taylor Carlisle

Where are you from?
After vagabond beginnings, I finally, finally came home to the Ozarks of Arkansas.

Describe in one or two sentences how being friends with a dog has enriched your life.
I can't imagine sadness, or celebration, work or cerebration without the presence of a dog whose character is so fine I can't hope to deserve their attention.

Do you have any other pets; if so, what are their breeds and names?
Two cats: Paul Verlaine and Bella. The dogs are Marcel Proust and XenaWarriorPrincess.

If you are a writer (either by trade or compulsion) what first drew you to the craft? If you're not a writer, why did you choose to write a piece for this anthology?
I was always a writer, a poet for the precision and because I most like to read poetry.

Almost Home Animal Rescue League is a non-profit 501(c)(3) organization dedicated to finding loving forever homes for homeless animals. Almost Home is a 100% no-kill shelter made up almost entirely of volunteers with more than 100 dogs and cats in our care at any given time.

Almost Home is a place where frightened animals need not be frightened. Where animals with special needs are not discriminated against. A place that radiates warmth and love to all animals whether they are young or old, sick or healthy, maimed or beautiful. A place to feel safe and "BE" safe. We rely solely on the generosity of animal lovers like you. Your donation could mean the difference between the life and death of an animal.

SHELTER HOURS FOR ADOPTIONS:
Monday-Friday 12:00-5:00pm
Saturday 1:30-5:00pm
Closed Sunday

LOCATION:
25503 Clara Lane
Southfield, MI 48034
248-200-2695
www.AlmostHomeAnimals.org
AlmostHome1965@gmail.com

www.ingramcontent.com/pod-product-compliance
Lightning Source LLC
Chambersburg PA
CBHW060807030726
47503CB00002B/378